Dedicated to my Roni

My one and only girl, my first reader always, and my partner in crime who always has bail money!

Love you beyond words

D1521091

ACKNOWLEDGMENTS

As I started the second book in the FRONTIER series, I knew exactly who I would turn to for advice, direction, and forbearance. I've been lucky that I have found some of the best in the business.

First, thanks to Sandra Haven-Herner, who takes her time and refines my stories to a razor's edge.

To Deirdre Stoelzle, who checked that the Western aesthetic was authentic and all the punctuation was in the right spots. And to Rafael Andres, who created a cover that made even me want to read the book.

Finally, to my wife Roni, who read each chapter numerous times and always nudged me back onto the trail when I had wandered into high grass and lost the story. Without you, Danny, Ben, and the entire book would still be a dream.

Chapter 1

Danny had been daydreaming as he ran, letting his mind wander over thoughts important and trivial. Preoccupied, he strayed from the dirt berm of the road into the gravel and directly into the truck's path. He didn't hear the rev of the truck's engine, and the crunch of tires sliding through gravel surprised him. The sound of impending doom caused him to whirl and throw his arms up. His hands landed on the grillwork as the truck slid to a stop.

"What in the Sam Hill's wrong with you, peckerhead," yelled the old man from the window of the red F-150. "You tryin' to get yourself kilt or something?"

The rooster tail the truck had left in its wake caught the Ford and washed over it. The dust passed over the old man and Danny like a crashing wave, varnishing all three in white dust particles.

A shudder passed through Danny's body. It'd been a near miss, and he knew it'd been stupid not to be paying attention. The shock wore off, and still leaning on the hood, he unpuckered the parts of him that puckered and ran an internal diagnostic.

The results told him he was uninjured and hadn't pissed himself, which was a relief. Wet running shorts would only add to his embarrassment at almost being roadkill. He pushed off the truck and approached the driver's door to apologize.

The man didn't wait for his arrival. He kicked his door open with a foot and hopped out of the idling truck. He was Nakota, and his face was a mountain range of wrinkles. A Hungarian pipe, fully bent, with a tall bowl hung comfortably from the corner of his mouth. He was thin and appeared constructed of equal parts bone and gristle. He wore jeans, a snap-button work shirt, boots, a straw cowboy hat, and a face like thunder.

"I'm going to kick your ass from here to Sunday. You almost put me in the ditch," said the man, jerking the pipe from his lips and getting his first good look at Danny. "Wait, you're a Wasi'chu." He stuffed the pipe back between his lips and puffed it to life. "You don't belong on the Rez. This ain't a goddam tourist spot."

Danny smiled at the insult. He'd heard it often enough, mainly from older residents of the Dead Horse Reservation. Wasi'chu was the Sioux word for non-Indian, and it was akin to being called Haole in Hawaii or cracker in the South. It was not a word that denoted affection.

"Sorry, sir. My mind wandered, and my legs followed," said Danny. He shrugged. "Just color me a dumbass."

The man squinted and gave Danny a suspicious look. "What are you doing out here? Don't they got roads to run on in Darwin?"

"They do, but I was running with a friend. Edmund Goodrunner, maybe you know him? He's with the Tribal Police," said Danny. "He's in much better shape than me and got tired of my turtle-in-molasses pace."

He'd hoped this joke would elicit a smile from the older man, but all he got was a more suspicious look from the Indian and dead silence.

Danny gave a surrendering exhale and held out his right hand, not knowing what else to do. He hoped the man would take it. "Again, I'm sorry, sir. Name's Danny Coogan."

The man's eyes narrowed. "Coogan, huh? You related to that Fish Cop from the Six Feathers shooting?"

"That's me," replied Danny with a smile. Inside his head, he frowned. Shit, is what went on at Six Feathers going to be my calling card from now on?

"Well, I'll be damned, imagine that. I'm Sonny Siebert. Sorry, I almost ran you down like a speed goat," said the man. His face erupted in an ear-to-ear grin. He reached out and gripped Danny's hand. "That was a hell of a thing you did, saving Nat and that white girl." He let go of Danny's hand and leaned back, thumbs in his front pockets. "Nat was a far-cousin of mine, so you got my thanks for ridding the world of them murdering bastards that tried to kill him."

Danny shrugged. He was uncomfortable taking praise for killing men. They'd been evil men who would have killed all of them if things had gone differently. He didn't regret what he'd done, but being congratulated for killing rubbed him the wrong way.

"Just doing my job," said Danny.

The man's eyes reflected shared experience, and he nodded knowingly. "It's a hell of a thing killing a man, but sometimes there ain't no choice if you want to live. I learned that lesson myself in Vietnam."

Danny stayed quiet, not knowing what to say. He agreed with the old Indian. He'd learned the same lesson in Afghanistan, but it didn't make living with the memory any easier.

The man pushed his hat off his forehead and puffed at his pipe.

"Sorry for the yelling. Scared the shit out of me, and I ain't got a driver's license," said Sonny. He spit into the gravel and reset his pipe. "Hitting you would have brought seven kinds of hell."

"No harm done to either of us, thank goodness," said Danny, relieved that the man had calmed down.

"I was headed into town for chicken feed," said Sonny. "Got a place up the road. Small for around here, but big enough for me."

"Big or small, every man needs a kingdom," said Danny.

"Ain't that the truth," replied Sonny. His smile melted a piece, and he added, "Too bad cancer took Nat, but at least you gave him a few months with what you done."

Danny nodded in agreement, but a chill passed over him. The second mention of last October and Nat brought memories fresh to his mind. He was being offered jobs because of the Six Feathers shootout. Sheriff Johnson wanted him as a deputy in Beckwourth County. The Montana DOJ's Criminal Investigation Division wanted him as an investigator working as a liaison with the reservations. Both jobs seemed to like him as a hired gun hand, something he was uncomfortable with.

He didn't know what he wanted, which was probably central to the problem. The best he had figured was that he wanted to marry Ruth; after that, it was all unmarked territory. He was sure he wanted more than being what he was, a game warden for Fish & Game, but the way forward eluded him. Or maybe I'm just pissing in the wind, he thought, and I need to stop half-assing my job and be content.

"Want a ride?" asked Sonny as he waved a hand in the direction of Tennant Creek.

Danny had just passed the eight-mile mark of his run. He knew he could power through the last two miles, but he'd choose four wheels over two legs any day of the week.

"Sure, why not."

He walked around to the truck's passenger side while Sonny climbed behind the wheel. A commercial for the upcoming Montana State Fair was ending on the radio as he pulled his door shut. As the commercial transitioned to a song, Sonny reached over to grab the button and turn the volume down. Danny recognized the tune as "Black Hills Dreamer," by Buddy Red Bow, a South Dakota Lakotan musician raised on the Pine Ridge Reservation.

"Leave it turned up. I like it," said Danny. He searched for a seatbelt and came up dry.

Sonny left the volume where it was and dropped the truck into gear. He eased back onto the center of the road and, at a leisurely pace, headed toward town.

"You know Buddy?" he asked.

"Edmund, the running partner I mentioned, introduced him to me," said Danny. He rolled his window down to let the breeze cool him. "Says it'll help me understand the people on the reservation better. Give me a different perspective."

"Ain't nothing wrong with that way of thinking. Too many people only listen to what goes on in their head," said Sonny. He took a pull on his pipe, wiggled in his seat to get comfortable, and asked, "You start running from town this morning?"

"We set out from the parking lot at Burbot Lodge," said Danny, referring to an upscale fish camp alongside the Spoon River. The camp comprised the lodge itself, a general store with a bait shop, and twenty cabins filled with tourists who caught fish and fed money into the Dead Horse economy.

"You young folk and running. You ain't got the sense God gave a goat," said Sonny with unconcealed contempt. "A hard day of ranching would do the same for you, and you'd have something to show for it." He glanced at Danny and winked, "And you wouldn't end up a hood ornament on an old man's truck."

Danny saw the logic and couldn't argue.

On the radio, "Black Hills Dreamer" ended, and Redbone began to sing "Custer Had It Coming."

Sonny leaned over and turned the volume to ten. He smiled in Danny's direction and said, "No offense, Wasi'chu."

Danny waved away Sonny's concern and bobbed his head in time with the rhythm. As the song hit the refrain, he cupped his head in his hand, leaned against the door frame, and closed his eyes. The breeze felt good, and he drifted into a half-sleep doze with a yawn.

He remembered he'd kissed Ruth goodbye this morning and driven to meet Edmund at the Tribal Police Headquarters in Tennant Creek. Ray Whitepipe, the Tribal Police chief and Edmund's boss, had offered to drive them out to the lodge and drop them off for the run back to town.

"Remember, I need you in town and on duty by nine," he'd said to Edmund as he stood beside his SUV and took the cellophane wrapper off a fresh pack of smokes. He placed one between his lips and lit it. "Stan's on light duty, Janine's in Darwin, and everyone else is off-duty after working the fire in Kimball."

"No worries," said Edmund. He poked Ray's belly, "Want to join us?"

"I'm too old for silly shit like running," said Ray. "Besides, I'm management."

Danny tied his running shoes, and when he finished, he stood up and studied the police chief. Ray was a large, grizzly bear-sized man, topping six-five. His hair was dark and cropped short, and his belly had grown over winter. He had brown, almond-shaped eyes that held wisdom and cleverness. He didn't look like much at a glance, but Danny knew you'd pay the price if you underestimated him.

Edmund glanced at Danny, motioned toward the general store window with his chin, and said, "He only drove us out here so he could get donuts from Hollis."

Hollis Haypenny appeared in the store window as if conjured, and they watched him set a tray of cream-filled, maple-topped donuts into the display case. He spotted the lawmen, flashed a nicotine-tinged smile, and waved hello. Hollis was pear-shaped, bald, and wore dark jeans and a black shirt. Danny always thought he looked like a pot-bellied penguin, but he had to admit that Ray wasn't wrong about the donuts.

Ray waved back. "It's not a morning worth a tinker's damn without coffee, a cigarette, and a donut." He saw the look Edmund shot him and added, "Piss off. It's the little things in life at my age."

"You're not gonna get much older if that's your everyday routine," said Danny. He leaned over to touch his toes, stretching out his hamstrings. "But glass half full, Edmund has an excellent chance for promotion if you keep it up."

Ray glanced at the game warden but spoke to Edmund. "If he dies on the run, mark the body and go back for it after your shift." He took a swipe at Danny, who dodged it. Ray smiled at him and joked, "We'll bury what the wolves don't eat."

With orders given, Ray crossed the parking lot, slipped into the store, and disappeared.

"Let's get to it," said Edmund with a predatory grin. "I'll take it easy on you today."

He paced Danny for the first five miles of the Redhawk Trail, then said he needed to pick up his pace to stretch out a cramp and not be late to town. This is where the turtle-in-molasses comment was mentioned. With a salute, the tribal officer accelerated like a goosed pronghorn and sprinted up a hill ahead of them. He crested the top, slipped over it, and disappeared down the other side, leaving Danny in the proverbial dust.

"That your friend?" asked a voice.

Danny jerked awake. He'd fallen asleep, and the sound startled him. It took him a few seconds to reorient and remember he was in a truck, and the voice belonged to Sonny.

He sat up and wiped the sleep blurs from his eyes. When he was able to focus, he saw Edmund. The Indian sat on the dropped tailgate of Danny's blue Power Wagon. He looked as he always did, relaxed and daisy-fresh as if he'd come from Central Casting, noble-savage department. His hair was coffee-colored and short, his six-foot frame solid, and his smooth, bronze skin unblemished.

He didn't look like a man who had just run ten miles at a sub-seven pace, and Danny both hated and admired him a little for that. Edmund casually kicked his legs while chatting to a woman on the sidewalk beside the truck.

"Yeah, that's him," said Danny.

Sonny gave Danny a sideways look and said, "Him? I was talking about the bit of sunshine with the great legs."

Danny couldn't disagree as he looked at the woman talking to Edmund. Demitta Sparrowhawk was beautiful.

She was also a reservation novelty; she'd left but had chosen to return, which told you everything you needed to know about the woman. She graduated from Stanford with a degree in art, then returned to take over one of the empty storefronts on Tennant Creek's main street. She wanted to establish a Dead Horse Cultural Museum and had gained support from the new chairman of the Tribal Council, Barrett Lodge.

She was as tall as Edmund, with an athletic build, thin hips, and brown hair, which she always wore in pigtails. Danny thought it was the pigtails and her unfiltered candor that attracted Edmund. But Edmund said her naughty mind and badlands curves stirred his interest.

Sonny pulled beside the Power Wagon and stopped to allow Danny to climb out.

Demitta noticed him first and said, "Good morning, Danny. Glad to see you safe. Interesting way to finish your run."

"Wasn't part of the plan," said Danny. He hopped up on the sidewalk beside her. "Sometimes us turtles need help getting out of the molasses."

"I'd about given up on you," said Edmund. He jumped off the tailgate and slipped an arm around Demitta's waist. He glanced at Sonny, then said, "Thought I was going to have to call Mountain Rescue, but I see somebody took pity on you."

"Edmund, this is Sonny Siebert," said Danny, motioning inside the truck. "He gave me a ride after we, uhm, met on the road."

"He means I almost ran over him. Boy's too polite for his own good."

Edmund smiled and said, "We're about to have breakfast at the diner. Want to join us? Payback for bringing in our lost turtle."

"Ain't got the time," replied Sonny. "But you could do me a favor."

"Be glad to," said Edmund.

"Tell Whitepipe that Joe Niland is squatting in his trailer in Crazy Buffalo Canyon. And things have begun to come up missing from surrounding ranches."

"I thought he was walking the straight and narrow," said Edmund.

"No such luck. Twenty years in prison didn't break him of bad habits."

"I'll let Ray know," said Edmund.

"Thanks." Sonny switched his eyes to Danny. "Be seeing ya, Wasi'chu." He then took a lingering look at Demitta before he waved and pulled away.

Danny watched him go, then turned back to Edmund. "Who's Joe Niland?"

"A bad penny," answered Edmund. "Hungry?"

Danny nodded, "Always."

Twenty minutes later, Sharla Lander, the owner of the Dan-Dee Diner, delivered breakfast to their table. Edmund had water, oatmeal, and fruit. Demitta opted for orange juice, granola, and yogurt. Danny picked the antithesis of healthy with black coffee, toast slathered in butter and jelly, and a full plate of biscuits and gravy.

"And you wonder why you're a turtle," pointed out Edmund as he swallowed a mouthful of oatmeal.

Sharla set the plate before him, and Danny sniffed the deep aroma of sausage and pepper. "Give me a break. Ruth never lets me eat this."

"Price you pay for living with a doctor," said Edmund.

"Not today," said Danny. He grinned like an eight-year-old on Christmas and quickly covered the biscuits and gravy in ketchup.

"You're ruining my food," barked Sharla, her hands on her hips. Sharla Lander was a force of nature known for her cutting tongue and spicy vocabulary. She was a squat woman with buck teeth and crooked legs. She'd married and buried three husbands, the first two Indian, the last a Mexican. "You know, there's the seventh level of hell for people who do shit like that to food."

"Save your breath. He's untrainable," said Edmund between bites. "He puts ranch on spaghetti."

With a whispered curse, Sharla twisted on her boot heels. She returned to the counter to wait on two ranchers who'd been watching and whose faces reflected a similar opinion of Danny's culinary behavior.

"How's Ruth?" asked Demitta, mixing her yogurt and granola.

"Good," answered Danny. "Back from visiting her folks in Indiana."

"What are their names again?" asked Edmund.

"Mike and Margery."

"Did she tell them she wasn't marrying rich?" asked Demitta.

"Pretty much," answered Danny. "A game warden a few rungs down from Devon Bridger."

Everyone at the table knew Ruth had been engaged to Devon Bridger, one of the wealthiest men in Montana, now that his father, Delmont, had died. She'd broken the engagement when Devon showed his true colors and lost out on millions, but everyone at the table knew she'd traded up when she and Danny had gotten together.

"What do her folks do?" asked Edmund, biting into his toast.

"Her dad was a Navy diver, retired a senior chief petty officer."

"When was that?" asked Edmund, leaning forward with interest.

"Years ago. Went home to Indiana after the Navy. Inherited the family farm."

"And her mom?" asked Demitta.

"Art teacher at the local high school," said Danny, glancing up at her and pointing a finger. "You two should get on."

Demitta's eyes twinkled, and her cheeks scrunched as she smiled. "Love to meet her."

Danny spun a piece of biscuit around his plate to get the last gravy and flipped it in his mouth. "Molly's planning a family dinner this Thursday after Ruth collects them from the airport in Great Falls. You're both invited."

The Whitetails had raised Danny after his parents drowned when Danny was seven. After the burial, with no relatives stepping forward to take him, Danny got in the Whitetails' car and went home. Ben had been Danny's superior with Fish & Game until his recent retirement and had been the driving force behind him even becoming a game warden.

"Wouldn't miss it," said Edmund, finishing his toast and reaching for his water. "Think Ruth convinced them you're worth marrying?"

"They didn't give a hard no, so I'm still in the race. Thought I'd show them around the county and the sights."

"What sights?" asked Edmund. "Beckwourth County is one big, empty, barren country. We got more pronghorns than people."

"Don't tease, Edmund," said Demitta. She smacked his shoulder. "Can't you see Danny wants to make a good impression?"

"I'm being serious," said Edmund. "The elevation is a bigger number around here than the population."

Demitta held up a palm to silence Edmund. "Ignore him. Bring them to the museum, and I'll give them a tour. Then you can take them out to Button Lake for the day."

"It is pretty out there," said Edmund. He reached out to take Demitta's hand, kissed her fingertips, and gave her a quick wink. "Maybe you and I should check it out tonight."

Demitta squeezed Edmund's hand back. "Cool your jets, mister. I'm not that kind of girl," she said, and then, with a wink, added, "Most times."

Edmund turned his attention back to Danny and asked, "What do you need us to bring?"

"Just your charming selves," said Danny as he licked gravy off his fingers. "I think Molly is more worried about Ben behaving himself. He has already nicknamed Ruth's dad Squidward."

"She's good to be on her toes. Ben's always one drink away from the devil," said Edmund, who knew how much Danny's stepfather liked liquor. Unlike some in the law enforcement community, Ben kept his alcohol consumption under control—most of the time, anyway. Edmund shook his head and smiled. "I can imagine the trouble he got up to in Italy."

"Speaking of Italy, tell Molly I want to hear about Tuscany. It must have been beautiful," said Demitta, glancing in Edmund's direction.

"Don't give me that look," he said. "Just two weeks ago, we went to Whitefish."

"To visit your sister," pointed out Demitta. "And we took your mother."

"Lay down, close your eyes, play dead," said Danny, whipping gravy from his chin.

Edmund started to speak but caught sight of Ray as he stepped into the diner. The look on the police chief's face ended all conversation at the table.

"I need you in uniform in five minutes," he said when he got to the table.

"No worries, I'll take care of breakfast," said Danny, tossing a look at Edmund.

"I meant both of you," said Ray, his eyes dark and his face as unforgiving as granite. "Got bodies outside Buckshot, one for each of you."

"Who?" asked Danny, feeling Ray's mood transfer to him. He knew Buckshot was no more than a collection of houses in the hills northeast of Tennant Creek.

"John Goodnight," said Ray. "Didn't come in for breakfast, so Ellen went to look for him. Found him dead in the north pasture."

"Jesus," said Demitta, putting both hands to her face.

"Got a steer dead downhill from him," said Ray, laying a Lincoln down on the breakfast ticket. He pointed a finger at Danny, "That's your department. I already called your boss and got special consideration."

Tribal Police and a multitude of local jurisdictions frequently assisted each other, but this time, the crimes appeared linked to both departments.

"Anybody else headed that way?" asked Edmund.

"I called Janine, and she's coming back from Darwin but thirty minutes out. I need you now. Ellen's by herself with John."

"We'll be as quick as we can," said Edmund. He slipped out of his chair and headed for the door.

Danny glanced at Ray and saw anger in the man's eyes. Without a word, he brushed past Ray's shoulder and followed Edmund.

Chapter 2

Danny and Edmund changed and were gone before Ray returned to the office. Danny wore hiking boots, jeans, and a brown shirt with the grizzly head game patch on each shoulder. He had taken to wearing a straw cowboy hat when the mood struck him, but it sat on the dash of the truck baking in the sun.

Edmund wore a dark blue uniform that bore the running white horse patch of the Tribal Police. He wore black Hi-Tecs and a blue baseball cap emblazoned with the reservation emblem perched on his head.

Ray radioed them with an update as they turned off Center Line Road and headed north toward the crime scene. He'd called Beckwourth County sheriff for assistance, and they, in turn, had called the Montana Division of Criminal Investigation.

Pat Palmer, a DCI lead investigator, was close by and rerouted to the crime scene. He'd done work on the Rez before and was heading back from a meeting in Great Falls with two technicians in tow. He promised to be there within the hour.

Twenty minutes after leaving the diner, Danny pulled the Power Wagon up to the gate of John Goodnight's north pasture. An old, blue Ford Ranger straddled the gateway and blocked him. The driver's door hung open, and the Ranger's engine sputtered and spat as it ran. A newer, harvest-gold Chevy Silverado with its tailgate down was fifty feet above the Ford. In its bed sat a pale-green water tank with black hoses attached that cascaded over the tailgate, dropping to the ground.

Danny touched Edmund's arm to get his attention and pointed at the empty rifle rack in the back window of the Ranger. Edmund glanced at the truck, grimaced, and reached down to unbuckle the retaining strap on his Glock. Danny did the same with the holster of his Sig Sauer.

"What do you think?" asked Edmund as he opened his door and stepped out. He pointed back into the Wagon at the M4 locked in the weapons rack. "You want to take it just to be safe?"

Danny considered it for a moment. The automatic rifles had become a standard issue since militia members had ambushed two wardens while investigating an out-of-season hunting complaint.

"Not just yet," said Danny. He pushed his door wide and hopped down. "I don't want to rattle anybody, and I don't want to get shot. On accident or on purpose."

"Just remember I gave you a chance," said Edmund. Apparently, the idea of getting shot had crossed his mind, too.

The two officers moved through the gate to the Ranger. Edmund leaned inside and turned the motor off. Danny motioned at the half-empty box of shotgun shells on the seat.

"Well, hell," Edmund said. "That's not good."

They linked up at the front of the Ranger. Edmund looked at Danny, who gave him the go-ahead, and the Indian called out in a loud voice, "Ellen. It's Edmund Goodrunner from the Tribal Police."

Nothing returned to them but the sound of wind through the grass.

"Maybe we should," started Danny, but a gunshot cut off his words.

Edmund ducked down and moved his hand to the grip of his pistol. Danny drew his Sig, brought it in front of him, and held it with both hands in the low-ready position.

"Power down, cowboy," said Edmund in a consistent voice. "Let's not make things worse."

The CH-CHUNK of a shotgun being racked came from the other side of the ridge.

"It's worse," said Danny. He lowered his pistol and let it hang in his hand along his thigh. He kept his eyes on the ridgeline. "How well do you know Ellen?"

"We used to buy horses off John when I was a kid," said Edmund. He had his eyes on the ridge also. "Never knew Ellen, but word is she's got vinegar in her veins."

"Hard woman?" asked Danny.

"Rancher's wife," said Edmund. "They don't come harder."

"Let's hope she didn't do the killing then. I hate the idea of shooting a woman," said Danny. He motioned up the slope with his pistol. "You lead out. If she shoots you, I'll arrest her."

"That doesn't make me feel better," said Edmund, but he turned and started to climb.

They crested the ridge and got their first look at Ellen Goodnight. She had her back to them and was twenty feet below. She was a little woman, rake-thin with no hips. She turned at their approach, and Danny saw she'd been crying. Her hair was ink-black, her eyes brown, and her face a wrinkled map from decades of outdoor work. She held a Remington 870 pump-action shotgun loose, pointed at the ground. Beyond her and downslope another sixty feet lay the body of whom Danny assumed was John Goodnight. Off to the side of the man was the dead steer.

Without a word, Ellen turned away and looked back down the ridge. She spit to the side, raised the shotgun to her shoulder, and fired. Danny had been fixated on her being the threat and had failed to see the three turkey vultures ten feet from John's body. Pellets from the shotgun peppered the birds. One fell dead while the other two hissed, rose, and flew away.

"Took you long enough," said Ellen. She chambered another shell, then turned to look at Edmund. "Been keeping the vultures away." She pointed at the dead steer that had five vultures crowding over it. "Seems like a few of them don't like beef."

"Ma'am," said Edmund. "Can you hand me the shotgun?"

Ellen made no move to hand the gun over but turned to stare at Edmund. "It shouldn't end like this. After twenty-eight years, it shouldn't end like this." She moved her gaze from Edmund to Danny and then to the pistol in Danny's hand.

"You scared of an old woman?" she asked. "Put that thing away. I'm shooting birds, not men. You need to be scared of the one that killed my John."

"How was he killed?" asked Danny. He holstered his pistol but didn't secure the retaining strap or take his eyes off the woman. He decided he'd show more trust after Ellen wasn't holding a loaded shotgun aimed in his general direction.

Ellen shrugged, stepped toward Edmund, and handed him the shotgun. "Go look for yourself. I can't stand to see it a second time," she said.

Danny started to ask what her husband had been doing this morning when he heard heavy breathing behind him and turned to see Janine cresting the ridge. She was tall, wore jeans and a denim shirt, had her hair tied in pigtail braids, and wore a ballcap.

Ellen nodded to her and started up the hill. She paused as she passed Edmund. With a flinty stare, she took his arm and said, "Don't let the birds get his eyes. Promise me."

"I promise," answered Edmund.

She released his arm and climbed the hill to Janine, who wrapped an arm around her and led her out of sight.

Both men watched her go, then turned downhill and started the hard work.

The body of John Goodnight was on its back. His eyes were open, and he stared at the thin, feathery clouds in the sky. His left leg was straight, but his right was bent at the knee and folded back under his body.

"Shirts got one hole punched in it. Not much blood," said Edmund. He crouched beside the body. "And he's got cow shit all over him."

"Can you see the wound?" asked Danny. One of the turkey vultures had returned, and he stayed between it and the body.

"Nope, just the hole in the shirt. Center-mass textbook kill shot to the heart." Edmund took his ballcap off to wipe the sweat away. He smoothed his hair, replaced his cap, and continued, "I'll never get used to seeing shit like this here."

"Let's hope you never do," said Danny as he pawed at the ground with a boot toe. He hit something hard and, with a few more kicks, unearthed a horseshoe with the opening aiming down. Poetic, thought Danny, since all of John Goodnight's luck had run out today.

"What do you think?" asked Edmund. He stood up and walked over to the stand beside Danny, who directed Edmund's attention on the now-two turkey vultures who stalked back and forth twenty feet away.

"Can't get a handle on it," he said. "The scene seems half a bubble off."

Danny looked back at the dead man and let his eyes travel the distance between John's body and the steer. He couldn't reconcile killing a man over a poached steer. He couldn't dismiss that as a motive; people kill each other for stupid reasons, but this seemed excessive and unnecessary.

A person convicted of felony theft in Montana, which included "any commonly domesticated hoofed animal," faced a fine of no less than five thousand dollars or incarceration for no more than ten years, or both.

Most of the sentences Danny had heard about seemed to come down heavier on the fine and lighter on confinement. So, if it was a poacher, what made those options so unpalatable to a person that they committed murder?

Even more puzzling was the dead steer. Why kill the steer instead of walking it away? You couldn't just toss a ton of beef over your shoulder and wander off. He searched the ground and saw no vehicle tracks. The scene had too many contradictions, as his father, Ben, would say.

"Danny," he heard Edmund say, shaking him out of his wool-gathering.

"Sorry," said Danny.

"Ray's here," Edmund said as he pointed up the slope at the police chief, who was lumbering toward them down the hill. Pat Palmer, the lead of the DCI field team, walked beside him, and two technicians loaded with forensics gear followed in their wake.

Danny leaned over to pick up the horseshoe, hefted it a few times to gauge weight, and flung it at the two turkey vultures. It struck the one on the left. It hissed in anger and took flight. The remaining turkey vulture looked at Danny, took stock of the situation, and followed its companion into the sky.

He turned as Ray and the DCI team walked up.

Pat had coffee in one hand and a clipboard in the other. "Morning, you two." He waved the two techs with him forward. "This is Monica Lewis and Bob Jennings, both transfers from Missoula. Monica, Bob, this is Warden Danny Coogan and Tribal Officer Edmund Goodrunner."

"Morning Pat, sorry to have work for you today," said Danny. He motioned to the body, "It's not a pretty one. Wife found the body."

Pat pointed at the shotgun Edmund held. "Murder weapon?"

"Only of vultures," said Edmund. He tossed a thumb over his shoulder at the two dead birds.

"One of these days, I want a call from you just to go fishing or hiking," said Pat. He set his coffee on the grass and pulled a pen from his shirt pocket. "When did you get here?"

Edmund glanced at his watch. "Just over an hour ago," he answered.

"And when was the body found?" asked Pat as he made a notation on his clipboard.

"Maybe thirty minutes before that," answered Edmund.

"Either one of you touch the body or move anything?"

"That's insulting," said Danny with a half grin. Then he remembered the horseshoe. "I did find a buried horseshoe and tossed it at the birds to keep them away."

Pat looked up from his scribbling. "What are you, five?"

Danny shrugged and looked to Edmund for backup, but the tribal officer was suddenly profoundly interested in the skyline.

"Cops like you are why I drink," said Pat. He clicked the pen shut and waved the two technicians toward the body. "Let's get to it, folks. You know the drill."

"Anything else you need?" asked Ray.

"Not now," said Pat. He pulled out a set of gloves. "I'll let you know the preliminaries as soon as possible."

The officers found Ellen in the passenger seat of Janine's Jeep. She was cradling a can of root beer and had been crying again.

Her window was rolled down, and she raised her head as Ray leaned on the door. He said in a gentle voice, "Ellen. I have to ask you a few questions. Then we can get you home."

Ellen nodded. "Go ahead."

"What was John out doing this morning?"

"He wanted to get water out for the cattle before it got hot," answered Ellen. "Said he'd be back by breakfast."

"What time was that?" asked Edmund.

Ellen shifted her eyes to him and said, "We get up at four-thirty. He was out by five."

"Go on," nudged Ray gently.

"When he didn't get back, I tried calling his phone. When he didn't answer, I figured he'd just left it in the truck. But after an hour, I got worried and went to look for him."

"Did you touch anything when you found John?" asked Ray.

Ellen shook her head no.

"You know of anyone who had a reason to hurt you or John?" asked Ray.

"Nobody," answered Ellen with a twinge of bitterness. "All we got is bills; nobody wants to take those from us."

"That's enough for now," said Ray. "I'm going to have Janine take you home. Do you have anyone who can come stay with you?"

"I can call my sister," said Ellen.

"Fine," said Ray. He looked through the Jeep at his daughter, who sat behind the wheel. "Janine will stay with you until she shows up."

"You think the council can help with the burial ceremony?" asked Ellen suddenly. "Don't have the money for it."

"I imagine it can be worked out," said Ray. "I'll talk to the new chairman."

"Trust my dad, it'll be okay," said Janine. She started the Jeep, slipped it into gear, and looked past Ellen to her father. "I'll let you know when the sister shows up."

As the three lawmen watched the Jeep pull away, Edmund turned to Ray and asked, "You think the chairman will give money?"

"Out of his pocket, I'm sure he will. But as for money directly from the council, those sanctimonious sons of bitches wouldn't give money to bury their mothers," said Ray. He pulled his wallet out, emptied it, and handed the contents to Edmund. "I expect everyone to give. Get with Levi Brown about arrangements. Tell him I'll cover whatever we're short."

Danny pulled his wallet out and extended the contents.

Ray looked him up and down. "I didn't mean you."

"Piss off, I'm giving," said Danny. He shoved the money into Edmund's hand. "Ranchers are the same on and off the Rez. Land-rich, cash poor. You'd do the same for Ben or me."

"He's got a fair point," said Edmund. He folded the money together and tucked it into his shirt pocket. "You two can fight it out later. Here comes Pat."

Danny replaced his wallet and glanced down at his watch. It was a quarter after eleven, and DCI had only been on-site for over an hour. This would be the preliminary report, a snapshot of information. Useful, but not detailed. The evidence collection would go on for hours, but any information was better than nothing.

Pat was writing on a clipboard as he approached them, not watching where he stepped. Almost to the gate, he walked into a fresh cow pie, and his left boot slipped sideways. He stumbled, nearly fell, but righted himself in a flurry of windmill rotations of his arms. The clipboard flew, clattered against the gate, and fell into the grass. Despite the circumstances, all three lawmen grinned.

Pat remedied himself, recovered his clipboard, and approached the three.

"Don't hold back on my account," he said as he wiped the side of his boots in the grass.

The three men had been smiling, but the smiles faded as Pat took the clipboard from under his arm.

Ray asked the question for them all, "What about John?"

"Mr. Goodnight was killed with a portable free bolt stunner fired through his heart. We dug the bolt out of the ground from under him," said Pat. He looked at Danny, who appeared confused. "A stunner is used for in-the-field euthanasia by veterinarians. It's comparable to a power-actuated nail gun."

"Fucking hell," said Edmund. "That's just evil."

"Never heard it being used to kill a man," said Danny, shaking his head and trying to reconcile someone doing this to another human being.

"It was in a movie some years ago. I forget the name," said Pat. "In the movie, it was used on the person's head, not their heart, but the results are comparable."

"Could he have done it to himself?" asked Edmund.

"No, it would have killed him instantly, and we found the stunner to the west, some thirty yards away," said Pat. "No way he could do this to himself and throw the stunner that far."

"How far away can you fire it from?" asked Danny.

"It has to be pressed against a surface to trigger," said Ray, answering the question before Pat could speak. Danny gave the police chief a look. Ray shrugged and said, "Grew up with cattle."

"No suicide, no long-distance shot. Whoever killed John walked up to him, pressed the stunner to his chest, and fired," said Edmund, understanding the ramifications. "He knew them."

"Worse than that," added Danny. "He trusted them."

"What about the steer?" asked Ray, shifting the conversation.

Pat looked back at his notes. "Same cause of death, but the bolt was through the skull."

"Opinion?" asked Ray.

Pat stared at the tribal chief with a straight-faced expression. "For Goodnight or the steer?"

"Jesus, Pat," said Ray. "I'm asking about Goodnight."

"Preliminary finding, homicide. We can rule out self-inflicted. Leaves us with a single avenue at present. We'll finish processing the site before I mark it on paper."

"Anything else?" asked Ray.

"Wallet, comb, and candy in his pockets. No keys, no money, no phone. His wedding ring was still on his finger," said Pat. "We found this; it was under him."

Pat pulled out an evidence satchel and drew a small rawhide pouch out with his gloved hand. It had a leather thong laced through notches in the top and cinched tight to prevent the contents from spilling. It had an intricate design in green, white, and tan embroidery, with a rainbow of glass beads dangling off the tails of a hide fringe that circled the pouch.

"Medicine bag," said Ray, not reaching for it. "Elk or deer hide."

Danny stared at the bag. It was beautiful. "John's?"

"No, he was a non-believer," said Ray. He gave a chin twitch toward Danny. "You white guys ruined him. Last I heard, he'd gone Catholic."

"Maybe he came back to his roots," said Edmund. "Old folks do that sometimes when they see the end coming."

"Maybe," said Ray. "But how would he know his end was coming?"

"We'll need to ask Ellen," said Danny. "Maybe he was sick and didn't want anybody besides her to know."

Ray nodded in agreement, then asked Pat, "Any chance for prints?"

"Remote at best. Environmental hazards."

"You mean cow shit," said Danny. His smile returned.

"Exactly," replied Pat with a smile. He slipped the medicine bag back into the evidence satchel. "We might have better luck with the items inside, but I want to do that back at the office. Controlled environment and better equipment."

"Anything else?" asked Ray.

Pat shook his head. "We bagged his hands in case he scratched his assailant, but don't pin much hope on that. Just not much to go on besides the medicine bag."

"You got to do better than that, dammit," said Ray. "Do your *CSI* magic."

"We could print the steer, but I doubt he did it," said Pat in an attempt at levity. Seeing the flat faces of the three lawmen, he cleared his throat and pressed on. "We'll go over the body again and walk the surrounding area a second time."

"Appreciate it," said Ray.

"I called for floodlights and generators. It'll be a long night. I'll ring you when I know more," said Pat. He turned to walk back to the crime scene, giving the slipped-on cowpie a wide berth.

Ray watched him go, then turned to Danny. "You think a poacher got the steer?"

"No," answered Danny. "Killing an animal you can't carry makes no sense. The vet could do a necropsy, give us an idea if it was hurt or sick."

"I'll have them collect the steer," said Ray, motioning his head in agreement. "What about neighbors?"

"Nobody close," said Edmund, rubbing his chin with a hand. "Lone Dog place is two miles east, but they're both in their eighties. The Stonechild boys live to the west. They have tempers, so they're worth a look." He hesitated, glanced at Ray, "And according to Sonny Siebert, Joe Niland is living inside Crazy Buffalo Canyon in that beat-up trailer of his."

Ray's head snapped up at the name. "I thought he settled with his daughter over on Rocky Boy's reservation after prison?"

"Don't know about that. Siebert gave me the heads-up this morning," said Edmund. He canted his head to one side. "He said things have come up missing. I think it was his way of giving us fair warning to deal with Joe before he and his friends find a rope and a tall tree."

"Fucknuts," said Ray. He started to say more when his radio sputtered to life.

Janine's voice came from the radio. "Unit one, unit five over."

Ray bent his head to the mike clipped to his chest. "Unit one."

"Dad, Ellen's sleeping, and Irene, her sister, just got here. Irene remembered on the drive that Joe Niland sometimes did hired hand work for John. It's a day-laborer thing. She doesn't know but thinks he might have been helping with the cattle this morning."

"What did Joe do time for?" whispered Danny to Edmund.

Edmund whispered back, "Killed a man in a bar fight. Got eighteen years."

Ray shushed them. "Anything else?"

"Just normal things. House is neat as a pin," she said. "Dishes are done, a basket of folded clothes. My God, she's organized. She said the bank has set the sale on their place for the end of the month. Considering how neatly she keeps house, she'll have no trouble packing."

"So, nothing out of the ordinary?" asked Ray.

"Nothing. By appearances, everything was normal before she went looking for John."

Danny spit into the grass and postulated, "So no reason for John to be dead then." He scratched his chin and asked the group, "Do we think John was mixed up in something Ellen didn't know about?"

"You got to stop binging *True Detective*," said Edmund. "It's warping your thinking."

"Finished it," said Danny with a smile. "Binging *Luther* now."

Ray gave them both a dirty look as he pressed the button on the radio. "I'm going to have Stan come and sit on Pat for answers. I need you here to relieve him in the field as soon as Ellen wakes up. She'll be fine alone with her sister."

"Roger, five out," said the voice, and the radio went dead.

"I'll stay here till one of them shows."

"And us?" asked Edmund.

"Go interview the neighbors."

"Niland first?" asked Danny.

"You read my mind. Be careful, though," said Ray. "He's a gun nut."

"And a convicted felon," said Danny. "Is he allowed guns?"

"I'm sure Joe doesn't give a rat's ass what he's allowed," replied Ray. "And he's not much of a rule minder. Probably got more guns than the National Guard."

"Awesome," said Danny.

Chapter 3

Driving the backcountry of Montana is never a straightforward proposition. The land is rough and untamed, with a need to test your resolve before it allows you to pass through it. The Dead Horse Reservation's hinterland was no exception. It was filled with sheer cliffs, rock-filled creeks, shifty hills, and truck-eating ravines. As the crow flew, it was seven miles from Goodnight's body to Niland's trailer in Crazy Buffalo, but it would be twice that far on the broken road Danny was currently driving on to get there.

In the old days, he and Edmund would have saddled up, packed supplies, and tracked their quarry through the land on horseback, he thought. True Western lawmen of the best tradition. He drifted left to avoid a hole, and a couple of problems with that scenario occurred to him. First, he didn't like horses, and second, he was absolute shit in the saddle.

"Do you have to hit every hole?" said Edmund in an annoyed voice. "I mean, for fuck's sake, they're not hiding from you. You can see them, right?"

Danny glanced over at the Indian. Edmund had his seatbelt fastened tight. One hand rested on the dash, and the other held fast to the ceiling grab bar.

"You're hurting my feelings holding on so tight," said Danny. The truck jittered over a washboard section of the trail. The tail went left while the front went right. Danny pulled his foot off the accelerator, steered into the slide, and the truck straightened.

He glanced over and asked, "You want to drive?"

"Watch out," yelled Edmund. Danny shifted his eyes back to the road in time to see the washout that spanned the width of the road. He winced as the front wheels struck it. They bronco bucked through it. Danny bounced up to hit his head on the ceiling of the cab while his groin contacted the bottom of the steering wheel.

The Wagon rolled to a stop on the far side of the washout. Danny's eyes watered; he was having a hard time breathing and was sure he was now a gelding. He glanced across the truck at Edmund, who also had tears in his eyes, but not from pain.

"Oh, shit," Edmund said through fits of laughter. "That was awesome."

Danny drew deep breaths and laughed at himself, even with the pain. He leaned his head on the steering wheel and massaged his crotch. "Cut it out. It's worse when I laugh," he said as his male parts went numb.

"We could get you some horse liniment," said Edmund, wiping his eyes. "Serves your Speed Racer ass right. You didn't rein in the speed, so you 'stirruped' trouble."

"I bet that sounded hilarious in your head," said Danny. He sat up, leaned back, and massaged the red spot on his head from the ceiling. "It's better now."

"Want me to drive?" asked Edmund.

Danny put his seatbelt on, tugged it tight, and breathed deeply. "I'll be all right. Just going to be high-voiced for a bit."

"Can I tell Ruth and Demitta about this?" asked Edmund.

"Sure," answered Danny. "If you want a tragically short life that ends with your death through an unsolved accident."

"Fair enough," said Edmund. But just before he turned up Marty Robbins singing "El Paso" on the radio, he added, "I'm still telling Ray."

Danny took a deep breath and flipped Edmund off, which only made the Indian start to laugh again. He concentrated on the road, pressed the accelerator, and eased the Wagon up to ten miles an hour. His groin still throbbed, but he was beginning to think he'd live and might even be able to father children.

After the song was over, he reached down and muted the radio. "What do you know about Niland?"

"Just what Ray's told me. He's in his fifties now. Went to prison back when you and me were in high school for killing a white BIA agent. Rumor around the Rez is he now claims to be a modern-day shaman with visions and shit."

"I thought BIA guys were Native?"

"Most are now, but this was a long time ago when the BIA was a lot paler."

Danny knew the Bureau of Indian Affairs had a checkered past in dealing with Native Americans. It had adjusted in many ways, so he figured glacial progress was still progress.

"Was Niland under investigation?" asked Danny.

"Ray didn't think so," answered Edmund. "The BIA guy was working a missing persons case and had a run-in with Joe at a bar. Kind of a bad-luck situation for both of them."

Danny maneuvered around a pile of large rocks. "Who went missing?"

"Joanna Parker and Ethan Iron Kettle, both fifteen. I remember them," answered Edmund. "Disappeared walking home from school."

"Why didn't Tribal Police handle the investigation?"

"Joanna was the daughter of a council member. Police chief at the time figured the BIA had more resources."

"They ever find them?" asked Danny.

"They found Joanna," replied Edmund. "Montana Power was stringing wires and found her body wrapped in a horse blanket in a culvert."

"Positive ID?" asked Danny.

"By the mother. The only thing missing was a turtle necklace her grandmother gave her."

"Turtle necklace?"

"The turtle represents Mother Earth," answered Edmund. "Lots of girls had them in school. I remember hers because it was blue with flecks of yellow."

"What about Iron Kettle?" said Danny.

"Never found him, alive or dead. Lots of folks think it was a love gone bad. BIA figured he killed Joanna, hid the body, and ran off."

"Don't sound like you buy that."

"Like I said, I knew them," continued Edmund. "Joanna was a pretty girl, a tad wild but sweet. I remember her walking the hall in the high school, all tight Wranglers, hat, and sass."

"And Ethan?"

"Skinny kid, kept to himself, and his interests didn't include girls, if you get my drift," replied Edmund.

"You can say gay. It's not the Dark Ages now," said Danny. He pumped the brakes as they descended steeply into a dry creek bed. "Did anybody ever think Niland was involved?"

"Not the BIA. He'd been in the local lockup for taking a swing at the postman over not getting his *TV Guide* delivered on time when the kids disappeared," answered Edmund.

"So, how'd the BIA agent end up dead?"

"He came into The Saddle and Spur Saloon half in the bag after they found Joanna's body. He'd promised the family they'd find her alive and took it hard when he couldn't deliver. Niland was half-drunk in the bar, and the two started picking at each other."

"How?" asked Danny.

"Racial shit, like always," replied Edmund. "According to Ray, the final straw was when Niland accused the agent of not caring because the girl was just another dead Indian."

"Did the agent throw the first punch?"

"Yep, but Niland had been a boxer before the bottle and ducked it. He comes back up, lands a few, and puts the BIA guy on the ground."

"But he didn't stay on the ground."

"Nope. This idiot BIA guy climbs off the floor, grabs Niland, says he doesn't know shit about how he feels, and tops it off by calling Niland an ignorant 'cherry nigger.' Ten minutes later, the agent's dead with a butterfly knife sticking out of his chest."

"Jesus," said Danny. "Didn't the lawyer claim mitigating circumstance? Ask for leniency?"

"Come on, Danny. This was rural Montana more or less a decade ago. Red guy kills a white cop; red guy goes to jail, and they lose the key; screw mitigating circumstances."

"So, he did his time, and now he thinks he's a shaman?" said Danny. "Do you believe in visions?"

Edmund gave Danny a blank glance. "Of course."

"What visions do you think Joe sees?"

"I doubt they're heaven-sent," answered Edmund. "Most likely come from a bottle. He drank at the professional level before prison, and I doubt he's retired from competition."

Danny slowed the Power Wagon and eased off the gravel road onto the glorified goat trail. "How do you know all this?" he asked.

"Family history. My uncle was in the bar that night and saw everything," answered Edmund.

Danny slowed down as they came to a washout that spanned the road width. He eased the Wagon down into the gully, gunned the engine on the other side, and resumed speed. The mouth of the canyon came into view as they passed over a slight rise.

The top of a camp trailer came into view ahead. Danny asked, "How do you want to handle this?"

Edmund thought for a moment. "No guns drawn, but let's unstrap and be ready."

"Agreed," said Danny. He steered past a sizeable rock, then cut back to the center of the road. "You take the lead and make contact. I'll circle and cover the back."

"Let me do the dangerous part, huh?"

"I'm just the tag-along here," said Danny. He pulled the Power Wagon to the side of the road and stopped. The two saw the trailer fifty yards ahead in a sparse cluster of aspens.

"Cover me while I pee," said Danny as he jumped out and swung the door closed on the Wagon. With relief, he unzipped his fly and watered a congregation of dandelions.

He zipped up and met Edmund at the truck's front bumper. Danny shrugged as Edmund glanced at him and wiggled a leg to adjust things. "No telling what Niland is going to do, but best to have an empty bladder whatever happens."

"Can't fault your logic," said Edmund. He tossed his chin at the camper. "I don't hear a generator."

Danny grunted in agreement and gave the camper a once over. It was a weathered 1970s-era Komfort trailer that Danny estimated was fourteen or fifteen feet long. It was colored a dirty white, with a baby blue stripe midway down that ran the length of its side. The windows were missing their screens and cranked all the way open.

"I think we've got probable cause covered," said Edmund. He gestured toward a makeshift corral to the far right of the trailer. It had four cattle inside it, all standing motionless and staring at the two lawmen.

"That's not suspicious at all," said Danny as he unstrapped his sidearm.

Edmund started to answer when the barrel of a long gun appeared in one of the open windows and fired. The round passed between the two men and punched a hole in the windshield of the Wagon. Danny dove to his left into the tall grass of the ditch. Edmund crouched and tried to move right, but a round struck the ground beside him. He hopped to the left, where his feet got caught in soft sand and fell in a heap, still in clear view of the shooter.

Danny rose from the grass in a shooting stance, his Sig Sauer out. His aim wobbled, and he fired two rounds. Both hit a water barrel at the front of the trailer, sending up a water geyser. He steadied his aim and fired a third round. The window beside the rifle barrel exploded.

A voice in the trailer cried out in pain or surprise, and the barrel disappeared.

Danny glanced over and saw Edmund had made it back onto his feet, drawn his service weapon, and was crouched in the high grass on the right side of the road. Danny turned to look at his truck, keeping his gun aimed at the trailer.

"Every fucking time," he yelled, referring to the busted windshield.

Edmund yelled to get his attention and motioned to their right and further off the road. "We need to get into the trees," shouted Edmund. "We can close in on the trailer from the nose end and avoid the window."

Danny spit and nodded. He and Edmund were combat veterans, and a few bullets didn't rattle them out of thinking tactically.

"Cover me, and I'll come to you," he said, preparing to dash across the open road. He moved to the edge of the grass, and as his foot touched gravel, he heard a vehicle engine rumble to life.

A green Jeep J10 with a Kaiser grill emerged from the butt end of the trailer. It bounced over the stump of what had once been a large oak, flattened a ceramic goose, and rumbled toward the lawmen. Danny could see the driver bouncing in the cab like a piñata, ricocheting off the cab roof and back down into the bench seat. *Guess I'm not the only one that doesn't buckle up*, he thought.

Edmund dropped to one knee, steadied his aim, and fired four times. The first shot went wide, and the second blew out a headlight. The third and fourth disappeared into the grillwork. As it passed him, he fired twice more, striking the rear rim with the first and puncturing the rear tire with his final shot.

At the same time, Danny raised his weapon and fired twice at the Jeep. His first round ricocheted off the truck's cattle guard and rocketed into orbit, but his second struck high on the Jeep's windshield. It passed through and hit the rearview mirror. The mirror cartwheeled into the driver's face, which made him take his hand off the wheel to grab his nose. The Jeep's front wheels turned in the gravel and veered toward the game warden.

Danny jumped to his left as the truck closed in on him. He winced as he hit the ground and continued to roll, hoping to avoid the tires. Suddenly, the ground disappeared beneath him, and he dropped into a two-foot-deep ditch camouflaged by high grass. He landed with a splash in stagnant, muddy water as the Jeep rumbled over the top of him. It fishtailed in the grass and almost hit a tree before the driver regained control and turned the wheel to climb back onto the road. Danny was soaked but uninjured and popped his head up just in time to see the truck clip the driver's side mirror off his Power Wagon and escape down the road.

Edmund ran to the passenger side of the truck and climbed in.

Danny climbed out of the ditch and moved to the Wagon. He picked up his crumpled mirror on the way and tossed it into the bed of his truck.

"Just once, I wish somebody would peacefully surrender," he said as he climbed in, started the truck, and spun around to chase the Jeep still in sight.

The Power Wagon closed the gap within a quarter mile and trailed the truck by only a few feet. Danny swerved to the right and prepared to draw up beside the Jeep, clipping the back rear end to send it into a spin.

"Get ready," said Danny.

Edmund holstered his weapon and placed his hand on the belt buckle. He would unclip the buckle the moment Danny initiated the spin of the truck. He'd jump free of the

Power Wagon and have the driver cuffed before they knew what was happening.

Just as Danny accelerated to make his move, the Jeep's tail kicked in the air like a bronco. It hung there for a moment, standing on its nose. Then, it slumped over onto its side like it had been poleaxed. It trundled off the road and slid down the slight decline to land upside down in the wide but only foot-deep Root River.

Danny slid the Wagon to a stop, and Edmund bailed out, side-hopping down the slope to get to the driver before he drowned. Danny glanced around to see what had caused the Jeep to bronco. His eyes found the sizeable rock he'd steered around on their trip the other way. The rock looked the same except for a large green paint smear and a piece of the Jeep's front bumper.

Danny jumped out of the Wagon and went down the bank to help Edmund. As Danny got to the vehicle, Edmund dragged a flailing man out of the Jeep.

The man reeked of pot and thrashed about, trying to punch anyone and everything. He gained his feet, broke free of Edmund, staggered, and took a weak swing at Danny. The warden caught the hand and twisted it behind the man's back. Edmund grabbed the man's other wrist and rotated the arm until the hands met behind the man's back. With a click, the cuffs snapped tight.

"Settle down," growled Edmund. He reached down to pick his hat out of the creek where it'd fallen during the wrestling match to get the man out of the truck. He jerked the hat down and away to knock water off and put it back on his head.

The man laughed a little, spit into the water, and said in a slurred voice, "What seems to be the problem, officer?"

"You think you're fucking funny, Joe?" asked Edmund.

Danny turned Joe to face him and looked at the man well while Edmund patted him for weapons.

Danny didn't see blood, but some swelling was starting on the man's right cheek. Joe was shorter than Danny and thinner in the middle. He had a smooth face, a hooknose, and long black hair tied in a ponytail with a bright blue shoelace. He wore no shirt under his denim jacket, and his pants were a pair of cargo shorts held up by a beaded belt. He had only one boot on and no socks.

"Officer," slurred Joe. "I'd like to report the theft of a boot."

"It's in the truck, along with the rifle you used on us," said Edmund. He'd finished his search and showed Danny the handgun and the six-inch skinning knife he'd found on Joe.

"I'm not feelin' too good," said Joe.

Before Danny or Edmund could grab him, Joe's legs wobbled, and he fell backward onto his butt in the creek. The water ran over his lap and covered his legs, soaking the bottom of his jacket.

Joe squinted at Danny, laughed, and said, "The water's cold. It tickles my rod and tackle."

"He's stoned out of his mind," said Danny. "I can smell the pot on him."

"He's on more than pot," replied Edmund. "Peyote would be my guess. I'm going to check the truck. You got him?"

"He ain't going nowhere," said Danny.

Edmund knelt into the water and crawled inside the overturned Jeep. Danny kept his eyes on Joe but heard

Edmund rummage around the inside of the truck. Edmund reappeared after two minutes and held up an M1 Garand, an M1911 Colt, and a Walther PPK tied down in a shoulder holster.

Edmund handed the pistol and shoulder holster to Danny. "Seems we caught the Native American James Bond."

Danny smiled, looked down at Joe, and asked, "You an international man of mystery?"

"I ain't international," answered Joe, confused. "I'm a local."

"Jesus," said Danny. He shook his head at the absurdity of the situation. He nudged Joe with the toe of his boot to get his attention, then motioned to the confiscated weapons and asked, "You expecting trouble today?"

"You had a Wakanpi stalking you," answered Joe with a shrug. His eyes shifted between Danny and Edmund. With a crooked smile, he said, "I saved your life."

"Was this Wakanpi sitting in my truck?" asked Danny, waving a hand up the bank toward the blue Power Wagon with its spiderwebbed windshield.

"Wakanpi are everywhere. Some good, some evil. An evil one hunts you," slurred Joe.

Danny looked at Edmund, "What's he talking about? What's a Wakanpi?"

"Spirit beings. They have the power over the earth and mankind," answered Edmund.

Danny gave a confused look at the Indian. "Come again?"

"You know about angels and demons?" asked Edmund.

"Of course."

"Same thing," said Edmund. He reached over to pluck a climbing crawfish off Joe's back, tossing it in the water. "Where you been this morning, Joe?"

Joe started to answer, then looked like he wanted to throw up. He leaned downstream to vomit, then raised an ass cheek and let loose with a long fart. Bubbles boiled between his legs, and Danny felt sorry for any nearby crawfish. Joe leaned upstream, drew in some of the creek water, swished it in his mouth, and spat it out. He looked up at Edmund, squinted his eyes briefly, and recognition rumbled across his face.

"Hey, Chief Whitepipe. You lost weight?" Joe swiveled his head to survey his surroundings. He sucked in a deep breath when he saw the upside-down Jeep. "What'd you do to my truck?"

"You did that yourself," answered Danny. Then, pointing up at the Wagon, he added, "And that."

Uncertainty trickled into Joe's eyes. "This is entrapment," he said.

"Freaking hell, we'll get no straight answers until the shit he's on wears off," said Edmund. "I'm going to radio in and request backup."

Danny leaned over to help Joe to his feet. "Might see if DCI can spare a tech to process the trailer and anything else we find."

"Good idea," said Edmund. He pulled his radio out and then pointed at the growing goose egg on the side of Joe's head. "And maybe an ambulance for the shaman."

Chapter 4

Two hours later, Ruth was examining the knot on Joe's head. He was sitting on the dropped tailgate of Ray's truck, handcuffed to a tie-down ring. Surrounding her were Danny, Edmund, Ray, and the just-arrived Tribal Officer Sotomayor.

Ruth had been hoping to catch Danny at the Tribal Police Headquarters and had been chatting with Ray when Edmund radioed. She'd volunteered to ride out with Ray so she could kill two birds with one stone. First, she'd examine and treat Joe; second, she'd tell Danny about her parents' change of travel plans.

"Did either of you see what he hit his head on?" she asked as her gloved fingers probed the knot on the man's forehead.

Edmund shook his head no while Danny said, "I assume he hit everything. He pinballed inside the cab during the getaway, chase, rollover, and trip into the river."

Ruth moved her hands down to the swollen cheek, and the half-asleep Joe flinched. "Well, the cheekbone is surely broken, but it'll heal. It's the hematoma that concerns me the most."

"You mean the knot?" asked Danny.

"Yes, the knot," replied Ruth. "Did you find out what he was on?"

"Tech found marijuana and peyote in the trailer," answered Ray. He tossed a wave at the DCI van parked beside the Power Wagon. "She's still processing the trailer but cataloged the drugs and weapons for us already."

Ruth leaned back on her haunches and stripped her gloves off. "My guess is peyote. Explains the vivid hallucinations of, what did you call it?

"Wakanpi," replied Edmund.

"Wakanpi, right," said Ruth. "Peyote effects can last for twelve hours or more. And since we don't know when he took it, we need to err on the side of caution. He needs to be under observation until he's lucid and can answer questions."

"Soto, put him in the back of your truck and keep an eye on him," said Ray to the junior tribal officer.

Soto undid the handcuffs and woke Joe up enough for him to drop off the tailgate. Joe stood, with support, beside him. "He needs to stay awake, right doc?"

"Yes," answered Ruth. "And I need to know right away if he starts feeling queasy or throws up."

"You get to have all the fun," said Edmund with a click of his tongue.

Ruth and the three remaining lawmen watched Soto half-carry Joe toward his used Ford Interceptor SUV, parked beside Ray's new Interceptor.

Danny watched them go and looked past them to admire the shiny SUVs. "You know the sheriff's department in Beckwourth put a requisition in for the same model Fords, and the county rejected it, said they cost too much."

"Federal grant," said Ray with a chuckle. "Money covers up all kinds of sins."

The police chief turned back to look at Edmund and nodded toward the corral. "Any ideas whose cattle those are?"

"No proof," said Edmund. "But I'd place a hundred-dollar bet they belong to Goodnight."

"They could be his," said Ray slowly. He stroked his stubble, and Danny could see tumblers falling into place in the man's eyes. "That's a tidy sum of money in that corral. And with John's money problems, losing them would hurt him bad."

"It would tie up real nice, wouldn't it," said Danny. "Joe's rustling some livestock; Goodnight catches him in the act and tries to stop him. One stun bolt through the heart later, Goodnight's dead, and Joe runs off with the cattle."

"It's a theory," said Ray. "But it doesn't hold water."

"How'd he get the cattle here?" said Edmund. "They don't fit in the bed of the Jeep, and I don't see a livestock trailer."

"And if he killed John, why not take all the cattle? Why kill the steer?" said Ray.

"And why get peyote high when you should be rehearsing your alibi," added Ruth.

The three lawmen turned to look at the doctor.

"What," she said. "I watched cop shows and live with a cop. I can have an opinion."

"Damn, rough crowd. Even the armchair detective shooting me full of holes," said Danny, but he smiled to show no hard feelings and slid an arm around Ruth. She leaned in and kissed his neck.

"Chief Whitepipe," came a female voice from the trailer.

The group swiveled their heads in unison to see the tech peeking out of one of the trailer windows. A headband was holding back her blond hair, but she'd pulled her face mask down and was waving for them to come over.

Ray and Edmund led out, with Danny and Ruth bringing up the rear and holding hands.

Ruth leaned close and said, "Just a heads-up, my folks decided to surprise us and are already here."

Danny raised an eyebrow and cocked his head to one side. "Is this a planned ambush to catch us unprepared?" He relaxed, and the smile returned to his face. "Sounds like the kind of dodgy shit a Navy diver would pull on an Army grunt."

Ruth laughed and poked him on the ribs with her free hand. "Be nice. Besides, it didn't work. My niece in

Indiana called to let me know they were coming. Ben and Molly are meeting them at the airport in Great Falls."

"Move and countermove," said Danny. "Molly will feed them into oblivion, and Ben will talk their ears off."

"That's me and Molly's plan, cowboy," said Ruth with a wink. She detached herself as they approached the trailer door. "You best get to work now. I'm going back to check on Mr. Niland." She leaned in, kissed Danny quickly, then turned away and sashayed back toward the parked vehicles.

Danny watched her go and was floored that a woman like her would acknowledge his existence in the world, let alone marry him.

"Danny," said Ray from behind him.

Danny turned to see the police chief smiling at him. "The power of a woman over a man's heart."

"We're just pawns in the game, aren't we," he said with a smile of his own and a glance at the confused face of the DCI tech standing in the trailer's doorway.

"Without a doubt," said Edmund.

Ray turned and gave his attention to the DCI tech and said, "Okay, Miss Lewis, what did you find for us?"

"Call me Monica," said the tech. She reached behind her, back into the trailer, and pulled out a large plastic shelf bin, the kind used for nuts, bolts, and washers. She tilted it forward, and the three lawmen leaned in to see the contents. Piled up on each other was an extensive collection of yellow, green, and blue button tags with different fifteen-digit numbers on them.

"RFID tags for herd management," said Edmund. He reached down and dug through the bin. "Some of these are Premise tags."

"What's the difference?" asked the DCI tech.

Edmund handed her one of the tags he was talking about. "A Premise tag has a unique number or code assigned to a single location."

"Like a farm or ranch," said Monica.

"You got it," said Danny.

Monica studied the numbers on the blue tag she held. "So, these tags would tell you where the animal it was attached to came from, right?"

"Exactly," said Edmund. "Even the standard RFIDs would be recorded if the animals are insured. It would take phone calls to the tag manufacturer, maybe the Animal Health Bureau. But they're recorded someplace."

"How many tags are there?" asked Danny.

"I stopped counting when I got to a hundred and only made it through a third of the pile," answered Monica.

"We're talking over three hundred stolen cattle," said Ray. He reached up to set his hat back farther on his head. "Joe's a hardworking thief. I'll give him that."

"The smart thing would have been to burn those tags," said Danny.

"That cinches it," said Danny. He took a bag of the still-cold money and held it up. "He's no criminal mastermind. He couldn't organize a thing this big."

"We have been around Joe all afternoon, and he hasn't done one smart thing yet," agreed Edmund.

"Where did you find them?" asked Danny.

Monica cocked her head before answering, "In a locked file cabinet along with a spiral notebook."

"What's in the notebook?" asked Edmund.

"Just lines of numbers," answered Monica. "Probably money-in, money-out kind of thing. We got financial forensics folks that can decode it."

"Locked up like he didn't want anyone to know about either of them," said Ray. Danny could see another tumbler fall into place in Ray's head. "I would hazard a guess he was either trying to protect himself or planning to blackmail somebody."

Monica handed the plastic bin to Danny, who set it beside him. She reached back into the trailer and pulled out a succession of clear Ziplock bags, each filled with stacked tens and twenties. "I don't know shit about how much a stolen cow brings, but I know it would be more than eight thousand."

"Where did you find it?" asked Ray.

"Stuffed in the icebox," answered Monica. "Just opened the door, and there it lay on top of the Chunky Monkey."

Edmund stepped to the side, stroked his chin, then said, "I remember a case I read about. Happened down in Oklahoma." He paused, then, with a deep exhale, and looking at Ray, continued, "This is just a guess, but do you think instead of stealing cattle off of Goodnight, they were in on it together?"

"You lost me," said Danny.

"I see the thread you're pulling," said Ray. "I don't believe it for a second, but it's a trail to follow."

Danny looked between the two and finally turned back to Monica and asked, "Do you have a fucking clue what they're talking about?"

Monica laughed. "Don't ask me. I'm a city girl."

"It's such an old game it's got whiskers," said Ray. He shoved one hand in a pocket and used the other to point at Edmund. "What he's saying is that Niland takes the cattle and finds a stockyard that will take them without papers while Goodnight files a claim with his insurance. Goodnight collects from both ends and pays Niland like an employee."

"But the Goodnights are broke," said Danny. "Janine said the bank set a sale for the end of the month."

"Well, it would be hard to explain where they got the money to settle the debt," said Edmund. "If they have been selling stolen cattle, they might be planning to disappear at the end of the month."

"Or maybe it's just John involved and Ellen's innocent," countered Danny.

"You two watch way too much TV," said Monica. "This isn't an episode of *Murder, She Wrote*."

"Monica is right, even with the ancient reference. You're both diving down gopher holes without proof," said Ray. "This could all be bullshit, and I'm not interrogating a wife that just lost her husband until we know some things."

"First, we track the RFID and Premise tags, see who owns what; second, if any tags come to John, we see if he had animal insurance and is collecting on stolen cattle."

"And if all that's true?" asked Danny.

"Then and only then will we talk to Ellen," answered Ray. "Understood?"

Edmund and Danny nodded in agreement.

"I can head back to town and start making calls," said Edmund. "I can have Soto take me and drop Joe and Ruth at the clinic."

Ray shook his head and fished out his keys. He tossed them to Edmund and said, "Leave the three of them with Danny and me. You can take Big Thunder."

Edmund shrugged, turned, and walked away, disappearing around the end of the trailer with the plastic bin under his arm. Out of view, they heard the new Ford Interceptor thunder to life and drive away.

Ray turned to face Danny and asked, "You mind sticking around with me?"

"Not at all," answered Danny. "Why'd you want Soto, Ruth, and Joe to stay?"

"Just a feeling," said Ray. "Like I said before, Joe might have kept those tags and notebook to protect himself or to blackmail somebody. Makes me uneasy, and I wanted to keep him close."

"You think whoever is heading up the rustling might catch wind you're here, and with Joe being the only link between them and the cattle," said Monica.

Danny saw the leap in thinking Ray had made and finished, "No Joe, no link."

"You're both right," Ray answered. He then looked up at Monica and asked, "Got anything else?"

Monica peered over her shoulder and into the trailer. "I got some piddly shit cowboy gear, a mountain of porn, whiskey, five cases of ramen noodles, and a flat of canned chili."

"I meant anything suspicious," asked Ray.

Monica turned her head, looked Ray in the eyes, and said, "Well, the ramen is all the same flavor."

Danny laughed while Ray cursed under his breath.

"I mean hell's bells, it comes in a million flavors," said Monica.

"Monica, focus on the evidence, not Niland's diet," said Ray. "It's getting on, and I'd like to get back to the main road before it's dark as the inside of a pocket." He gestured toward Soto and Danny. "Make sure those cattle got feed and water enough until we can arrange transport."

Both men nodded and headed off toward the makeshift corral.

"Nothing much else to go through," replied Monica. "We could come back out in the morning and dust for prints, but with no lock on the door and no screens on the windows, it'd be a long shot."

"Crank all the windows closed, and we'll look around for something to secure the door shut," said Ray. "Then we can saddle up and get the flock out of here."

Monica closed all the windows while Ray searched the area for a makeshift door lock. Ray found a length of log chain in the burn pile, and after Danny finished with the cattle, he remembered he had a padlock in the Power Wagon that was meant for the cellar door at Ben's but hadn't been delivered yet.

Twenty minutes later, the caravan of Danny's Power Wagon with him, Ruth, and Joe in it, the DCI van with Monica, and the remaining Interceptor with Ray and Soto headed down the gravel trail toward the main road, all with their headlights on.

Ruth had wanted Joe with her in the Power Wagon to keep an eye on him. He was still stoned but was starting to get more lucid. She sat in the passenger seat and was twisted to face the rear. She tried to keep him talking and yelled at him occasionally when he drifted to sleep.

Joe leaned over to look out the window. The Root River was running below them, and the far bank rose quickly to form a high slope parallel to the river and them. Danny looked in the rearview mirror and saw Joe squinting into the darkness.

"You see something, Joe?" he asked.

"You are in danger," said the Indian.

Danny studied the man in the mirror. "Is it something real, or is the Wakanpi back."

Joe rotated his head to look at Danny in the mirror. "The evil spirit is here, but it stands to the side. A human Wakanpi hunts you now."

"What is he talking about?" asked Ruth. She turned and stared into the darkness. "I don't see anything."

Danny glanced past Ruth and into the black of the slope himself. He caught a flash of light, immediately followed by a rifle shot crack.

"Get down!" he yelled, reaching across the cab and grabbing Ruth's shoulder. But the bullet never impacted the Wagon. Instinctively, he dropped into military mode. He knew the truck gave him mobility, and by doctrine for lethal force encounters, he should use it to create distance from the shooter.

He heard three more rifle shots, then closer sounds of gunfire behind him.

He glanced over his shoulder at the two trailing vehicles, and his plan to run went to shit. The DCI van had careened down the bank and was sitting in the Root River, but at least it was still wheels'-side down. Soto's Interceptor sat crossways on the road, its lights pointing across the river. The officer had his door open and was crouched behind it, firing his Beretta at the slope.

Danny couldn't see if Ray was firing back, had been hit, or was dead.

"Fuck, fuck, fuck," he said. He slammed the brakes, and the Wagon skidded sideways to a stop. He unlocked the M4 and three loaded magazines from the center-mount gun rack. He slid the first magazine in and charged the weapon.

"Climb over the console and drive," he barked at Ruth.

He hit the switch to cut off the dome light, opened the door, and jumped out. He unholstered the Sig and pressed it into Ruth's hand as she settled behind the wheel.

"Go, and don't stop until you get to Tribal Headquarters," Danny ordered.

With a warning in her eyes, she nodded and said, "Keep the stupid shit to a minimum."

She slammed the door shut, and with a roar from the Wagon's Hemi, she, Joe, and the truck were gone.

Danny started to run toward the DCI van.

Three more rifle shots came from the slope, and Danny heard each thump into the Interceptor's metal.

Time for stupid shit, he thought.

He crouched, raised the M4, took aim, and waited for the muzzle flash. When the shooter fired again, Danny sent three rounds in return. There was a lull, then another muzzle flash, and a round impacted the road where he'd been crouching.

But he had already been on the move. He reached the river and splashed through the shallow water toward the van. Another rifle round threw up a water geyser at the rear of the vehicle as Danny made the cover and pressed his shoulder against the side of the van.

From above him, he heard Ray yell out, "What the hell is your dumb ass doing?"

"Giving them something else to shoot at besides you," yelled Danny back. He traveled the van's length, leaned out around the tail end, and fired three more rounds into the slope where he'd seen the muzzle flashes.

He started to yell at Ray again but stopped short when he heard the sound of an engine start, rev, and move away.

Danny tapped the side of the van, "Monica, can you hear me? Are you all right?"

"Is the shooting over?"

"I think so," answered Danny. He stood up, walked around the back of the van, and opened the doors. Monica lay on the floor in the back, between the shelving. She had a cut on her forehead, and blood had soaked through her shirt at the left elbow.

Monica sat up and pushed a whiteboard off her legs. She rummaged for a first aid kit, found it, and pulled out a gauze roll.

"Does stuff like this happen a lot?" she asked, pushing her shirt sleeve up.

Danny looked up at the empty, dark slope, thought about the previous winter, and answered, "Now and then."

Ray appeared on the bank above Danny, his limping backlit by headlights.

"You and Soto okay?" asked Danny.

"Twisted my ankle jumping out the truck, but I'll live," said Ray. "Soto got cut up pretty ugly by flying glass, but the truck took all the bullets."

"Ruth and Joe?" asked Danny.

"Haven't heard anything yet," replied Ray. He looked across the river at the slope. "The shooter was here, so I imagine they got away clean."

"Somebody wanted to kill Joe bad to shoot at us also," stated Danny.

"It would appear so. He's lucky Ruth wanted him to ride with her," replied Ray. He waved with his right hand in the direction of the shot-up Interceptor. "First three rounds went right in the back door. He might have been dead as a hammer with a larger caliber."

"Shows serious intent to shut Joe up permanently," said Danny. He helped Monica out of the van, and they crossed the river and began to climb the bank to Ray.

"Hey, boss," came Soto's voice as they made their way up. "What's that back down the road?"

Ray turned to look in the direction they'd come from as Danny and Monica made it to the road and stood beside him.

They couldn't see the flames, but they could see the glow of the fire that lit up the western sky.

"It's the trailer," said Ray. "If we hadn't got to Joe first, I'm sure he'd be burning with everything else in that trailer." He turned to look at Danny with tired eyes. "Like you said, no Joe, no link."

"No way the shooter could have made it back there yet to start the trailer fire," said Danny.

"Nope," said Ray. "We need to be looking for at least two folks."

"These are some serious fuckers," said Danny. He rested the barrel of his carbine on his shoulder.

Ray looked at the bullet holes in the Interceptor and the cuts on Soto's face. His eyes changed from tired to angry, and he said, "So are we."

Chapter 5

After the shooting had stopped and they'd heard the vehicle drive off, Danny and Sotomayor had hot-footed it across the river and climbed the hill to ensure the scene was clear. Soto's face was cut up, and he'd lost some of his Rico Suave looks, but Ray's ankle limited him, and Danny needed backup.

Ray radioed Tribal Police Headquarters just as Danny and Soto started up the hill. Danny heard the conversation coming across Sotomayor's radio. The officer asked Danny if he wanted him to mute it. Danny thought about it for a moment. He was almost positive the shooter had run, and Danny was desperate to know if Ruth had made it to town.

"Leave it turned up," he told Soto as they climbed. "We need to know what's going on."

Stan Satchwell, a Tribal Police officer and Ray's nephew, handled the night desk. "Last calling station, this is Tennant Creek Base. Say again, you're breaking up. Over."

"Stan, this is Ray," said the police chief. "We got a shooting just outside Crazy Buffalo Canyon on Buck Trail. I need all available officers sent to this location."

"No shit. Do you need an ambulance?" asked Stan with excitement.

"Negative. And don't cuss on the radio," replied Ray.

"Oh, yeah, shit, sorry," said Stan. "I'll get Janine to call the sub-station at Medicine Hat, and I'll call the one in Brokenrope. We should be able to send troops your way soon. Give me five, and I'll call back. Tennant Creek Base Out."

A familiar voice came across Soto's radio. "Ray, it's Edmund. I'm almost in town. I can swing around and be there quicker than anybody."

"Keep going," said Ray. "Ruth and Joe are headed your way, and I need you to watch over them in case somebody tries for Joe again."

Danny could hear the frustration in Edmund's voice, but he said, "Acknowledged; anything else?"

"Work the phones on those tags. We need to know where those cattle were stolen from. Over," said Ray.

Edmund sounded a little less frustrated and replied, "Wilco. Out."

While they waited to hear back from Stan on reinforcements, they found the area Danny thought the shooter had been in. They patrolled the site to ensure it was abandoned, and then Danny borrowed the hand mic from Soto and called Ray.

"Ray, it's Danny," he said. "Shooters cleared out, and it's too dark to search. We will mark the area and return once it's daylight. Agreed."

"Agreed. Head back down."

Danny handed the mic back to Soto. He pulled the powder blue handkerchief from around Sotomayor's neck to mark the area. He tied it around a tree limb, and they headed back down the hill.

As they descended, Stan came back on the radio. "Ray, I got four folks heading your way, but it's gonna be an hour at least."

"We're safe enough for right now," said Ray. "Let me know if anything changes."

"Will do," answered Stan.

By the time Danny and Sotomayor arrived back at the vehicle, Monica was sitting in the backseat of Soto's Interceptor. She was talking on her phone to her boss, Pat Palmer. He'd just packed up and was heading in from the meadow with John Goodnight's body. From the one side of the conversation Danny heard, it was apparent Monica and Pat had more than a working relationship.

Danny wondered if his phone had a signal. He pulled it out and saw the display read NO SERVICE. He glanced up to see Monica still talking to Pat and decided he needed a new phone. Or service. Or both.

The Brokenrope sub-station was the closest to their location, so Ray had expected to see Lucinda Battles and Archie Red Crow when the patrol car rolled up. But it was Stan who climbed out from behind the wheel while Ruth appeared from the passenger seat.

"What the hell?" said Danny as Ruth jumped out of Stan's car and ran to hug him. "I wanted you out of danger."

"Joe is locked up in jail and fine," said Ruth. She squeezed him tighter. "And don't try telling me what to do. I'm not your wife yet, and even then, it wouldn't work."

Danny looked at Stan, and the big man just smiled. "Said she'd kick my ass if I didn't bring her."

Danny looked at the man skeptically. Stan was a walking mountain of a man. He had a bull-neck, close-cropped black hair, dark eyes, and the body of an NFL lineman. But as Ruth squeezed the air out of him, he agreed that the big man had probably made the right choice.

"When you're done fondling your fiancé, I got customers for you," said Ray. He pointed at Sotomayor's face and Monica's head wound.

Soto returned the favor and pointed at Ray's ankle.

Ruth gave Danny a peck on the cheek, then shoved him away and headed over to start treating her assorted patients. She popped the hatch on the back of the Interceptor and, using the dome light to see, ran a makeshift emergency room with the first aid kit taken from the DCI van.

She dug the glass out of Soto's face, treated the cuts for infection, and had him hold a bandage to a large gash in his cheek that refused to stop bleeding. She was working on the wound to Monica's forehead after treating and rewrapping the dressing on the DCI tech's elbow when the next patrol car approached and joined the party.

It turned out to be Lucinda Battles and Archie Red Crow from Brokenrope. They would have beaten Stan and Ruth, except for the bison roadblock.

"We came screaming around the bend of the river on Two Brothers Road," said Lucinda. "All the sudden, in the headlights stood hundreds and hundreds of those shaggy sons-a-bitches. Blocked the whole road."

"We tried using the horn," said Archie. He pointed at the dented front quarter panel. "A bull took exception and rammed us."

"Took twenty minutes to weave through them and get to clear road again," said Lucinda.

"Montana problems," said Ray. He shook his head and had to laugh.

"But we're here now," said Archie. "Where do you need us, boss?"

Ray sent them along with Stan to check out what was left of Joe's trailer. They radioed back and reported that the fire had burned out, and the trailer was as good as gone.

"Nothing left but the steel frame undercarriage," said Archie.

"What about the cattle?" asked Ray over the radio.

"What cattle?" asked Archie back.

"Never mind," said Ray. "Stay up there and search the trailer remains with flashlights. At daybreak, do a perimeter search for footprints and vehicle tracks."

"Roger," replied Archie, and the radio clicked off.

"So, they ran off with the cattle or scattered them at least," said Danny.

"And burned the trailer," said Ray. "Somebody wants to tie up loose ends."

Another set of headlights appeared down the road, coming from the direction of town.

The patrol car slid to a stop, and Officers Mike Talon and Matt Bringloe from Medicine Hat stepped out.

Talon walked up to Ray and offered his hand as he said, "Came as quick as we could. Glad to see everybody up and vertical."

"Good to see you, Mike," said Ray. The police chief took the offered hand, shook it, and looked over the car's hood at Bringloe. "Morning, Matt."

"Morning, boss," said Bringloe. "What do you need us to do?"

"I need you two to stay here and mind the store. Keep an eye on the doc and her two patients," said Ray. "As soon as it starts getting light, Danny and I will head up and search where the shooter shot from." He pointed at Danny. "He and Soto cleared it last night, and Danny marked it, so it should be easy to find again."

"I think we can handle our end of the log," said Bringloe. The lanky young officer walked back, opened the rear door of the patrol car, reached in, and drew out two Benelli M1014 semi-automatic shotguns.

"Nice guns," said Danny.

"Sure as shitting they are," said Talon as Bringloe handed him one. "Your buddy Goodrunner turned us on to them. They work on the ARGO system as in auto-regulating gas-operated. The action is smooth as silk."

"An Italian firm designed them for the Marines. Specs required them to be low-maintenance and simple. They only got four working parts," said Bringloe with a grin. "But they're durable as hell. Rated at twenty-five thousand rounds before you need replacement parts."

"Expensive?" asked Danny.

"Couple grand a piece," answered Talon.

"Let me guess," said Danny. "Federal grant?"

"Got to be a few perks to being an Indian," said Talon with a smirk. He turned to Ray and said, "Me and Bringloe got this covered for a bit. If anyone shows up with bad intent, we'll make them wish they hadn't. Go close your eyes, boss."

Ray didn't argue. He nodded in appreciation and headed to the front seat of the Interceptor to stretch out.

Talon motioned to Bringloe, and the lanky man moved into position to watch the road in the direction of town. Talon turned back to Danny and said, "Crawl into the cruiser's backseat and get some sleep. We'll wake you when it's time."

"Much obliged," said Danny, and he moved to the back door of the cruiser, opened it, and unslung his carbine. He laid himself on the seat and the weapon on the floorboard. He knew nothing else until Bringloe shook his foot ninety minutes later.

"Coogan, time to get hopping," he said.

Danny grabbed his rifle and crawled out of the cruiser. The sleep had felt good, but there had been far too little of it, and now he felt groggy and stiff.

He turned to the east and watched as morning twilight began to appear low in the sky. He yawned and glanced at his watch. It read five twenty-eight. Time to make the donuts, he thought with a smile. He checked his ammo for both his M4 and his Sig and glanced up to see Ray standing at the front of the patrol car, waiting for him.

"I thought your ankle hurt?" he asked as he slung the carbine and holstered his Sig.

"Not enough to let my men take all the risk," said Ray. He turned and started to walk toward the riverbank. Over his shoulder, he said, "And I knew your dumb ass would want to go, and I didn't want to burden any one of them with the white guy."

Danny had to admit Ray was right. He'd been on the hill, knew the shooter's location, and damn sure wouldn't miss out on going back up. But was there more to it? he wondered. Was it the thrill, the danger, the unknown he was seeking? Did he miss combat that badly?

Well, shit, he thought with a shrug. At least he'd have plenty of new problems to discuss with his counselor at his next VA appointment.

He detoured to the Interceptor's back hatch and kissed Ruth on her cheek as she slept. She was curled up and using the first aid bag as a pillow. Monica lay beside her, and Soto was snoring in the backseat.

He turned and started for the riverbank when someone spoke his name.

"Coogan," said Talon. He was standing ten feet away and held a small pack. He walked over and handed it to Danny. "Packed it with binos, bottled water, and protein bars."

"You're a saint," said Danny. He unslung his rifle, threw the pack on his back, cinched down the straps, and wiggled his shoulders to center the weight.

"Thanks," he said as he slung the carbine back on and over the pack.

"No worries," said Talon. He pointed at the weapon on Danny's back. "Don't hesitate to use the rifle."

"Think it'll come to that?" asked Danny.

"We got somebody not afraid to kill cops," said Talon. "So, yeah, I fucking think you'll need it."

Danny nodded and jogged over to Ray, who waited on the bank at the river's edge. Together, they turned and waded into the cold water of the Root River.

Forty minutes later, they'd reached just below the slope's summit. They stood amongst young pine trees and tried to catch their breath. From their vantage point, they had a good view of the river, the road, and the vehicles below them.

While he let Ray try to stop hyper-ventilating, Danny lifted his eyes, looked east, and saw the shadowy outline of the Bear Paw Mountains. They were an island range in isolation from the other mountains in the area. Danny had always thought they seemed more defiant than the other, higher mountains in Montana. Baldy Mountain, the highest of the Bear Paws, only reached six thousand nine hundred and sixteen feet. They weren't tall, but they were broad-shouldered and beefy.

Ray pulled him out of his wool-gathering by saying between gasps of air, "Good spot for a sniper."

Danny dropped his eyes to the Tribal Police chief and saw he'd taken his hat off, had half unbuttoned his shirt, and had his hands on his hips.

"If you have a heart attack, I ain't carrying you. Just going to roll you down the hill and into the river."

Ray smiled at Danny and, with his breathing almost regular, replied, "I'll shoot your ass and claim self-defense if you even try it."

Danny laughed and began to study the ground and surroundings. "You're right, in any case. This is a solid spot for a sniper. Whether by luck or planning, they had us dead to rights."

"Are we close to where you left your marker?" asked Ray.

"A little to the left, I think," said Danny. "But we can spread out and work back just under the summit, and we should find it."

It took them just over fifteen minutes, but they found the handkerchief tied to the branch and searched the ground for the exact location the shooter had fired from. It was Ray who saw it. The pine nettles under a thick fir tree had been pressed down to reveal the outline of where a body had lain. Danny found two of the neighboring trees had gouges and bark blown off.

"I think we did more than hit trees," said Ray. He pointed to a small pool of what looked to be dried blood in the nettles.

"You thinking solid hit or ricochet?" asked Danny.

"Ricochet," replied Ray. He knelt and scooped the stained pine nettles into an evidence bag. "With a solid hit, we'd have a body."

Danny drifted right, and something reflecting the sun caught his eye. He knelt beside a bush and saw a bright, shiny casing winking back at him in the morning light. He pulled his jackknife from the front pocket and extended the thinner blade. He reached through the leaves on the bush, slipped the knife into the casing where the projectile had been, and drew it back to him.

Ray walked over and joined him as he stood. They both looked down as Danny rotated the end of the casing toward them so they could read the writing on the bottom.

"Shit," said Ray. He held out another bag, and Danny dropped the casing in. "The .308 Winchester is the standard caliber for hunters in the U.S. Doesn't thin the herd much on tracking down the rifle."

"Not by much," said Danny in agreement. He caught Ray's annoyed look, shrugged, and added, "At least we can narrow down the field some. No need to look at folks packing AR-15s or buffalo rifles."

"You're just a constant ray of sunshine, you know," said Ray. He folded the evidence bag in half and slipped it into a shirt pocket.

"You're right, though," said Danny. He folded the jackknife and slipped it back into his pocket. "Everyone and their grandma have a .308 in Montana. Maybe we'll have more luck with the blood?"

"I'm not holding out hope," said Ray. He wiped the back of his hand across his lips. "Damn, I'm thirsty."

"Shit, I forgot. Talon gave me water and food," said Danny. He pulled the carbine off his back and leaned it against a tree. He unslung the pack and pulled out two bottles of water and three protein bars. He handed one bottle and two bars to Ray, who accepted it like manna from heaven.

The lawmen finished breakfast, and Danny stuffed the trash in the pack. He handed Ray another protein bar and ate one himself before shouldering the pack and carbine.

Ray pointed toward the top of the hill. "Let's follow the trail and see what we can find."

Danny adjusted the pack and rifle so it rode comfortably on his back and said, "I'll follow you. This is your circus, and I'm just one of the monkeys."

They followed the route left by the shooter in their haste to escape. Danny was not near Ray's level regarding tracking, and he accepted the man's expertise. Ray followed a winding route, pointing out places where the shooter had lost his footing, where spiderwebs had been broken, and where they'd followed a game trail.

They summited the hill, crossed over, and halfway down the backside, came to a broad, grassy spot the size of a boxing ring. The trail continued down the hill. It turned to the east and was lost to view as it disappeared into the underbrush. A stone campfire ring was in the center of the grassy spot. Trash was scattered everywhere, with one large pile to the side.

"If I'm not mistaken," said Ray. "This is the endpoint of Euphoria Trail."

"Never heard of it," said Danny.

"I don't doubt it. It's a local nickname," said Ray. "Kids come up here on four-wheelers, dirt bikes, and the like. Get high, howl at the moon, fornicate."

"Not sure we're going to find much here," said Danny, heading to one side of the large trash pile as Ray took the other. He bent over the trash pile and started sorting through bottles and cans. As he dislodged a large, empty vodka jug from the pile's perimeter, a small avalanche of cans and bottles ensued, revealing a blue-jean-covered leg and a single boot.

"What the hell…" Danny began to say but was cut short as a figure rose from under the pile of trash, jumped on him, knocked him to the ground, and landed on top of him. The buttstock of the carbine strapped across his back punched him in the kidney, and he felt the bottled water burst in the pack.

Danny struggled to grasp the figure, but they were covered in runoff from the pile and slippery as an eel.

"Dammit," yelled Danny as the figure dropped a knee into his stomach, forcing him to give up his grip on a flailing forearm.

Ray had caught the motion with his peripheral and then heard Danny yell out. His handgun had barely cleared his holster when the figure ran into him at full speed. Ray stumbled backward from the impact, found a large root with one boot, and toppled over. The figure ran past him as he fell, and he reached out to snatch a handful of shirt.

The shirt tore in two and fell off. The last thing Ray saw before the figure disappeared was long black hair and the straps and back of an orange sports bra.

Danny was beside Ray before he could get up, pulling the big man to his feet. He unslung the carbine and tossed it to Ray.

"Stay here," he said and turned to chase the figure.

Ray grabbed Danny's arm, and the warden spun his head to look at the police chief.

"It's just a kid," said Ray. "A girl, I think."

"Does that matter right now?" asked Danny. He pulled out of Ray's grip. "Whoever it is just kicked the shit out of both of us."

Danny stumbled, righted himself, and sprinted down the trail. His back throbbed from landing on the carbine, and his stomach still felt the lingering effects of the knee, but whoever this was might be the shooter or maybe a witness to identify the shooter.

Thankful for all the miles he'd put in with Edmund, Danny caught the figure within a quarter-mile. He saw them running along the path ahead and sprinted to close the gap. He almost had them and was preparing his tackle when the figure stopped, spun to face him, and dropped into a crouch.

Danny skidded a dozen feet away to a stop and got his first good look at who'd attacked him.

Ray had been right; it was a girl. She was small, maybe five-five, and had an athletic build that was mainly legs. She had on an orange sports bra, jeans, and a pair of boots. Her eyes peered out through a tangle of dark hair. The eyes glared at Danny but flashed left and right, looking for escape at the same time.

She held a short knife in her raised hand and waved it at him. "Stay back. I didn't see nothing and don't know nothing."

Danny held his hands out, palms-up, to show the girl he didn't have a weapon. Slowly, as he inched forward, he said, "Let's all relax."

"Don't come any closer, asshole," said the girl. She took a few quick steps backward, bumped into a tree, and glanced behind her in surprise. Danny hurled himself at the girl, and as she turned to face him, he caught the wrist of the hand with the knife and twisted it. The girl screamed, and the knife fell into the grass.

He stepped in, still holding the wrist, and hip-tossed the girl away from the fallen knife onto a patch of bare ground. The girl rolled over, causing him to release his grip on the wrist, or he'd break it. She got her feet under her and sprang at Danny, head-butting him in the chest and clawing his face.

He swept her feet with a leg, and she crashed to the ground, knocking the wind out of her lungs and leaving her gasping for breath. Not letting the spitfire get another chance at him, Danny flipped her over, pulled out his cuffs, and snapped them shut on both wrists.

Ray hobbled up as Danny used the toe of his boot to roll the girl over onto her back.

"Is she hurt?" asked Ray. He favored his bad ankle and leaned on a tree to relieve it.

"I fucking hope she is," said Danny. "Then we'd be even." He was breathing hard and had long, jagged scratches on his face from the girl's nails. "You recognize her?"

"Now I do," said Ray. He smiled and looked at the girl. "Her name is Andrea Saltes. Got reported by her parents as a runaway a month ago."

"How old?" asked Danny.

"Sixteen," replied Ray.

Danny leaned over, lifted Andrea, and dropped her onto her feet. He did a quick check for weapons and, besides the dropped knife, found nothing.

"So, Andrea," said Danny. "What haven't you seen, and what don't you know?"

The girl's eyes ping-ponged between Ray and Danny. She finally settled on Ray and said, "You need to protect me. I ain't getting killed over some bullshit."

"We'll keep you safe," said Ray. "Just tell us what you know."

Andrea looked over her shoulder at Danny and said, "Take the cuffs off, and I'll talk."

Danny rubbed his chest where she'd head-butted him and said, "Not a chance in hell."

Chapter 6

By noon, everyone was back at headquarters in Tennant Creek. Battles and Red Crow hadn't discovered anything significant on the perimeter of the burned-out trailer. After their report, Ray sent them back to Brokenrope but kept Talon and Bringloe at headquarters.

Once Pat visited Monica in the medical clinic to ensure she was okay, Talon escorted him and his DCI underling, Bob Jennings, back to the trailer to process the site. Ray and Danny agreed it was a long shot that DCI would find anything, but a long shot was better than no shot.

Sotomayor had been checked out at the clinic and given a clean bill of health. Danny told him that he was sure the scars from the glass would add to his roguish charm. Soto wanted to come back in, but Ray sent him home for the rest of the day to be nursed back to health by his wife.

Stan returned to staffing the front desk and grumbled about how everyone got to have all the fun except him. He would have complained more, but a call came in, and he headed over to Silverheels Sinclair Gas Station to take a report of a fill and fly.

Ruth had cleaned the young and feisty Andrea Saltes up, and both were asleep on bunks in one of the holding cells with the door handcuffed open. Ray called Alvin Saltes to tell him they had found his runaway daughter, and she was at the jail if he wanted to pick her up. Alvin said that was a good place for her and hung up.

"So, what's that mean?" asked Danny. He sat his feet on Ray's desk and sipped his third cup of coffee.

"Not sure," said Ray. He scribbled a reminder on a notepad by the phone. "I'll call back later and ask for Glenda, the mother. Maybe she's more forgiving of Andrea's sins."

"When do you want to question her about what she doesn't know and didn't see?" asked Danny.

Ray looked at his watch as his stomach growled. "After she wakes up. You hungry?"

When it came to food and Ray, Danny knew the proper response. "I could eat."

"Janine," yelled Ray. He leaned around his desk and called for his daughter, "Janine, get in here a minute."

All six feet of her appeared in the doorway. She smiled her gapped-tooth grin and leaned on the doorframe. "Already ordered everybody something from the diner."

"How'd you know what I wanted you for?" asked Ray.

"Daughter radar," she said as she returned to her desk. "Besides, I was hungry a half hour ago."

Danny wanted to ask what they were having, but Edmund walked into the office before he could get the words out. He dropped into the blue Elgin Atomic side armchair that matched the one Danny sat in and rubbed his eyes with the palms of his hands.

"Rough night," said Ray, more rhetorical than as a question.

"Not as rough as yours," replied Edmund. "But I'm going blind and deaf looking at computer screens and talking on the phone."

"Any luck?" asked Danny. He nudged Edmund and passed him his remaining coffee when the Indian looked at him.

"Thanks." Edmund took the cup and downed the contents. "Must be the last cup from the pot. More mud than liquid." He handed the empty cup back to Danny. "Not getting anyplace with the insurance companies. They want paperwork before giving up client information."

"For Pete's sake," said Ray.

"I did have a thought, though," said Edmund. "Since the local brand inspector quit, they haven't filled the job. I want to go over to Big Sandy and see Charmayne Lucas. I gather she's filling in for now."

"Why not just handle it over the phone?" asked Ray.

"It's a shit-ton of tags. Too many to try and handle remotely," Edmund answered.

"I could show her the tags and help run them to ground. Interview some of the ranchers who lost cattle and see if we can get a lead. Whatcha think?"

"I think that shows outstanding initiative and bravery," said Ray with a thin, almost hidden smile.

Edmund glanced at Danny. He wasn't hiding his smile at all.

"What's the joke?" asked Edmund.

"No joke," said Ray. "You've never met Charmayne. Have you?"

"No, but I hear she's a good inspector," said Edmund. "She got a write-up in the paper for busting that rustling ring over in Teton County. Sounds like she'd be perfect for helping out."

"She'll be perfect, and I want you to see her," said Ray. "Just a few things to know about her. She's politically incorrect, swears like a sailor, and is tough as kangaroo leather."

"You've been warned," said Danny. He got up to make a fresh pot of coffee.

Edmund looked from the police chief to the warden, then back to the police chief. "This is a put-on. She can't be that bad."

"Oh, she's not bad. She's spectacular," said Ray. "Tinkerbell looks, Calamity Jane disposition. Been married three times and on the prowl for number four."

Edmund got up from his chair and grabbed the keys to Ray's Interceptor. "You're both bullshitting me." He crossed the room and walked out the doorway. He flipped the bird over his shoulder before he got out of view and yelled back, "I'll let you know if I get any leads."

Danny finished pouring water into the coffee maker, added copious amounts of grounds, and hit the little red button. He sat back down in his chair. "I can't wait to hear back from him."

"We warned him," said Ray.

Janie walked in with three large paper grocery bags. "Chow's here. I gave Edmund his when he walked out. You know he took your truck, right?"

"He's going to see Charmayne Lucas," said Ray. He took the wrapped hamburger from Janine and stole a bag of fries from the grocery bag. "Thought he deserved a perk."

"Charmayne, huh? You warned him, right?" asked Janine. She handed a sandwich to Danny and took the fries back from Ray. "Your cholesterol, Dad. Limits on the fried foods."

"We did, and I didn't have donuts this morning, so I should get to have fries."

Janine handed the fries to Danny, stuck her tongue out at her dad, and dropped into the vacant blue chair. "Do you want me to wake up Ruth and Andrea? See if they're hungry?"

Danny bit into his cheeseburger, wiped the ketchup off his mouth, and answered, "We can let them sleep for a bit if it's okay with Ray. Ruth will need it. Ben, Molly, and her parents finally made it to the ranch and are expecting us for supper."

"You don't have to wake us up. My mom's call did that," said a voice.

All three lawmen looked up from their burgers to see Ruth and Andrea standing in the doorway.

"Dinner's at eight sharp," she said. "But we're hungry now."

Ruth crossed to sort through the remains of the grocery bag while Andrea moved to the couch and eased down. Danny watched the girl's every move.

"I called your house, Andrea," said Ray. He took a drink of his soda to wash the burger down. "Talked to your father."

"I can just imagine what he said," replied Andrea. Ruth handed her a burger and fries. She looked up and smiled at the doctor. "Thank you."

Ruth sat beside the girl on the couch and opened up her sandwich.

"I'll call back later and talk to your mom. Maybe I'll have better luck," said Ray.

"You wouldn't," said Andrea through a mouthful of burger and fries. "She's the one who kicked me out."

Danny wanted to ask the girl about the night they found her and why she'd attacked him but noticed a man standing in the doorway with his arms crossed and a patient look on his face. He was shorter than Danny, with a clean-shaven face and short black hair. He wore weathered jeans, a denim shirt with sewn-over rips, and a bandana tied around his neck, cowboy style.

"Ray," he said. "You've got company."

Ray glanced at the door, swallowed his burger, and said, "Shit. Sorry, Barrett. Didn't see you walk up." Ray stood up, scanned his desk for a napkin, came up dry, and leaned over to wipe his hands on his pants. "What can I do for you?"

The man walked over to the desk and pulled back the side of a grocery bag to peek inside. "You could give me a burger if you got one not spoken for. Been in the saddle overnight and all morning tending cattle."

Ray sat back down, "Help yourself."

"Much obliged," replied the man. He grabbed one of the three left and a bag of fries, then turned, leaned against the desk, and surveyed the room. "Not sure I know everybody."

Danny knew Barrett wasn't talking about the Indians in the room, so he introduced himself, "Danny Coogan, Montana game warden."

"And I'm Ruth Beebe," said Ruth from beside Andrea. "And you're Barrett…"

"Barrett Lodge," said the man. He chewed his burger slowly and studied Danny and Ruth. He seemed to be taking the measure of each of them.

A memory slipped into place in Danny's head, and he made the connection. "You're the new council chairman."

"That's me," said Barrett. He wiped his mouth on his bandana. "I know I don't look the part. That might be the reason they elected me."

"Or it could be you were the only no-show at the meeting and got elected in absentia," said Janine.

"That's closer to the truth," said Barrett as he reached up and touched the tip of his nose. He shifted his eyes to the girl. "Afternoon, Andrea. In trouble again?"

The girl had finished her burger and was picking at her cold fries. "As always, Uncle Barrett." She leaned over to see Ray behind Barrett. "You called him, didn't you?"

Before Ray could say anything, Barrett swallowed the last of his burger, took a long pull from an unclaimed soda on Ray's desk, and answered. "He didn't call me. I'm here on council business. But I can deal with you when I'm done."

"You want an update on John Goodnight," said Ray. "Is that why you're here?"

"The council just wants to stick their nose in and get in the way, as usual," said Barrett. "Give me something I can toss to them to get 'em off your ass and let you do your job."

"Not a lot to tell," said Ray. "A dead rancher, killed in a unique but brutally effective way. A convict who decided to have a gunfight with police, and finally, a sniper who has an arsonist sidekick."

Barrett crossed his arms and craned his neck so far that his chin almost touched his chest. "Motive?"

"None that I can point to right now," said Ray. "We got some ideas but are running down specifics before I'm comfortable saying what they are."

"Tell me about Niland?" asked Barrett.

"We got him locked up," said Ray. "He's sleeping off peyote. We'll question him once he comes down from his high."

"I understand Andrea gave you a go last night," said Barrett.

Ray pointed at Danny. "It was him she whooped up on."

Barrett glanced up and locked eyes with Danny. "You pressing charges? No pressure either way. Just want to know if I need to get a lawyer for her."

Danny glanced at the girl, at Ray, and then back to Barrett. "I don't think so. It seems she has enough to deal with right now."

Barrett slapped his knees and stood up. He turned to shake hands with Ray and said, "I'll let the council know you have someone in custody and are building a case. That should be enough red meat to satisfy them for the moment."

"I'm pretty sure Niland is not the one who killed Goodnight," said Ray.

"Never said he was," replied Barrett. "I said you have someone in custody and are building a case. Never said the two were related." He gave Ray a wink. "If the council wants to make assumptions, it's not our fault."

"Smooth," said Danny. "Keep it up, and you'll get reelected."

"Bite your tongue, Coogan," said Barrett.

"There is one more thing," said Ray. "Andrea is going to have to stay with us for a spell. She might be a witness to the shooting last night."

Barrett turned to glare at the girl.

"I didn't do anything," she said.

Barrett and Ray looked at her with raised eyebrows.

She wilted some and sunk into the couch. "Well, I might have seen somebody."

"Let me give you all some privacy," said Ruth. She stood up and collected her and Danny's empty sandwich wrappers and fry bags. She walked over to the trash can and tossed them all in. She moved to Danny, kissed him, and said, "I'll be at the clinic checking on Monica. Come get me when you're done here."

"No worries," said Danny. He patted her butt as she drew back from him.

"Remember, we need to run home to shower and change clothes before supper," said Ruth. She gave a wave to Janine and slipped out of the room.

Barrett glanced at Ray, then looked at Danny and asked, "You here officially?"

"I'm not sure. Officially, this started with me checking out dead livestock," he answered. "Things have been happening fast since then. I haven't had a chance to check with headquarters on jurisdiction. Probably something I should do."

"I'll make a call and request assistance, proper-like," said Barrett. "That is, if you want to be involved?"

"Got no place else I have to be," said Danny.

Ray moved from behind his desk and crossed to close the door. When it was shut, he asked, "Andrea, what were you doing on Euphoria Trail last night?"

She shot a look at her uncle and then answered, "Just hanging out."

Barrett stood up from leaning on the desk and said to Ray, "Maybe I should step out." He moved to the door and opened it. Before he left, he looked back at Andrea and said, "I know why Alvin and Glenda kicked you out. Makes no difference to me." He glanced at Ray. "Once he says it's safe, you come live with Aunt Nina and me. Okay?"

"Okay," answered the girl.

The door closed, and the room was quiet enough that they all heard the sounds of Barrett's boots moving away down the hallway.

"Were you alone, or was someone else with you?" asked Ray.

"With someone," she said. "But she was gone by the time the shooting started."

"She," said Ray in an even and calm voice. "Was she the reason you got kicked out?"

Andrea stared at her feet. "Yeah. My mom said she already had five boys and didn't want another one. She wanted a girl who acted like a girl."

"We don't much care about any of that, Andrea," said Ray. "But we need to know who if you saw the person doing the shooting and what happened after the shooting ended."

Andrea lifted her head and stared first at Ray, then moved her eyes to Danny. "I don't know who it was, honest."

"Just tell us what happened," said Danny. He scooted forward on the edge of his chair.

"I heard a shot on the other side of the hill. Then all hell broke loose. Sounded like a war movie or something," she said. "Got scared. I had no idea who was shooting at whom or for what reason. So, I put the fire out and moved back into the trees to wait for everyone to go away."

"But they didn't, did they?" asked Janine.

"No," said Andrea. "Pretty soon, somebody came down the trail all crazy-like. They were swaying and bumping into trees like they were drunk."

"Or been hit by a ricochet," Danny said to Ray.

"Did you get a look at them?" asked Ray.

"Not really," answered Andrea. "I'd been around the fire, so my night sight was shit. But they were dressed in that camouflage bullshit hunters wear and carried a rifle."

"Can you describe them at all?" asked Ray. "Anything would help."

Andrea thought momentarily, then said, "They were taller than me but smaller than him." She pointed at Danny. "They were thin, had long legs, and had hair tied back. It hung down the side from under the hood they were wearing."

"What color was the hair," asked Janine.

Andrea shrugged, "I don't know, dark."

"Did they say anything?"

Andrea shook her head.

"What happened next?" asked Ray.

"A while later, I heard an engine start, and whoever it was took off like a bat out of hell."

"So, why'd you attack me?" asked Danny.

"Me and Becca were getting ready to leave the Rez," said Andrea. "She left me at Euphoria to get her brother's car."

"Are you talking about Becca Paulson?" asked Ray.

"Uh. Yeah, can we forget I mentioned her?" said Andrea. "Anyway, she was coming back by noon, and we were heading for Missoula. I heard you and got scared it might be the shooter coming back and buried myself in the pile." She shot a side glance at Danny. "I never thought anybody would start sorting through empty beer cans."

"And I never thought a girl could take me down and whoop me," said Danny. He gave Andrea an embarrassed smile. "Guess we both got surprised."

Andrea relaxed and smiled back. "No hard feelings?"

Now Danny smiled outright. "None at all. Just please don't go spreading it around."

"Deal," replied Andrea. She shifted her eyes to Ray. "So, what now? Can I leave?"

Ray moved behind his desk and sat in his chair. "Not yet. We have somebody on the loose who may hear about us pulling you in and be interested in what you told us. That puts you in danger."

"But I didn't see who the shooter was," protested Andrea. "This is bullshit."

"No way around it," said Ray. "But I'll make you a deal. Go with Janine, and she'll let you give Becca a call. So she knows you're all right."

"No fooling."

"No fooling."

Danny watched the two leave the room, then said to Ray, "That was nicely done."

"Andrea's got enough on her plate without me adding to it," said Ray. "And I've got a daughter, so I know how hard that age is."

"What are you going to do about her parents?"

"Not a damn thing," said Ray. "I figure Barrett has that handled."

"How long do you figure until Edmund gets back?" asked Danny.

"Couple days," answered Ray. Then he grinned and said, "That is, if he survives Charmayne."

"If he gets a list of the ranches those cattle disappeared from, it will be a place to start," said Danny.

"Don't forget we still got Joe. When he sobers up, I have hard questions for him, but you need to get going to make supper with the folks."

"You're right. I had best get Ruth and the wine, then head home. Got future in-laws to impress," said Danny. He climbed out of the chair and headed to the door.

As he reached the doorway, he turned and asked, "How much danger do you figure Andrea's in?"

Ray leaned back in his chair and chewed his lip for a bit. He finally said, "Sizeable. We got an individual not afraid to shoot police, so I figure they wouldn't give a tinker's damn when it came to killing a young girl."

"You keeping her here and guarded?" asked Danny.

"Yup. I'm not sleeping at home until it's over," said Ray. He rolled his chair over to the coffee pot, poured his cup full, and rolled back to his desk. "I'll call you tomorrow and let you know if Barrett got you cleared to assist."

"I'm coming back either way," said Danny.

Ray looked at him and said, "You could fool around and get fired doing shit like that."

"Yeah, I know," said Danny. He turned and started walking away. "Maybe that's what I'm angling for. Be seeing you, Ray."

"See you in the morning, Danny," said Ray.

Chapter 7

Danny and Ruth drove to his parent's house in Ruth's green Subaru Forester. Danny had dropped the Power Wagon off at Abracadabra Body Shop. A new windshield had been ordered to replace the one ventilated by Niland, the side mirror had been reattached, and the dents and dings were being buffed out. It would look showroom-new when Danny got it back, ready to be damaged again in the line of duty, he thought with a frown as he put the Forester in park.

"I'd rather not get into what's going on out on the Rez," Danny said. He reached behind him and collected the wine from the backseat. "I don't want your folks to worry about my job."

Ruth gave him an amused look. "I'm sure as hell not telling them you spent the last few days getting shot at. I got enough trouble with my mom thinking I'm pregnant."

"Wait, what?" said Danny, as a stunned look traversed his face. "Are you?"

Ruth leaned across the console and planted a deep, curl-his-toes kiss on Danny's lips. When she drew back, she smiled, winked, and said, "Of course not. But it's something we could talk about."

Leaving him with an even more stunned look on his face, she opened her door, climbed out, and shut it behind her. She bent over and looked back into the vehicle at Danny. "Close your mouth, sweetie. You look like some trout."

He was still trying to wrap his head around Ruth's words and their meaning while they walked toward the house when Ben opened the door.

"Well, there he is. Rooster Cogburn reincarnated," exclaimed Ben. Ruth's father, Mike, stood behind Ben and peeked over the retired warden's shoulder. Ben turned and spoke to the man, "See, I told you. None the worse for having some bullets thrown his way."

So much for leaving the Rez on the Rez, thought Danny.

He hugged Ben and whispered, "Way to kick the hornet's nest."

Danny handed his father the wine and moved past him to extend a hand to Ruth's father. "Good to see you again, Mike," he said.

"Daniel," replied the man with a curt nod as he took Danny's hand.

The tone of the voice was friendly, but Mike's eyes held an appraising look, and he didn't smile. He was a short man, cresting at five-seven or five-eight. He had white-blond hair, a burly physique, and a face chiseled from granite. As Danny released his hand, he realized Mike reminded him of the Nakota. Both were friendly and watchful at the same time.

Danny turned to ask Ruth something and found her hugging Ben. She was on her tiptoes and whispering into his ear. He had no doubt she was scolding him for spilling the beans about Danny's adventures on the Rez. He turned back to Mike and found that the man had pulled out a thick cigar and a small box of wooden matches.

"Thought I might smoke out by the horses before dinner," he said. "I'd like you to join me, Daniel."

"Be my pleasure," answered Danny. *Here comes the inquisition*, he thought, as he let the man step past him and head for the small corral to the side of the barn.

Danny twisted his neck to look at Ben when Mike was out of earshot. "What the hell were you thinking?"

Ben shrugged and placed a hand on Danny's shoulder. "Best get to the rat killing first thing so that you can have clean air between you and him. Your job is his only worry when it comes to you and Ruth. No sense dancing around the landmine in the room."

Danny glanced at Ruth. She gave her own shrug and said, "I wanted a nice, quiet evening, but that's shot to hell now. And there is an illogical logic to what Ben is saying."

Danny pointed a finger at Ben, "If I come back a gelding, I'm doing the same to you, old man."

Ben gave Ruth a side hug. "Makes no difference to me," he said. "All the lead in my pencil comes from a blue pill."

"Jesus," said Danny.

Mike was leaning with both forearms on the top rail of the corral as Danny walked up. He'd gotten his cigar lit, and smoke drifted from the tip.

Danny leaned a shoulder against a corral post and waved away the offer of taking a puff.

"I do my best thinking with silence and the whiff of tobacco," said Mike.

Danny nodded. "Never was one to smoke, but I get the connection with silence."

Mike took a draw on the cigar, then knocked some of the ashes off the tip. "These two got names?"

Danny glanced into the corral at the horses. Ben hadn't had horses since Danny was a teenager but had bought these two after he retired. Ben had figured he and Molly could ride together, maybe join the local sporting club, and take in one of the week-long rides along the Missouri River. That was the plan, but so far, all they'd done was name them.

"Johnny is the big bay, and the paint is June," answered Danny. He smiled, "My parents have a thing for country music royalty."

"Johnny and June," said Mike. "Nothing wrong with that." He took another pull from his cigar and asked, "Do you ride?"

"Badly and only when I can't get out of it," answered Danny. He stared down at his boots and used one to kick a rock. "But you don't want to stand out here and talk about horses, do you?"

"Not really, but they're damn interesting animals," replied Mike. He knocked some more ash off his cigar and lifted a leg to rest on the bottom corral rail. "I wanted to talk about your chosen profession and whether you'd change it if given the chance."

And there it is, thought Danny. He knew Mike was concerned about what Ruth would be buying into with being the wife of a lawman. Shit, he was worried about it too. And given his uncertainty about what he wanted his future to be, Danny did the stupid thing and told the truth.

"Honestly, Mike," he said in slow, measured words. "I got no idea what I want to do tomorrow or for the rest of my life outside of being married to your daughter."

Mike gave him an appraising look again, frowned, and shook his head. "Ruth told me you were honest to a fault, even when it didn't put you in the best light."

"I'm too lazy to lie. It's too much work remembering them," said Danny.

"Last year, because Ruth was with you, she was almost killed," said Mike. Danny noticed an undercurrent of emotion and anger in the man's voice. Mike asked, "Can you promise me that will never happen again?"

Now would be the perfect time to lie, and because it was the perfect time, Danny told the truth instead: "No, sir, I can't promise that."

Mike took a deep breath, dropped his cigar, and crushed it with a boot heel. He turned to look at Danny. The vein of the man's jaw was dancing, and Danny was sure he was about to get thumped by a roundhouse punch. With an effort, Danny saw Mike force himself to relax.

"Do you know what I did in the Navy?" asked Mike.

"You were a diver," replied Danny.

Mike gave a thin smile. "I was a little more than that, but it doesn't matter. What matters is Ruth, how she feels about you, and what goes through her mind each time you walk out the door to do your job."

"I understand her feelings, sir. I had it each time Ben left when I was growing up."

"Then you're one up on me, and you and Ruth may do fine. I shipped out time and time again without any thought as to what it was doing to my wife or Ruth. Being so focused on my job almost cost me a marriage, and it took a long time to get back into both their hearts."

Mike went back to watching the horses while Danny considered his words. Johnny and June crossed the corral and took a long drink from the water trough. Johnny lifted his head and turned to look at them as a shiver ran across his chestnut coat.

At length, Danny said, "Ruth is strong-willed, brave, and has a mind of her own, so I can't promise you she'll never be in danger again," said Danny. "But I can promise you that if it ever comes down to the job or Ruth, it's Ruth always, forever, period, the end."

Mike seemed to consider it, then held out his hand. "Well, shit. I guess that'll have to do. Welcome to the family, and good luck with Ruth. She takes after me and has a lot of renegade in her."

"I got no complaints," said Danny. He shook the offered hand and asked, "Does Margery know anything about the shootings on the Rez?"

"Oh, sweet Jesus, no," replied Mike. His grin spread across his face. "And don't ever let her know I know about them. She'd have a conniption, and I'd be divorced. Shit, I'm still trying to convince her Ruth's not knocked up."

Danny laughed, shoved his hands in his pockets, and kicked at the rocks in the dirt. He glanced at Mike and said, "Ruth told me about that. She said it was something we should talk about."

"Well, I ain't in no hurry to be a grandpa, but that's between you two," said Mike. "All I ask is you figure out what future you want before you bring a little one into the mix, capiche?"

"Heard and understood," replied Danny. He rocked his hips toward the house. "Reckon we need to head in for dinner."

Mike slapped him on the shoulder, the grin still holding fast to his lips. "I reckon so. Built up an appetite, standing with you, solving the universe's problems."

"What if Margery asks what we talked about?"

"Tell her I was trying to corrupt you with tobacco."

"Sounds like a plan."

Ruth opened the front door as Danny and Mike approached it and walked out. She gave her dad a peck on the cheek and slid an arm around Danny's waist.

"So, did you two figure out my future for me?" she asked.

Mike shook his head, "No, darling. I stopped trying to tell you what to do when you were eight."

Ruth shifted her eyes to Danny and asked, "What about you?"

Danny hugged her and answered, "The only thing I want you to be is Ruth Coogan. After that, it's all gravy."

Ruth shifted her eyes from one man to the other. "I call bullshit on both of you."

"I just wanted to find common ground with your man, Ruthie," said Mike. He patted Danny on the shoulder. "You got a good one in him." He let his hand drop and started toward the front door.

Ruth watched her father walk away. "What the hell did you say to him?" she asked.

"Nothing really, we just talked some," replied Danny. "Why?"

Ruth turned her head to look up at Danny. "With most boyfriends, he talks about having a shotgun and a shovel."

"Maybe he's mellowed," said Danny.

"He doesn't know the word's meaning," said Ruth. She shook her head. "That's not the dad I grew up with."

Danny shrugged. "Let's call it FM, declare victory, and move on."

"FM?"

"Fucking magic," said Danny. "It was how Ben let me cuss around Molly without her knowing it."

"Okay, I like it," she said. She kissed him and pulled him toward the door. "Let's get inside. Dinner's on the table, and I'm hungry."

They walked into the dining room just as Molly laid the bread on the table. Danny noticed she'd changed into a sleeveless, pastel-pink farm blouse to show off the tan she'd gotten in Tuscany. Her ginger hair was pulled back in a ponytail from cooking, and teardrop earrings hung from her ears as always.

Margery stood by Mike at the end of the table. Danny thought she was pretty, if not a bit hard-looking and cold. She was taller than her husband, had bronze hair, and was dressed in slacks and a jacket like she'd shown up at the wrong party. She'd been a Navy wife, and now she was a farmer's wife, but Danny felt Margery always marched to her own drummer.

She glanced over, saw Danny and Ruth walk in, and gave them a quick wave. She moved past Mike and came over to provide Danny with a hug. She kissed Ruth on the cheek and said, "Doesn't the table look perfect? Molly has been cooking for hours, and the food smells delicious."

"Don't let her fool you," said Molly. She pulled out a chair at one end of the table and sat down. "She was working in the kitchen just like me."

"Pshaw, I peeled potatoes and mixed the salad. Your mom is the founder of the feast," replied Margery. She moved back to Mike. He pulled her chair out, let her sit, then sat in his chair beside her.

Ben wandered in with four bottles of open wine. He sat the bottles in the middle of the table, relocated to the opposite end from Molly, and plopped down in his chair.

"Good-looking food, ladies," he said. "I think I'll keep you both on the payroll."

Danny and Ruth found their seats on the far side of the table.

Danny said Grace for the family, and they all ended with an "Amen" and the sign of the cross.

Molly began the passing by lifting the plate of roasted sliced ham and handing it to Danny. "Take some and hand it on. You know the drill." She speared an end piece with a lot of pineapple glaze on it before Danny could move the plate and said to Ruth, "Did your mom tell you we ran into Father Matt yesterday when we were showing off Darwin?"

"Really," said Ruth. She took the ham from Danny. "Where did you run into him?"

"I believe it was at St Paul's," said Molly. She handed Danny the baked beans. "Keep the potholder under the dish. It's hot," she said.

Danny took the beans and gave his mother an amused look. "Imagine that. Running into a priest in a Catholic Church." He spooned some baked beans onto his ham and then passed them to Ruth. "Imagine the odds."

"Oh, Ruth, it is just the prettiest church," said Margery. "The stained glass reminds me of that chapel we went to in Crete when your dad was stationed there."

Ruth glanced back and forth between the two mothers and then looked at Danny. "I think we're being manipulated into having the wedding at St. Paul's."

Ben finished filling his plate with ham and handed it off to Mike. "That's nothing. Wait till you find out where they decided you're taking your honeymoon."

Mike took the plate, slid two slices off, and passed it to Margery. "And guess which two mothers want to tag along?"

Danny froze with a forkful of cheese and cabbage casserole an inch from his lips. "You're kidding, right?"

"Of course he is," said Molly. Then, just before she took a bite of scalloped corn, she added, "At least about the last part."

When the plates had been cleared, and the rhubarb-crisp and ice cream had been served, it had all been hashed out. Molly and Margery had been victorious on the location and would talk to Father Matt about dates in September. Danny and Ruth declined the idea of Hawaii for the honeymoon and chose Denali in Alaska, while Ben and Mike guaranteed the couple they'd keep the mothers from making the honeymoon a quartet.

Later, the three men gathered on the front porch for whiskey. The older men occupied the chairs while Danny leaned on the railing. Mike pulled out two cigars and a guillotine cutter. He snipped the end of both, put one in his mouth, and offered the second to Danny, who waved it off.

"How about you, Ben? You feeling sporty?" asked Mike. He extended the hand holding the cigar. "Last one I got, interested?"

Ben took the cigar and turned it over in his hand. "What denomination are they?" asked Ben.

"Punch Clasico Lonsdale," said Mike. He lit his cigar, took a couple of puffs, and tossed Ben the box of wooden matches. "They smoke smooth in the evening with a glass of good whiskey."

Ben lit his cigar, took a few puffs, rolled the cigar in his mouth, and took a few more. "Well, Mike, the whiskey is middling, but your smoke is pretty good."

"Thanks," said Mike. He crossed his legs and shifted his attention like a shark to Danny. "So, explain to me the shootings out on the reservation."

Danny had been expecting this ambush when Mike had suggested cigars and whiskey on the porch. Since Ben wasn't saying anything, Danny figured he was in on it.

"Not much to tell," said Danny. He recounted the finding of Goodnight's body, the chase with a peyote-high Joe Niland, and the surprise attack after they left the trailer.

Mike listened to it all but didn't cut in or interrupt to ask questions, which Danny appreciated.

Danny wrapped his story up with Edmund going to see Charmayne Lucas to track down the cattle tags.

"And that's all the news worth telling," he said. "Chairman Lodge said he'd get me cleared officially to aid the investigation. I'll head back out to the Rez in the morning."

"Charmayne Lucas, huh," chuckled Ben. "You did warn Edmund, didn't you?"

"Repeatedly, but he didn't believe us."

Ben rolled the cigar between his lips. "Killing someone with a cattle stunner is brutal. Ray's got real trouble if whoever did it gets to like it. Not many of Whitepipe's men got experience with that kind of evil."

Danny nodded. "I think that's why Ray was glad for my help. I could probably get you hired on as a consultant if you want some beer money and a little excitement."

"I have retired from active competition, my boy," said Ben in his lecturing voice. "Besides, I got an unbreakable appointment to pick out a new bedspread in town tomorrow with Molly, then lunch at the Dream Bean Café."

"Just thought I'd ask," said Danny.

Ben tried to blow a smoke ring, but it floated away, looking more like a hazy halo. He batted his hand back and forth to clear it, then glanced at Mike. "Kind of quiet. Everything okay?"

Mike stood and stepped over to stand by Danny at the railing. After a minute, he glanced at Danny and said, "Thank you for thinking of Ruth first. Getting her out of there."

"She's a tough woman, Mike," said Danny. He felt he should tell the whole truth here and not just part of it, so he plunged in. "Whoever did the shooting was gunning for Niland. She left me to save him. Without her needing to get Niland out of harm's way, there would have been nothing I could have done to get her to leave me. I just wanted you to know the kind of woman you raised."

Mike stared at Danny while he puffed on his cigar. The smoke curled and coiled between the two. But his eyes never left Danny's. At length, he pulled the cigar from his mouth and said, "I got no doubt the kind of woman I raised. And I think she's found the man worthy of her.

Chapter 8

Danny was back on the Rez the following day
before the sun rose. The Power Wagon was still in the
body shop, waiting for a new windshield, so he had to pick
up some transportation. Ruth couldn't give up her Subaru
due to making her medical rounds to the county's indigent.
Ben was next on his list, and Danny knew it would be hard
to convince his father to loan him his restored, harvest-gold
2000 Ford Expedition.

The Expedition had been the first new vehicle Ben
had ever bought, and he lavished attention and money on it.
It sat high on a van frame, was in pristine condition, and
was affectionately known as "The Beast." Even after
Danny vowed not to drive over fifty and avoid parking
under trees with birds in them, it was touch and go. Ben
was reluctant to lend Danny his pride and joy because
whatever the boy drove seemed to attract rifle and pistol
slugs.

In the end, Ben had made Danny promise, on pain
of death, that "The Beast" would get no bullet damage. As
Danny drove past the reservation sign, he prayed he could
keep his promise to his father. He and Ruth would have to

elope to Canada, change their names, and start loving hockey if he couldn't.

Danny had an errand to do before going to Tribal Police Headquarters. He first drove out on Redline Road and turned off onto the lane that led to Burbot Lake, Hollis Haypenny, and Ray's favorite donuts.

"I need twelve of your Maple Bismarck's," he told Hollis, who stood behind the display cases.

"Anything else?"

"Cup of coffee if you can spare it."

"I can. Fresh pot just came up," Hollis said. He put a dozen donuts in a cardboard box and handed Danny a Styrofoam cup of coffee and a thirteenth Bismarck. "My treat."

"Thanks," replied Danny. He took a big bite and was instantly overwhelmed by sugar, maple glaze, and crème. "These are silly good. I see why Ray likes them so much."

Haypenny straightened and asked, "You getting donuts for Chief Whitepipe?"

"Yes, sir," answered Danny. "Helping him out with a case. Want to get on his good side straight away."

"Then you best take two dozen," Hollis said as he reached for a second box.

Later, as he sat in one of the blue chairs opposite Ray's desk, Haypenny had been dead correct, thought Danny. One cardboard box was now empty and sat tilted sideways in the trash can, while the second was open on Ray's desk and already had three missing.

"Donuts on your first day," said Ray. "I might have to arrange a trade with Fish & Game for you."

"I'm for it," said Sotomayor. He sat in the other blue chair before Ray's desk, devouring his second pastry. He still had bandages on his face but had recovered enough to annoy his pregnant wife, so she'd sent him back to work.

Ray took a large bite and followed it up with a slurp of coffee. "You think they'd take Stan for you in an even trade?"

"Not a chance," answered Danny. "They couldn't afford to feed him." He sipped his coffee, crossed his legs, and watched Soto finish his donut and drain an energy drink. Danny couldn't understand it. The kid had broad boxer shoulders, a flat belly, and muscular arms, all on a diet of junk food and syrupy drinks. Shit, thought Danny, I have a notion about a cookie and gain three pounds.

Getting older sucks, thought Danny. He glanced out the window and saw a young mother walking on the street, holding the hands of two little ones. Ruth and I should talk about kids, he thought, but Soto brought him back from his daydreaming.

"You think Niland would rat on his buddies for one of these?"

"Joe's getting nothing but frozen burritos from the icebox out back until he tells me who the head rustler is," replied Ray.

"Speaking of your lodgers, how's Andrea getting on?" asked Danny.

"Fine. Although she hates being cooped up," answered Ray. "But I can't let her leave just yet. Not sure how much danger she's in."

"So, she's staying here happily?" asked Danny.

"I wouldn't say that," replied Ray. "But her uncle, Barrett, came by yesterday and made things clear to her, and her girlfriend Becca has been to visit her a few times."

"Any news from Edmund?" asked Soto, changing the subject.

"He called just before Danny showed up with breakfast," replied Ray. He wiped his mouth and finished his coffee. "Those tags come from stock all over central Montana; most of it reported stolen and insurance claims submitted."

"Then it's like we had it figured," said Danny. "Well-organized cattle rustling mixed with insurance fraud."

"Cattle rustling," laughed Soto. "I thought that shit was just something in the movies until now."

"A fair amount of it still goes on, and a good bit of money can be made," said Ray. He got up and filled his cup. "Edmund said he traced at least thirty tags back to Goodnight."

"So, we got probable cause to look around the Goodnight place then, right?" asked Soto.

"My gut says yes," said Ray as he folded himself back into his chair. "It looks and feels like our dead rancher was into some shady shit."

"Then I guess Ellen will need to be questioned," said Danny.

"You want me to do it?" asked Soto.

"I want you both to go. Soto, you're the lead, and Danny, you watch and gauge Ellen's reactions. We still don't have concrete proof that Goodnight was dealing dirty. And even if he was, Ellen might have been blind to it all."

"But if it walks like a duck and talks like a duck," put in Danny.

"I know, I know, then it's a fucking duck," replied Ray. "But let's go gentle with Ellen. She just lost her husband, and it sounds like she's losing the ranch. If we go charging in making accusations that are wrong, there will be hell to pay. And I'll be footing the bill."

"Understood," said Danny. He saw the logic of not ruffling feathers until more evidence was locked down.

Soto stood and adjusted his holster, then glanced at Danny. "I can drive." Danny didn't let the relief show but was thankful to leave the Expedition in town.

Soto's Interceptor slowed as he approached the Craftsman-style house. He pulled in beside Ellen's blue Ford Ranger and parked. The front door was partly open with its window broken, and the screen door swung on one hinge.

"Radio for backup," said Danny as he unsnapped his holster strap.

Danny exited the Interceptor and drew his firearm. Soto finished his radio call and joined Danny at the chain-link gate that opened into the grass yard. They did a quick visual reconnaissance of the playing field: Fiery yellow, red, and orange blanket flowers filled beds along the perimeter of the porch. A bay window was to the right of the front door, and a high window was to the left. Soto had his weapon in his hand.

Danny ran through what he knew about Soto, and all he could remember was him being married and a Marine. "We go in the front door. I'll clear right, you clear left. Got it?"

"Got it," replied Soto without fear or emotion.

Danny glanced at the man and saw that Soto was calm and poised for action. "If you have to shoot, shoot to kill," said Danny. "The people we're dealing with got no problem shooting at cops."

"Don't worry, I'll hold up my end." Soto winked before moving forward.

They went through the gate and fanned out to avoid being an easy target. Both kept their weapons low and scanned for signs of movement.

They reached the porch and stationed themselves on either side of the open door, Soto to the left and Danny to the right. They peeked in and saw an entryway table had been knocked over, and a large, iridescent-green carnival fruit bowl had fallen and shattered. The hardwood floor showed scuff marks, and the wall on the opposite side of the room had a head-sized depression in the drywall and smears of what Danny hoped was not blood.

Danny nodded to Soto, and the tribal officer shouted, "Ellen, this is Officer Damacio Sotomayor of the Tribal Police."

No answer came. Soto led through the door and stayed left. He stepped over the broken bowl and scanned the living room. A fireplace was on the right wall. A framed print of what looked like a Remington painting hung above it.

A couch was to Soto's immediate front, framed by two recliners. A flat-screen television sat on a stand against the entry wall, turned toward the couch, and played the old Western *Wanted: Dead or Alive* with a very young Steve McQueen.

Danny entered behind him, weapon up. He went right and inspected the room.

"Tribal Police. Anybody here?" yelled Soto. The only reply came from the TV, where McQueen was talking to a teenage Michael Landon.

Soto glanced at Danny, shrugged, and pointed his gun at the dent in the drywall and the archway beside it. "Kitchen must be through there."

Danny nodded. "Cover the room. I'll clear the kitchen."

Soto nodded and swiveled to cover the living room while Danny moved forward to get a better kitchen view.

He moved past the furniture and slid along the wall, seeing more and more of the kitchen as the angle improved. A yellow Sunbeam Mixmaster sat overturned on a counter with what looked like pink cake icing in the mixing bowl. A wooden table with two chairs sat in the middle of the room. Beside the table, Pyrex bowls lay spilled on the red-and-yellow checkerboarded vinyl floor, some broken, some whole.

Danny took another step forward and stopped as something heartbreaking came into view. "Fucking hell," he said with misery.

Soto snapped a look at him. "What?"

Danny's eyes never left the kitchen. "Body," was all he said.

Both men were stunned to silence and lost the impetus for action until a sputter of static from Soto's radio made them jump. "This is Stan. I just pulled behind the house between the grain bin and the detached garage. Where do you need me?"

Soto reached up to key the mic. "Roger, stay put."

The static went, "Roger, Ray's on his way. The ambulance is ten minutes out."

"Roger, wait one," said Soto into the mic. He took a guard position in the doorway.

Danny moved forward to kneel beside the body. He checked for a pulse. After a minute, he glanced back at Soto, shook his head, and stood. "She's dead, but the body's still warm."

"You think the shooter is still here?"

"Maybe." Danny surveyed the room. "Kitchen is the only room that looks tossed. We might have spooked them."

"Or they're still here," said Soto.

"Or they're still here," replied Danny. He lifted his weapon. "Better warn Stan."

Soto radioed Stan and briefed him on what they'd found and how the perpetrator might still be onsite.

"Roger," replied Stan. "I'll let Ray know about Ellen and cover the back. Radio the all clear if you don't find anyone."

It took ten minutes to clear the Goodnight house, but the only person Danny and Soto found was dead on the kitchen floor. They holstered their sidearms and radioed to Stan the "all clear."

"Acknowledged. I'll move to the front gate and let you know when Ray arrives," replied Stan.

"Thanks, Soto out."

Danny and Soto came back to the kitchen and started documenting the scene. Ellen had a deep cut along her hairline. Her eyes were open, and she stared at the ceiling fan as it spun clockwise on the ceiling. Blood had run down the right side of her face, pooled beside her head, and flowed in rivulets across the floor and under the cabinets.

Danny knew head wounds bled a lot, but they usually don't kill you. He knelt beside the body and, starting with her feet, moved his eyes north, looking for the cause of death. He found what he was looking for when he got to her chest. Ellen would have survived the head wound, but the two bullet holes just to the left of the sternum were another matter.

"Two shots," said Danny. He gestured at the holes in the dress.

Soto shook his head, "She never had a chance, did she?"

"No," said Danny. "Dead before we even drove up."

Danny made sure they didn't touch anything. He wondered if Ray had contacted DCI yet and how long Ellen would have to lay here. He leaned farther over the body to inspect the cut at the hairline. He wasn't sure, but he guessed the depression in the drywall would be a match for Ellen's head.

"I'm guessing a nail or wall stud," he said, referring to the cut.

Soto took his notepad out and scribbled as he replied. "Any ideas?"

Danny stood and looked down at the body, the head wound, and the two bullet holes. "Not sure. Feels off." He looked up and scanned the kitchen. He saw Ellen's purse hanging on the back of one of the chairs. He took two steps and peeked inside without touching the bag. He saw a set of keys, a wallet, a checkbook, and the crisp end of two folded twenty-dollar bills.

"Looks like everything is still in her purse," he said. "Kinda nixes the robbery angle."

Soto pointed at the bullet wounds. "I don't know nothing about nothing, but those holes look like they were made at close range."

Danny walked over and hovered above the body. "You may not know anything, but dollars for donuts, you're right," he said. "Killed just like John, up close and personal."

"I was afraid of that. With Ellen dead, another loose end is tied up," said Soto. He slipped his notepad and pencil back into his pocket. "And whatever information she could've given us is gone." He leaned back and looked through the living room at the screen door hanging by one hinge. "If they wanted to kill her, why not shoot her straight away?"

Exactly what I have been thinking, thought Danny. He mulled it over, then said, "What if they wanted something from her and only killed her after they got it?"

"Or after they didn't. Either way, John and Ellen are dead, and we're no closer to knowing who did it," Soto said.

Danny stared at Ellen's body. I've got to be missing something, he thought. He began at the woman's head and traced his eyes down her face, chest with the twin bullet holes, and each leg and foot. Nothing. He moved up to her shoulders and down her arms to her hands. The left hand was unmarked, but he froze when he got to the right hand.

He glanced up at Soto. "Is the stove on?" he asked.

Soto looked at Danny, confused. "What do you mean is the stove on?"

"Just tell me if the fucking stove is on?" growled Danny.

Soto shifted his eyes to the electric stove top. He held a hand over the left-front burner, but nothing. He then held it over the right-front burner. "Dammit," he said as he snatched his hand away. "Hot."

"Look at her right hand," said Danny. He felt sick, so he walked out of the kitchen and into the living room.

"Jesus Christ," came from behind Danny as he made it to the front porch, stepped through the open door, and took a deep breath to clear his head.

Soto joined Danny on the porch and vomited over the side into the fiery yellow, red, and orange flowers. He sniffed deeply and spat to clean out his mouth. He used the back of his hand to clear the saliva around his lips.

The two men saw Stan climb out of Soto's Interceptor. He waved at them and yelled, "Ray's a couple of minutes out."

"Thanks," yelled Danny back.

"Enough time to get straight," said Soto.

"Gum?" asked Danny. He tossed over a pack of Fruit Stripe gum.

Soto turned the pack over in his hand, stared at Yipes, pulled a stick from the pack, and tossed the remainder back to Danny.

Danny pulled a stick out, unwrapped it, and shoved it in his mouth. *Shit, melon-flavored*, he thought as the taste filled his mouth. Melon was his least favorite, but he chewed it anyway.

Danny wondered how he'd break the news to Ray when he got here. The killing the police chief already knew about, but Ellen being tortured could tear the department and the Rez apart if it got out.

"When we found Ellen, I didn't think it could get worse," said Soto. "Then I saw her hand. I thought I left that shit behind in Afghanistan."

"We both did, brother," said Danny, placing his hands on the smooth porch stone and leaning over to rock back and forth on his bootheels.

"What the fuck is going on?" asked Soto behind him.

"I don't know, but it sure as shit just got worse," said Danny.

"Sorry for throwing up. Can we not let anyone know about it?"

Danny waved away the words like smoke. "They wouldn't hear about from me. Shit, I almost did the same."

Stan waved to get their attention, then pointed at dust in the distance. Ray's Interceptor soon came into view. Its light bar flashed, but the siren was silent. Danny watched Ray pull up beside Stan, shut the engine down, and climb out. The passenger door of Ray's vehicle opened, and Monica stepped out. She had a bandage around her head, but the DCI tech seemed to have recovered from her injury.

Heavy storm clouds had chased Ray to the ranch house, and Danny smelled the sweet, pungent aroma of ozone. Lightning lit up a portion of the clouds, and a deep-throated thunder raced ahead across the prairie to announce coming rain.

Heavy raindrops began to fall, but Ray moved without urgency. It was clear he knew Ellen was dead. But he doesn't know everything about how she died, thought Danny.

"Bad news never gets better with time," said Soto. He headed down the steps and into the rain.

"Yeah, I reckon so," said Danny, and he followed Soto.

They met Ray halfway between the porch and the fence. Ray had a defeated look on his face and asked, "Just say it straight."

Soto glanced at Danny, then said, "We arrived and found the door open and signs of forced entry. We found Ellen in the kitchen. She took two bullets in the chest."

Monica had her shoulders hunched, and rain was wetting her hair.

Danny looked at her and asked, "How did you get here so fast?"

Rain was splatting her face, and she squinted and answered, "Never left. I was still at the clinic. Dr. Benteen hadn't released me yet."

Danny shifted to Ray. "Did you call for Pat?"

"Look," said Monica, breaking in. "I know you're all outdoor lovers, but can we move this to the porch before I drown."

"Soto, can you take Monica to Ellen?" asked Ray. "I want to talk to Danny."

"Sure, Chief, no problem," answered Soto. He glanced at Danny, then at Monica, and said, "She's in the kitchen, toward the back of the house."

After they climbed the porch steps, Ray asked, "Tell me the rest."

"It's bad," said Danny.

"I know it's fucking bad," said Ray. His control over his anger slipped. "Else you wouldn't come out in the rain to tell me."

"Ellen wasn't just killed," said Danny. "Somebody burned her hand on the stove."

Ray went stone-faced. "What do you mean burned her hand?" he asked.

"They tortured her, Ray," replied Danny.

Chapter 9

Danny and Ray sat in silence on John and Ellen Goodnight's front porch in two of the wicker chairs. Ray stared at his boots while Danny stared off at the distant mountains. Both listened to the rainfall. A low glass table holding a snake plant, two empty coffee mugs, and a set of reading glasses sat between them.

Ray shifted in his chair, and Danny glanced over at him.

"Good to get rain," said Ray. His eyes had shifted from his boots to the drops bouncing off the edge of the cement porch. "Been dry this summer. Lucky we haven't had any fires."

"Lucky," said Danny.

The two of them went silent again. It was as if the effort to speak was too much for them in light of the day's events. It'd been ninety minutes since Ray and Monica had arrived. Monica was inside, with Soto helping her, doing a preliminary on the body. She'd called Pat, the DCI lead, and he was heading to the house to investigate the death.

They saw a patrol vehicle appear on the road. It would be Stan back from getting coffee and bringing some equipment Monica had requested. The car pulled up beside the front fence. Stan climbed out, grabbed a tray of drinks and a gear bag, and joined Danny and Ray on the porch. He handed them each a tall coffee.

"How are they doing in there?" he asked.

"In the kitchen now," answered Danny, but not elaborating. He took the cover off his coffee and let the steam and the aroma pass over his face. He pointed with his free hand at the duffel bag. "I'm sure Monica could use that gear."

Stan nodded, shouldered the bag, and headed inside.

As the door closed, Ray spoke. "Got a call from Barrett and Tribal Council while you walked the house with Monica. They wanted to know if I made any arrests yet."

"Jesus Christ," said Danny. He sipped his coffee. "Not expecting much, are they?"

Monica interrupted their discussion by leaning out the door and motioning for them to follow her inside. The lawmen replaced the lids on their coffees, set them on the small table, and followed Monica.

The kitchen looked the same as the last time Danny had been in it. The colored bowls were still broken on the floor, and Ellen was still dead. Monica had bagged Ellen's hands to maintain any trace evidence from her fingernails.

"Let's start with the obvious," said Monica. She knelt beside Ellen and pointed at the two bullet holes in the woman's chest. "It was close range, less than three feet. You see the black halo on the dress; that's soot and shows where the heat scorched the fabric."

"Whoever it was was ruthless," said Soto. He had gloves on like Monica and had been acting as her assistant. "They knocked her to the floor, stood over her, and executed her."

"Now for the not-so-obvious," said Monica as she moved up the body. She lifted Ellen's head and twisted the neck to the left to expose the side of her head. It had a deep gash in it and globs of congealed blood. "I thought this was from the drywall or a nail from the living room." She pulled back Ellen's hair to expose an egg-shaped depression above and behind the temple. "Then Soto found this."

"What caused it?" asked Stan. He leaned in and canted his head. "Ball bat?"

"I don't think so. The wound is symmetrical and oblong," said Monica. She reached over to the counter and picked up a small plastic baggie with blue dust and the remnants of what looked to be broken glass beads. "I found this in the wound and mixed in her hair."

"Could it have been a hammer?" asked Danny. He was still looking at the wound and not the baggie.

"No, I don't think so. The skin on a person's head is thinner and less pliable. Coupled with the spherical shape of a head, hammer strikes usually result in lacerations and have specific fracture patterns. None of which I see here," said Monica. "And besides, if the weapon was a ball bat or hammer, then some things I found don't make sense."

"What things?" asked Ray.

"First. The broken glass beads," answered Monica. "Not something you find on bats or hammers."

Danny now eyed the baggie.

"And the second?" asked Ray.

"That we found the same injury on John Goodnight. It was hidden by his hair and farther back on his head," said Monica. "It's part of the formal report. Sorry, you haven't got it yet."

"So, is it the murder weapon?" asked Stan.

"No," answered Monica. "The shots to the hearts from the stunner and the firearm did the killing, but the knock in the head did significant damage and is virtually identical in both cases."

"If not a bat or hammer, then what did it?" asked Soto.

Monica glanced at Danny and then Ray before she said, "I got an idea. But it's a little far out."

"It's a war club," said Ray, frowning as he lifted his eyes off Ellen's body and stared back at the DCI technician.

Danny glanced at Ray to see if he was serious and found Ray's face hard and unsmiling.

"I was leaning that way but wanted your opinion first," said Monica. She pulled her gloves off, wadded them, and tossed them in the open bag beside her. "Saw

something similar in Missoula a few years ago. I had a
wife go whack-a-mole on her husband's side girlfriend.
We found an antique war club beside the body. Husband
said it belonged to his great-grandfather."

Ray stared at Monica and, to Danny, it seemed the
police chief was reassessing his first impression of the
woman. Finally, Ray said, "You seem too smart just to be
a techie working for Pat. Why'd you leave Missoula?"

"It's a long story," answered Monica.

"Give me the footnotes," said Ray.

"Okay," said Monica. "There was this hotshot
prosecutor who would make his bones convicting two boys
from the Flathead Reservation for murder. He was in the
papers and said he was interested in politics after the case.
I proved it wasn't them. Embarrassed the shit out of him."

Danny shook his head. "I'm sure that made you
popular at the DA's office."

"That's an understatement," said Monica. "Ended
up that the little prick did have some pull, and I got let go
during a so-called reduction-in-force when the reduction
was only one person in the department. Me. I needed a
job. Pat offered one, so here I am."

"Missoula's loss is our gain," said Ray. He pointed down at Ellen and the twin holes in her chest. "Getting back to work, any idea on the caliber?"

"Not yet," answered Monica. "The entry wound can rule out some calibers, but I need the slugs. Stan, Soto, can you help me?"

Monica knelt with the two officers beside her, and they rolled Ellen gently toward them and onto her side. Stan held her in place while Monica examined the linoleum floor. Two holes, matching the ones in Ellen's chest, pierced the floor and stared up at them all like the dead eyes of a possum.

"I imagine we'll find what we're looking for in the basement," replied Monica.

They lowered Ellen back onto the floor, and Monica, Ray, and Danny headed into the basement.

It was a dirt-floor basement with walls made of lichen-covered cinder blocks. An oblong, wooden workbench leaned against the left wall. A toolbox sat on it with well-worn wrenches, rachets, and hammers scattered across its surface.

On the right wall nested the mechanicals of the house. The water heater hummed and popped while the furnace waited silently for fall. Both were brand-new and bore yellow, new EnergyGuide labels.

"I thought Janine said they didn't have any money?" asked Danny.

"She did," said Ray.

Monica halted and pointed at two holes above them in the kitchen floor. She tracked downward to find two more holes in the lid of a chest freezer. "Bingo." She flipped the freezer lid open and said, "Holy shit."

Danny leaned around her and glanced into the freezer. He saw the carton of ice cream with two holes in it from the slugs, but he also saw the zip-locked bags of cash the ice cream was resting on.

"Son of a bitch," he said. "What the hell is it with people hiding money in the freezer?"

Monica slipped on new gloves and lifted the ice cream carton high enough to see the unperforated bottom. "Looks like the Rocky Road caught the slugs. I'll dig them out and see what we got."

"And the money?" asked Ray. "Can you get prints?"

"Doubtful," said Monica. "Rare to get usable prints off plastic bags. I'll let Pat try when he gets here."

Ray thought they should know the amount, so he and Danny donned gloves and opened one of the zip-lock bags to count the contents.

"Five thousand a bag," said Danny. He stacked the twenties and fifties back into piles and inserted them into the bag. "How many bags do you think are in there?"

Ray hovered over the open freezer. "I can see at least twenty-two," he said.

"That puts it over a hundred thousand," said Danny.

"And there may be more buried under what I can see," said Ray. He reached up and closed the freezer lid. "More than enough to kill somebody over."

They called Stan down to guard the money in the freezer and headed upstairs to check in with Soto. They told him what they'd found in the basement and that Pat and his team would arrive soon to process the entire house. Monica stayed in the kitchen, still mining for the slugs in the carton. Danny and Ray walked out onto the porch to await Pat.

Ray pulled out a pack of cigarettes, tossed one in his mouth, and drew the smoke deep.

"I thought Janine wanted you to quit those?" said Danny.

"She does, so to maintain Anglo-Indian relations, you best not tell her," said Ray.

Danny walked over and sat in the wicker chair he'd been sitting in before Monica called them in. "You think Ellen knew about the money?"

Ray pulled out a second cigarette, lighting it with the stub of the first, and said, "I don't see how. You saw her hand. She would have told."

"I reckon," said Danny. His eyes drifted off the porch and to the horizon. Midday had come and gone, and it'd stopped raining. Danny thought everything looked fresh, the colors all more vivid and deep. The sun shone and hit the water droplets on the leaves and flowers, and the world seemed new. Danny would call this a picture-perfect moment if he could forget what had happened in the house behind him.

He started to ask Ray if Edmund had called with more information when the police chief's phone rang. He heard Ray say hello and then start pacing the porch as you do sometimes when you need to work off pent-up energy. Danny returned to watching the horizon until Ray shoved the phone at him.

"It's Janine with Niland on the line," said Ray. "Says he'll talk, but only to the Wasi'chu."

Danny put the phone to his ear. "What do you want, Joe?"

"Is it true about Ellen?" he asked. "Is she dead?"

Danny glanced at Ray, then drove forward with the truth, "Yes, Joe. She's dead."

"Did they kill her?"

"Yes."

"Then I walk the dark road now," said Joe. "I'll tell you all I know. But only to you, Wasi'chu," and he hung up.

Danny briefed Ray on what Joe had said. Ray didn't say anything but hollered at Soto to get Stan and come out to the porch. Once they were assembled, Ray let

Soto and Stan know that he and Danny had to head back to headquarters. He warned both officers to be on the lookout for whoever was still looking for the money to come back.

"Soto, I want you in the living room watching the road. Stan, you in the kitchen to cover the back. The only folks showing up should be Pat and the rest of his DCI team."

"And if anyone else drops by?" asked Stan.

"Arrest them," said Ray. "I'll sort it out later. Got it?"

"Got it," the two said in unison.

Ray and Danny went down the skinny road and back onto the Redline. Ray powered his Interceptor up to fifty before Danny asked, "So, you going to tell me what Joe meant when he said he walked the dark road now?"

Ray set his cruise control and shifted in his seat. "Wallace Black Elk, an Oglala Sioux holy man, taught that there are two roads. The red road and the dark road."

"You mean like heaven and hell?" asked Danny.

Ray glanced at him as he drove. "Not really. The dark road is the road of self-destruction, while the red road is the path to healing."

"Healing?"

"If you walk the red road, you embody the Seven Sacred Virtues. You are connected to everyone else on the road in a circle, a sacred hoop," said Ray.

"Why do you think Joe believes he's on the dark road?" said Danny.

"My guess," said Ray, "is he knows Ellen was innocent and got killed, and he could have prevented it."

"You know," said Danny, "the more I learn about your beliefs and religion, the more I think your people have gotten it right from day one."

"A convert," said Ray. He tapped the brake as they entered the edge of Tennant Creek. "After this shitstorm, we need to have a long, far-reaching talk then."

"I'll pencil it into my calendar," replied Danny as they pulled up to headquarters.

In headquarters, Janine sat at the dispatcher's desk. She swiveled around and pointed toward Ray's office. "He's in there."

"You left him alone?" Ray snapped.

"Not at all. The door's open, and I can see him from here. Plus, he's handcuffed to the radiator," replied Janine. Then, in a pissed-off tone, she added, "You left me here alone to cover phones, walk-ins, and prisoners. You're lucky the place isn't on fire."

Ray kissed her on the top of her head as he passed and said, "Bad day, honey. Sorry I barked at you."

"If you think you'll get around me with that excuse," she said. Then a sad smile touched her lips, "You probably will."

The two men entered Ray's office and shut the door, blocking out the rest of the world.

Ray moved to sit behind his desk while Danny relocated one of the blue chairs in front of Niland and settled into it. "What can you tell me, Joe?"

Joe Niland was a defeated man; Danny saw it as if it was printed in bold lettering on his forehead. He sat limp and listless in his chair, staring at the carpet.

"Tell me true," said Joe. Only his lips moved. "Ellen's dead?"

Danny leaned forward in his chair and put his elbows on his knees. "She's dead, Joe," he said. He glanced at Ray, who gave him the go-ahead. Danny turned back to Joe and asked, "Somebody hurt her bad before they killed her, Joe. Do you know who did it?"

Niland lifted his head and stared at Danny. The man had dark eyes, and they seemed to be empty and dead. A chill passed over Danny as the eyes locked on him, but the man's voice was calm, even when he said, "I was wrong about the Wakanpi. It came for me; it knew I would let an innocent die. I'm on the dark road now."

Danny now saw fear in the man. "Can I help you against the Wakanpi?" he asked.

"No," answered Niland.

"Can I help you find the way back to the red road?"

Niland's head came up at the mention of the red road. "You know about the red road?"

"Only a little," said Danny. "Helping us catch who did this to Ellen is the first step back to the red road."

"I don't know who did this. I never knew who was in charge of things," said Niland, looking down again.

"How did you get instructions, then?"

"They would leave notes and money at my trailer. Along with liquor and noodles."

"So how can you help us?" asked Danny.

Niland's eyes came up again to look at Danny. "I know where they hide the cattle."

"Where?" asked Ray from his desk.

Niland shifted his eyes to Ray, and for a moment, Danny thought they'd lost him. But his eyes drifted back and settled on Danny. "Cornerstone Canyon."

"How many are watching them?" asked Danny.

"Two, maybe three," said Niland. "Charlie Prince will be there for sure." The man reached out to grab

Danny's leg. "Be careful of him. He's a mean son of a bitch. Most likely, it was him who shot at you that night."

Danny felt an eagerness to head out wash over him, but he had to ask before he left, "Why did you want to tell *me* about this?"

"I wanted to tell you about the Wakanpi so you wouldn't have to walk in fear," said Niland. "And to say I'm sorry."

They thanked Joe for the help, got up, and walked outside Ray's office.

"Charlie Prince," said Ray in a low voice. "He's a whole new level of bad. Did twelve years for manslaughter. Been accused of a few more killings, but the evidence was never there."

"You figure he's our shooter?" asked Danny.

"He did a stint in the Army," answered Ray. "Trained as a sniper, so you do the math."

"What about Cornerstone Canyon? You know how to get to it?"

"It's a box canyon up in the corner of the Rez," answered Ray. "Rough country. There are no roads, just miles of prairie, secret valleys, canyons, and buttes. Perfect place to hide things you don't want found."

"With no roads, how are they getting the cattle out?" asked Danny.

"Drive them north on horseback. I figure they move them to the Rez border and meet up with trucks off the highway," answered Ray with a smile.

"So, how do we slip up on them? And why are you smiling?"

"They'd hear us coming miles off on anything with a motor," replied Ray. "We're going to have to move up on them, quietlike."

"Be serious," said Danny. "Horses?"

Ray just smiled bigger and walked away. Over his shoulder, he said, "Time to saddle up, Hopalong."

"You know I could stay here and answer phones," yelled Danny. He glanced over at Janine, who was laughing. "I'm sure Janine would love to go."

"Not me," she said between laughs. "I hate horses."

Chapter 10

The following day, Ray and Danny were parked along the side of the road in one of the Tribal Police cruisers. They sat in front while Matt Bringloe from Medicine Hat was stretched out in the back, dozing with his hat over his face. Ray had pulled him in to ride with them. He'd been in rodeo and was the best rider on the force. They had the windows down, but the air was still, and all three wore the shine of sweat.

"Going to be a hot one," said Ray. He glanced at the sun, then at his watch. "He should be here by now."

Danny glanced in the rearview mirror and saw a truck and horse trailer come around the corner a quarter-mile away. "Speak of the devil."

The truck slowed, pulled to the side of the road, and parked behind the cruiser. Barrett Lodge climbed out of the driver's seat, and two younger Indians climbed out the passenger side.

Ray and Danny exited the cruiser and met Barrett at the back of the car.

Ray and Barrett shook hands. "Beginning to wonder if you got lost or something," said Ray.

Barrett gave a morning nod to Danny, then said, "Had a hard time getting my grandsons off their asses. But we're here now, and we can get started."

"We?" asked Ray. "You coming with us?"

"Course I am," said Barrett. "You think I'll loan out horses and hope to get them back?" He turned and told his grandsons to drop the gate, run the horses out, and get them saddled. The two strolled away to do as ordered, and Barrett turned back to Ray and Danny and asked, "Got your gear ready?"

Bringloe opened the back door before they could answer. The man climbed out of the cruiser, set his cowboy hat on his head, and stretched. He was rough-looking and angular, with long dark hair and an aura of relaxed danger.

"Morning, bright eyes. Glad to see you join us," said Ray. "Barrett, this is Matt Bringloe. He's one of mine from down in Medicine Hat. Matt, I think you know Barrett Lodge."

"Morning, Chairman," said Bringloe.

"Bringloe," said Barrett, turning the name in his mouth. "Didn't you used to rodeo down in Wyoming and Colorado?"

Danny thought he saw the man blush, but it was hard to tell. Bringloe tucked in his shirt and said, "That was a fair bit ago, but yeah, I rode the circuit for a few years."

"Thought so," said Barrett. The barest of smiles came to his lips. "Saw you ride at Cheyenne. Covered all three broncs you rode. Got second place, if I remember right."

"Yes, sir," said Bringloe. "Closest I even come to a buckle."

"Well, good to have you," said Barrett. He looked at Danny. "Nice to have a proper horseman along."

Danny saw Barrett glance at Ray, and the smile became more defined on the chairman's face.

Danny shifted his eyes from Barrett to Ray, who didn't hold back and had a broad grin. "You're an asshole. You know it."

"That's the rumor," said Ray. He popped the trunk on the cruiser. "Let's get going."

The lawmen got their rifles, bedrolls, and saddlebags from the trunk. Ray left the keys on the trunk lid so one of the grandsons could drive it back to Tennant Creek. They walked to the back of the trailer and found four horses saddled and ready and one pack mule standing by himself.

Bringloe chose a sorrel named Rojo; Ray loaded his gear on a blue dun named Winchester. Barrett's grandsons had loaded his pack on his horse, another sorrel with the given name Thunder. This left Danny with a buckskin called Fred.

"Why is he called Fred?" asked Danny as he tied down his gear. The grandsons were smiling and pointing. "And why do they think it's funny?"

Barrett came over to check Danny's saddle, reins, and gear. He adjusted here and there, then said, "He was named after a much-venerated relative who has passed on."

"Why do they think it's funny."

"Because Fred is my wife's horse," said Barrett. Danny started to protest, but Barrett held his hand up. "He rides smoothly and doesn't spook. Besides, my wife wanted you to ride him. She said she knew your mother and always liked her."

Danny was at a loss for words, so he pointed at the pack animal and asked, "What about the mule?"

"That's Dammit," said Barrett, who turned, walked over to Thunder, and pulled himself aboard. Ray and Bringloe were already astride. "He had another name, but it didn't stick."

Danny looked at the three men in the saddle and had a flash of nostalgia for how this job used to be done. He gathered Fred's reins, slipped his foot in the stirrup, stood up, and swung his leg over the saddle.

He looked up to see the three men staring at him. "What?" he asked. "I never said I couldn't ride. But I don't like it, and I'm not good at it."

Ray shook his head and smiled; Barrett tossed the keys to the truck at the taller grandson. Bringloe clicked his tongue, flinched his legs, and walked Rojo to the mule. He took the reins of the pack animal from the shorter grandson and said, "Be seeing ya."

He rejoined the other three and pointed to the northeast. "Cornerstone Canyon is roundabout twenty miles." He looked at Barrett. "You figure on coming in from the west?"

"I do," said Barrett. Thunder stamped the ground some, ready to get moving. "More cover that way. We'll tie up the horses below and come up in the tree line on the west ridge of the canyon."

"We could do it in a hard day of riding," said Bringloe. "But neither us nor the horses would be worth a damn when we got there. I say we break it in half. Ten miles a day." He looked at Ray, "What say, boss?"

"Ten a day sounds fine to me," answered Ray.

"I know a good place to hole up overnight," said Bringloe. "Old hunter's cabin. The roof was half caved in last I knew, but it might give some cover if the weather turns."

All agreed, so Bringloe led off as point man, taking them to the north and into the scattered trees. Barrett followed, with Danny trailing him and Ray pulling drag.

They traveled for a few hours and came to a creek, so they paused to rest the horses and let them drink. Danny found a toppled-over tree to sit on, and he opened his canteen and drank his fill.

Ray and Barrett stood talking by the horses, but Bringloe approached Danny and offered him some raisins and granola from a large bag.

Danny took a handful. "Thanks."

"No problem," said Bringloe. He squatted on his haunches and tossed a handful of the mix into his mouth. "What you doing this for, Coogan?" he asked. "You ain't from the Rez, and you ain't no Indian."

"Well, Ray asked my boss for my help."

"Nah, you know what I mean. Why are you taking risks for us?"

Danny had to admit he admired the man's straightforward way of going at things, but he didn't have an answer to this question. "No idea. Just seems like the right thing to do."

Bringloe was quiet for a bit, then stood. He offered Danny more granola, which he took. He noticed the man staring at him while he chewed. Finally, Bringloe said, "Most folks find reasons not to do the right thing. I guess you ain't one of them."

"Time to go," called out Barrett from beside the creek.

As Bringloe walked over to help with the horses. Danny reflected on what the man had said, not knowing if he'd just had his motives or his resolve tested.

They rode through the afternoon and into the early evening before they found the cabin Bringloe had told them about. He'd been wrong about the roof. It wasn't half collapsed. It'd been blown off completely and laid behind the cabin.

Bringloe stepped out of the saddle, shrugged, and said, "Well, it has been a good four years since I've been by this way."

They tended to the horses and the mule, and once they were fed and picketed, the four men tended to themselves.

Barrett pulled two gas-fueled portable stoves from the supplies Dammit, the mule, had been hauling all day. He made coffee with one, and once everyone had a cup, he and Ray commenced cooking dinner. He cooked beans and rice on one stove and boiled water for more coffee on the second. Once the beans and rice were warm, Ray cut in slices of summer sausage and divided the meal into fourths.

Later, Bringloe and Danny cleaned up and stowed the gear while Ray and Barrett relaxed and smoked around a small fire from parts of the fallen roof. Dammit had been staked out close to the ruins of the cabin and watched the goings on with little interest. Soon enough, the two younger men joined them at the fire, and the conversation turned to tomorrow.

"We'll start before dawn. Get a jump on the ride," said Ray. "That'll get us to the canyon by mid-afternoon."

Danny nodded his head. "Gives us time to see what's what in the daylight to deal with it."

"Good plan. Until the shooting starts," said Bringloe. He poured a touch of coffee in his canteen cup. "You know Charlie Prince won't go easy."

"I know. He'll fight if we give him a chance," replied Ray. "The others might not, but Prince will no matter what."

"What's the story on him?" asked Danny. "Niland seemed buffaloed by even his name."

"He was born with all bad bits, I suppose," said Ray. "In and out of jail as a teenager. Then killed a man down in Utah and got locked up."

"Tatankan Gnaskiyan," said Bringloe. He stared at the fire and did not look up.

"Yes," said Ray. "Crazy Buffalo runs deep in him."

"I've heard that name before," said Danny. He looked at Ray.

Ray poked the fire with a stick. "Tatankan Gnaskiyan, or Crazy Buffalo, is an evil spirit that brings all kinds of miseries."

"I know the Prince family. His mother swore he was born under a dark star," said Barrett. "She said he was a right bastard and as mean as they come."

Ray leaned to the side and gave a long look at Barrett. "You know this is police work. You don't have to join in when we get to the canyon."

Barrett looked insulted. "Not join in? What the hell you think I brought my rifle for, gophers?"

"Just wanted to give you the chance to step away," said Ray.

Bringloe tossed what was left of his coffee out, stood up, and said, "I'm headed to bed."

They peeled off and climbed in their bedrolls one by one until only Dammit was left around the fire.

The following day, after a breakfast of granola, coffee, and leftover summer sausage, the men packed, saddled up, and headed toward Cornerstone Canyon.

As planned, Barrett had them approach from the west and pull up in a stand of fir trees. They picketed the horses, drew their rifles, and packed extra ammo into their belts and rucksacks.

Ray slipped a set of lightweight binoculars around his neck, then watched Danny throw his pack on. "Looks heavy. Think you got enough rounds?"

"Enough and more," replied the warden. "If it comes down to a fight, I don't want folks saying I died due to a lack of lead."

"You said it," said Bringloe as he walked up. He already had his pack loaded and carried his rifle in one hand. He turned to the council chairman, "You ready, Barrett?"

"Just about," he answered. He was standing by Dammit and had a flap open on a saddle bag. He drew out a length of rope, coiled it, and stuffed it in his pack. He shouldered the pack, picked up his rifle, and walked to the three waiting lawmen.

"A man without a rope is a man without arms," he said.

"We plan on arresting them," said Ray. "Not roping them."

"Even so," said Barrett. "A little rope always comes in handy."

With everything set, they started in a single file up the slope through the sparse trees. Forty minutes later, the four lay on the rim of Cornerstone Canyon and looked down on a herd of roughly a hundred cattle, three wranglers, and one ramrod, Charlie Prince.

"Four of the bastards," said Ray. He stared down at the herd with the binoculars.

"We could pick them off from here," said Bringloe. "Course, that's not strictly legal."

"At ease with that bullshit," said Ray. He handed the binoculars to Danny and scolded Bringloe, "We're supposed to be the good guys."

Danny sighted the herd with the field glasses, then scanned its perimeter and saw where the wranglers were stationed. "Which one is Prince?" he asked.

"He's on the blue roan paint," said Ray. "Off to the right."

Danny shifted his elbows and aimed the glasses at the man and horse. Charlie Prince was not as advertised. Danny had built Prince up in his head, but the binoculars settled on an ordinary man sitting low in the saddle of the paint. He wore a cowboy hat with a heavy sweat ring, working clothes, and weathered chaps. He had pistols on both hips, and Danny could make out the butt of a rifle poking out of a scabbard.

As if reading his thoughts, Ray said, "I know he don't look like much, but don't let that fool you."

"Recognize anybody else?" asked Barrett.

"One of the riders to the south is Davy Haugestuen. He's a no-account from down by Square Butte," answered Ray. "I don't know the one with him."

"The one to the west is Levi Littlejohn. I can tell by how he sits the saddle," said Bringloe. "Rodeoed with him some."

"How you think we should do this?" asked Barrett. "We could go straight at them, but it'd be messy."

"I want to take them alive," said Ray. He glanced at Danny, who had lowered the glasses. "What are you thinking?"

Danny pointed and said, "Littlejohn is closest and by the tree line. We could make our way down through the trees and take him. Once we get Littlejohn, we'll have the other three in a crossfire and can take them peacefully," said Danny. He gave a crooked grin.

"I like your optimism," said Ray. He thought for a moment, nodded in agreement, and said, "Bringloe and me will go the other way and cover the canyon mouth. Chairman, you go with Danny." He exchanged glances all around. "Let's get to it."

The men slipped over the lip of the canyon and melted into the trees. Halfway down, they separated. Ray and Bringloe broke south to cover the canyon mouth while

Danny and Barrett went straight. They got to the edge of the tree line behind Littlejohn.

Littlejohn faced the herd and sat relaxed in the saddle. Danny began to move out from cover and toward the wrangler, but Barrett stopped him. The warden looked at the Indian who held his rope in his hand. He'd fashioned a lasso on the end, pointed at the rope, and then at Littlejohn.

Danny mouthed the words, "You're shitting me."

Barrett smiled, gave Danny the rope's end, pointed deeper into the trees, and made a runaway motion with two fingers. Not having a better plan, Danny leaned his rifle against the tree, moved behind Barrett, and nodded that he was ready.

The chairman stepped to the left, twirled the lasso around his head, and threw it. It arched toward the wrangler, who'd heard something and had begun to turn. But the rope got there before he knew what was happening. It dropped over Littlejohn's head and fell around his chest. Barrett slapped Danny in the shoulder, and the warden sprinted into the trees. Littlejohn was towed from the saddle and landed with a thud in the grass all so quickly it stole his breath, and he couldn't call out. The rope held him tight, and he was dragged into the trees into the waiting arms of Barrett, who put a foot on his chest and pointed a rifle at him.

"Afternoon, Levi," he said.

Danny jogged up, flipped Littlejohn over, and handcuffed him. He looked up at Barrett and said, "That was some crazy shit."

"Funny how often crazy shit works, though," said Barrett.

Danny stood and moved out of the trees to see if they'd been spotted. "Looks like everything is," he said when he heard the crack of a rifle. The side of his face was stung by bark shrapnel as the slug tore into the tree inches from his head. He dropped like a stone and scrambled behind the wounded tree. He grabbed his rifle and peeked around the tree's edge to locate the shooter.

He saw Prince with his rifle up and riding toward them. The other two wranglers hadn't moved, but both pulled handguns from holsters.

"Where the hell is Ray?" asked Barrett. He raised his rifle and fired at Prince. The shot went wide but caused both man and horse to flinch and turn away to the left toward the stirred-up herd.

The answer came as a voice yelled out of the trees. "Drop the rifle, Prince, or I'll blow you out of the saddle."

Prince pulled his horse to a halt and scanned the trees for the location of the voice.

"Who's hiding behind that tree threatening me?" said Prince. "I see you. You're too fat for all of you to get behind that pine."

Danny heard Ray call out, "It's Ray Whitepipe. We got four rifles on you. No sense in dying today. All three of you throw the weapons down."

Prince still scanned the trees but yelled, "If you know me, you know that ain't going to happen."

Danny moved to a kneeling position, raised his rifle, and aimed it at Prince. Barrett held his rifle low, leaned on the tree, and called out, "Prince, this is Barrett Lodge from the council. Do as you're told."

Prince snapped his head around at the new voice. Danny saw on his face that he recognized he was in a crossfire and was figuring out how to escape. The other two still held their pistols but seemed uneasy about gunplay.

Prince began to back his horse toward the cattle.

"Don't make me shoot you," yelled Ray.

Danny then saw Prince do the bravest and dumbest thing he'd ever seen a man do. Like a striking rattlesnake, the man snapped the rifle high and fired two shots into the woods toward Ray and Bringloe. Danny fired, and the bullet would have knocked the ramrod from the saddle if he hadn't moved like greased lightning. As the warden's bullet sped toward him, Prince ducked down, swiveled in the saddle, and swung his rifle under his horse's neck to fire at Danny and Barrett.

The bullet missed Danny, but he heard a thump, and Barrett cried out.

He heard Ray and Bringloe firing their rifles, but all their shots missed high. Both Indians had too much love for horses to bring themselves to kill one.

Prince hung off the side of the saddle and used the horse for cover. Danny didn't like horses, but like Ray and Bringloe, he couldn't kill one out of hand.

Prince was moving the horse backward into the herd. The cattle were spooked now, and seeds of stampede had been planted.

Danny couldn't fire at Prince, so he stood and aimed at the wranglers. It was then that he got his second surprise of the day. Davy Haugestuen rose in his saddle and fired two pistol shots toward Ray and Bringloe. He then spun and aimed in the direction of Danny. The warden sighted in on Haugestuen's chest and began to squeeze the trigger when the wrangler was tackled off his horse by the other wrangler.

The herd, frightened by the falling men, broke for the canyon mouth.

The unknown wrangler lifted Haugestuen from the ground. Davy tried to shoot him, but the man caught the wrist with the gun and brought the butt of his pistol down on Haugestuen's head. The wrangler dropped like he'd been pole-axed. Danny switched his aim to the unknown wrangler, who tossed his gun away, smiled, and held his hands up.

Danny turned to find Barrett on the ground. He was holding his side, and blood seeped through his fingers.

"Go, go," he moaned through gritted teeth. "I'll live. Go get the bastard."

Danny didn't need to be told twice and sprinted out of the trees and toward the stampeding herd that was getting away. The cattle moved like a flock of birds, tight-knit together, gathering speed and flowing like an unstoppable force. As they ran, thick dust began to rise.

Danny couldn't bring himself to shoot a horse, but a steer was another proposition. He aimed at the steer directly before Prince and pulled the trigger. It went down like a switch had been flipped. Prince spurred his mount hard, and it jumped over the fallen steer and ran on.

"For fuck's sake," cussed Danny.

He saw Prince climb back up in the saddle after the jump and looked back at him. The bastard had a smile on his face. Danny raised his rifle again, steadied his aim, and fired just before the dust got too thick to see Prince.

"Think you got him?" asked Ray once he and Bringloe had joined Danny.

"Not sure," said Danny. He had his rifle now trained on the unknown wrangler who had his hands up.

"Barrett caught a slug, says he'll live, but he needs a doctor."

"Bringloe, go check him," said Ray. "Danny and I will tend to things here."

"Aye, Chief," said the man, and he dashed off toward the trees.

Danny motioned with his rifle toward the standing wrangler. "What about this one?"

"Let's go ask," said Ray as he started to walk toward the man.

"Decide to switch sides?" asked Danny as he approached the man. He still had his rifle aimed at him.

The man glanced at the moaning Haugestuen, the rifle, then Danny. "Never was on their side."

"Then this is a funny place to find you," said Ray.

"Not really," said the man. "Name is Rune Jacobsen, U.S. marshal. And you just blew a four-month undercover operation."

Chapter 11

It turned out a bullet had not shot Barrett. Prince's round had struck the stock of the rifle Barrett had been holding, fragmenting the wood and driving large splinters into the man. Bringloe had removed the ones he could get hold of, then bandaged him the best he could until they could get the first aid kit from the pack loaded on Dammit. By the time Danny and Ray returned to the trees, with Haugestuen and Jacobsen in tow, Bringloe had Barrett up and back on his feet.

"Thought for sure I was punctured," said Barrett. He lifted his rifle to show off the jagged end. "Ruined a good gun, though." He lowered the rifle and inspected the two handcuffed wranglers. "Who's the white boy?"

Danny smiled. For once, the white boy in question wasn't him.

"Claims to be a U.S. marshal," replied Ray. He pointed past Barrett at Littlejohn, who was trussed to a tree with the rope that had lassoed him off his horse. "How's the one you bulldogged?"

"Says his ass hurts, but that's a long way from his head, so he'll live," said Barrett. It was his turn to point now, so he aimed a finger at Jacobsen. "You figure he's telling the truth?"

"I am telling the truth," said Rune. His handsome looks were a little battered from his tussle with Haugestuen, and his blond hair stuck out at odd angles from under his cowboy hat. He held his cuffed hands out. "Now, how about some common courtesy for a fellow lawman."

"You got a badge or something?" asked Barrett.

"Undercover doesn't work that way," replied Rune. He shifted his eyes to Ray. "You can call the office in Billings. Ask for Tom Heck."

"Do we want to believe him?" asked Bringloe.

"Leave him cuffed," said Ray. "He's a criminal till we can prove different."

"Goddam it," stammered Rune. "I'll have your jobs for this."

Danny laughed, "You'll have to get in line. Lots of folks want to fire us." He turned and looked at Barrett. "Can you ride?" he asked.

"Funny question coming from you," replied Barrett with half a grin. He swayed a bit, waved off help, and said, "Of course, I can. Why don't you younglings hike back and get the horses while I heal up some."

"I'm warning you," said Rune with a face like thunder.

"One more word and I'll gag you and leave you for bear bait," said Ray.

Barrett was left to guard Haugestuen and Jacobsen, who joined Littlejohn in being tied to the tree. Ray went after the wrangler's horses, which had wandered north, deeper into the canyon, and grazed on ryegrass. Danny and Bringloe climbed back the way they'd come to gather their horses and Dammit.

They rode around to the mouth of the canyon and rejoined Ray, who'd caught all three horses and sat astride the one Haugestuen had been riding.

"Any sign of the cattle?" asked Ray as they rode up.

"They're south about a mile off," answered Bringloe, pulling up.

"What about Prince?" asked Ray. "Did you find a body trampled to shit?"

Danny reined his horse and said, "No such luck. If I clipped him, it wasn't enough to knock him out of the saddle."

"You want to track the man or drive the cattle?" asked Bringloe. "I could scout for sign of his horse moving off."

"No, we stick with the cattle," answered Ray. "We got prisoners, cattle, and a hurt man. Much as I want him, Prince will have to wait."

"You're the boss," said Danny.

They joined Barrett and the wranglers in the trees, packed the confiscated weapons on Dammit, and passed around some food since the day was going to be long.

Thirty minutes later, everyone was up and aboard and riding toward the herd. Ray and Barrett were in the lead while Danny and Bringloe brought up the rear and kept an eye on the three wranglers who rode handcuffed to the saddle. Rune had complained about still being handcuffed but clammed up once Ray pulled out his bandana.

Barrett halted everyone as they approached the herd. He'd questioned the wranglers before heading out, and Levi had fessed up the route information. He said they'd always taken the herds from the canyon and north along the ridgeline to the highway. Barrett assigned himself to ride point. Ray and Bringloe had experience with cattle, so they'd drawn the flanks. Danny was the greenest, so he drew riding drag. He pulled double duty as he also needed to keep a weather eye on the prisoners.

They rode the remainder of the day, pushing the cattle north. It was hard work and made more difficult since the stolen cattle were from different ranches and not used to being herded together. Countless times, Ray and Bringloe had to corral misbehaving steers back into the fold while the herd seemed poised on the edge of stampeding.

Danny had hours to contemplate the life of a drover since the three wranglers weren't chatty. As appealing as the nostalgia of a cowboy's life seemed, he quickly decided the trail life wasn't for him. Bringing up the rear, covered by the dust of plodding hooves, the decision was easy.

At twilight, Barrett led them into a shallow draw with a three-foot-deep creek running down its middle. Red-tailed hawks circled above them, diving at mice and snakes escaping from the herd, and the air smelled faintly of smoke from a far-off fire.

"Nice place to tuck in for the night," said Barrett. They moved the cattle into the draw and let them rest. Some spread out and grazed, some laid down, and others moved to the creek to cool their feet and drink.

Twenty minutes later, Barrett declared the herd bedded for the night, and all the men on both sides of the law rode to the top of the north ridge above the draw and looked into the distance.

They saw headlights traveling back and forth on the highway when they reached the top. Danny estimated it was two or three miles away. Down below them, maybe a quarter mile, was a light pole standing sentinel beside a white mobile home. Lights were on inside the trailer, and behind it was a huge corral with a single horse.

Danny and Ray pulled their cellphones from their packs, checked for bars, and came up empty.

"Mostly landlines this side of the Rez," said Bringloe. "I could ride to the trailer and see if they got a phone."

"I wouldn't if I were you," said Rune.

All eyes turned to look at him with astonishment. Since Ray had dangled the bandana, he'd been silent as the grave, not even talking when they took a noon break.

"And why not?" asked Danny.

Rune ignored Danny and looked straight at Ray. "Chief, I am a real U.S. marshal and want to warn you about going up to that trailer. It ain't safe."

"Speak plain," said Ray. He moved his horse over beside Rune. "And fast."

"I've been undercover for four months. We've moved cattle from the canyon to the highway five times to load them on trucks. Each time we came to that trailer."

"Think Prince would've come this way?" asked Danny.

Rune twisted in his saddle to look at Danny. "Every day of the week and twice on Sunday," he replied.

"You're beginning to convince me about being a marshal," said Ray.

Rune lifted his cuffs as far as they would go, since they were connected to the saddle.

"Not that much," he said and looked off at the trailer. "How many do you figure?"

"Besides Prince," said Rune, "no idea. Never went inside."

"Two," said a voice. They all turned to see who'd spoken. Haugestuen had his head down, but Littlejohn was looking right at Danny. "The Salamander brothers."

"Archie and Elliott?" asked Danny.

"Uh-huh," said Littlejohn. "They work for Charlie."

"You know them?" asked Ray.

"Only by reputation," answered Danny. "They both got five years for poaching and illegal outfitting. I didn't know they were out."

Ray turned to look at Littlejohn and asked the man, "What else do you know about the trailer."

Littlejohn shot a side look at Haugestuen. "I never went inside, just to the corral. But Charlie sent Davy in one time to fetch the brothers."

Haugestuen raised his head at the mention of his name. His eyes bore holes in Rune, and he said, "Charlie had you pegged as the law. We just hadn't figured out how to get rid of you without causing a stir."

"You want to help yourself out?" asked Ray. "Buy some grace when you go before the judge?"

"Fuck you, fat man," said Haugestuen. "Charlie will fix your wagon soon enough." He shifted his eyes to Rune. "You're all dead men."

"I guess that's a no," said Danny. He drew his rifle from its scabbard. Ray did the same. Danny fed bullets into his rifle and said, "Plan on three in the trailer. Prince and the two brothers."

"We can swing east, work through the juniper, and get close," said Ray. "Bringloe, fix things up here for Barrett."

Bringloe stepped out of the saddle and pulled the three wranglers to the ground. He had them sit in the grass. He returned to his horse, pulled leather strips from his saddle bag, moved back to the men, and tied their feet.

"Come on now," started Rune. "*They* even thought I was the law. You're going to need my help to take Prince."

Ray looked down and said, "If you are a marshal, I'll apologize afterward. But I'm cautious about giving somebody I don't know a gun."

Bringloe climbed back aboard Rojo and ambled over to Dammit. He leaned in the saddle and drew a rifle and ammunition box from the top pack. He moved to Barrett and handed the man the rifle and ammo.

"To replace yours," he said. "Be seeing you, Barrett."

"Watch yourself, Bringloe, and keep those two from getting killed," the council chairman motioned with his chin at Danny and Ray. "The chief ain't as young as he thinks, and Coogan is reckless."

"Yes, sir," answered Bringloe. He tossed his handcuff keys to Barrett and said, "Just in case you decide to trust the man."

He rejoined Ray and Danny, and the trio moved east for a mile, then turned north and rode until they came to the trees. They got off their horses and led them by the reins through the trees until they could see the glow of the light pole ahead of them.

They secured the horses and moved forward until they were near the corral. The lone horse gave a friendly nicker and stared at the three. It was a paint like Charlie had been riding, so Danny figured it was even money Prince was in the trailer.

Ray had just started to whisper when the trailer's back door was flung open. Light from inside the trailer flooded the rear yard, and a large man wobbled out the door. He took two steps down the stairs, slipped, and dropped to his ass like a sack of potatoes.

"Goddam it, Archie," came from inside the trailer. "You're too high to go to town."

The now-identified Archie climbed to his feet. He turned around, gave the finger to someone inside the trailer, then fumbled in his pocket for his keys. "I'll be fucking fine. Charlie needs a doctor for that shoulder. He's bleeding like a stuck hog."

Charlie Prince's voice came from inside the trailer. "You ain't going nowhere. We got trouble coming and need to get ready. I can take the pain till it's over."

A second man, a smaller copy of Archie, appeared in the open door. That must be Elliot, thought Danny. He maneuvered the steps without falling on his ass and grabbed Archie by the elbow. "Get your happy ass back…" he said but paused when he eyed the corral.

"Fucking hell," said Ray, and all three lawmen dropped.

"Charlie!" yelled Elliott. He let go of Archie, who lost his balance, fell backward, and smacked his head on a rock. Elliott reached behind him and pulled a pistol from his belt. "Trouble's here."

He leveled the pistol and fired four rounds. One round went high, two struck the corral railing above the lawmen, and the last threw up dirt at the feet of the paint. The horse panicked and ran to the south side of the enclosure.

Elliot was backing toward the trailer door when Bringloe jumped to a knee and fired twice with his rifle. The first round missed to the right and struck the trailer siding; the second hit the man in the thigh, and he went down screaming in pain.

Ray and Danny jumped up to rush the trailer but dove to the ground as Prince emerged from the door, firing an assault rifle. Rounds impacted the dirt around Danny, and he felt he was in a hornet's nest of lead. He heard rifle fire to his left and realized Bringloe was still up and firing at Prince. Brave, he thought, fucking stupid, but brave.

Danny looked to his immediate left and saw Ray behind a water trough full of new drain holes. Ray didn't move, and a blood stain spread on the back of his shirt.

The fire shifted to Bringloe, and Danny took the chance to peek his head up. Prince was firing the assault rifle with only one arm. This gave him no accuracy, and he was throwing lead in hopes of getting lucky and hitting one of them. The other arm was in a sling, and stains of red covered his shirt, shoulder, and arm.

Prince was using the gunfire to cover Elliott, who got back on his feet and climbed the steps to get back inside the trailer. Danny saw the man limp inside and return immediately with a second assault rifle. Unlike Prince, Elliott had the use of both arms and standing in the doorway, he raised the gun and sighted in on Bringloe.

Damn you to hell for making me do this, thought Danny as he rose to his knee, aimed at Elliot Salamander's forehead, and fired. The man's head snapped back, and he fell heavily to the floor, laying half in and half out of the trailer. The automatic rifle fell from his hands onto the steps between his feet.

Prince ran out of ammo. He tossed his rifle away and turned to sprint back in the trailer.

Danny shifted his aim to him and yelled, "On the ground, now!"

To his left, he heard Bringloe yell, "Where the hell is Ray?"

Prince picked up the rifle between the dead Elliott's feet and spun to fire at Danny. The warden didn't have time to shout a warning again and fired a round into the man's stomach. The slug staggered him, but Prince didn't go down. He took two steps forward, raised the automatic rifle, and fired. Danny heard the rounds pass him like zippers, but none struck home. He aimed at the man's chest and started to squeeze the trigger, but Bringloe beat him to the shot.

The automatic rifle fell from Prince's hands, and he staggered forward one, two, three steps. Danny heard him singing his death song as he moved, then Charlie Prince smiled and keeled over dead.

Danny stood, his rifle still tracking for targets. Elliott and Prince were dead, and Archie wasn't moving. Fuck them, he thought and ran to where Ray lay face down.

He threw himself down on his knees beside the police chief. Blood soaked the back of Ray's shirt. Danny whipped his knife out and sliced the shirt in two to see the wound. It was large, and bright red blood spurted with every beat of the man's heart. Bringloe ran up, slid to a stop, and dropped to his knees on the other side of Ray.

Danny saw the dog-ear of the bandana in Ray's pocket and jerked it free. He wadded it up and packed it into the wound. Danny applied pressure, looked up at Bringloe, and saw the panic on the man's ordinarily calm face.

"Run to the trailer, find the phone," yelled Danny. The blood had already drenched the bandana and flowed between Danny's fingers. He risked letting up on the pressure, leaned back, pulled his shirt over his head, and pressed it into the wound to staunch the bleeding.

Bringloe jumped to his feet, sprinted around the corral, through the rear yard, vaulted over Elliott's body, and disappeared inside the trailer.

Danny heard Ray moan softly, then listened to the approach of fast-moving horses. He glanced up and saw Barrett and Rune riding toward them, hell-bent for leather. Barrett had a rifle in his left hand, and Rune held a pistol in his right.

They reined in the horses and jumped clear before they'd even stopped. Together, they ran to Danny. Barrett stood, rifle at the ready, and scanned the surroundings. Rune pulled the handkerchief from around his neck and knelt beside the man. He shoved a hand and the cravat under Ray, searched for a moment, then pressed upwards.

"I got the entry wound," he said. Rune and Danny now had Ray pressured both front and back, entry and exit wounds both covered. There was precious little else they could do.

"How'd you get a gun?" asked Danny.

"I gave it to him," said Barrett. "Thought we needed all the help we could get."

"If you're a real marshal, call for a medivac," said Danny. "He's dying."

"Barrett, take my place," said Rune. "Don't let the pressure up."

Barrett tossed his rifle to the side, fell to his knees, and replaced Rune's hands with his own. Bringloe rushed up. He had a laundry basket of towels tucked under one arm. With his free arm, he aimed his rifle at Rune. "What the hell is he doing here?"

"Being trusted," snapped Danny. He looked at Rune, "Go!"

Rune sprinted toward the trailer, and Danny wondered how much time Ray had.

Bringloe tossed the basket to the ground and pulled a yellow-topped bottle of Wonder Dust out of his back pocket. Danny focused on it and saw it said, "Wound Powder for Horses and Show Stock."

Bringloe twisted the top off and said, "Found it in the kitchen. Prince must have been using it on his shoulder. How much you want?"

"Pour it all in the wound," said Danny. He tossed his soaked shirt away and grabbed the top towel from the basket as Bringloe emptied the bottle. Danny pressed the towel into the wound and looked at the trailer's back door as Rune appeared.

"Check his pulse and keep checking it," ordered Danny.

Bringloe jumped over Ray's outstretched arm and knelt to feel the side of the man's neck. "It's weak. I can barely find it."

"Keep your finger on it," said Danny. "Tell me if it changes."

Danny glanced up and saw Rune dashing toward them. The man skidded to a stop and said, "I got through to the Marshals Service. A medivac from Darwin was already in the air coming back from a transport. ETA is five minutes."

Danny nodded. "Sorry we didn't believe you."

"Fuck it," said Rune. He pointed at Ray. "Just make sure he lives to apologize to me."

It seemed like an eternity passed before Danny heard the whop-whop-whop of the medivac. The red and white helicopter came in fast, hovered above the trailer, switched on its landing lights, and slipped sideways toward the corral to land. The side door flew open, and two men in blue jumpsuits carrying trauma kits leaped out and raced toward them.

"I lost his pulse," yelled Bringloe. The rotor wash blew his hat off.

"Goddam it, Ray!" shouted Danny.

Chapter 12

Danny sat in a chair in the waiting room of Darwin County Hospital. He'd washed the blood off his hands and wore a well-worn, denim, pearl-snap Western shirt the night nurse had given him from the lost-and-found box. His rifle was with Bringloe, but his Sig still sat in its holster on his belt.

Back at the trailer, he had hesitated to leave Bringloe and Barrett, but Rune urged him onto the helicopter by saying that if Ray woke up, he needed to see a friend. It had been at that moment when Danny turned to look at Rune and saw fear and pain that he decided to trust the man fully.

On the flight, he watched as the flight medics revived the police chief twice in the air. As the lights of Darwin appeared beneath them, Danny felt the pilot flare the helicopter and decelerate. For a flash, he was in Afghanistan and heading into a hot LZ. Then the memory passed, and Ruth, with a nurse and another doctor he didn't know, raced toward them as they touched down on the pad. Ruth had checked Ray and shouted orders, and the other doctor and nurse dashed away, pushing the gurney and Ray into the elevator to head down to surgery.

Ruth had buried her head in Danny's chest and hugged him. He'd wrapped his arms around her and never wanted to let her go. Too soon, she'd loosened her grip and leaned back. Danny could tell she'd been crying. He'd tried to say something but had no words for his feelings.

She had hugged him tight again and, as if she'd read his mind, whispered into his ear, "I know. Me too." Then she was gone, sprinting to the door beside the elevator that led to the stairs.

The automatic doors of the surgery center opened, bringing him back to the present, and the doctor Danny didn't know walked out. He strode across to Danny, who rose to shake his hand.

He was taller and thinner than Danny, with a red beard, a bald head, and long fingers.

"I'm Dr. Oliver," said the man. "You're Ruth's fiancé and the man who flew in on the medivac with Chief Whitepipe?"

"Yes, sir, I'm Danny Coogan. How's Ray?"

"We've given him blood to replace what he'd lost and are trying to stabilize him so we can operate," said Dr.

Oliver. "I want to be honest. His odds of survival aren't good."

"You don't know him like I do," said Danny. "He'll take those odds and beat them."

"From your lips to God's ear. I'm an atheist, but I'll take the help," replied Dr. Oliver. He tried to smile and give reassurance, but Danny thought it made him look like a corpse. "Have you contacted his family?" he asked.

"I called the Tribal Police. They broke the news to Ray's daughter, Janine. She should be here within the hour."

"Very well," said Dr. Oliver. He retook Danny's hand and clasped his shoulder. "I have to get back in there. I promise we'll do all we can."

"Thank you," said Danny. He watched the man walk away and disappear behind the automatic doors.

Danny was thinking of raiding the vending machine when the whoosh of the emergency room door caused him to turn. He saw Janine, Stan, and Andrea Saltes rush in and make a beeline for the information desk. The nurse behind the desk stood and started to come out to greet them.

Janine spotted Danny, grabbed Stan by the arm, and hurried toward him. Andrea trailed in their wake.

"Where's Dad?" asked Janine.

"They are getting ready to operate on him," said Danny. He wondered how much he should tell her, how much he could say to her. As always, for better or worse, he chose the truth. "He's in a bad way."

Janine tensed and squeezed Stan's arm.

"What are you trying to tell me?" she asked.

"The surgery is going to be rough on him," said Danny.

Janine glanced behind Danny. He turned and saw Ruth standing there. Ruth gave a quick nod to affirm Danny's words.

"No," said Janine. Her hand dropped from Stan, and she backed away from Danny and bumped into Andrea. "No."

"He's a fighter, Janine," said Ruth. She walked to Ray's daughter and took her hands. "He's holding on. Dr. Oliver is operating now." She glanced at Danny and then back to Janine. "But Danny's right. The surgery will be hard on him."

"He fought to make it here," said Ruth. "Something in him won't give up. That should give us hope."

Janine glanced between Danny and Ruth, then melted into the arms of Stan and let the tears flow.

"Thanks for being here for Janine, Stan," said Danny. Then he remembered that Stan was Ray's cousin. He shifted his eyes to Andrea. "How are you doing?"

Andrea looked mousy and answered, "Chief Whitepipe was trying to protect me. Is this my fault?"

Danny was stunned at her words but didn't let it show on his face. With everything going on with her, the last thing she needed was to feel guilty for Ray. He touched her shoulder and replied, "No, Andrea, this isn't your fault. It's the fault of two people. One who can't hurt anyone anymore, and a second who was in charge of them."

Andrea melted with relief, and Ruth wrapped her arms around the girl.

Danny looked at Stan holding Janine, Ruth holding Andrea, and at the doors that led to the room where Ray lay almost dead. He knew it was wrong, but deep inside his chest, an ember of anger, revenge, and retribution stirred to life.

The surgery took two and a half hours, but Dr. Oliver was able to give cautionary good news when he walked out to talk to them.

"Chief Whitepipe made it through surgery and is in critical but stable condition. We're moving him to recovery." He held up a hand to stop the rush of questions. "You can see him through the glass in a little while, but no visitors in the room. We won't know more for a few hours."

They started heading through the recovery room's automatic doors when Danny's phone went off. He pulled it out, glanced down, and saw it was the Montana State Police.

He waved them on. The others followed Dr. Oliver through the doors, and as the doors closed, Danny raised the phone to his ear. "Coogan."

"Warden Coogan, this is Trooper Brett Hawkins. I got a Tribal Police officer who needs to speak to you."

Danny heard the phone switch, and Bringloe's voice came on the line. "Danny, it's Matt. How's Ray?"

"He's out of surgery. Doc says he's critical but stable," answered Danny. "Janine and Stan are here. We won't know more for a few hours."

"At least he hasn't curled his toes," said Bringloe. "And he's one tough son of a bitch."

"How are things there?" asked Danny. "Did the brand inspectors show up to collect the cattle?"

"That's the second reason I called. We need you back here."

Danny shook his head. "Not a good time. Can't you and Barrett handle it?"

"It's Barrett that asked me to fetch you."

"What's happened?" said Danny. "Is he okay?

"Yeah, got his hide patched up fine." Then Bringloe took a deep breath on the other end and dove in. "The livestock cops showed up with trailers and are loading the cattle. The state police are here to handle the traffic on the highway. That's how I got Hawkins's phone."

Danny switched the phone to his other ear and reached into a pocket for his small spiral notebook and pen. "Go on."

"Rune had the calvary on speed dial, so we got federal marshals and DCI headed this way. Be here within the hour."

Danny took all this down, then said, "Sounds textbook. Why does Barrett want me?"

"Council caught wind of goings on and wants to call the FBI. Barrett talked them down by promising you'd oversee things."

"What the hell," said Danny. "I'm not Tribal Police. I'm just helping out."

"Don't seem to matter much," replied Bringloe. "You're the flavor of the month with them, and they agreed as long you take charge."

"Shit fire," said Danny. His mind fired off down multiple paths. This should be a simple rustling case. Now men are dead, Ray might be joining them, and the Tribal Council wants to put him in charge. "I'm not an Indian."

Bringloe laughed and said, "Don't seem to matter to anybody, given the present situation."

"You could run things," said Danny.

"Coogan, I appreciate that, but I'm just a retired bronc rider who breaks up bar fights and writes tickets. Barrett needs you, and he's promised you to the council."

"Give me a minute," said Danny, and he let the phone fall from his ear. He curled it in his fingers and rubbed his forehead with the heel of his hand. Him being in charge, what the hell is Barrett playing at? Danny knew the reputation of the FBI on the Rez and the residents' pure disdain for it, but in his mind, he was no better than them. He used the calming technique the counselor at the VA had taught him.

With his eyes closed, he let his three top fingers form a skirmish line from the bridge of his nose upwards. He breathed deeply and felt the world slow. He peeled back the uncertainties and reasons for not accepting the job until he got to the essential fact: Barrett needed him, and duty was a way of life for him.

He shifted the phone back to his ear. "Tell Barrett he's got me. I'll find a vehicle and head your way," said Danny. The doors swung open, and Ruth walked out and up to him. She was in scrubs, had her hair in a ponytail, and was sans make-up. She was beautiful. "Give me two hours," Danny said and hung up.

Ruth stepped up on her toes and wrapped her arms around his neck. She smelled of antiseptic and perfume, but Danny buried his face in her hair and hugged her until his mind settled.

She dropped her arms from around his neck and moved them down to hug him around the middle. She leaned her head against his chest and gave a deep sigh. Danny was sure she could hear his heartbeat and asked, "How's Janine?"

"Scared," replied Ruth. She raised her head and looked into Danny's eyes. "So am I. That could be you in there."

Danny tried to think of something to say that would be reassuring, but he knew his girl. He knew what she expected of him, so he told her, "I know."

"Mom lived through this with my dad, and it almost broke them," she said. "Living in fear, hoping to see him come home."

"Do you want me to quit?" asked Danny. His voice was even and calm. No anger, no resentment, just a simple yes or no question that he was willing to abide by.

Ruth let her arms drop and stepped away from Danny. She gave him a long look and said, "'I promise you that if it ever comes down to the job or Ruth, it's Ruth always, forever, period, the end.' That's what you told my dad, right?"

"Yes, and I meant it."

"I know you did," Ruth said. "I love you for the man you are. I would never remove any part of you and make you less."

"So, what do you want?"

"I want you to be you," she answered. "Your only job is to be Danny Coogan. If you change to please me, it'll piss me off."

"Message received," he said, drawing her back into his arms. "Love you."

"Love you back," she answered, pressing the keys to her Subaru into his hand.

A nurse came down the hallway and saw the two but lowered her head and passed by without a word. Danny and Ruth stayed huddled together for quite a while.

Two and a half hours later, Danny pulled off the highway and onto the long drive that led to the Salamanders' trailer. He passed five parked livestock trucks with brand inspectors processing the evidence, in this case, cattle, before he got to the state police roadblock that blocked the drive.

He stated his name and flashed his badge to a female trooper who said, "Coogan, huh? You must be the cat's meow; the marshals and the head Indian been waiting on you."

Danny asked, "Has Montana DCI shown up yet?"

"Drove in an hour ago with a contingent of marshals," answered the woman. "You better get going and join the party."

"Yes, ma'am," he said. She waved him past, and he drove up the long drive.

Danny parked beside two black Suburban SUVs and climbed out of the Subaru. Next to them, Ruth's car squatted like a calf among bulls. He knew the vehicles were not the standard version. They'd been modified with armor, thicker windows, and state-of-the-art electronics. Each cost more than any tiny house Ruth and he were looking to buy.

He thought of his tax dollars at work as he made his way around them and toward the trailer and assembled lawmen.

Barrett saw Danny walking toward them and moved to intercept him. The chairman extended a hand and said, "I know it's hard to leave Ray, but thanks for coming."

Danny shook his hand and nodded. "Stan is taking care of Janine, and Ruth will call me if anything changes, good or bad." He tossed a chin at the gathered lawmen and techs combing the rear yard of the trailer. "How's the living Salamander brother?"

"You mean Archie?" asked Barrett. "He came around after you and Ray flew off. Bringloe cuffed him and tried to question him, but the dead brother lying beside him put him off cooperating. Paramedics checked him out. He'll live, unfortunately."

Danny surveyed the glut of evidence flags that marked expended brass. In places, the flags looked like they'd been sown solid. We should all be dead, thought Danny.

"Where'd they take him?" he asked.

"Sheriff Johnson had him transported to county jail after he was cleared," answered Barrett. "He took Littlejohn and Haugestuen also. He reckons you'll be by to talk to them."

Talking to Archie was at the top of Danny's to-do list, but that could wait until they got done here.

He followed the flags until he came to the bodies. Charlie Prince and Elliott Salamander lay where they'd fallen, Elliot in the doorway of the trailer and Charlie by the corral.

Rune was squatting next to Charlie Prince's body and talking with a DCI tech when he glanced up and saw Danny. He gave a quick wave, finished with the tech, and jogged over.

"How's Chief Whitepipe?" he asked.

Danny passed on all he knew and watched the man take it in.

"Fucking hell," Rune said. He glanced back at Prince and spat. "Bringloe told me how the fight went down. You took Elliott, and he finished Prince."

"No choice on either one," said Danny, not wanting to relive it. "The Salamander kid had a bead on Bringloe. If I hadn't shot him, Bringloe would be lying in a bed beside Ray or in the basement of Darwin Hospital."

"And Prince?" asked Rune.

"As Ray said, if given the chance, he'd fight," replied Danny. He reflected on Prince's final moments, the death song, the smile. "It was like he wanted to die."

"He's been trying to die for years. He yearned for it, talked about it," said Rune. His voice had a tinge of sadness in it. "Don't get me wrong; he was an evil man, irredeemable. I only knew a tenth of what he did and knew he deserved a bullet from that alone."

Danny and Barrett furrowed their brows and stared at Rune. "That's a surprising and politically incorrect comment coming from a federal law enforcement officer," said Barrett.

Rune turned to watch two DCI technicians put Prince into a body bag. He turned back to stare back at the men. "Maybe. But I don't always walk a fine line politically and want no misunderstandings between us." He shifted his eyes to the trailer and the technicians working on Elliott Salamander. "Besides, his ass is dead and beyond my concern now."

Rune walked off in the direction of the trailer. Danny and Barrett watched him go.

"He's been saying things like that the whole time you've been gone," said Barrett, still watching the man walk away. "Spooky shit if you ask me. The undercover job and proximity to criminals have tainted his outlook on the law some."

"We all get world-weary," said Danny. He saw Rune stop on his way to the trailer and talk to a man in a blazer with U.S. MARSHALS stenciled on the back. "Worn down by the realities of a hard world." Barrett turned to stare at him, and Danny glanced at him and said, "For me, I just try to hang on to why life is beautiful."

A slight smile came to Barrett's lips. "You sure you're not Nakota down deep inside?"

Danny matched his smile. "Not that I know of. I'll take that as a compliment."

They started to walk after Rune when Danny's phone went off. He pulled it free from his pocket and looked at the screen. The display showed an unknown number, and he almost treated it as spam, but with Ray in the hospital, he thought he should answer it.

"Warden Coogan," he said. "How can I help you?"

The voice on the other end made Danny stop cold. Barrett walked another two steps, then halted and turned to look at the warden, concern digging deep grooves in his face. His concern grew as he heard Danny's side of the conversation.

"Sir, yes sir, I know who this is."

"Yes, sir. The council has asked me to take over the investigation. How did you hear about it?"

"I'm sorry they woke you when they called."

"No, sir, I wouldn't return to duty. Chief Whitepipe is in the hospital, all shot to shit. I plan on getting the bastards responsible."

"Sir, you can call it insubordination, disobeying orders, or whatever you want. I'm not going to leave the investigation."

"Then, I guess we've got ourselves a standoff."

"You do what you think you have to, but I'm staying on the Rez."

"Yes, sir. Goodbye."

Danny punched the button to end the call and dropped his hand.

Barrett approached him and asked, "Was that what it sounded like?"

"That was the Director of Fish, Wildlife, and Parks," answered Danny. "He just fired me."

Chapter 13

Danny woke with a jerk as Rune opened the door of the Suburban he was asleep in, and the late-day sun hit his eyelids. He lay across the backseat, covered in a blue microfleece bearing the marshals logo. He'd kicked off his boots and used a wadded blazer as a pillow. He gave Rune a rude look and rolled over.

"Evening, deadbeat," said Rune. He held two Yeti Rambler cups by the handle. Both had the marshals logo on them. "I brought coffee. Barrett needs you over at the trailer."

Danny pulled the blanket over his head to block the sun. "I'm not a warden anymore. Just want to get enough sleep so I can think straight and not be a zombie."

Rune pulled the fleece off him and hovered one of the cups above his face.

"We'll have to settle for the zombie," replied Rune. "Shake a leg. We've got things to get settled."

Danny sat up at the words. He searched for and found his boots. He tied his laces and asked, "What are we settling?"

"You'll see," said Rune.

Danny jumped out of the truck, and Rune handed him the coffee. "Nectar of the gods, thanks."

"I got to get back to my team," said Rune, heading off toward a huddle of blue blazers. "I'll see you after."

Danny found Barrett standing outside the back door of the trailer. Bringloe was with him, along with two older Nakota he didn't recognize.

The taller one was thin and had his hair in two long braids that fell below his shoulders and were wrapped in colored thread. He wore jeans, a button-up shirt, and a buckskin jacket. A black stone pendant hung around his neck from a leather lanyard and had the shape of a sitting dog. He didn't smile and seemed keen to be anywhere but here. Danny thought the man was trying too hard to look like an Indian.

The shorter man was stocky, the muscles beginning to shift to fat. His face was broad and open, and he smiled with a mouthful of teeth and genuine Western charm. He looked like a rancher who just placed the winning bid on the prize bull at the auction. He reminded Danny of Nat Long Soldier, a good friend who was gone now.

He instantly disliked the tall man but was warming to the short one.

Elliott's body had been moved from the doorway, and DCI technicians moved in and out of the trailer.

Danny sipped at his coffee as he walked up. He nodded to Barrett. "Rune says we got stuff to hash out." He motioned with his cup at the technicians and asked, "They find something?"

"They did," answered Barrett. "Boxes of drugs, weapons, and more cattle tags."

"Evidence of rustling, but still no idea who's in charge of the operation?" asked Danny.

"Exactly, but that's not why I had Rune wake you up," said Barrett. He smiled slightly as he spoke. "I need you to answer one question for these gentlemen."

Danny shifted his eyes across the assembled group and went on edge. His mind sounded the alarm, and he replied with caution. "What's the question?"

"Why did Fish & Game fire you?" asked Barrett.

Danny took a sip of coffee, then answered, "Does it matter?"

"Trust me, it matters," said Barrett.

Danny shrugged and answered, "For insubordination and failing to follow orders."

"Why were you insubordinate, and what order didn't you follow?"

"They wanted me to report back to duty and leave the investigation. I said I owed it to Ray to find the men that did this and couldn't step away. They said to report back or get fired. I said no, and that pretty much settled things."

Barrett looked at the two other men and said, "Satisfied?"

The taller one gave a curt nod while the shorter man smiled and said, "Offer it to him."

"What's he talking about?" asked Danny.

Barrett turned to face Danny and spoke. "We wanted to offer you a job."

"What job?" said Danny in a wary voice. "You've seen me, I'm shit on a horse, and I'd be a poor excuse for a wrangler."

"Tribal Police officer," replied Barrett. His smile deepened as he saw Danny's eyes go wide. "I understand you have some law enforcement experience, and we thought you might be worth the risk."

"You're joking, right?" asked Danny. His eyes shifted from Barrett to Bringloe, who was grinning ear to ear.

"Not at all. I can offer you half what you made as a warden plus medical. Sorry, no dental," said Barrett. "Got a badge and everything right here."

Danny sipped his coffee and moved through the eyes staring at him trying to figure out if it was all a put-on. Finally, he shrugged and said, "Council would never approve it."

"We already did," said the shorter of the unidentified men.

Danny twisted to look at the man and caught him with the same slight smile Barrett was wearing. His mouth opened, but he couldn't figure out what to say, so he shut it.

"Barrett says you're vital to finding who's doing all this." The man waved a circle above his head. "You've got a good name with the council and are trusted."

Barrett gestured at the taller man and said, "This is Jonathan Redwing." He shifted to the shorter, rounder man. "And the one who just complimented you is Andy Banner. Both members of the council."

"Hold on," said Danny. "What do you mean we already did?"

Barrett pulled out a Tribal Police badge and held it out to Danny. "You were approved, eight to two."

"Winnie Whitefeather doesn't like you," added Andy Banner. "Got something to do with last year."

Winnie was the head nurse at the town's medical center, and she and Danny had a run-in the previous year over the Oxendine boys.

"And I voted against you," said Redwing. "We need to police our problems, not have a white savior ride in to save the day. But the council decided otherwise."

"Let it rest, Jonathan," said Barrett. "You had your say, got outvoted, and the decision stands: Coogan's hired."

"Wait a second," said Danny. He ignored the insult from Redwing as a parade of obstacles ran through his mind. First and foremost, he wasn't Native American. "I'm not an Indian."

"Normally, that would be a problem, but we're going to overlook that shortcoming for the moment," said Banner. "Based on how things have played out, it's either you or the FBI, and I'll take the devil I know every time. No offense."

"The hire is provisional, and for the duration of finding out who the hell is responsible for the Goodnight killings and shooting Ray," said Barrett.

"But I reckon if you solve the case, the job would be offered permanent," said Banner. "Regardless of your skin tone."

"This is all pretty quick," said Danny. He started to say more, but the chairman cut him off.

"God dammit, Coogan, take the badge," grumbled Barrett.

Danny reached out and took the badge. He twisted it in his hand and stared at the seven points of the star and the enameled horsehead in the center. "Well, I sure enough thank you, but I'm not sure how this will work."

"You let us worry about making it work," said Barrett. He took the coffee out of Danny's hand. "There is one thing you need to know about the badge before pinning it on."

Danny looked up, and Barrett nodded at Banner, who stepped forward, his earlier smile replaced with a look of reverence.

"The badge has a star with seven points, each representing one of the Seven Sacred Virtues," he said. "You will need to study them, practice them, and honor our ways."

Barrett added from behind, "The virtues are prayer, honesty, humility, compassion, respect, generosity, and wisdom."

Danny felt something grow in his chest, and he held the badge more reverently.

"We received these virtues from the White Buffalo Calf Pipe Woman," said Barrett. "Only accept and wear this badge if you can uphold each one."

The badge was weighed with solemnity and spirituality in his hand, and Danny hesitated, then reached up and unpinned the Fish & Game badge from his shirt. He slipped it into the front pocket of his jeans. He replaced the bare place it had hung with the Dead Horse Reservation Tribal Police badge.

He looked down at it on his chest, smiled, and glanced up at Barrett. The old rancher's slight smile had blossomed, and he said, "No more calling you Wasi'chu, I reckon."

Bringloe laughed and clapped Danny on the shoulder. "There goes the neighborhood."

"Chairman," yelled someone behind them, and as a group, they turned.

Still with a bandage on her head, Monica Lewis of the Montana DCI leaned out of the open trailer door and waved them over.

"Get to work, officer," said Barrett to Danny. He pulled out his phone and started to walk away toward the corral. "I got calls to make. Trying to manage a ranch remotely is a son of a bitch."

A problem came into Danny's head, and he asked, "Who do I work for? I mean, with Ray in the hospital, who's in charge?"

"For now, the council," said Barrett over his shoulder. "But as soon as she feels up to it, Janine Whitepipe will be acting chief."

"Good choice," said Bringloe. "She's tough and knows the job after watching her dad growing up."

Danny nodded in agreement, then shook hands with Redwing and Banner. He watched them trail off after Barrett. He knew Barrett wasn't calling to manage his ranch but making calls to justify selecting a white man to serve on the Tribal Police and a woman to be acting chief. Politics. He sighed, but as they said, none of that was his problem.

Bringloe nudged his elbow and motioned toward the trailer. "We best get at it."

"Got to get to it, to get through it," said Danny. They started walking in the direction of the trailer. "You want to lead?"

"Not really," said Bringloe. "You got a shit-ton more practice than me at investigations. I want to hang back and learn."

"You're grading me on a curve," replied Danny. "Let's both learn how to do this."

"Fair enough," said Bringloe.

They climbed into the trailer, being careful what they touched and stepped on. Monica was in the small kitchen, and they joined her.

"First off, the Salamander brothers and Prince eat the same ramen and canned chili as Niland," she said, shaking her head. She pointed at a stack of magazines on the counter, "But their porn is of higher quality."

"What does this have to do with cattle rustling?" asked Bringloe.

"Nothing," replied Monica. "I'm just amazed how men live without women."

"We live poorly and without joy," said Danny. He lifted one of the magazines, then another, then another. "Notice anything about these?"

"Not my area of expertise," answered Bringloe. He leaned over Danny's shoulder. "But the redhead's cute."

"Not the covers. I meant the delivery address. It's not here."

"222 Lodge Pole," replied Bringloe. "That's the backside of Tennant Creek."

"We'll have to check the address," said Danny. He pulled his phone out and took a picture of the address. He looked up at Monica, "Anything else?"

"Assorted handguns, rifles, and shotguns," said Monica. She knelt, picked up a large evidence bag, and sat it on the counter beside the magazines. "And this."

Danny stared down at the war club sealed inside the bag. Its rock head was wrapped with rawhide sewn with sinew onto a hickory branch. The end of the piece trailed a coyote tail and owl feathers with glass beads on the ends of knotted rawhide thongs. Head to tail, it looked to be roughly two feet long.

"Guess this connects Prince and his posse to the two Goodnight killings," said Monica.

"Reckon so," said Danny. He glanced at her, shook his head, and said, "But I'd still like to nail down the how and the why. You going to test them?"

"We'll check for blood and DNA, cross-match it against that of the Goodnights. Also, analyze the impact points to see if they match."

"How do you do that?" asked Bringloe.

With a straight face, Monica answered, "We hit a too-inquisitive lawman in the skull."

"What about the rest of the trailer?" asked Danny.

Monica pointed across the small living room and down the hall. "Got two bedrooms and a bath. Whoever had the back bedroom had a girl here now and again."

"Why do you say that?" asked Bringloe.

"Women's clothes in the closet. She is size four, so I hate her already. Pink Venus razor and coconut shampoo in the shower," replied Monica. "Unless the Salamander brothers lived a life we don't know about yet, there was a girlfriend."

A younger female Danny didn't recognize walked up to the group. She held out an evidence bag with a photo booth strip in it. "Found this stuck in a paperback on the nightstand." She handed the bag to Monica and said, "Could be the girlfriend."

The DCI woman examined the photos and then handed the bag to Bringloe. "Any ideas?"

Bringloe flipped the bag over and stared at the pictures. "Son of a bitch," he said and handed the strip to Danny.

Danny took the strip, rotated it, and saw Elliott Salamander in four poses with a girl. They were laughing and mugging for the camera. The girl looked to be in her teens, had long dark hair, an athletic build, and was pretty, but not in an obvious way.

He handed the strip back to Bringloe. "You know her?"

"So do you," said Bringloe. "Or at least you know her mother."

"What are you talking about?"

"The female vote against you from the council."

"You're shitting me," said Danny. He leaned his head back and stared at the ceiling.

"That is Marguerite Whitefeather, daughter of Winnie Whitefeather and apparent girlfriend of one very dead Elliott Salamander," stated Bringloe.

Still looking at the ceiling, Danny asked, "How old is she?"

"Seventeen," answered Bringloe.

"Elliott Salamander was thirty-four, according to his arrest record," said Monica.

Danny dropped his head and stared at her.

Monica shrugged and said, "I assumed that's what you were going to ask next."

Danny flicked his eyes at Bringloe. "This is bad, isn't it?" he asked.

"Daughter of a councilwoman involved with folks that may have killed a husband and wife, and for sure as hell tried to kill us," summed up Bringloe. "This is Granite Peak bad."

Granite Peak was the highest point in Montana, so Danny quickly grasped Bringloe's point: the situation was unrivaled in its level of badness.

Monica reached out and poked the Tribal Police badge on Danny's chest. "Statistically, the first day on a new job is always challenging and stressful."

Danny glanced at Monica and saw the toothy smile. "I'm sure you think you're hilarious," he said. "If you don't have anything else, we got to drive to Tennant Creek and break a mother's heart."

"Daughters and bad boys. Makes me glad I don't have kids," said Monica. She waved at them and said, "I'll call if we find something else."

Danny and Bringloe left the trailer and headed for Ruth's Subaru.

As they got to the car, Rune walked up.

"You get something from DCI?" he asked.

"Got a lead to follow," said Danny. "An address in Tennant Creek."

"My guys are auto-piloting the evidence," said Rune. He leaned on the hood. "Need me to ride shotgun?"

"I've already got shotgun," said Bringloe. He frowned at the marshal and climbed in the passenger side.

"We got it handled," said Danny as he climbed into the car and started the engine. "It might be a waste of time anyway."

Bringloe waved as Danny turned the car around and headed for the highway.

"I noticed you didn't tell him we had Marguerite Whitefeather's name and who she's related to," he said.

Danny side-eyed him and replied, "He's not local. He helped save Ray, but it doesn't mean he gets a free pass to know everything."

"Already don't trust the feds," laughed Bringloe. "We'll make an Indian out of you yet."

Danny and Bringloe made it to the highway. The stock trucks were gone, and female Trooper Rankin had been relieved by a male trooper. He waved them by, and soon Danny had the Subaru up to sixty and heading for Tennant Creek.

He settled in and started to move for the radio when Bringloe spoke up.

"Can I ask you something?" he said.

Danny left the radio off and leaned back in his seat. "Shoot."

"Barrett said you smiled when you got fired," he said. "Didn't you like being a game warden?"

"The job was fine, and God bless the folks who love it and do it," he said. "It was a bad fit from the start."

"Bad fit, how?" asked Bringloe.

"I was pretty lost after the Army and drifted into Fish & Game because Ben recommended me. I stayed as long as I did because I didn't want to disappoint him, but my heart was never in it."

"What will Ben say about you being Tribal Police now?"

"I think he will say it's the second-best decision I ever made," answered Danny. Then, with a grin, he added, "Then he'll laugh himself silly."

"What's the best decision?"

"Ruth. Without a doubt," said Danny. He shifted in his seat and slowed down as they passed through the gas station, saloon, and seven houses that constituted the town of Darby. As they passed the last house and he started to speed up, he said, "My turn. Why's a rodeo gypsy like yourself a tribal officer? With your experience, you could work the circuit as a pick-up man and make twice the money."

Bringloe stayed quiet and looked out the front window at the prairie. His eyes went distant, and Danny was sure he'd asked the wrong thing.

"Oh, shit. I'm sorry, Matt. Look, if I went a place I shouldn't have with the question, my apologies."

"Nah, it's all right," said Bringloe. He turned to look at Danny, and his eyes were in the present. "I was a big deal for folks around here when I rodeoed, a hometown boy done good. Lots of folks were kind to me, but I got a big head and didn't appreciate it. Got thrown in Billings. I did something to my back that I can't pronounce, but it was the end of the rodeo for me. Came back here feeling sorry for myself, and even though I wasn't a big deal anymore, folks were still kind to me."

"Not something you find everywhere," said Danny. "Montana is a unique place."

"So, when the job of tribal officer was offered to me here on the Rez, I figured I could handle being a little deal and start appreciating the folks around here and their kindness."

They drove in silence for ten miles. It was like they had been embarrassed by sharing secrets and baring souls. Finally, Danny couldn't take it anymore and blurted, "Can you believe who the Broncos drafted this year? We needed a tight end, and they used the first-round pick on a guard from Michigan."

"I liked the pick," said Bringloe. "He's a great run blocker, and we got a stud at running back."

Back on safe ground, Danny and Bringloe talked about the Broncos, Avalanche hockey, hunting, and country music for the remainder of the ride.

They pulled into Tennant Creek just after noon and parked in front of the medical clinic. No patients remained from the morning in the waiting area, and the afternoon crowd hadn't arrived yet. Leotie sat at the reception desk and, as always, gave the lawmen a frosty reception. Danny had learned from Ray on a previous visit that Leotie's boyfriend was serving five years at Deer Creek courtesy of the Dead Horse Tribal Police and that she still held a grudge.

"Good day, Leotie, you're looking well," said Danny. He leaned on the counter and gave his best smile.

"Put it away, Coogan. I don't have time for your nonsense," she said without looking up from her paperwork. "What do you need, Matt? I got work to get done."

Bringloe pushed his hat back on his head and said, "We wanted to see if Winnie was on duty today. We need to speak with her and her daughter."

At the mention of Marguerite, Leotie's head rose, and she looked first at Bringloe and then Danny, who wilted some under the hard stare. "What business you got with Maggie?"

"That's between Winnie, Maggie, and us," said Bringloe. He'd come off leaning on the counter and cocked his head to one side. "Do you know something about Maggie we don't know?"

"She doesn't know anything," said a voice behind them.

Danny and Bringloe turned to see Winnie Whitefeather standing in an open doorway in her white nurse's uniform. She looked older than Danny remembered, more threadbare, and worn down by life. She was shorter than Ruth and had that later-in-life spread around the middle that older women get. She held a cigarette between her fingers, and smoky tendrils curled toward the vent in the ceiling.

"She's in here but sleeping," said Winnie. She stared at Danny, first at the badge, then at his face. "You here to rub it in my face that the council hired you."

"No, ma'am," answered Danny with a glance at Bringloe. "We're here to ask your daughter about the Salamander brothers and the last time she saw them."

"They're the reason she's here," said Winnie. "That piece of shit, Elliott, especially."

Bringloe took a step forward, but a glance from Winnie stopped him cold.

"I heard he's dead," said Winnie. "Along with that red trash, Charlie Prince."

"Not the time to talk about all that," said Bringloe. "It's an ongoing investigation."

"You don't get to talk with my daughter until you tell me what's happening."

"They're both dead, ma'am," said Danny. "Archie is in custody."

Winnie raised her chin and stared hard at the newest tribal officer. "You do it?"

"Danny shot Elliott to save Ray and me," said Bringloe. "I put down Prince."

"Nobody'll cry over their graves," said Winnie. She turned to look back into the room behind her. With a sigh, she turned back to the lawmen. "Maggie made all bad choices and will have to stand for it. I want consideration since she's young, stupid, and thought she was in love."

Neither Danny nor Bringloe knew what to say, so a loud silence filled the hallway. Behind them, Leotie cleared her throat.

"I need consideration," repeated Winnie.

"Ain't ours to give, ma'am," said Danny. "But anything she tells us would help wipe some of the bad off her slate."

Winnie took a drag from her cigarette and tapped the ash into her free hand. She sighed deeply, then said, "It was my daughter and the Salamander brothers that caused all this, but you, Coogan, put my daughter in the bed behind me."

"What are you talking about?" asked Danny, genuinely confused.

Winnie had the beginning of tears in her eyes as she said, "You shot her."

Chapter 14

Danny stood beside Maggie Whitefeather's bed and looked down at the young woman. She was sleeping on her back, and her chest rose and fell with each breath. She had her mother's looks without the mileage of hard luck and disappointment. She was small, thin, and had dark hair cut at the shoulders. The face was unblemished, naïve, yet fierce in a way, and at another time, Danny could imagine her outfitted in a beaded buckskin dress and riding a pony bareback.

He glanced at the monitors and watched the green images dance in response to her heartbeat. His eyes shifted to the side she favored, and he knew the wound he'd given her was under the blankets and hospital gown. She gave a quiet moan, licked her lips, and turned her head to one side before falling into a deep sleep.

She'd shot at him, tried to kill Ray and Sotomayor, but he couldn't bring himself to hate her. According to Winnie, she'd done it for love, and Danny knew the list of stupid things people do for love was endless. So, he couldn't hate her.

He had sympathy for her. She'd destroyed her life for Elliott Salamander and for a love that most likely wasn't even returned. After this, he'd try to help her as much as possible. Try and get some leniency at sentencing or at least have her serve her time close to the Rez so Winnie could visit more often. After it was all over, he thought, but that time hadn't come yet. It wasn't even close.

"Here ya go," asked Bringloe. He handed Danny a waxed paper cup from the vending machine. "It tastes like shit-filled mud, but it's all I could find."

"Thanks," said Danny. He sipped the coffee; it was terrible, but he'd had worse a hundred times.

"This ain't your fault, Coogan," said Bringloe, reading Danny's mind.

"I know," replied Danny. He looked at the other man and said, "It don't make me feel better about it, though."

Winne came into the room and walked to her daughter's bedside. She peeked at the monitors and adjusted one of the lead wires tangled between the girl's fingers. She caressed the hair out of Maggie's face, then turned to face Danny.

"You'll go gentle?" she asked.

"As gentle as we can," answered Bringloe. "But we got folks being killed."

"And Ray might join them," put in Danny. "We need answers to stop it."

Winnie stared at Danny with a rough look that melted into resignation as reality sunk in. She turned back to her daughter and gently shook her awake.

"Maggie, wake up," she said. "The police are here and want to talk to you."

Maggie opened her eyes, and a flash of panic passed through them as she saw Danny and Bringloe standing at the end of her bed. Confusion replaced panic as she saw the badge on Danny's chest. "You're not Indian," she said through a dry throat.

Winnie handed her a soda and answered, "It's a long story, but he's tribal now."

Maggie drank the soda as Danny said, "Sorry for putting you in here."

The girl waved away the words and asked, "You here to arrest me?"

"Should I be?" asked Danny.

"I did shoot at you," said the girl. She pulled herself up, and Winnie slid two pillows behind her back so she sat up more. "Ain't no use in denying it."

"Yes, you did shoot at me," said Danny. "But I got a funny feeling it was no accident that you missed us."

"This is Montana. She was raised with a rifle," said Winnie. "She hits what she aims at."

"I have no doubt," replied Danny. He risked a glance at Winnie. "Which makes my point that she wasn't aiming at Joe Niland or any of us."

"I knew Niland was in the truck with you. I saw him climb in at the camper, then I got ahead of you, across the river, and up the ridge. I knew it was safe to shoot at Ray's back door and not hit anyone."

"Why did you do it?" asked Bringloe.

Maggie dropped her eyes and picked at the fuzz on the blanket with her fingers.

"Charlie said I had to do it, or he would hurt my mom."

"Charlie Prince?" asked Danny.

"Uh-huh."

"How did you get mixed up with Elliott?" asked Danny.

Maggie looked at Winnie, then Danny, and then back at the blanket.

"I work at the Coin O' Clean, and he would sometimes come in to wash his clothes. We talked now and again, and he seemed nice. He was always polite, telling me how pretty I was and how he'd like to take me out. Not many boys notice me at school, so I liked it."

"But then he wasn't so nice?" asked Danny.

"No," answered Maggie. "After a few weeks, he started asking me to do things for him and Charlie. Then it was Charlie who did the asking."

"And then Charlie doing the threatening," Bringloe guessed.

Winnie hissed, "Charlie Prince was a bastard, and Elliott was no better than him. They can't ever be dead enough for me."

"Mom, don't," said Maggie. She reached out to take the woman's hand. Winnie's eyes welled up. "It's my fault as much as theirs. I should have gone to Chief Whitepipe right away, but I got scared when they said they'd hurt you."

She shifted her eyes to Danny and Bringloe and went on.

"Charlie said you had Niland, and he could cause a lot of trouble for them if he talked. He told me they'd leave me and Mom alone if I did it. I didn't believe them, but I knew they'd kill you all themselves if I didn't agree to do it."

"So, you took on the job and made sure every shot missed?" said Danny.

"Only thing I could think of," answered Maggie. "I thought you'd taken off in that big blue truck of yours, so I got up on one knee, and a ricochet got me. You surprised the shit out of me."

"He does that to a lot of folks," said Bringloe. "Do you know who gave Charlie Prince and the Salamanders orders?"

"No, as far as I knew, Charlie was in charge," answered Maggie.

"Is there anything else you can tell us that might help?" asked Danny.

"Nothing I can tell you. But I can give you something."

"What?" asked Danny.

She pointed to the corner behind Danny and Bringloe, and they turned to see a well-worn backpack sitting on a wooden chair. It had patches sewn onto it in various places and was stained with what looked like tree sap and blood.

"Can you hand me that?" she asked.

Bringloe moved to snatch it and sat it on the bed beside the girl.

She unzipped one of the outer pockets, pulled out a cell phone, and handed it to Bringloe.

"It's Prince's," she said. "I took it when he wasn't looking."

Bringloe took the phone and hit the button to bring up the screen. Danny moved to look over his shoulder. The background showed a picture of a derelict saloon with the name Last Round painted on the wall above the broken windows. A desiccated hitching post was in front of it, and the building's skeletal remains stood on both sides.

"That's in Marmont," said Danny.

"You mean that ghost town to the west?" asked Bringloe. He looked up from the phone to stare at Danny. "We call it Long Hope. It's a place we avoid."

"Why's that?" asked Danny.

"It was home to the Indian Agency years ago, and folks held a long hope it would dry up and die." He glanced back at the image. "Looks like we got our wish."

"Got to be a reason Charlie Prince had a picture of it on his phone," said Danny. "You willing to check it out with me?"

"Not on my list of places to see before I die," said Bringloe. "But I'll go with you."

Danny turned back to Winnie. "I need you to know that I got no idea what the charges will be for Maggie, but if what she says is true, then she's got a chance."

"Thank you for that," said Winnie.

He shifted his focus to Maggie. "I'll call over Tribal Headquarters and have them send someone over to keep an eye on you."

"You mean to arrest me," replied Maggie.

"Yes," answered Danny.

The girl touched her side where she'd been shot. "I ain't going no place." Then, with a smile, she added, "Tell them to bring pizza."

Winnie walked them out and shook hands at the door of the clinic.

Danny had a thought and asked, "Who treated Maggie's wounds?"

Winnie stiffened and said, "Dr. Benteen, but he doesn't know the truth. We told him it was an accident. I don't want him charged in all this."

Danny thought about Milo Benteen. He'd been an emergency room doctor in Butte and had served as a combat medic for four years in Vietnam. He was pushing ninety and had seen more gunshot wounds than Carter's had liver pills. His wife had been born in the area, and even though she'd died, he retired here and volunteered at the clinic. Danny knew the man wasn't stupid and knew the story he'd been given was a lie, but he'd also been around long enough to know the true story wasn't any of his business.

"He won't be charged. I can promise," said Danny.

"Thank you, Coogan," said Winnie. "I still don't like you, but thank you."

After they climbed back into the Subaru, they sat for a bit, taking stock of all they'd learned and all the lives lost or ruined.

"You believe in God, Danny?" asked Bringloe suddenly.

"Sometimes," answered Danny honestly. "Depends on the day. You?"

"I used to," he answered. "But I don't think he cares anymore. I think he packed up and moved on."

"Could be he wants us to figure things out on our own," said Danny.

"Well, we're doing a shitty job of it," said Bringloe. He pulled out Prince's phone and punched up the photo gallery. As he scrolled through the images, he said, "You want to check out the address in town or go to Long Hope first?"

"I want to go to the station first, tell Janine about Maggie if she's there, and get an update on Ray," said Danny.

Bringloe nodded in agreement and kept scrolling through the pictures.

Danny's phone rang.

"When were you going to let me know you got fired?" asked Ruth with an edge to her voice.

Son of a bitch, thought Danny. He winced and said, "I thought it was something we should talk about in person."

"I also heard you're a tribal officer now," said Ruth with less animosity.

"Again, something I wanted to talk to you about in person," said Danny. "How the hell did you hear about all this?"

"I got it from Ben, who got it from Molly, who heard it from Rosalee down at the Dream Bean Café," said Ruth. "Small towns, Coogan. You can't keep any secrets."

"I guess not. Are you mad?" asked Danny.

The line went silent momentarily, then Ruth laughed and said, "Of course not. You're finally where you should have been all along."

Danny finally allowed himself a breath and asked, "What's the vibe about me being tribal now?"

"Rosalee thinks it's groovy, Molly is house-hunting for us on the Rez, and Ben laughed himself silly."

"What about you?" asked Danny. "It's a lot less money."

"Piss on the money, Coogan. I'm low-maintenance," answered Ruth. "If you think you can help more people this way, I'm behind you."

Damn, he loved this girl, he thought. More every day and more than any words he could ever string together.

But now was not the time for all that, with Bringloe listening in, so he jumped into another furrow.

"How's Ray?" he asked.

"Somebody is with you, and you can't talk. Well, I love you too," replied Ruth with a laugh. "He's conscious and off the monitors. Still in a bad way, but all prospects point to him recovering."

Danny relayed the message to Bringloe, who looked up from Prince's photos, tilted his hat back, and, with a big grin, said, "About time we got some good news."

"Any chance you could swing by?" asked Ruth. "Been some time since I've seen my husband-to-be, and my dad would like a word."

A touch of panic rose in Danny as Ruth spoke about her dad. "Has he changed his mind about me?" he asked.

"Not at all," laughed Ruth on the other end. "If anything, he's more impressed. You might have even passed me as his favorite. He told me the other night not to let you get away."

"We'll try," said Danny. "Headed to Tribal Headquarters to see Janine, then out to an old ghost town called Marmont or Long Hope, depending on who you ask."

"I never knew we had a ghost town, and just so you know, Janine isn't at headquarters," said Ruth. "With Ray conscious and off the critical list, she left this morning to do her acting chief job. She's over at the sheriff's office interviewing the two that were along with Prince."

"She might get something out of Littlejohn, but Haugestuen is pretty hostile," said Danny. "But I doubt Archie will talk. He went mute once he knew his brother was dead."

"Oh, you don't know then?" said Ruth.

"Know what?" asked Danny.

"Archie Salamander escaped," said Ruth.

Danny pulled into a spot in front of the Tribal Headquarters and shut off the Subaru.

"Shit fire," said Danny.

Bringloe caught the tone and glanced up from the phone. "What happened?" he asked.

Danny hit the speaker button and asked, "How'd Archie escape?"

"He had a knock on the head and complained about being nauseous, so they ran him to the emergency room," said Ruth. "He clocked the deputy with a chair, stole his patrol car keys, and disappeared."

"So much for good news," said Bringloe. He went back to flipping through the photos.

"We got to get on this, honey," said Danny.

"Just stay safe, Coogan," said Ruth. "See you when I see you. I love you, Danny."

"Love you too, Ruth," replied Danny. "Have your dad call me if he wants."

"Will do. Bye," said Ruth, and she hung up.

Danny hopped out of the car and went inside the Tribal Headquarters. Bringloe stayed in the Subaru, scrolling through the photos and noting places he recognized or people he knew. Danny found Sotomayor staffing the desk and gave him the information on Maggie.

"The councilwoman's daughter," said Sotomayor. "This will be a hornet's nest once the council finds out."

"Keep it quiet for now. Go over and take a statement, but she'll need to stay in the clinic for now," said Danny. "Let Janine know that I'd like to talk to her before she writes up charges."

"What are you going to do?" asked Sotomayor.

"Got an address to check out in town, then making a run to Long Hope," answered Danny. "It's on Prince's phone, so he might have hidden something there."

"I'll have Janine call you when she's done at the sheriff's office," said Sotomayor.

"We got anyone else around?" asked Danny.

"Stan is out on patrol, and Barrett is asking the council to bring a few retired officers back to active duty for the short term. We're stretched thin."

Danny nodded and started to leave.

"Hey, Coogan," said Sotomayor.

Danny stopped and looked back at him.

"Glad to have you on the team," he said with a smile.

"Glad to be on the team," said Danny, and he walked out the front doors and back to the Subaru.

He climbed in, and Bringloe handed him the phone.

"Archie and Elliott were in Long Hope, along with somebody else," said Bringloe. "Time stamp had it over a month ago."

Danny looked at the phone and saw a photo pulled up that showed Archie and Elliot Salamander standing beside a red F-150. Between them stood Sonny Siebert, pipe in his mouth and wearing the same jeans, snap-button work shirt, and straw cowboy hat he'd had on when he'd nearly run over the distracted Danny less than a week ago. All three men were not looking at the camera, and Danny suspected the picture was taken without their knowledge. He guessed the picture-taker had been Maggie.

"Fucking hell," said Danny as he returned the phone to Bringloe. "I know the old man in the middle."

"Me too, and he's a nice old cowboy," said Bringloe. "I'm trying hard to find an innocent reason for him to be with the Salamander brothers and Prince and be out at Long Hope, but I can't come up with one."

"Ain't many folks we meet lately that have been innocent," said Danny. "We need to talk to him before going to Long Hope. Agreed?"

"Yeah, I reckon," said Bringloe. "Him going bad would be enough to drive me back to the rodeo. What about the address we got from the magazines?"

"Let's hand it off to Stan. He's on patrol," answered Danny. "I'm done in and dead in my boots, can't even think straight. We can track down Archie in the morning after we get Siebert to explain this picture."

"I know where he lives," said Bringloe. "But something to eat and a bed sounds better right now. It's been a long haul with no breaks since Corner Canyon."

"We can go to my place and rack out," said Danny. "Ruth has the overnight shift. I got beer in the fridge and pizza in the freezer, plus a couch for you to crash on."

"Talked me into it," replied Bringloe.

Danny fired the car to life and pulled out onto Tennant Creek's main street. Traffic was light, as always, but no one waved at him since they didn't recognize Ruth's car.

He handed Bringloe his phone and had him text the magazine address information to Stan and got an acknowledgment from the big Indian that he'd run it down before the end of his shift. Stan also sent a welcome aboard to Danny about being hired on as Tribal Police. He said the beers were on him at a later date, but tonight he was headed to check on Ray after his shift.

Danny had Bringloe text him thanks and to let them know how Ray was doing.

He smiled to himself then. He'd been a tribal officer less than a day, and it already felt more like family than being a game warden for the year before ever had.

God or the Great Spirit or whatever directed the trail of his life had a strange sense of humor, but Danny was glad it'd taken this turn.

Chapter 15

The next day while Danny was making coffee and Bringloe had a shower, Stan called. He had two updates. First, Ray had improved but still had a long road to travel before he'd be back in the saddle. Second, the magazine address was a bust. The address was a small, vacant house.

"Looks like a mail-drop site," said Stan. "The brothers probably didn't want visitors out at the trailer considering the crooked shit they were into."

"You're likely right," replied Danny. "But can you check and see who owns the property? Maybe it will give us somebody to go after."

"No problem, my light-skinned brother," joked Stan. "And again, welcome to the team. I always knew we'd get you in the end."

"Glad just to be employed. Talk at you later," said Danny, and he hung up.

He filled Bringloe in on Stan's updates as they drove out of Darwin and headed in the direction of the Rez and Sonny Siebert's place. The sun glowed, and a few feathered clouds floated high. They drove through a rolling prairie scattered with wildflowers. In the distance, mountains rose to scrape the underbelly of a bright blue sky. If he could put aside all the things going on, Danny would've felt it was a perfect morning.

As he drove, Danny realized it was now July. Fourth of July in Darwin meant a VFW-sponsored carnival, a craft bazaar at the Catholic Church, a one-day rodeo, and fireworks at the County Fairgrounds. He hoped he'd get a chance to take Ruth and her parents, but it all depended on what Sonny told them and what they found at Long Hope.

Bringloe pointed at the old mailbox sitting on a tall stump with the silhouette of a running horse and the name SIEBERT painted on it in red lettering.

"I hope he's around and not chasing chickens," said Bringloe. "I want to put to rest which side he's on."

"You and me both," said Danny. He had a bad feeling in the pit of his stomach but hoped he'd been right about Sonny and this was all just a big mistake.

Danny turned off the road and into the narrow gravel driveway of the small ranch house.

A small creek ran beside the house, and a thicket of juniper grew beside a small corral with a large, weathered barn. Danny saw two horses, one a red roan, the other an Appaloosa with a black and white dappled hindquarter in the corral. The red roan was a pretty horse, but the Appaloosa was breathtaking. It harkened back to the "old-time" Appaloosas. It was tall, narrow-bodied, and had a rangy, tough-leather look of a horse with no quit.

The house was painted light blue and gray, so it looked like thunderclouds in a summer sky squatting in the grass. A stone porch ran along the length of the front with the windows open and the curtains waving in the breeze. But the curtains didn't hold Danny's interest; Sonny Siebert did. He sat in a rocking chair beside the front screen door with a rifle across his legs and a pipe between his lips.

"Shit," said Bringloe. He reached down and undid the safety strap on his sidearm. "I was hoping for a peaceful day."

Danny stared at the man and said, "Could he be running off coyotes bothering the stock?"

"Maybe. Or it could be he's waiting for us," said Bringloe.

"Could be," admitted Danny. "You think Archie's hiding out here?"

Bringloe seemed to consider for a moment, then said, "I'd call it even money."

"We're not going to figure it out sitting here," said Danny. He glanced at Bringloe. "Let's go nice and easy. No need to draw until we know for sure. I still think Sonny's one of the good guys."

"Me too," replied Bringloe, "but I ain't dying today, so nice and easy only goes so far."

They exited the car, and Danny heard music from a radio inside the house. He smiled when he realized it was Chris LeDoux singing "Ten Seconds in the Saddle."

Sonny couldn't be all bad if he listened to rodeo ballads, he thought. It was broken logic, but it was all he had to bolster his courage, so Danny grabbed onto it, walked across the grass, and stopped before getting to the porch. Bringloe stepped a few paces away and crossed his arms over his chest.

"Afternoon, Mr. Siebert," said Danny. "Danny Coogan. You remember me?"

"Name's Sonny, and of course, I remember you," said the man. He pointed a crooked finger at Danny. "You're wearing the wrong badge."

"Got a better offer," said Danny, glancing at Bringloe.

"Bullshit," said Sonny with a faint smile.

"We need to talk to you about the Salamander brothers," said Bringloe.

Sonny shifted his eyes to him and said, "Not much I can tell you. The way I hear it, Elliott's dead as a hammer, and I just chased Archie off with my rifle. Bastard stole my truck."

"How long ago?" asked Danny. He looked around as if Archie would materialize.

"An hour or so," answered Sonny. "Been waiting for you lot to show up." He motioned down at the cooler beside him. "You want a beer?"

Danny ignored the offer and asked, "Did he have a weapon?"

"Yeah, a shotgun and a pistol," answered Sonny. "I reckon he got it from the Beckwourth sheriff's cruiser parked out back. Do I get a reward for turning it in?"

"There's a sheriff's car here?" asked Bringloe.

"Yep, parked behind the barn," Sonny grinned.

"Jesus," said Danny. "Why didn't you call somebody?"

"Ain't got a phone," replied Sonny. "Besides, I figured somebody would come looking for Archie, him being on the run and all, and here you are."

"You could have taken the cruiser for help," said Bringloe.

"No keys," said Sonny. "In all the excitement, Archie drove off with them."

Danny ran a hand through his hair to avoid strangling the old man.

Sonny's grin faded, and he asked, "You are hunting Archie, ain't you?"

"Not precisely. We came to ask you some questions," said Danny. "How do you know the Salamander brothers?"

"We worked together every so often," replied Sonny. His eyes hardened, and granite filled his face as he asked, "Are you accusing me of something?"

"Got a picture of you and the brothers out at Long Hope," interjected Bringloe.

"Not a crime to go out there," said Sonny, but Danny noticed the man lost his grin.

"You're right; it's not a crime," said Danny. "But the Salamanders never made an honest dollar in their lives, and it makes me wonder what you three were up to."

The man's eyes become softer, saying, "It weren't legal what we were up to. Just a bit of side money, nothing you'd care about."

"The brothers were partnered with Charlie Prince," said Danny. "Prince may have killed the Goodnights, and I watched Elliott shoot Ray."

"Got nothing to do with me!" said Sonny, too quickly and too loud.

Danny stared at the man until he glanced away.

"We can tie you to the suspects in two murders and the shooting of a police officer," said Danny. "I think you should tell me the truth. Now! Before I pull cuffs out, and we do this the hard way."

Sonny stared at Danny, and the former warden could tell the wheels in the man's mind wavered between telling the truth or spinning a lie. After a minute, Sonny shifted a foot and lifted the rifle from his lap. Danny and Bringloe stiffened, and both men slid their hands to the butts of their sidearms. Sonny watched them, shook his head, and then twisted in the rocking chair to prop the rifle against the side of the house. That done, he bent over and pulled a beer bottle out of the cooler.

"You know you spooked me on the road that morning, and it wasn't just about almost hitting you," said Sonny. He took a sip of his beer. "I thought the brothers or Niland had let something slip."

"Let what slip?" said Danny. "Tell us what's going on in Long Hope."

"It don't matter now, I reckon. It's all gone to shit, and folks are dead," said Sonny. He took another sip of beer. "Psilocybin mushrooms. Been growing them in the saloon basement for a year now."

"Magic mushrooms? That's a Schedule I controlled substance," said Danny. "It's a felony just to possess them. Guaranteed jail time. Why risk it?"

"'Cause I'm broke and an inch from losing the only home my family's ever known," said Sonny. He finished his beer with one swallow and stared Danny straight in the eyes when he said, "There're worse things than going to jail, Coogan. Live long enough, and you'll know them."

"How did you get mixed up with the brothers?" asked Danny.

"Joe Niland," answered Sonny. "He told them about my money troubles, and they came and offered cash just for me to watch the mushrooms grow. Tend to them. They'd already figured out that the basement of the Long Hope Saloon was ideal for a fair-sized crop."

"You knew what kind of men they were," said Danny. "What were you thinking?"

"I was thinking that this was my grandparents' place. I was desperate enough to do anything to save it," said Sonny. He reached into the cooler and pulled out another beer. He twisted the cap off and tossed it in the coffee can by the screen door.

"Anything?" asked Bringloe.

"I meant anything short of killing," said Sonny. "I ain't got the sand for that anymore. Got my bellyful in the war." He took a swallow. "Shit, I don't even hunt anymore."

"If Niland helped you, why'd you bird-dog him to the Tribal Police?" asked Danny. "You put Edmund on Joe's scent by telling him Joe was squatting in Crazy Buffalo Canyon." Danny needed more of the puzzle, and Sonny gave him more pieces with each answer.

"Niland help me out?" said Sonny. "He had my money, but I never got shit."

"I'm guessing you were looking to get about eight thousand," said Danny.

The bottle paused on its way to his mouth. "How'd you know?" asked Sonny.

Danny turned to look at Bringloe and said, "That's the exact amount we pulled out of the freezer at Niland's trailer."

Bringloe whistled, "He cheated you good, Sonny. You did all the work, and he kept all the money."

"When I was a kid, you could trust everybody on the Rez," said Sonny. He let his eyes drop to his boots. "But we got old and desperate and forgot our honor. Ended up on the wrong trail."

"The dark road," said Bringloe.

"The dark road," said Sonny. He lifted his head and, in a soft voice, said, "I swear I knew nothing about the killing."

Danny and Bringloe gave Sonny a penetrating, appraising look, then moved their hands away from their guns.

Danny believed the man. Sonny had admitted to a felony and had to answer for that. But as for the murders, Danny made a judgment call that Sonny didn't have that evil in him. Desperation and need had been behind him breaking the law, but Danny believed the old man still had a few lines left he wouldn't cross.

He glanced at Bringloe, who gave a slight nod of agreement, and he then turned back to Sonny and said, "We'll talk about things later. Right now, you can help yourself by helping us."

"Anything I can do?"

"Where do you think Archie went in your truck?"

Sonny didn't have to think long. "He'd go to Long Hope."

"Why there?" asked Bringloe.

"That's where the Salamanders kept their money. In the vault of the bank," replied Sonny. "Building caved in, but the vault still worked. Elliott got the combination from his grandfather. Said it was his own personal Fort Knox."

"Sounds like Archie is going to take the loot and run," said Danny. He turned and headed toward the car.

"You two going to try to stop him?" asked Sonny.

"Ain't nobody else around, and the Tribal Police are running pretty thin right now," said Bringloe. He turned to follow Danny. "I guess we're elected."

"You going to need more than pistols to get the job done," said Sonny. He opened the screen door and ducked inside and out of sight. Danny heard him hunting through the house. He heard a heavy thump followed by a string of curses, and then Sonny reappeared, holding two M14 rifles, four twenty-round magazines, and a half-dozen boxes of ammunition.

"Archie's a gun nut," said Sonny as he handed a rifle to each man. "He'll have more than a shotgun when you find him."

Twenty minutes later, Danny was driving the Subaru toward Long Hope over a single-lane gravel road that was an insult to the word road. Bringloe sat beside him. Both M14s lay in the back seat with four magazines loaded and ready.

Danny suddenly smiled and laughed.

Bringloe looked at him like he'd slipped a cog. "You okay?"

"I'm fine. Just wondering how I will explain bullet holes in Ruth's car."

They crested a hill an hour later and saw the remains of Marmont or Long Hope below them in the shallow valley. The saloon was the only building intact, with seven other buildings in various states of decay. One building sat isolated at the west end of town. The roof had collapsed, and only two walls remained standing, but the words MARMONT SAVINGS COMPANY were visible on the street-facing façade.

"Sonny was right about Archie. There's his truck," said Bringloe. He pointed at the rear of the bank, and Danny saw the familiar grillwork of the red F-150.

"You don't suppose he'll come peaceful?" asked Danny.

Bringloe gave him a frown.

"Me either," said Danny. He drove to the east end of town and pulled the car inside a long-forgotten corral with half its rails missing. Beside the corral was a pile of kindling that had been a livery. And beyond it was the saloon with the crop of mushrooms in the basement.

As Danny got out of the car, he heard the sound of a generator running.

"To run lights and ventilation for the mushrooms, you think?" said Bringloe.

"No idea," answered Danny. He opened the car's back door and drew out the two M14s. He tossed one over to Bringloe. "But the noise will cover our movement."

Danny slung his rifle across his shoulder and leaned in to collect the four magazines. He handed two to Bringloe, who now stood beside him.

"This is when Edmund would remind me not to do anything stupid," said Danny. He unslung the rifle, slid a magazine home, and chambered a round.

"It does seem to be our go-to," said Bringloe. His rifle was ready, and he slid his spare magazine into his pocket.

"Ready?" asked Danny.

Bringloe nodded, and they headed toward the back of the livery. Danny thought there was no sense in walking in plain view down the main street. The back alley would keep them hidden until they reached the open area between the last building and the bank.

They skirted the back of what was left of the livery, reached the rear of the still-standing saloon, and drew up when they heard the sound of Sonny's truck start.

"Son of a bitch," said Danny. With Bringloe beside him, he rushed past the last two buildings and into the open to see Archie loading canvas bags into the back of Sonny's truck.

"Tribal Police. Hands in the air!" yelled Bringloe.

Archie turned to look at them in surprise. He glanced left and right and seemed to have realized that only two lawmen existed. He smiled and took a step toward the far side of the truck.

"Don't try it!" yelled Danny. "You're not that fast!"

Archie took another step backward.

"Don't make this worse than it already is, Archie," said Danny. "Nobody wants to get shot today."

"How'd you find me?" asked Archie.

"Just a lucky hunch," answered Bringloe.

"I don't think so. Old man Siebert put you on my trail. Didn't he?" said Archie. "I should have shot him when I had the chance, but I had to get to the money," he pointed at the canvas bags. "No worries, though, I reckon I got time to settle up with him once I kill the pair of you."

"I need you to raise your hands and drop to your knees, or I'll have to shoot," ordered Danny. As he said it, he knew Archie would make the wrong choice, but he still had to let it be the man's decision.

"Are either of you interested in a bribe?" As he finished speaking, he turned and, quick as a rattler, dove behind the truck. Bringloe got off two shots, both of which hit the bank's side behind where the man had stood.

Archie burst up from behind the truck bed and fired three rounds from the shotgun he'd stolen from the sheriff's cruiser.

Danny and Bringloe would have taken pellets if they'd stood their ground, but the shot only hit the side of the hotel. Both men had moved like spooked jackrabbits, Danny behind the wall of the collapsed hotel and Bringloe to a hole that might have once been a root cellar.

Danny aimed through a broken window and cracked a shot over the head of Archie, who ducked down out of sight.

"That's your last warning, Salamander," yelled Danny. "Give it up, or this only ends one way."

"Yeah," shouted Archie. "You two dead and me driving off into the sunset with the money."

Wood from the window frame exploded next to Danny's face as a hail of bullets from an automatic rifle pin cushioned the hotel wall. Danny dropped to the floor and felt the splinters bite into his cheek and neck. Blood flowed onto his shirt, and he scrambled to the side as more bullets tore into the hotel wall.

Danny found a knothole and aimed through it to fire three shots. Two struck the truck's tailgate, and one struck the cab's rear window, exploding the glass. He hadn't come close to hitting Archie, but the shots from the automatic rifle at least paused.

"Ain't you dead yet?" laughed Archie. Another barrage of bullets hit the wall. The wood ruptured with each hit, and pieces poured down on Danny. Broken glass fell like rain, and Danny curled into a ball to make himself as small a target as possible.

He heard another burst from the rifle, but nothing hit the wall. Must be trying to keep Bringloe pinned down now, thought Danny.

An idea came to Danny, and it was something so stupid it would have impressed Edmund. He moved to the double doors at the front of the hotel, out of Archie's view, slipped through them, and out onto the wooden sidewalk at the front of the building. He raced to the corner of the building, peeked around, and saw the truck fifty feet away. Archie leaned over the hood, firing at the hole Bringloe had dived into.

He raised his rifle. He didn't have a chance at hitting Archie, but he intended to get the man's attention. He fired twice into the tailgate of the truck.

Archie immediately ducked down.

Now for the stupid part, thought Danny. He hoped Bringloe would take advantage of the chance he was about to give him. Danny put a hand to his mouth and yelled, "You shoot like shit, just like your brother. Too bad I had to put him down."

The firing stopped, and Archie shouted, "What'd you say?"

"I said too bad I had to put your brother down," yelled Danny.

"Makes us even. Your buddy here's dead, Coogan," shouted Archie. "I got him in the head when he popped up like a gopher. Whatever your plan was, it's fucked. Show yourself, and I'll finish you quick."

Bringloe dead? It can't be, thought Danny. He didn't believe Archie but hadn't heard any gunfire from the tribal officer's position. He leaned around the corner of the hotel and yelled, "Come and get me if you got the balls."

A wave of slugs struck the corner of the hotel, and Danny ducked back to avoid them. He heard the thunk of Archie's weapon going empty and knew the man would be changing magazines.

Danny swung around the corner and loosened five quick shots from the M14. Three hit the truck's body, one struck a side mirror, and the last sailed into the distance.

He's ripe for it, thought Danny as he ducked back. He yelled, "You're a coward, Archie, a yellow coward. Your brother was a coward, too."

"Keep talking, you son of a bitch," shouted Archie. "Keep talking. I'm brave enough to kill you."

Danny eased around the corner and saw Archie was at the back of the truck, ready to rush him. He almost had him mad enough to make a mistake.

"You call hiding behind a truck brave?" yelled Danny. His mind hunted for insults to goad the Indian. "You're scared stiff and know you can't take a real man."

Something snapped in Archie, and with a roar, he sprung from behind the truck and charged Danny. Danny fired twice. He hit Archie in the leg with the first but missed with the second. Archie kept coming and fired the automatic rifle from the hip. Slugs impacted the wall and sidewalk. Danny felt one round clip his shoulder, and another stuck the buttstock of the M14, knocking it from his hands and spinning Danny onto the ground and into the open.

Danny flashed a look at Archie and knew he couldn't draw his Sig in time. So, this is how it ends; I wished I'd lived to marry Ruth, thought Danny.

Archie limped toward him, a smile on his face. He raised the rifle to kill Danny, but before he could squeeze the trigger, his head snapped to the side, and he went down in a cloud of dust.

Danny hadn't recovered from the shock of not being dead when he saw Bringloe pull himself out of the hole. He had a bright red line on his forehead and staggered as he got to his feet.

"Next time," he yelled. "No stupid shit."

Chapter 16

The sun was deep in the west as Danny stopped Sonny's recovered truck behind the Tribal Police Headquarters. Bringloe parked behind him in Ruth's Subaru, got out, and walked up to the truck. He had a blue bandana tied around his forehead to cover the track Archie's bullet had traveled across his brow. Bringloe stumbled as he took a step and was unsteady on his feet, but he'd been stubborn as a mule when Danny asked how he was and had insisted on driving the car back to town.

I'm not in much better shape, thought Danny, and took inventory. He had splinters from the hotel wall on his face and neck, a bullet crease to the right shoulder, a twisted knee from being thrown into the street, and his left thumb might be broken.

But did you die, he thought, just like he had felt after every firefight in Afghanistan. Yet this wasn't a war zone. This was Montana back home; once again, it had become a shooting gallery.

Bringloe walked up and leaned against the side of the truck. He swayed back and forth some and seemed to be struggling to stand.

"I feel as bad as you look," said Danny. He gripped the man's forearm from the truck window to keep him from falling backward. "You got a concussion sure as shit. We need to get Doc Benteen and have him patch us both up."

"We got to take care of the money first," said Bringloe. "And get Archie into the icebox." He pointed at the wrapped, dead body lying on the money bags in the truck bed. "He's gonna ripen up out here in the heat."

"We can do that after Doc Benteen takes a look at you," said Danny. "Now ease yourself down, and I'll get some help."

Bringloe sank slowly to the ground until his legs buckled, and he flopped onto his rear end in a cloud of dust. Danny had jumped out of the truck as he lost purchase of Bringloe's arm. He prevented him from falling back and striking his head on the ground, but Danny's dodgy knee betrayed him, and he ended up lying beside the sitting man.

"I feel like I been bronc stomped," said Bringloe.

Danny heard the rear door to headquarters open, and he leaned his head back to see an upside-down Janine Whitepipe staring at them. She had her hands on her hips and a look of unrestrained fury on her face.

He tipped his head back forward and poked Bringloe in the shoulder. The man turned to look at him, and Danny said, "Chief's here, but I think we're fired."

"No worries," replied Bringloe. He smiled crookedly, and right before he slumped forward and passed out, he muttered, "Rodeo always needs clowns."

An hour later, Bringloe was in a bed at the medical clinic under Dr. Benteen's care. He'd been ordered not to step out of bed for forty-eight hours, and a nurse named Enola had appointed herself clinic warden to ensure he complied, or she'd give him a second concussion.

The money had been counted, inventoried, and locked in the evidence room of headquarters. Archie had almost escaped with over three hundred thousand dollars, a dozen assorted guns, and a satchel full of receipts from cattle auctions.

As for Archie himself, he was lying in a bed of his own at the medical clinic, but there was no chance of him stepping out of bed. The hole in the side of his head just forward and above the ear had ended his time on Earth, and he'd taken all his secrets with him.

Danny had the splinters removed from his face and neck, and the wounds bandaged to ensure any more leaking didn't end up on his shirt. The bullet crease to the shoulder hadn't broken the skin, but his whole shoulder throbbed. He looked like a hot iron had branded him, and his arm didn't work properly.

The good news was that his thumb wasn't broken, but it still hurt like hell. The twisted knee was another matter. He could stand on it and walk, although with an unmistakable limp. Dr. Benteen was confident he had tendon damage and said he would need an orthopedic surgeon to check it out whenever possible.

"Possible" wasn't going to be soon, thought Danny a half hour later as he sat in Chief Whitepipe's office, drank a soda, and listened as Janine tore into him for violating a dozen Tribal Police standing orders.

"What the hell were you thinking, Danny?" asked the acting chief.

Danny's face stung as he said, "I thought we needed to get to Archie before he disappeared."

"And it never occurred to you he would be heavily armed?" asked Janine. "Just like his brother and Charlie Prince were when they shot my dad."

Fair point, thought Danny. She had every reason to be pissed at him and Bringloe, and he knew it. He wondered if his résumé was current as he told the truth: "Never occurred to me, honestly. I thought Archie was our last live link to whoever is pulling the strings of this shitshow."

Danny watched Janine start to say something, then wave it off and flop into her father's desk chair. "You may have been right to go without backup. Considering I was still in Darwin, Stan was patrolling to the south, and Soto isn't supposed to leave the office."

Danny saw an opening and took it, "So me and Bringloe aren't in trouble?"

"Course you're in fucking trouble," said Janine. "You two dumbasses almost got yourselves killed. I'm just saying if you'd waited for backup, Archie would be gone now."

"You want my badge back?" asked Danny.

"Fuck you," replied Janine as she flipped him the bird.

Danny ventured a smile. "If nothing else, you've got your dad's temper and cursing down. How is he, by the way?"

Janine released a sigh. "They moved him to a regular room, and he's able to eat on his own now, so we'll declare victory and walk away." She rolled under the desk and shuffled the scattered papers into a neater pile. "How's the knee and thumb?"

"Both will let me know if rains are coming," answered Danny. "But I'm good enough to keep going."

"Good, 'cause we got more officers in the hospital than healthy," said Janine. "Good news is Edmund should be back by morning. He tracked the ranchers who claimed stolen cattle, and four of them identified the Salamanders as folks they saw in the area before the cattle went missing."

"What about Prince?" asked Danny.

"Nobody says they saw him, but I suppose he was careful not to be seen," replied Janine. "Maybe you should talk to your marshal buddy Rune and see what he'll let slip.

He's been working out of the council building with Barrett."

"I could do that," said Danny. He levered himself up out of the chair he'd been comfortable in and hobbled toward the door.

"Shit, hold on a minute," said Janine. She searched through her pockets, found a set of keys, and tossed them at him. "Your future father-in-law brought your truck out a couple of hours ago. I forgot once a dead body showed up."

Danny looked down at the keys, and a sense of having an old friend back beside him ran through his veins. Be good to be back in a proper vehicle again and return the Subaru to Ruth without bullet holes.

"Demitta Sparrowhawk was here when he showed up, and she volunteered to give him a tour of the Cultural Museum, then they were going to have lunch at the diner," said Janine. She went back to her paperwork. "They might still be there."

Danny thanked her and started to hobble to the door again when it occurred to him that he didn't know where his Power Wagon was parked. He turned back to ask, but

Janine said, without looking up from her papers, "Parked out front." Then she did look up and winked at him, adding, "Get going before Doc Benteen sends Enola over to put you beside Bringloe."

He found the Wagon right where Janine said it was parked. He unlocked it, walked around, and opened the passenger door on the driver's side. He saw that they had relocked his Fish & Game M4 in its place, and he remembered he was supposed to have turned that in already, along with his badge. But what could they do about that now? Fire him?

He flipped the floor mat up and opened the floor storage bin, rummaged through the tiedown straps, and located the treasure he'd been searching for. He popped open the top of the container and shook out four of the 500 mg acetaminophen. He knew the dosage was supposed to be two, but he figured he'd take one each for the splinters, the bullet crease, the dodgy knee, and the not-broken thumb.

He dry swallowed them, shut the door, and hobbled between a truck with a stock trailer and a slow-moving 4Runner toward the Dan-Dee Diner, where he hoped to meet up with Demitta, Ruth's dad, or at least a couple of cheeseburgers.

Danny saw them through the front window as he climbed onto the sidewalk. Demitta had a stunned look on her face, so Danny figured the bandages made his injuries look worse than they were, even though he had to admit they were pretty bad. Mike had an unreadable look, but Danny figured he was calculating how much worry Danny's latest adventure would cause his daughter.

"How's the other guy look?" asked Mike when Danny settled beside Demitta.

"Dead," answered Danny. He was bone-tired, busted up in too many places, and too worried about Bringloe to lie or have playful banter.

"Oh my God," said Demitta. She gingerly touched the side of his face. "Does this hurt? Does Ruth know? Was anybody else hurt?"

Danny felt the bottom drop out when Demitta mentioned Ruth. It gave weight to all his thoughts when he looked at Mike. He knew the man was reevaluating his daughter's life with a lawman who seemed to attract trouble like a magnet.

He turned to look at her and said, "It does hurt; no, I haven't told Ruth yet; and Matt Bringloe was hurt and is in a bed over at the medical clinic." He stood, moved to the side, and continued, "Do you mind if I have a moment alone to talk with Mike some?"

Demitta flashed her eyes between the two men and seemed to sense a reckoning was coming. She collected her purse and wide-brimmed straw hat and slid out. "I'll go to see if Matt needs anything. I won't say anything to Ruth, but you should call her."

"Thank you, Demitta," said Danny, and he slid back into the booth.

They watched her leave the diner and head down the sidewalk toward the medical clinic.

"I don't feel like doing this right now, Mike," said Danny. "But I don't want it to fester. So, ask me anything you want."

Mike stared at him momentarily, then said, "Tell me what happened."

Danny started with Winnie and her daughter and getting Prince's phone. He went on about how the phone led to Sonny Siebert, who led to Long Hope and Archie.

As he got to Archie, the waitress wandered by, and he ordered coffee and two cheeseburgers loaded with everything. After she'd stepped away, he'd finished telling Mike the story of the shootout with Archie, the drive back to Tennant Creek, and the update on Ray and Edmund he'd gotten from Janine.

"You've had a busy day," said Mike. He took a sip of his coffee. "You mind if I make some observations?"

"Sure, fuck, why not," said Danny. The exhaustion, the wounds, and the body count had finally hit a tipping point for him; future father-in-law or not, he was tired of taking shit.

"First, I think you were lucky beyond hope to survive," said Mike. "Second, I don't think you had any other option if you wanted to stop this Archie fellow from getting away. Third, even though you might have a short life based on your ability to find trouble, I got no issues with you marrying my daughter."

Silence filled the booth, and the waitress arrived with two cheeseburgers and a mug of coffee.

Danny ate his burgers silently, glancing at Mike occasionally, only to see him staring back or sipping coffee.

When finished, he wiped his mouth and took a ten out of his wallet to pay. Mike put his hand on his and said, "Put it away, officer. It'd be my honor to pay for your meal."

Danny said, "I don't do this on purpose. It's not like I want this."

Mike pulled his hand back, pulled two twenties from his pocket, and laid them on the table.

"No true warrior does," he said. "But we can't pass it on and have someone else take the risk. We couldn't live with it if it went sideways and they got hurt or killed. But remember, it's our families that bear the heaviest weight. You and Ruth memorize that. Never lie to each other about the risks, and always make it home no matter the odds."

"You sound like Edmund when he talks about the warrior societies," said Danny.

Mike nodded, "Read about them. The Dog Soldiers would fit in with the unit I served with."

"What the hell did you do in the military?" asked Danny.

"Just this and that," answered Mike with a faint grin. "Where you going next?"

"I'm heading over to see Marshal Jacobsen and Chief Lodge at the Council Hall," said Danny. "Update them on Archie and the investigation. They want to be kept in the loop."

"Mind if I tag along?" asked Mike. "You look like you could use a friend, and it would get me out of going antiquing with Margery and Ruth. Just let me hit the head first."

Navigating the distance between the Dan-Dee Diner and the Council Hall took fifteen minutes. They could have taken the Wagon, but Danny had felt his knee tighten up, and he wanted to stretch it some and keep it limber.

They crossed paths with Jonathan Redwing and Andy Banner as they walked into the hall.

"Jesus, Coogan," said Banner. "What the hell happened to you?"

Danny gave the short version of the events to the council members. He left out Winnie and Maggie in hopes he could talk to Ray once he was better about lowering the charges. He wrapped up and waited for the questions he was sure would follow.

"With the Salamanders dead along with Charlie Prince, how do you find the head of the snake?" asked Redwing.

"I'd say we make a run at Joe Niland again. I feel he knows more than he's told us so far. We also have the two wranglers in custody with the sheriff," answered Danny.

"Niland's unreliable, and the wranglers have been shipped out," said Redwing. "Something about warrants from a sheriff down in Wyoming."

"But they're accomplices in all this," said Danny. "Couldn't you have stopped it?"

"The council voted not to challenge the extradition," answered Banner. "It was a prickly issue. But we were assured they could be returned if we needed them."

"That doesn't do us any good if we need to question them," said Danny. His anger got the best of him, and he railed, "With everyone either dead or shipped to Wyoming, who do you suggest we go after?"

"What about Maggie Whitefeather?" asked Redwing. "I've heard she might be tangled up in all this."

Banner gave Redwing a double take and asked, "You never told the council about that."

Redwing turned to the shorter man and, looking down at him, said, "I wanted to get it from an official source before I said anything." He turned to Danny and said, "She's disappeared, from what I've heard, and her mother doesn't know where she is. Do you have any information she's involved?"

Danny studied Redwing for a span of seconds before answering. Redwing might be asking a legitimate question. Or he might be wanting dirt on Maggie to use against Winnie. He might be starting a power play on the council. Or he might want to locate Maggie and find out what she knows for an entirely different reason.

"Her name hasn't come up in the investigation," lied Danny. It was time to be strategic with his information. "Do you have any reasons we should be looking at her?"

Redwing glanced at Mike, who stood beside Danny, then at Banner, and then back to Danny. "Just rumors."

Danny decided that whatever the reason was for Redwing to ask the question, he didn't like the man. He looked at Banner, who seemed confused by all this, then looked at Redwing and said, "We like to deal with facts, not rumors, but we'll keep an eye out for her."

"She and her mother aren't to be trusted. I got a feeling they're in this up to their necks," said Redwing. He smiled at Danny and added, "I'd look at Sonny Siebert harder. I think he's your man."

Danny did not smile back when he answered, "I seriously doubt Sonny's a criminal mastermind."

"Give it a look," he said. "For the council. We need to wrap this up so we can get back to business."

The two councilmen walked away, and Mike leaned in to say in a quiet voice, "Go your own way, but I'd keep two eyes on that fucker."

"Way ahead of you," replied Danny.

The two went down the long hallway and turned right into the last office. They found Barrett sitting behind his desk with Rune standing beside him. Both men were poring over a map of the Rez and looked up as Danny and Mike walked in.

Barrett stood and reached out to grab Danny's hand. "Damn good to see you alive, Coogan," he said. "I heard about things with Archie, damn shame. He might have told us something." He dropped Danny's hand and gazed at Mike. "Who's this?"

"Chairman Barrett Lodge, this is my soon-to-be father-in-law, Mike Beebe," said Danny. "And Mike, this is Deputy U.S. Marshal Rune Jacobsen."

There were handshakes all around, and once everyone was settled in a chair, Danny was asked to tell the story of what had happened. He told the same abbreviated story he had with Redwing and Banner, leaving out Maggie and her involvement with Elliott. He figured he'd spill it on Barrett when he got him alone.

"Sorry about Bringloe," said Rune. "How's he doing?"

"Concussion and enforced bed rest for forty-eight hours," said Danny. "They got the nurse Enola watching him, so he doesn't try to escape."

"So, you're the last man standing," said Rune.

"I suppose you could say that."

"You think the receipts from the cattle auctions could lead anywhere?" asked Rune.

Danny shrugged. "I got no idea, but it was one of the things Archie came back for, so they must be important to somebody."

"Or blackmail material for Archie if some of those receipts have the name of our mastermind on them," said Barrett.

"Spot-on what I was thinking," said Danny. He was half-asleep in the chair. Between the beating he'd taken, the bleed off of adrenaline, and the two cheeseburgers warming his belly, he found it hard to keep his eyes open.

"Rune," Barrett said. "You mind if I talk to Danny alone for a few? Some tribal business has come up. Nothing to do with this, but it's private."

Rune gave Barrett a bothered look but rose out of his chair. He slipped his hat on and said, "I'll walk over and talk to the acting chief. See if she got anything from those wranglers before Wyoming shanghaied them." He nodded to Danny and Mike and left, shutting the door behind him.

"All right, what are you holding close?" asked Barrett. "It ain't just being tired. You're getting picky with who you talk in front of."

"There is something else," said Danny. He told Barrett about Winnie hiding Maggie at the medical clinic and Maggie's involvement with Elliott. Neither seemed to surprise the man, but his eyes widened as Danny told him it had been Maggie on the ridge the night of the ambush.

"You're shitting me," said Barrett. "That little girl was the one who tried to kill you all?"

"That's the rub," replied Danny. "She claims she only did it because they threatened her mom and says she missed every shot on purpose."

Barrett leaned back in his chair. "You believe her?"

Without hesitation, Danny answered, "Yes, sir, I do."

"I need to think on this some," said Barrett. "You go home, get a good night's sleep, and meet me back here at seven in the morning."

"Too dead on my feet to drive back to Darwin," said Danny. He struggled to get out of the chair with his bad knee, but with Mike's help, he did it. "I'll sleep in one of the empty cells in the jail," said Danny.

"I'm sleeping at the jail," said Mike. "I'm taking you over to your friend Edmund's house. Ruth is there with clean clothes and everything else you need."

"I just need her," said Danny with an exhausted grin.

Mike smiled and glanced at Barrett. "How can you not just love this kid."

Barrett smiled and replied, "I can get you a better place to stay than a cot in a cell."

"Don't bother with it. Slept on worse for years in the service," said Mike. He helped Danny hobble to the door. "Besides, this is the most fun I've had since I retired."

Chapter 17

The following day, Danny was sitting with Ruth at the Dan-Dee Diner when Mike walked in and slid into the booth opposite them. Danny gave him a nod, then speared a strawberry out of Ruth's fruit bowl with his fork. He flipped it in his mouth and asked, "How was the cot?"

"Slept like a baby," said Mike. He winked at Ruth and said, "Morning, sunshine."

"Morning, Dad," said Ruth.

Mike pointed a finger at Danny and asked, "You get Superman here back in working order?"

Ruth nudged Danny with her shoulder, smiled, and said, "He's not showroom-new, but I think he's roadworthy."

"She thinks I need to get my knee looked at by a specialist," said Danny between bites of his honey-covered oatmeal. "Might be something torn that needs to be stitched up."

"Always trust your doctor," said Mike.

The waitress came by, and Mike ordered pancakes with sausage and coffee. Ruth gave him a disapproving look as she walked away, and he said, "I'm old. I get to eat whatever I want." He winked at her, "Just don't tell your mother."

Danny started to protest why Mike got to eat what he wanted, and he got oatmeal, but he swallowed his words along with the oatmeal after a stern look from Ruth.

The polite sparring about breakfast entrees between father and daughter continued for a few minutes until Ruth surrendered and accepted that her father would eat whatever he wanted when her mom wasn't around.

Mike turned serious and asked, "You two talk about what happened? Come to an understanding?"

"Danny told me everything," said Ruth. She poked at the bowl of fruit in front of her. "He's promised to rein in the stupid stuff when he can, and I got him to agree to dance lessons for the wedding."

"Blackmail, I like it," said Mike. "But are you both on the same music sheet about Danny's job?"

"For fuck's sake, Dad, let it go," said Ruth. "It's not much different than when you were deployed and let Mom worry, and you two survived it."

"Only just," replied Mike.

"We're fine, Mike, I promise," said Danny. "You raised a strong woman who is not shy to call me out on my bullshit. An old sailor told me to never lie to each other about the risks and always make it home no matter the odds."

Ruth kissed Danny on the cheek and turned to collect her backpack, her to-go coffee, and the Subaru keys. "I've got an early shift at the hospital and need to get going." She slid out of the booth. She adjusted her backpack and leaned over to give Danny a curl-his-toes kiss.

She glanced at Mike. "You want a ride back to town?"

"I think I'll stay until Superman here gets a partner to go places with him," said Mike. "Try to keep him out of trouble."

"That's a laugh," said Ruth. She leaned over, gave her father a peck on the cheek, waved at Sharla behind the counter, and walked out of the diner.

Danny and Mike finished breakfast, with Mike letting Danny pick up the tab this time, and walked the few blocks to the Council Hall to meet with Barrett. He was late, but his office door was open, so they decided to wait comfortably in his office instead of on one of the benches in the hallway.

As they waited, they admired the pictures on the wall. It seemed Barrett had been an athlete of some repute in his youth, and the images recounted a history of achievement in football, baseball, and rodeo. There were pictures of him holding footballs, throwing baseballs, and standing beside corrals wearing chaps and a vest with a number pinned to it.

Danny pointed at one in which a younger version of Barrett was on the back of a bull in mid-leap. The bull was a red, striped brindle of mixed breed. Both rider and animal seemed to be at the height of their youth and power in the captured moment of the past.

"Not for all the treasure in Montana," said Mike.

"That's Red Rock," said a voice behind them. They turned to see Barrett standing in the doorway. "I drew him at the Nationals in my last year on the circuit."

"Looks like a hell of a ride," said Danny.

"It wasn't," replied Barrett with an embarrassed look. "And it didn't last long. I got tossed off in four seconds and bounced off a chute gate. Broke three ribs and cracked a bone in my back. Decided after I recovered that I'd rather raise 'em than ride 'em."

"Can't blame you," said Mike. "Never been to a rodeo, but I've seen it on TV, and it's damn impressive what riders can do."

"Had them up at the house, but the council wanted me to personalize my office," said Barrett. "Try to impress folks when they visit. I think it's all bullshit, but to shut them up, I hung a few."

"They are impressive," said Danny. He itched above his nose and asked, "What did you want to go over this morning?"

"Maggie Whitefeather," said Barrett. He motioned at Mike. "We're getting into some Reservation business here, so I'd appreciate it if what gets said here stays here."

"I can step outside if you like," said Mike. He put his hands on the arm of the chair and started to stand.

"No, it might be best if you hang around," said Barrett. "I get the feeling you want to keep watch on

Danny until Edmund gets back to town, which is smart. The boy needs someone to mentor him in risk avoidance."

Mike sunk back down into his chair. "I know how to keep secrets, if that's what you're worried about."

"If Danny trusts you, I trust you, so enough said about that," replied Barrett. "I went and spoke to both Winnie and Maggie last night."

"And?" asked Danny.

"I believe her," answered Barrett. "Her link to this died with the Salamanders and Charlie Prince, but we shouldn't let on about her. Whoever is behind this might think she knows something she doesn't."

"Same as our young runaway, Andrea," put in Danny.

"Like Andrea," parroted Barrett.

"Maggie'd be safer at Tribal Headquarters if she's healthy enough to be moved," said Danny.

"Exactly what I brought up to Winnie last night, and she agreed," said Barrett. "Janine is moving them over this afternoon."

"All the witnesses protected in one basket," said Mike. Danny and Barrett turned to look at him, surprised he'd spoken. He glanced at each of them, then said, "What? I watch cop shows."

Barrett smiled and asked Danny, "With all that's happened, where do you think we should be looking?"

"Tell me about Jonathan Redwing," said Danny.

Barrett got a surprised look on his face and asked, "Why?"

"Just throwing shit on the wall to see if it sticks. Tell me about him."

Barrett took a deep breath and said, "Not much to tell. He grew up on the Rez and went to college back East, Cornell, I think. He made a lot of money working the gas fields in Canada, and then, last year, he moved back."

"He worked the gas fields?" asked Danny.

Barrett smiled. "Not on the platforms. Jonathan's never done a day's hard labor in his life. He was management, white-collar all the way."

"What about family?" asked Danny.

"Folks are dead, no wife, no kids, no siblings I know of," replied Barrett.

"How'd he get on the council so quick?" asked Mike. "I mean, if he just moved back and has no family here."

"Same way as everywhere else: money," said Barrett. "The new addition that's being built onto the Two Moons Tribal Hall and Sports Center. It'll contain a pool and a movie theatre. First of each on the Rez. Redwing is paying for it."

"So, for that, he got a council seat?" asked Mike.

"It's a lot of money," answered Barrett. "I'm sure the council thought it was the least they could do when he asked."

"All that may be true," said Danny. "But he just strikes me wrong. And it's not just his voting against me or the white savior bullshit."

"Speak plain," said Barrett.

"He caught me before I saw you yesterday. He wanted an update on the investigation, so I filled him in. But I got a bad feeling from how he was acting."

"How bad?" asked Barrett. His surprise had changed into suspicion.

"Bad enough that I left out the part about Maggie," said Danny. "Funny thing was, she still came up."

"Who brought her up? You or him?" asked Barrett. He leaned forward in his chair.

"Redwing did. He said he'd heard rumors she might be involved. I'd left that part out, as I said, so my antenna went up when he mentioned her. It was like he already knew the answer and wanted to see what I knew."

Mike added, "He seemed to want to know if Danny knew where this Maggie had disappeared to. Between you, me, and your wall full of pictures, I don't like the man, and not just because he seems like a dick." He glanced at both men who were staring at him. "Not that my amateur opinion counts for anything." He saw they were still staring at him. "Okay, I'll shut up now," he said.

Danny looked at Barrett. "Amateur opinion or not, I agree with Mike. Redwing seems too interested in Maggie for it not to be something. He also told me to ignore anything Niland told me, said he was unreliable."

"I would take anything Niland told me with a grain of salt, but I wouldn't ignore it," said Barrett. "I know he has no friends on the council or the Rez."

"Why is that?" asked Mike. Danny glanced at him. His future in-law was incapable of staying shut up.

"He wants to bring a casino and five-star hotel to the Rez. He's got an idea to make Dead Horse the Reno of the Rockies. Boasts about how much money it will bring in, like that would solve all the Rez's problems," said Barrett. "Don't take this the wrong way, but money is a white man's solution to problems, not an Indian's."

"No offense taken," said Mike. "Throwing money at problems is like sowing seed. It just grows more problems."

"And he brought this to the council for a vote?" asked Danny.

"And it was voted down in favor of a plan to bring in fishing, hunting, recreation, and tourism instead. That's what the Cultural Museum is all about," answered Barrett. "We wanted to keep to the old ways. Not as much money, but more in harmony with the land and keeping with who we are as a people."

"Who brought the alternative plan to the council?" Danny asked, but he was almost positive he knew the answer.

Barrett paled. "Son of a bitch."

"Winnie Whitefeather, right?" said Danny.

Barrett didn't say anything, just nodded.

"So, anything Redwing could do to discredit her would work in his favor. If he could get her off the council and replace her with one of his own, it would get him closer to a yes vote on the casino."

"But I don't see the connection between him, the Salamanders, or Price," said Barrett. "What proof do you have?"

"Honestly, I got nothing concrete right now," answered Danny. "Just a feeling that something's not right when it comes to him."

"You think he'd do all this for a casino?" asked Barrett. "People have been killed."

"His plan could be worth millions," said Danny. Then, thinking of what he'd seen in Afghanistan, he added,

"I've known men who have killed for far less. Even killed for sport."

"This is all just half-ass guesses," said Barrett. He stood and walked to the walnut sideboard. It held a collection of binders, a pair of worn chaps, some rope, and a coffee maker. He poured a full porcelain cup and offered Danny and Mike some, but they declined. He walked back and settled into his chair.

"We're going to need proof before we accuse Redwing of anything," said Barrett. "He's on the council, and that counts for something when it comes to accusations. It ain't right, but the rules are different for people in power."

Mike interjected. "Meaning your proof needs to be so tight, it doesn't squeak."

Barrett raised his cup in salute. "Exactly."

Danny thought on the situation for a minute, then said, "I think he's worth a hard look. If for nothing else than to eliminate him as a suspect."

Barrett picked up his coffee, blew on it, and took a sip. "Then you best find some proof one way or the other before the Rez has another decrease in population."

Danny knew a "get off your ass and go do your job" order when he heard one, so he nodded, stood, and started to say he'd call in later, when Barrett stopped him.

"We can't wait to figure this out, but I can't let you wander around the Rez alone," said Barrett. "I don't want you to disappear and me find your bones in six months."

"Edmund is headed back today," replied Danny. "I should be fine till then."

"It's not a suggestion," said Barrett.

"The department is stretched to breaking," said Danny. "No one is left between the hospitalized, the hobbled, and the ones protecting Andrea and Maggie."

Barrett let his eyes wander to Mike. "You sure about that?" he asked.

Danny glanced at Mike, who was smiling.

"You're going to hire *him* now?!" said Danny. "He's on vacation."

"Only as your driver and," Barrett covered his mouth to hide the grin, "to keep you clear of trouble."

"Him, keep me clear of trouble." Danny turned to look at Mike and said, "You know Ruth is going to blame me for this."

"Blame you for what? I'm just getting to know her fiancé better," said Mike. Danny started to protest, but Mike waved to quiet him and said, "Oh, shut up and give me the truck keys."

Danny wanted to go back and talk to Niland first, and as they made their way from the Council Hall to Police Headquarters, Mike asked him about the Long Soldier case the previous fall. Danny gave him the *Reader's Digest* version and played down the parts where Ruth had been in danger.

"Is this investigation anything like that one?" asked Mike as they walked past North Star Pub & Package.

"Except for the dead bodies, no," said Danny. "I got through last fall by dumb luck and despite not knowing what I was doing."

"How have things changed?" asked Mike.

"Been taking a criminal investigation course online with Montana State," answered Danny. "Pat, the lead from DCI, put me on to it."

"Good course?" asked Mike.

"Good enough," said Danny as they got to Tribal Police Headquarters and walked inside.

Andrea was at the counter talking on the phone, and Soto was at a desk but got up to walk over and say hi.

Danny made the introductions then asked Soto if Andrea was doing all right.

"Better than all right, she's working part-time for Janine," he said. "Taking calls, running errands. She's a good kid."

Andrea hung up and walked over to the trio.

"That was Bobby Blackmore out in the trailer park," she said. "He wants someone to come out and arrest his ex-wife."

"Arrest her for what?" asked Soto.

"She stole his dog," answered Andrea. She looked at Danny and then at Mike. "Is it 'bring your dad to work' day?"

"Not my dad," said Danny, but before he could explain more, the phone rang, and she hurried over to answer it.

"The dueling exes are at it again," said Soto. "Last time, it was her calling in on Bobby, who stole her propane tank."

Soto shook Mike's hand and collected his hat and cruiser keys. As Danny watched the officer leave the building, he reflected that maybe his case wasn't the worst one on the Rez to be working currently.

Andrea covered the phone receiver and said, "You look worse than after we first met. You tangle with a mountain lion or something?" But whoever was on the other end came back on the phone, and she started writing on a pad of paper.

"Funny girl," said Mike. "What happened when you first met her?"

"She kicked my ass," said Danny. He pointed to the door that led to the cells. "Niland will be in the back."

They found Niland in the corner cell with the number one stenciled on the concrete floor in front of the door. There were only three cells, but the corner one had a barred window and allowed more light to enter. Niland was covered up and asleep with dirty, socked feet sticking out toward the bars. Danny pulled his pen out and ran it up the bottom of one exposed foot. Niland jerked awake and sat up, exclaiming, "What the fuck?"

Mike laughed and asked, "Was that part of the course?"

"Lesson one," said Danny before he turned his attention to Niland. "We've had some developments, Joe," and he explained everything that had happened since they last spoke.

"They're all dead?" asked Joe. "Archie, Elliott, Charlie Prince?"

"Every last one," answered Danny. He gave the man a minute to digest the news, then asked, "Why didn't you ever tell us about Sonny Siebert and the mushrooms?"

Joe gave a halfhearted shrug and stared at Danny.

Danny smiled and said, "You didn't want us to know about Sonny, the mushrooms, or what the Salamanders had in the vault in Long Hope."

Joe didn't shrug this time. His eyes went flinty, and the stare got meaner.

"You seem less remorseful than last time," said Danny. It snapped into view for him now that it had been an act when Joe had blamed himself for Ellen Goodnight's death and given up Prince and the Salamander brothers. Joe knew Prince wouldn't go easy and that he and the brothers would likely end up dead, leaving everything in Long Hope to him.

"When did you figure out the combination for the vault in Long Hope?" asked Danny.

Joe continued to stare.

"You might as well tell us. The three hundred thousand is locked up in evidence, and you're facing new charges." The last part was less true than the first, but Danny was looking for a threat to open Joe up, and more jail time seemed as good as any.

"Six months," spat Joe like it had been forced from him.

A sensation of dread hit Danny.

"Did you get it or did Sonny?" asked Danny.

"Sonny," replied Joe. "Archie had a bad memory for numbers and had it wrote down."

"Fuck," said Danny under his breath. He looked down and away. He had wanted Joe to tell him Sonny was just an old man watching mushrooms grow, but deep in his head, he must have had doubts, or he wouldn't have even asked the question.

He looked back at Joe with a look that would split diamonds. "Tell me the plan."

"Sonny came to visit me just after Ellen was killed. He figured that with Charlie and the two brothers gone and nobody else knowing about the vault, we could split everything in it. I got some serious debts with my suppliers in Great Falls. They want me dead; I needed that money."

"They can't get you in here," said Danny. "Now tell me the rest."

Joe glanced between Danny and Mike, settled on Danny, and went on. "Sonny told me to act broken up about Ellen, say I blamed myself, and then let slip where the stolen cattle were hidden."

"How'd he get in here?" asked Danny.

"It was after I got brought in with your girlfriend. He was outside and talked to me through the window."

"And you don't know who they stole the cattle for?" asked Danny.

"Nuh-huh," answered Joe. "Neither did Sonny. We didn't care. We wanted Prince and the brothers dead, so we had free rein to get the vault money."

Danny took a shot in the dark. "Ever heard the name Jonathan Redwing?"

Joe shook his head no and said, "Who's that?"

"Never mind," said Danny. He glanced at Mike. "We need to get to Sonny right away. Are you up for that?"

"Sure," answered Mike. Danny started for the door, but Mike looked at Joe and shook his head. "This Sonny must be a cold-hearted bastard to set those boys up like that."

"It wasn't about the Salamanders," said Joe. "It was Charlie. Sonny hated him something awful."

Danny stopped in his tracks and walked back to the cell. He leaned in and asked, "Why did he hate Charlie Prince?

"Shit, don't you know?" said Joe. "Charlie killed his grandson."

Chapter 18

"Damn it to hell," muttered Danny. He pounded a hand on the dash of the Power Wagon. "Damn it to hell."

Mike was behind the wheel, and the Wagon pressed eighty as they raced down the two-lane blacktop toward Sonny Siebert's house.

There were still a lot of unanswered questions in Danny's mind. Did Sonny have a part in the killing of John and Ellen Goodnight? If he didn't, did he know who did? Did he know who the head man was? Or was he the head man? Who was his son?

Niland didn't have any of the answers but had given Danny enough for him to be sure that Sonny was eyeball-deep in everything that had been happening on the Rez.

"Danny," said Mike. He slowed to turn onto a side road. "It's all right. Nobody would have figured it out."

"It's not that," said Danny. It wasn't, he realized. "I liked the old man. I wanted to believe he wasn't guilty. I wanted to believe he was just a desperate man."

"I think he is," said Mike. "Desperate for revenge. Desperate to avenge his boy."

Danny glanced at Mike, "Why'd you say that about Sonny anyway?"

"I've known many bad people in my day," said Mike. "And most of them were charming as hell, which is why it is so hard to reconcile when they turn out evil."

"I reckon," said Danny. He pointed at the upcoming house and said, "This is it. Just pull in the front."

Mike gave him a double take, "You don't want to come in a little less conspicuous?"

"I can guarantee he knows we're coming," said Danny. He reached down and unfastened the strap on his SIG. "Not to insult you, but do you want to stay with the truck?"

Mike laughed and slowed the Wagon to turn into Sonny's yard. "That was an insult, and, no, I don't want to stay in the truck. Barrett said I was your driver and your bodyguard."

"Then," said Danny, and he opened the console and pulled out a Beretta M9 in a belt clip holster, "You better strap this on."

Mike glanced down at the pistol, then back up to turn into the yard. "Got an extra magazine?" was all he said.

"Two," answered Danny as the Wagon rolled to a stop.

As Mike slipped the holster into the waist of his jeans, he scanned the porch, the house, and the outbuildings for signs of movement. Nothing moved except for the Appaloosa in the corral. The horse had trotted over to the corral rail as the Wagon turned in and now stared at them like they were a bright and shiny new toy come to play.

"What do you think?" asked Mike.

"A horse is missing, but I don't think he's gone," said Danny. "I think he's got eyes on us right now."

"My bet is the top of the barn."

"Why do you say that?"

"It's where I'd be," said Mike. He opened his door. "Elevated position, open fields of fire and observation, use the hay for cover."

"If we make it through this," said Danny as he opened his door. "We need to have a come-to-Jesus meeting about what you did in the Navy."

Mike smiled and stepped out of the Wagon and into the yard's grass. Danny did the same on the other side of the truck, and they moved forward. They kept a reasonable distance apart, the instinctive military training to spread out and not provide a single target.

Mike moved ahead and stationed himself at the edge of the porch where he could back up Danny and keep an eye on the corral and the barn. Danny climbed up on the porch and peeked in the window. Nothing. He whistled at Mike to get his attention and motioned inside. Mike nodded and went back to watching the corral and barn.

Danny drew his Sig, took position beside the screen door, and said in a loud voice, "Sonny, it's Danny Coogan. We need to talk."

"Not sure there's much to talk about," Sonny said from inside the house.

Mike spun at the sound of the voice, and Danny was amazed at Mike's speed at getting the Beretta out. Danny hadn't even seen him draw it.

"Who you got with you?" asked Sonny.

"Mike Beebe," said Danny on reflex. He then realized Sonny had no idea who that was. "He's my financée's father."

"That's a hell of a person to bring to an armed standoff," said Sonny. "Ray is recruiting folks off the street now."

Danny peeked in through the screen door. He couldn't see Sonny, so he must be deeper in the house. "Why don't you come out, and we can talk?"

"I can hear you fine from here," said Sonny. "And I reckon you don't want to see what I plan on doing."

Danny flinched at the words and glanced at Mike, standing just off the porch. It might have been better if Mike had been right, and Sonny had been waiting for them in the barn. It would have given Danny hope to bring the man in alive. But he wasn't in the barn. He was in the house, and by his words, he planned on not seeing the next hour.

"Heard you killed Archie," said Sonny. "Is it true?"

"We did," said Danny. He needed to keep him talking, he knew, and give himself more time to think of a way out of this fucking mess. "We talked to Joe Niland. He told us about your grandson."

There was silence from the house, and Danny peered in again. He was worried he'd say the wrong thing and push too quickly or hard. He expected to hear a gunshot, but the silence lasted a minute.

"Tell me about your grandson," said Danny. "What was he like?"

"I failed him. Just like I failed his mother," came the voice. "Didn't even have the guts to kill the man who killed him."

"Charlie Prince?" asked Danny.

"Yeah."

"How'd you find out?" asked Danny. He moved to one side and looked in a window. He saw a living room with a couch, two chairs, and a coffee table. He didn't see Sonny, but he did see a large bottle of whiskey and a glass. The bottle was three-quarters empty. Shit, he thought, if Sonny were half in the bag, he would be more prone to do something impulsive.

"We were drinking out at Long Hope one night, and he let slip how he first killed someone when he was still in high school. Said it didn't matter none; it was just some fag who deserved it."

The memory of something Edmund had told him about the disappearance of two teenagers years ago came flooding back. "You're talking about Ethan Iron Kettle, aren't you?"

"He was my only grandchild," said Sonny. "Lilly, my daughter, had him while she was still in high school. Father was a young Crow boy working in the gas fields. He got himself kilt in a blowout before Ethan was even born."

"What was the Crow boy's name?" asked Danny. He needed to keep Sonny talking.

"Noah Yellowtail," answered Sonny. There was a long silence, and when the man spoke again, death was in his voice. "Lilly was never the same after that; when Ethan disappeared, she just gave up."

"What happened?"

"Tried to drink herself to death, but it was too slow," replied Sonny. "Hung herself in the barn out back."

Jesus Christ, thought Danny. He caught movement in the shadows of the house interior and squinted, but the image disappeared.

"Why not kill Prince yourself?" asked Danny.

"I wanted to know where Ethan was buried. I tried to get it out of him, but he got suspicious and threatened me."

"You could have killed him then," said Danny.

"Couldn't bring myself to do it," answered Sonny. "I tried. Had a gun on him half a dozen times and couldn't pull the trigger. Vietnam took all the killing out of me, I reckon."

"So, you set me up to do it for you. You had Joe tell us where to find them," said Danny. "You knew Prince wouldn't give up without a fight.

"Ashamed of myself for that, but I did it."

"And the money in Long Hope?" asked Danny. He started moving past the door to the other window and glanced at Mike to ensure he was covered, but Mike was gone. He froze. What the fuck, he thought.

"That was my last throw of the dice," said Sonny. "Didn't want it for me, wanted to give it to the school. But that's all turned to shit now. Nothing good left in me."

Danny heard the hopelessness in the voice. He's made his choice, Danny thought. He started to open the screen door. The pistol led the way. "You can still have good things, Sonny. Let's talk about Ethan some more, what he was like."

"No. No more talk. I've been fooling myself for years. Thought I would get over it, but the hurt never goes away," said Sonny with death in his voice. "Only one last thing to do."

Danny threw the door open and stepped into the entryway of the house. He heard the sounds of a scuffle, and then two shots rang out and stung his ears. He raised his Sig and aimed at the doorway that led to the next room.

"Clear," came Mike's voice. "Coming out, don't shoot."

Sonny appeared in the doorway with his hands at his sides. Mike walked behind him.

After Danny had cuffed Sonny and placed him in the back of the Power Wagon, Mike handed him the snub-nosed .38 that Sonny had intended to do himself in with.

"You could have told me what you planned to do," said Danny.

"No time," replied Mike. "You had him talking, and I took the chance."

"Thanks for stopping it," said Danny.

"Stopping what?" answered Mike as he handed Danny back the Beretta and holster. "If anybody asks, I stayed with the truck."

Danny smiled and said, "Understood."

Mike looked at Sonny in the back of the Wagon. "Can't blame him for wanting revenge. I'd have no problem shooting someone who hurt Ruth or Margery."

"Like he said, he couldn't bring himself to do it," said Danny. He turned to look at Sonny, who had his head down and was crying. "And he hates himself for it."

The ride back to Tennant Creek was a quiet one. Mike drove and resisted the urge to turn the radio on.

Danny rode shotgun and spent the ride lost in his thoughts. Both men left Sonny to his uninterrupted hell in the back.

They placed Sonny in cell three, farthest from Niland, and had Soto stay with him to ensure the man didn't hurt himself. They'd give him time to reconcile with the fact he was still alive, and then they'd start the interview that had to happen if they wanted to solve this shitstorm. Danny dreaded questioning Sonny and the pain it would bring the man.

But Danny also had a niggling feeling in the back of his head about Ellen Goodnight. The deeper they got into the case, the stranger and more pointless her death became when you figured in all they now knew. Something about the neat state of the house irritated him; it was out of place and an incongruity.

He checked his watch; it was high noon. Shit, it wouldn't take long, and he wanted to walk the crime scene again to nail down what was bothering him about it. He asked Mike if he wanted to take a drive until it was time to talk with Sonny. Mike pulled out the keys to Danny's truck and said, "Sure, where to?"

They drove to the Goodnight house and parked just off the road. Danny asked Mike again if he wanted to stay in the truck.

"A woman was killed here," he said. "It's not a pretty scene."

Mike shut the truck off and looked at Danny. "I've seen the same, or worse; I'll be fine. What is it pestering you about his place?"

"The money," said Danny. He stepped out of the truck and joined Mike at the front bumper. "We assumed whoever did this was looking for the money we found in the basement freezer. I'm not so sure now."

"Why?" asked Mike as they climbed onto the porch.

"It was hidden in a freezer. Simple to find it," said Danny. "I think whoever killed Ellen and started searching the kitchen before we interrupted them was after something specific and not the money. They either found it, and we're shit out of luck, or they didn't, and it's still here waiting for us."

"So, what do you think we're looking for?" asked Mike.

"I have no fucking clue," said Danny. "But my radar goes off whenever I think about finding Ellen dead and nothing missing. The house wasn't even tossed."

"Or it was tossed by someone who doesn't like a mess," replied Mike.

Danny gave him a quizzical look.

"People can't change who they are," said Mike. "I was a neat, orderly kid. Everything had its place, so the military wasn't a hard adjustment for me. Might be the same way with who you're looking for."

"Somebody military?" asked Danny.

"Maybe," answered Mike. "Or someone meticulous, orderly, and precise."

"I never thought of that," said Danny. "Prince was in the military, so this might be his work. He's damn sure mean enough."

"Just consider me a son-in-law whisperer," said Mike. He lifted the police tape and let Danny twist the knob. The door swung open, and the smell of stale air hit them. Danny slipped under the tape and stepped into the living room. Mike followed and left the door open to vent the house.

The house was precisely as DCI had left it on the day Ellen had been killed. The blood had dried and was shadowy on the drywall in the living room, while it had thickened to the consistency of tar where it had pooled on the kitchen floor. Fingerprint dust covered most of the surfaces in the kitchen, and a heavy, oppressive silence filled each room.

They went through the drawers in the kitchen, careful to return the contents as they'd found them and to leave no clutter in their wake. Nothing struck either of them as out of place or suspicious. They stepped over the broken bowls on the floor and knelt by where Ellen's body had been found.

"How did she go out?" asked Mike.

"Bludgeoned in the head with a war club, then finished with two shots to the heart," replied Danny. His eyes drifted up to the stovetop. "She was tortured before she died."

"No shit, a war club, huh," said Mike. "Does that mean an Indian?"

"Maybe," replied Danny. "Or someone wants us to lean that way."

Mike stood and crossed his arms. "Lots of unknowns in your business."

"Ain't there, though," said Danny. He walked to the back of the kitchen and saw that the door led to a small sunporch with a loveseat, chair, and a small desk. Danny searched the desk and found bills, late notices, canceled checks, and sales receipts for cattle.

On top of the desk were a glass paperweight, two bone-handled skinning knives, a pair of well-worn work gloves, and an old coffee tin. The tin was short, about half the size of a regular can. It was muted yellow and had black lettering with red shadowing that read SAVAGE, and then below in only red was the word COFFEE. Between the two words was the head of an Indian with a full headdress of feathers.

"Funny thing for him to keep," said Mike. He had leaned on the doorframe and watched as Danny had sorted through the desk. "Not culturally sensitive."

Danny shook the coffee tin, and something rattled inside. He levered his thumb under the edge of the top and forced it open. A wave of aromas filled the sunporch.

He tipped the tin up and poured out the contents. Small amounts of tobacco, sweetgrass, sage, and cedar spilled onto the desk's wood. Teeth, from what Danny guessed came from wolves and mountain lions, were mixed in with the herbs, but it was what lay on top that interested Danny. On a broken leather cord was a blue turtle with flecks of yellow.

Danny stared at the turtle, and its ramifications reverberated in his head. He then leaned back in the chair and felt sick to his stomach.

Mike straightened in the doorway and said, "You look like you just saw a ghost."

"In a way, I did," said Danny. He replaced the contents of the coffee tin and resealed the lid. The scent of the herbs still hung in the air, but it was the image of the blue turtle that Danny couldn't shake.

"We need to get to town to see if Edmund is back yet," said Danny. He held the tin in his hand and pushed past Mike into the kitchen. "You mind driving still? I need to make a call."

"No problem," said Mike, but he reached out and took Danny by the arm. "What did you find?"

Danny said, "Maybe the answer to a decades-old mystery."

As they walked through the living room, Danny dialed Janine's phone number, hoping she was visiting her dad. He needed to ask Ray about Joanna Parker and Ethan Iron Kettle's disappearance.

Mike opened the door, and Danny ducked under the police tape as Janine's voicemail picked up on the other end. He waited for the beep and got out, "Janine, it's Danny," before a bullet smashed into the side of the house where his head had been a second ago.

He dove to the ground and heard a loud thump as Mike hit the floor back in the house. Danny instinctively rolled to the left and behind the cover of the concrete porch wall. Bullets struck the floor and followed Danny until he was behind the cover, then hit the wall he was hiding behind three times. Chunks of the wall were torn off with each strike, and dust covered Danny.

He drew his Sig and yelled, "Are you hurt?"

From inside the house, Mike yelled back, "No, the television broke my fall."

Another round hit the wall, and Danny saw a crack begin to appear. He rolled further to the left, popped up, and fired two rounds in his best-guess direction of where the shots were coming from. A barrage of rounds hit the wall and column around him.

"Mike!" he yelled. "I need you to spot for me. Stay behind something. When I fire, look for muzzle flash."

"Hold steady," yelled Mike. Danny heard movement in the house. "In position."

Danny took a deep breath, rolled to the right until he cleared the wall, and fired twice past the Wagon and into the high grass across the road. Bullets struck the porch again, but Danny had continued his roll right and was now behind a different wall on the other side of the porch.

"What do you got?" he asked.

"Rock formation with two cottonwoods halfway up the hill," said Mike. "At your one o'clock. The range is two-fifty at least."

"Fuck," said Danny. His pistol was worthless at that range. He might as well chuck rocks at them. Then, an idea came to him, and it was on a whole new level of stupidity.

"Mike," said Danny. "I'm going to toss you my pistol, and I need you to lay some fire down, just enough to keep them honest."

"And what are you going to be doing?"

"I'm going to run for the Wagon and the M4," said Danny.

He heard Mike move to the window right behind him. "Hey now, let's think this through," he started.

But Danny said, "No time," and tossed the Sig through the window. "Moving," he yelled, jumping to his feet and sprinting off the porch in a crouch.

He must have surprised the shooter because the first rounds came his way as his feet hit the grass. He heard the strike of rounds behind him. Then, a ceramic gnome exploded in front of him. Shit, he's getting the range, thought Danny, but he sprinted on.

He waited for the impact of a bullet, then heard firing coming from the house, and the fire from the cottonwood wilted. The assailant wasn't in danger from the pistol, but the firing must have worried them. The pause was all Danny needed, and he urged his legs forward and flung himself down behind the truck as the shooter opened up again. Bullets hit the mailbox and skipped off the road, but he didn't hear any solid thumps hit the Wagon.

He climbed to his feet and opened the side door. Two more shots rang out but impacted the side of the house. Mike's pistol fire had unnerved the shooter more than Danny had hoped.

He climbed in the truck, unlocked the M4 and the ammunition box, and pulled two magazines out. He dropped back out of the truck, loaded the rifle, and made his way to the truck's rear.

He saw a muzzle flash from the cottonwoods, and a puff of dust rose from underneath the Wagon as the round skipped under the truck and tumbled into the ditch.

Danny raised the rifle and aimed where he last saw the flash. As the shooter leaned out to fire again, Danny squeezed the trigger and heard them cry in pain and disappear.

He heard movement behind him, and then Mike was beside him, the pistol in his right hand, the coffee tin in his left, and a glare in his eye. "Never do that again," he said. "You scared the shit out of me, and that takes some doing."

"Seems to have worked," said Danny. He stepped out into the open and glanced between the cottonwoods and the side of the truck. To his amazement, the Power Wagon was hole-free.

Chapter 19

If the shooter was still on the hill, at least now, we have him outgunned, thought Danny as he and Mike fanned out and began to climb.

They found no dead body or wounded shooter amongst the rocks or the cottonwoods. Damn, thought Danny, I was sure I hit them. While Mike circled to search the other side, he searched where he thought the shooter had been.

Danny scanned the area before moving ahead to search for evidence. The grass covered almost everything, but bare spots from the game trail led off to the north. Satisfied, he walked through the grass, and unexpectedly, the sun reflected off something. He parted the blades, and there lay a spent cartridge. A few inches forward were two more, then a pile beside a leather pouch with the strap broken.

"Over here," called out Mike.

"Just a sec," replied Danny. He looked around, found a twig that had fallen from the cottonwood, and collected the brass back into the pouch. He then moved to the far side of the position to stand beside Mike.

He showed Mike the brass and the bag. ".308," he stated, but Mike ignored him and pointed at the rocks. Specks of blood painted one of the rocks, and a trampled trail through the grass led away to the west, parallel to the hilltop.

"They can't be that far ahead," said Danny. He stuffed the bag inside his shirt and headed out. He hurried but didn't run. He fell in on the trail and followed it with the M4 held ready. Danny's head swung left and right on a swivel. The grass was tall here and provided good concealment. They'd been ambushed once today; he didn't want it to happen again.

Mike walked behind him, his eyes on the horizon. "Shit, you hear that?" he asked.

Danny had heard it. The sound of an engine starter grinding. He and Mike dropped all pretense and worry and sprinted forward. They neared the end of the hill, and the ground began to slope downward, and they saw a small dirt road running between the hill they were on and the next.

They heard the engine catch and then the sound of gravel being thrown as a vehicle sped away. Danny went around the tail of the hill just in time to see the back end of a green Jeep disappear around the far side of the next hill.

He pulled up, breathing hard, and turned to look at Mike. "You see it?"

"Yeah," replied Mike. His breathing matched Danny's, and he took a deep breath before he said, "Jeep, green, older. The dust and distance were too much for my old eyes. No idea about the plates."

"At least we got a vehicle to look for now."

Mike walked over to stand beside him, "And we got brass. They must have panicked when they got hit. Snagged the bag on something."

"Little clues put together are usually what cracks the case," said Danny. He turned and headed back up the trail toward the shooter's nest and the Power Wagon. "That's what the criminal investigation course taught me."

"So, what do a turtle necklace, a green Jeep, and .308 brass tell you?" asked Mike as he dropped into step with Danny.

"That this whole thing is about more than stealing cattle," answered Danny. He slung the M4 across his back and stepped off the road and back in the direction they'd come.

They walked the grass the shooter had fled through, sweeping over it for any further evidence, but found nothing. At the shooter's nest by the cottonwoods, packed down in the grass, they found a few threads of shirt coated with blood and a single button. Danny collected them and slipped them into his pocket.

He stepped back and almost ruined the perfect imprint of a right-footed boot print. It showed a square toe, a riding heel, and a clear brand imprint that read ROCKY.

"Bingo," said Danny. He pulled out his phone and took a picture of the print.

Mike wandered over and gazed down at the print. "That will come in handy."

"Rocky brand working boot," said Danny. "Size ten, I'd say."

"How do you know?" asked Mike.

Danny stepped forward and placed his right foot alongside the print. The length was identical. "I'm a ten."

"Still, not much to go on. Lots of folks wear a ten," said Mike. "The brass and Jeep might lead us someplace."

"You never know. Add enough up together, and we got 'em," said Danny.

Mike lifted his nose and sniffed the air like a dog tracking a scent. "What the hell is that smell?"

Danny did the same, and soon he was tracking the same scent. "That is something not found in nature," he said. He bent over, then laid on the packed grass to sniff. Then it stuck him, and he rolled over to look at Mike. "It's men's cologne."

"They wore aftershave to a shooting?" Mike shook his head in disbelief but knelt beside Danny. "The shit you folks do out here in the West."

Danny rolled over to take a big whiff. "Do you know it?"

Mike closed his eyes, sniffed deep, and seemed to think for a minute. He opened his eyes and stood. "No idea, you?"

"Unless it's Old Spice, I'm useless," said Danny. He drew in the fragrance again. "It does smell familiar."

Danny stood, brushed off his pants, and readjusted his duty belt.

"You okay?" asked Mike.

"Sure, why?" said Danny, not paying attention to Mike.

"Just asking," said Mike.

Danny gave Mike a calm look. "I'm fine. Folks have been shooting at me so much lately that I'm getting used to it."

"Not sure that's a good thing," replied Mike.

"I'm positive it's not, but it gives me shit to talk about with my VA counselor," said Danny. He squared up to Mike. "No more bullshit, Mike. Between you, me, and any bird that can overhear us, what did you do in the Navy?"

Mike considered Danny, then said, "I suppose you deserve an answer."

"I think I do," said Danny. "I've been banking on you to back me up."

"I was in Naval Special Warfare Command," said Mike.

Danny had anticipated this answer but was still surprised he'd been right. "You were a Seal."

Mike shrugged.

"Why not just tell me?" asked Danny.

"Danny," stated Mike. "I told you my job almost broke my marriage and lost me my daughter for some time. Besides the pension deposited once a month, I've turned the page on it." He frowned and finished, "I had to learn to be human after all I saw. I wanted to leave it behind me. So, I go with the diver story."

"Then why are you out here doing this with me?" asked Danny.

Mike grimaced and said, "'Cause deep down in places I keep hidden, I miss it."

Danny reflected on how he had felt during the fight. The clarity, the simplicity, the thrill of the moment. He looked into Mike's eyes, and the two shared a deeper understanding of each other than words could convey. "I do, too," was all he could get out.

"Ain't we a fucked-up pair," laughed Mike quietly as he picked up a rock and chucked it. "Lucky for us, we got women who put up with all our bullshit."

Danny wanted to say more, but his phone rang and when he answered it Janine was on the other end. As they walked down the hill to the Wagon, Danny filled her in on the shooting, the brass, the bloody shirt fibers, the green Jeep, the boot print, and the coffee tin.

"Holy shit," said Janine in response to learning what was in the tin. "After all these years, her necklace pops up."

"I know," said Danny. "And somebody isn't happy we found it first."

"I'd sure as shit say so," said Janine. "I'll have Soto check on green Jeeps registered on the Rez."

"I'd widen out to include the whole county," said Danny. "No guarantee our shooter's an Indian."

"Good point," said Janine. "Anything else?"

"Whoever shot at us was wearing men's cologne," said Danny. "Smelled it on the grass where they laid."

"Weird," said Janine. "Do you know what brand?"

"It's on the edge of my brain," said Danny. "I've smelled it before but can't place it."

"Okay, get back here, and I'll rally the troops," said Janine. "By the way, Bringloe got released from the hospital. I got him watching over Sonny."

"Great news," said Danny. "How is he?"

"Madder than a hornet that he missed out on things. See you soon," she said, and the line went dead.

Danny and Mike walked back to the Wagon. Danny opened the door, relocked the M4 in its cradle, then thought of something and said, "Wait here a minute." He grabbed a pocketknife from one of the rear seat cup holders and jogged to the porch. Five minutes later, he was back.

"What was that about?" asked Mike.

Danny opened the console and reached in. He pulled out a handful of small empty pill pouches Ruth had dropped in it.

"Benefits of being with a doctor," he said as he dropped three slugs into one of the bags. One was shaped like a daisy from hitting the concrete wall, while the other slugs had maintained most of their shape and been pulled from the doorframe wood.

He reached into his pocket, pulled out the bloody shirt threads and button, and slipped them into a second pouch. "Lots of little things added together break the case."

"Amen, brother," replied Mike, and he leaned back to relax as Danny pulled away from the house.

They returned to town and saw Edmund's car in front of Tribal Police Headquarters. It was a black El Camino SS of the 1966 vintage, and Mike whistled at the gleaming finish and glistening chrome.

Danny told Mike the car had belonged to Edmund's grandfather. He explained that the car had been bought with money the government had been forced to pay the grandfather after violating his civil rights during a protest against the "Termination Policy" enacted in 1953.

"What was that about?" asked Mike. He slowed down the Power Wagon and parked behind the El Camino.

"It formally ended the federal recognition of over one hundred tribes," answered Danny. He reached down to collect the coffee tin between his feet. "It was the government's attempt to force the Indians to assimilate."

"How'd it go?"

Danny smiled and replied, "About like everything else the government tries to do, it failed. But it was successful in one way."

"How so?"

"Pissed off every Indian coast to coast. It got them to band together and organize. The policy led to the formation of AIM, the American Indian Movement, and a dozen other groups." He opened the truck door and jumped down onto the sidewalk.

Mike jumped out on the street on the other side, and they met at the tailgate.

"You are studying this or something?" asked Mike.

"No, but an old Indian named Nat Long Soldier, an AIM OG, told me about it," answered Danny. "And I find it interesting when the underdog gets a few licks in."

"And in your current job, it doesn't hurt to understand the Indian mindset regarding the feds and whites in general," offered Mike.

"Spot on. I think you have figured out my thinking."

They started to walk inside the police headquarters but heard the voice of a woman calling them.

Danny and Mike turned to see Demitta leaning out of the Dan-Dee Diner's door and waving for them to come over.

"If you're looking for that sorry excuse for a tribal officer and my boyfriend, he's in here, having a late lunch," she shouted.

Mike looked at Danny and asked, "Hungry?"

"I could eat, but we need to get it to go," replied Danny, and the two of them walked across the street and into the Dan-Dee Diner. Edmund sat at a table in the back, devouring a bacon cheeseburger and tater tots drenched in ketchup.

Sharla walked over from the counter with two menus, but Danny stopped her and said, "Two of whatever is on the grill and pick a side for us." She gave him a squinted-eye stare, and he added, "Whatever you got, we're in a hurry, thanks."

"Fine," she said as she walked back to the counter and yelled at the cook to box up whatever was burning on the grill: fries and the leftover cherry pie.

Edmund frowned through a mouth full of cheeseburger, pointed a finger at Mike, and asked, "This your future outlaw?"

"Sorry, I forgot, you two never met," said Danny. "Edmund, this is Mike Beebe, Ruth's dad. Mike, this is Edmund."

The two exchanged a handshake, and Edmund went back to his sandwich.

"When did you get back?" asked Danny.

"Drove in this morning from Big Sandy," said Edmund. He drained his soda and reached over to steal Demitta's coffee. "Got the livestock report from Charmayne. You know she's not as bad as you and Ray made her out to be. She tracked most of the tags Niland had with stolen cattle from half the counties in central Montana." He took a swig of coffee and asked, "What have you been up to this morning?"

"Getting shot at," answered Danny with a deadpan face.

The cheeseburger stopped midway to Edmund's mouth. "Say again?" he asked.

"Getting shot at," repeated Danny.

"You're joking," said Demitta.

Danny glanced at her and said, "Sorry, Demitta, I'm not joking, and I'll have to steal Edmund from you." He looked at Edmund and continued, "Can you get that to go?"

Sharla showed back up as Danny and Mike got up and pushed their chairs back under the table. She'd bagged the indeterminate sandwiches, two orders of rough-cut fries, and half a cherry pie. She was well known for keeping her patrons well-fed and didn't seem to want to lose her reputation. Mike pulled out his wallet, but she told him to put it away.

"Have Janine settle with me at the end of the month," she said. "Napkins and plastic forks are in the bottom." She directed her eyes at Edmund. "You need a box?"

Edmund said no. He left the tots, finished his burger and Demitta's coffee, and slid out of his chair.

"Call you later," he told Demitta. He kissed her on the top of the head, then nodded to Danny, and the three men left the diner and headed across the street to police headquarters. Danny detoured to the Wagon long enough to grab the yellow Savage Coffee tin that held the clue to the disappearance of Joanna Parker a decade ago.

When he rejoined Edmund and Mike on the sidewalk, Mike handed him a foil-wrapped sandwich. "It's interesting."

Danny unwrapped it and saw what looked like a burger. "It's a burger," he said.

"It's a bulgogi beef burger. Korean," said Mike. "Edmund says the chef watches too much YouTube and gets adventurous."

Danny took a bite and was flooded with the taste of beef, soy sauce, sesame oil, sugar, ginger, and garlic. He finished it before he spoke again. "Damn, I love YouTube."

Janine and Soto greeted them as they walked into tribal headquarters.

"Your Jeep was driven by a dead man," she said as Soto held out a sheet of paper.

Edmund took the paper, read it, and handed it to Danny as he wiped his mouth with his sleeve. He read it and said, "Why can't anything be easy."

"I think it's a long-lost relative out for revenge," said Soto. Janine scowled at him. "Or not," he added.

"Who is it?" asked Mike.

"The Jeep registration comes back to John Goodnight," replied Janine. "Victim number one in this goat rodeo."

"Is he the guy who got the stunner bolt through the heart?" asked Mike.

The assembled lawmen turned to look at him, and then Edmund and Janine shifted their eyes to Danny.

"Remind me to talk to you about the Tribal Police procedures on giving out information concerning ongoing cases," said Janine, quoting directly from a manual Danny hadn't read and didn't even know existed.

"In my defense," said Danny. "I didn't work here when I told Mike."

Janine frowned and stared at Danny. Then she flipped a switch, turned to Mike, and with her best gap-toothed smile, said, "Thank you for being there for Danny. We've got Edmund back now, so he can back Danny up. I can get you a ride to Darwin if you need one."

Danny cut in and said, "Barrett hired him on to be my driver and bodyguard. He's on the payroll." Janine now frowned at Mike, who shrugged and looked at Danny. She shifted her gaze between them.

"What are you two, a double act?" asked Janine. She didn't let Danny answer before she threw up her hands in surrender. But the smile returned when she said, "Shit, fine, whatever. The more, the merrier. Let's head into the office, put a pot of coffee on, and figure out what the hell is going on."

They adjourned to the office and got comfortable while Soto made coffee. Danny and Edmund settled into chairs, Mike sat on the couch, and Janine was behind Ray's desk. Ray's desk, thought Danny. He could think of it no other way. It was strange to see someone else behind it, daughter or not.

Concern about Ray filled his mind, and it was out of his mouth before Danny could stop it. "How's your Dad?" he asked.

"Better," answered Janine. "He might be able to go home next week."

"Is somebody with him?" asked Danny.

"Andrea and Stan got the duty tonight," answered Janine. "Monopoly until somebody goes broke."

"If he's going home, then he's on the mend, right?" asked Edmund.

"Not so much," countered Janine. "The nerve damage isn't responding to treatment. He may never walk right again."

Damn, thought Danny. Another misery to add to the growing list this case had caused. "Then you'll be in the saddle as chief for a while."

Janine nodded her head. She accepted a cup of fresh coffee and a glass sugar dispenser from Soto. She poured at least a quarter cup of sugar into her mug before saying, "Looks like."

Danny stood, got a cup of coffee with no sugar, and returned to his chair. "It suits you," he said after taking a sip.

Janine gave him a long look. By her stare, Danny saw that she knew he meant it.

"Thanks," she said. She stirred her brew, blew on it, took a large taste, then asked, "So what do we know?"

Silence filled the office like the woods after a heavy snowfall. Each officer looked at the one next to them, but no one ventured to be the first to talk.

Danny glanced at Janine and saw the nervousness. She was trying to live up to her father at this moment, and it was slipping away.

He cleared his throat and said, "We know that Charlie Prince killed Ethan Iron Kettle a decade ago."

Edmund and Soto were stunned and looked toward Janine.

She nodded her confirmation. "Ethan Iron Kettle was Sonny's grandson. Prince confessed to Sonny about the killing without knowing about the relationship. Which made Sonny want to avenge his grandson's death."

Danny explained further, "Sonny then ratted out Prince through Niland, who told us where to find Prince. Sonny knew Prince would never surrender. So he spun us up and sent us out like hitmen to eliminate Prince and the Salamander brothers."

"Holy shit," said Edmund. He turned to look at Danny. "But Archie didn't die at the trailer."

"No," said Danny. "And that wrecked the second part of Sonny's plan."

"What do you mean?" asked Soto.

"The money," said Mike, to the surprise of everyone.

Danny smiled at Mike, then explained, "The Salamanders had around three hundred thousand dollars hidden in the bank vault in Long Hope. Kind of their retirement fund. Sonny knew about it, ferreted out the combination, and hoped, with everyone dead, to take the money and split it with Niland."

"Only that didn't pan out. And Sonny tried to kill himself afterward, but Danny and Mike stopped him," said Janine.

Edmund peered at Janine, then shook his head in shock, "You see the shit I miss when I get sent out of town?"

"Then you better buckle up, buttercup," said Danny. He stood and walked over to the desk with the Savage Coffee tin in his hand. "'Cause you ain't seen nothing yet."

He removed the top and gently poured the contents on the desk's wood. The smell of the herbs filled the room, and the blue turtle with flecks of yellow on a broken leather cord came to rest on the pile of animal teeth.

Edmund stood, walked to the desk, and hovered over the turtle necklace. By his clenched jaw, Danny could tell he recognized it.

"Where did you find it?" asked Edmund.

"On John Goodnight's sunporch," said Danny. "Sitting in this old coffee tin."

Soto joined Edmund and peered down at the necklace. "I don't understand."

"This necklace was on a girl who was found murdered long ago," said Edmund. He turned around and stared at the pictures on the wall. "Joanna Parker."

"Jesus Christ," said Soto. "Do you think Goodnight did it and kept the necklace as a trophy?"

"No proof either way," replied Danny. "The Goodnights are dead, and Sonny has arranged for everyone else who might know something to be dead as well."

"But do you think he did it?" asked Janine. Her voice held an edge to it.

"If I had to give a guess, I'd say 'no,'" said Danny. "Somebody threw shots at us today, and I imagine it's about what's in this tin. I think Goodnight had the necklace as blackmail, and it got him and Ellen killed."

"What about the two wranglers that got sent to Wyoming," said Soto. "You think they might know something?"

"That is another thing that niggles at me," said Danny. "The council gave the go-ahead on that. Strange when they were folks who we still needed to ask hard questions."

"Who pushed for Wyoming to be able to take them?" asked Edmund.

"I heard it was Redwing," replied Janine. "Made the case they'd still be in custody, and we could always get them back if needed."

"That man's name is popping up too often not to mean something," said Danny.

"We've also been getting phone calls from Rune Jacobsen," said Janine.

"Who's that?" asked Edmund.

"Deputy U.S. marshal, he was working undercover as a wrangler to bust Prince," answered Janine. "He's hot to help. Got in trouble for getting his cover blown without an arrest and is looking to dig himself out of the hole he's in with his boss."

"I don't know what he can do," said Danny. "Shit, I don't even know what the next step should be."

"Can I say something as an outsider who doesn't know anybody on the reservation beyond the people in this room and that museum gal?" said Mike from the couch.

Janine rolled her chair to the left to see Mike beyond Edmund and Soto. "Go ahead."

"Danny told me most of this, and I listened to everything said here." Mike stood and walked to the desk. "I think all the killing is due to desperation."

"What do you mean?" asked Janine.

"Whoever shot at us today was desperate enough to kill lawmen because they wanted what was in that coffee tin," rationalized Mike.

"So how does that help us?" asked Danny.

Mike shrugged. "Figure out who's still alive and connected to what's in that coffee tin."

Chapter 20

The meeting in the chief's office broke up before suppertime. Soto returned to the cells to relieve Bringloe, who had an appointment. He was still having headaches, and Dr. Benteen had threatened to sic Enola on him if he didn't check in at least once daily.

Edmund headed out to see Demitta and bring back an evening meal from the diner for the two prisoners, along with something for Winnie and Maggie, who were being bunked on cots in the TV room. Danny would have loved to see Ruth, but when he called, she said the hospital had a full emergency room from a bus-versus-guardrail accident, and it would be the following day before she'd get home.

Danny listened as Mike called Margery. She said Molly, Ben, and she were headed to Sun Prairie in Cascade County to eat at The Lucky Lemon, a vegan health food café. Molly was excited to show it to her, and Ben was going but planned on stopping for a burger on the way home. Danny heard Margery ask Mike if he wanted to come along, and Mike declined and said that he and Danny had plans.

Mike hung up, slipped the phone into a shirt pocket, and looked at Danny. "You ever eat at that place?" he asked.

"The Lucky Lemon, sure, Ruth loves it," said Danny. "The veggie hummus wrap is great."

"Maybe so, but I'm with Ben. A burger sounds good right now," replied Mike. He turned to look at the acting police chief. "Hey, Janine, you hungry? I'm buying."

Janine didn't hear him. She had a pile of paperwork to filter through. She had discovered, much to her annoyance, that while her father was an outstanding Tribal Police chief in most regards, he was a terrible bureaucrat. Some of the reports were due a year ago, and the federal government threatened to repossess the Ford Interceptors due to a missing certificate. Janine found it on the bottom of the third pile, unsigned.

"I love my dad, I love my dad," she whispered in a mantra as she moved another stack of papers.

Danny got up and crossed to the desk. He rapped twice on it to bring Janine out of her paperwork-induced trance. She looked up and gave him a surprised look. She'd forgotten he was still here.

"What?" she said in an annoyed voice.

"Let it lay for now," said Danny. "We've been going balls-out since this started and need a break to recharge." He gestured to Mike, who stood by the door. "We're headed to the Western Spur for a burger and beer. He's buying."

"I got too much to do," she said. She started to search through the papers again.

Danny laid a hand on the pile she was sorting and said, "This is a non-negotiable request from a friend. I don't want to come back and find you keeled over from a stroke due to stress."

"I got to get this done," she protested.

"The feds are closed for the night, the Tribal Council has gone home, and our only suspects are locked up, so get your shit and come on. Don't make me carry you to my truck."

"I should fire you for being insubordinate," she said. But she smiled and stood up.

Danny shrugged and smiled back. "Wouldn't be the first time it happened this week."

Janine walked back to the cells and told Soto where they'd be if anything came up and joined Danny and Mike by the front doors.

The ride to the Western Spur Diner was slow and leisurely. The radio played "Thirty Dollar Cowboy," from Chris Ledoux, then switched to a few songs from Teri Clark. Danny drove and demoted Mike to the copilot, while Janine first lounged in the back but soon slumped over and fell asleep.

Mike glanced in the backseat at the sleeping woman and said, "She's pushing herself hard."

"Her dad is a lot to live up to," said Danny.

They drove on, each in their thoughts and careful not to wake Janine. Danny watched the sun drop more on the horizon and thought about Sonny. The man had lost his grandson and wandered off the Red Road for revenge. The deaths of Ethan Iron Kettle and Joanna Parker had been indelibly linked because of their proximity in time. But were they?

Danny doubted Charlie Prince had killed the girl. He'd bragged about killing Ethan to Sonny, and Danny didn't believe Charlie would be shy about bragging that he'd killed Joanna also. So, who had done it? The necklace had been found at Goodnight's, but Danny didn't believe John did it either. So, who had shot at him and Mike? Did the shooter want the necklace or something else hidden in the house?

Danny frowned. The answer was clear as mud. It had to be someone with a motive Danny hadn't figured out yet. Whoever it was, Danny agreed with Mike's assessment. They needed to look for whoever was left that was desperate.

A germ of a plan cropped up in his head. It might flush out the killer and give Sonny some redemption.

He started to say something about it to Mike but saw that he had fallen asleep.

Little Jane and the Pistol Whips came on the radio with "All I Need to Know." Danny tapped his foot along to the song and watched the prairie go by as a plan began to form in his mind.

He slowed as he approached the diner. The parking lot was half full of pickups, old sedans, and motorcycles. Above the low-slung building hung a ten-foot-tall, neon-blue cowboy boot kicking back and forth. The boot had a yellow spur with a W on the button, riding along to give the place its name.

Willy Whitepipe owned the Western Spur and the Blue Swan Motel beside it. He was also Ray's brother.

Danny parked his truck in the gravel away from the building and made sure it was pointed in a direction that allowed him easy egress or regress, depending on the situation. He knew this habit was due to convoy duty in Afghanistan, but it had also served him well in Montana, so he stuck to it.

Danny switched the truck off, and Mike's eyes burst open like he had a button on his ass. "Shit," he said. He sat up and rubbed his eyes with the heels of his hands. "Sorry about that."

"Nothing to worry about," said Danny. He turned to jostle Janine awake. "At least now I know who Ruth gets the 'sleeping with her mouth open' thing from."

They walked in and surveyed the surroundings.
The Spur had the classic dinner layout. Booths around the
outside along windows, a long counter with stools opposite,
and tables and chairs filled the in-between. The motif was
mid-century modern paired with a pinch of a Western
saloon. The mid-century part was the green Formica and
chrome tables with vinyl chairs and booths. In contrast, the
Western pinch was the converted counter now serving as a
bar.

Bars aren't a usual accouterment of diners, but the
Spur occupied a fuzzy no-man's-land between the county
and the reservation jurisdictions. Willy used this to his
advantage since neither the Tribal Police nor the Sheriff's
Department seemed to mind.

Janine saw Barrett at a table toward the back and
told Danny and Mike to follow her. They weaved through
the tables and behind the stools and walked up to Barrett as
he pushed his plate away and wiped his mouth.

He looked up, and concern passed over his face, but
Danny held up a hand and said, "Nothing happened, just
here to eat."

Relief replaced concern, and Barrett motioned for them to sit. Danny and Mike took the chairs opposite him, and Janine settled beside him.

"Looking for a heavy dose of meat," said Mike. What do you recommend?"

"Double cheeseburger with onions and an over-hard egg, plus a side of Western-seasoned, rough-cut fries," said Barrett without hesitation. "You can feel your arteries squeeze shut as you eat, and it'll cut an hour off your life, but I figure the taste is worth it."

A man walked up to the table. He held a pink pad of paper in one hand and a yellow Ticonderoga pencil in the other. "Well?" he asked with no explanation.

Danny glanced up at the man. He was tall, razor-thin, with a long-stemmed churchwarden pipe that hung from his mouth.

"Evening, Willy," said Danny. "Sorry about Ray."

"Coogan," said Willy. He gave a tight nod to Janine and ignored Mike.

"Bring them three of what I had," said Barrett. "And a round of Coors."

"Make mine a Moose Drool," said Danny.

Mike glanced at him. "What the hell kind of drink is that?"

Danny smiled. He was used to the reaction. "It's a brown ale. Made here in Montana."

"Switch me to that," said Mike. He glanced at Willy. "Love to give the local brew a go."

Willy scribbled the order on his pad, gave Janine a long look, and walked away.

"He's a charmer," said Mike.

"He's my dad's brother, and he's pissed off at me," said Janine. "Figures I should be at the hospital."

Mike leaned back and looked across the room at Willy. The man was tearing the order off the paper pad and sliding it through the pass-through window to the kitchen.

"He and Ray don't look anything alike," he said.

"Growing up, folks on the Rez always said my dad was prime beef while Uncle Willy was the scraps," said Janine. "They live at the reverse ends of everything, but he's family."

The food and the beers came, and after eating, the four talked about everything but cattle rustling and killing. It was a broad conversation and drifted from comparing ranching to farming, which was mainly from Barrett and Mike, to the beauty of Montana, where Janine kicked in most, and the spiritual side of the Nakota people, which entailed Mike asking Barrett and Janine unending questions.

Danny, for his part, kept quiet. His mind kept wandering back to the contradictions of the case. He'd wanted to get Janine out of the office and away from the pressure she was under for a few hours. As she laughed at something Mike said, it was clear it had worked. But for him, the case was still first and foremost in his head. His head was so immersed in thinking that he didn't notice the man and woman who walked up to the table.

When he returned from his grain-of-sand counting, he saw DCI's Pat Palmer and Monica Lewis standing beside the table. Pat was in jeans with a hubcap-sized belt buckle, an aqua paisley shirt, and a pair of Wilson boots with a tulip-and-leaf pattern. Next to Pat, Monica looked understated. She wore jeans, a pink, snap-button shirt, and sneakers. Her head wound had healed, and she radiated beauty.

"I asked how you are doing, Danny," said Pat.

Embarrassed, Danny said, "Oh, fair to middling." He ran his eyes up and down the couple and asked, "Not dressed like I see you show up most times. Pat, you're looking good enough to be buried. What's the occasion?"

"Headed to Augusta for the American Legion Rodeo," said Pat.

"You're a little early," said Barrett. "It ain't for a week or so."

"We've got a little side trip to take first," said Pat. He looked at his boots and then glanced at Monica. "We got married yesterday and are headed to the Scapegoat Wilderness for a hiking honeymoon."

A collective shock rolled over the table, and Janine was the first to recover. She screamed, stood, and enveloped Monica in a hug.

Danny and Barrett regained their senses, rose to shake hands with Pat, and hugged Monica. Mike held back, not knowing anyone, so he smiled, gave his congratulations, and kept his distance.

As Danny stepped back, he asked, "If this is your honeymoon, what are you doing at the Western Spur? How'd you know we'd be here?"

"It was my doing. We stopped at your office, and Soto said you were here," said Monica. "The report on both John and Ellen Goodnight was finished, and I wanted to make sure you got it."

"Well, shit," said Barrett. "You could have dropped it in the mail. You two got bigger fish to fry."

"We knew the case took on a new importance once Ray got shot," said Pat. He glanced at Janine as Monica dug him in the ribs with an elbow. "Sorry, we just wanted you to have it as quick as possible. We'll be out of cellphone range for a week and didn't want to leave any unanswered questions."

Pat reached behind him and pulled a folded manila envelope from his back pocket. He handed the envelope to Janine and said, "The bodies of John and Ellen didn't turn up much, but we confirmed the head wound was the same on both."

"What about the other items found?" asked Edmund.

"No prints on anything," said Monica. "But we cataloged and photographed it all. I never saw a medicine bag before. It was interesting."

"Well, thanks for dropping it off," said Janine. She rose, hugged Monica again, and kissed Pat on the cheek. With a smile, she said, "Now get out of here, turn your phones off, and start honeymooning."

They watched them wind their way through the tables and, with a final wave, disappear out the front doors.

"You could have knocked me down with a feather," said Janine. She finished what was left of her beer and waved for another. "I thought Pat was a confirmed bachelor. I didn't even know they were seeing each other."

"It got out that she got a knock on the head, and he came to see her in the hospital," said Danny. "She was thinking about moving back to the big city." He smiled and finished his beer but didn't wave for another. "Guess Pat figured out a way to make her stay."

"Speaking of staying," said Janine. She looked at Mike and continued, "Have you and your wife ever considered moving to Montana?" She gave a warning glance toward Danny. "Your future son-in-law could use some guidance and help to stay out of trouble."

Mike gave the same look at Danny. "He does seem to be a magnet to conflict."

A waitress brought another beer for Janine and Mike, while Barrett declined, and Danny ordered a diet soda.

"What's Indiana like?" asked Barrett as the waitress walked away. "All that flat would unhinge me. I can't imagine not waking up and seeing mountains."

Mike laughed and started telling Barrett about Indiana, his family farm, and living on land as flat as the dinner table.

Danny listened, but his attention was drawn back to the manila envelope on the table between two empty glasses and a stack of plates. On impulse, he reached over, took it, and tore open the top.

He pulled out the report and skimmed it as Mike joked about why so many button-fly jeans get sold in Indiana. Danny stopped reading and looked up. Mike paused for effect, laughed at the punchline to himself, then steadied himself and said, "Because sheep can hear a zipper a mile away."

Barrett and Janine broke into fits of laughter, Janine so much she had to wipe tears out of her eyes. Danny smiled at the joke and figured alcohol had multiplied its comedic effect on Mike, Barrett, and Janine.

He returned to the report and flipped to the appendix that held all the photos. He ensured no one was behind him who might get an accidental look at the autopsy photos and then went through the ones of John and Ellen. The notes to the side all dovetailed with what Pat had told them at the crime scene.

He flipped back and came to pictures of the stunner and the bolt that had traveled through John's body. Also, there were pictures of the slugs that had killed Ellen, passed through the kitchen floor and the top of a freezer, and ended up in a tub of rocky road ice cream. The notes gave the caliber as .45 ACP.

He let the report droop and glanced up to hear Janine joke about a female hunter, a cowboy, and a horse mistaken for an elk. Now it was Mike's turn to laugh till he cried.

The caliber was a .45, thought Danny. They'd taken an M1911 off Niland that fired .45 ammunition. But he'd been in custody when Ellen had been killed. He thought about Charlie Prince and the Salamander brothers. He was sure they would kill someone without regret, even a woman, but what would be their motivation?

Not the coffee tin, he thought. Whoever wanted it wouldn't discuss what was inside it. That would replace one blackmailer with a new blackmailer.

He flipped past the pictures of the two murder weapons and came to the secondary items found at each crime scene. He turned page after page through the photos, then paused, thunderstruck at the pictures of the medicine bag and its contents.

"Well, I'll be double-damned," he said.

He glanced up and found all three sets of eyes looking at him.

"I think I just found something to make our night," he said.

"What?" asked Janine.

"A piece of evidence of who our main suspect should be," said Danny.

"You mean the head cattle thief?" said Mike.

"No. I don't know, maybe, but this is something bigger," said Danny. He stood and said, "I meant the guy who might have killed Samantha Parker."

All three of the others stared at him. Janine raised an eyebrow, "Are you going to make us play twenty questions?"

"It's Jonathan Redwing," said Danny.

"Arc you drunk?" asked Barrett. "Look, I know you don't like him, and I'm with you on that, but you got to have proof before you go after someone as powerful as him on the Rez."

"But we do have proof—or at least a link that he needs to explain," he said, slamming the report on the table. "It's right here in the DCI report." He pointed at the photo, and all three leaned forward to look.

Barrett was the first to see it and leaned back in his chair. Janine glanced at him in confusion. Barrett stretched out his hand and pointed with his index finger to a segment of the picture. Realization traversed her face, and she said, "Holy shit."

Mike looked at them and then at Danny. "I'm new. Somebody want to clue me into what I'm supposed to see?"

Danny pointed at the photo, and Mike leaned forward again to see a black stone pendant shaped like a dog.

"Redwing has one exactly like that hanging around his neck," said Danny.

Barrett said quickly, "It's not proof positive, but it's pretty dammed close considering what else he's doing."

Danny's ear pricked up. "What are you talking about?"

"He's called for an emergency meeting of the council. He wants Winnie off the council, and I think he's got the votes for it."

"Why didn't you tell us?" asked Danny.

"I thought this was just a nice night out," said Barrett. "I honestly thought it was just a political sideshow. I didn't think proof would show up against Redwing."

"Is there anything else he's up to?" asked Janine.

"He's bringing up the casino again," said Barrett. "The vote was close last time, and if Winnie gets voted out, it will depend on who replaces her."

"Seems like the council should be concentrating on solving the killings and protecting the folks on the Rez," said Danny.

"Remember," said Mike. "Figure out who's still desperate."

"You think Redwing is desperate to get the casino approved?" asked Janine.

"He is if he's got all his money tied up in it," said Danny. "It would break him if it didn't go through."

"And if he has backers who gave money, they expect a return," said Barrett.

"We need to see his financials," said Danny.

Janine snorted. "Never happen. That's a court order; any judge worth their salt would tell us to pound sand. They'd say this is all circumstantial pie in the sky, nothing concrete."

"And they'd be right," said Barrett. "Sorry, Danny."

"Maybe I know a guy," said Danny. He pulled out his phone and started searching.

"Who?" asked Janine.

"Our friendly neighborhood deputy U.S. marshal," said Danny. He found the number, hit the dial icon, and put the phone to his ear. He looked at Janine. "If this works, can he have credit for the arrest? He needs it to get out of the doghouse with the Marshals Service."

"I'll credit the man on the moon," said Janine. "I just want the shit to end."

"Hello, Rune. It's Danny Coogan. Can you meet me at Tribal Headquarters in an hour?"

Chapter 21

On the drive back to Tribal Police Headquarters, Danny laid out his plan. Barrett had hitched a ride with them and left his truck in the parking lot. He said he was one beer past driving and didn't want to get a DUI, seeing as two officers would watch him drive away. He sat in the front with Danny while Mike and Janine rode in the back.

"You expect Redwing to confess to killing the girl?" asked Barrett. He took a drink of the Coors he'd smuggled out of the diner. "He ain't the sharpest tool in the shed, but he'd know enough to keep his mouth shut."

"I don't think so. Not if he thought he could get the evidence back," said Danny. "If I got this figured right, he's got too much to lose to risk it."

The Wagon ran up quickly on an old, slow-moving, mint-green Ford pickup, and Danny was forced to slow down. He let an oncoming Mazda pass, hit his turn signal, and pulled into the passing lane to slip by the slow-moving vehicle.

Eugene and Pearl Thunderhawk sat inside the old truck. The couple were well into their eighties and known to all. They smiled and waved as the Power Wagon passed them. Eugene always said he didn't like to drive beyond his ability, and with the daylight dwindling, his ability was forty miles an hour.

"Didn't Eugene used to be the council chief?" asked Danny. He pulled back into the right lane and accelerated.

"He was chief for twenty years before Charles Falling Star pushed him out," said Barrett. He fished out a cigar but couldn't find his lighter. He searched the switches and knobs on the dashboard but came up dry. "Where's your goddam lighter?"

"Didn't come with one," said Danny. "Besides, it's a non-smoking truck."

"Shit, I guess I should have taken the chance and driven myself," said Barrett. Unable to smoke, he put the cigar in his mouth and chewed the end. "Eugene could be chief again if he asks, but Pearl won't wear it."

"Getting back to your harebrained plan," said Janine from the backseat. "Why would we use Sonny to bait the trap?"

Danny frowned at his plan being described as harebrained but replied, "Redwing would clam up like a monk if one of us tried to blackmail him with the medicine bag and turtle necklace. Niland is too squirrelly for Redwing to take seriously. So, it has to be Sonny."

"This plan is more complicated than the moon landings," said Janine. "I say we arrest his ass, show the jury the dog figurine and medicine bag found with Goodnight's body and book him long-term lodging at Deer Lodge. The hell with all this cloak-and-dagger."

"Deer Lodge?" asked Mike.

Barrett turned to look back at Mike. "Montana State Prison."

"What do you think, Mike?" asked Danny. "Back another white guy up."

"Sorry, but it does sound like something out of an Ian Fleming novel," he answered. He leaned forward and put a hand on the back of Danny's seat. "Best to live by the hard and fast rule of KISS."

Now, it was Janine's turn to be confused. "Who's Ian Fleming?"

Mike looked at her and said, "Sorry, I forgot you're twelve. Ian Fleming wrote the James Bond books."

"There are James Bond *books*?" she asked, then shook her head. "Never mind, what's KISS? If you're talking about the band, I don't understand."

"He means 'Keep It Simple, Stupid.' It's a military thing," said Danny. He looked at Mike in the rearview and added, "You may be right. I'm overthinking it."

"Only by a mile or so," said Barrett. He stuffed his cigar back in a shirt pocket.

The wagon took the wide turn just before Tennant Creek, and Danny slowed as the outskirts of the town began to close in around them. The sun was below the horizon, but the last gasp of the day burned in lilac and ginger colors behind the mountains to the west.

"You don't get a sunset like that in Indiana," said Mike. He turned to see Janine looking at him. "Most of ours involve corn."

"Be something different to see," said Janine. "Never been out of Montana, so that sunset is all I know."

"Once Ray is better, you two should drive over," offered Mike. "The Midwest is awful pretty in fall."

Janine considered it and said, "I think we'd like that."

Danny slowed the Wagon and turned down the street that led him around to the back of Tribal Headquarters. He pulled into the spot marked FOR OFFICAL VEHICLES ONLY and switched off the truck. Danny frowned. The rear entry door to the building stood wide open, and a light shone out. What the…? Through the opening, they saw a pair of legs lying just inside on the floor.

Janine was first out of the truck. She drew her weapon and headed toward the open door, her pistol pointed ahead. Danny opened the console, pulled out the Beretta, and handed it between the seats to Mike.

He drew his Sig, dropped out of the truck, and ran to catch up with his chief.

When they reached the door, they paused with Janine to the right and Danny to the left. Danny smelled the tang of pooled blood and the acrid smell of modern propellant. The legs didn't move, and he dreaded the thought of who might be lying on the floor.

Janine nodded to him, and Danny covered her as she moved around the doorframe and peeked inside.

"Fuck," she said and leaped through the doorway. She holstered her weapon on the fly, landed beside the body, and fell onto her knees. "Soto, can you hear me?"

Danny followed Janine on instinct and had his Sig up and aimed down the empty hallway. He glanced at the uniformed man lying on the ground as he moved into position farther down the hall. Soto lay face up with his arms spread wide on the coolness of the cement floor. A deep red gash stretched from his eye to his ear on the left side of his face.

Both eyes were open, but the left one would never see again. It had ruptured, with the pupil hanging like a dropping teardrop, and its fluid had run down the side of Soto's face.

Janine was on her radio calling for an ambulance.

"Stay with him. Pull your weapon," said Danny. "The shooter might still be here."

Janine redrew her pistol as an acknowledgment came from the clinic that an ambulance was coming. She nodded, and Danny swung his attention back down the hallway.

He kept his Sig aimed down the hall and listened for the sound of movement. Nothing but the sound of the circulation fans came to his ears.

He moved quickly down the hall and came to an intersection. Straight ahead were the cells. To the right was a hallway that dead-ended after twenty feet with a door on either side. Danny knew the left door opened onto the laundry room, and the right door entered the lavatory and locker room.

To the left was the corridor that led to the offices and front lobby. A body lay face down on the floor, arms splayed over its head.

"Edmund!" shouted Danny. He abandoned all hesitation and rushed to the man's side. He dropped to his knees and slid into position beside the body. Edmund was unconscious but breathing. Danny searched his body but found no bullet wounds. He checked the head and saw a small amount of blood had pooled beside the man's jaw. A thin line of blood ran up the side of Edmund's face and disappeared into his hairline.

Danny ran his fingers gently through the hair on the back of the head, and when he pulled his hand back, it was blood-covered. He sighed deeply in relief at the realization that Edmund had just been knocked out and not shot.

He was about to shout for Janine when a soft moan came from the vicinity of the cells. The Sig came up, and he surged forward. The sound was louder now, more urgent, and came from cell three on the end by the hall. Sonny's cell, thought Danny.

"Shit," he said. He glanced down at Edmund and figured he'd be all right until he got back. He stood, kept the weapon ready, and rushed forward. The cell door was open, and he raced in. "Sonny, are you all right?"

But it wasn't Sonny. Deputy U.S. Marshal Rune Jacobsen lay on the cell floor with a blood-covered chest and belly.

Barrett ran up beside Danny with Mike trailing. Both looked down at the wounded marshal. Danny pushed Barrett in the shoulder and yelled, "Get the trauma kit! Hanging on the wall outside the chief's office! Fucking go!"

Barrett gave him a double take, then sped down the hall toward the offices and disappeared. Mike held the Beretta high, took a protective stance, and scanned for targets.

Danny dropped to Rune's side. The man coughed, and his eyes opened to slits.

"Stay still," said Danny. He tore the man's shirt open.

"Fooled me," Rune gasped. "Fooled me good."

Danny found three bullet wounds. Two in the belly and one high on the chest. He leaned over, tore the sheet off the bunk, bundled it, and applied pressure to the two belly wounds leaking the most blood.

"What happened?"

A pounding and the echo of muted shouts came from the basement. Winnie and Maggie: Danny recognized the voices.

Barrett returned, tossed the kit on the bunk, flipped open the lid, and pulled out QuikClot gauze.

Danny looked at Mike and said, "Go tell Janine we need more help."

Mike nodded and sprinted in the direction of the police chief.

"Fooled me," Rune repeated. "Fooled me good."

Danny moved the sheet up to the chest wound and applied pressure while Barrett worked to seal the gauze around the more severe belly wounds and hold pressure there as well."

"It was Sonny," said Rune, and his eyes closed.

"What about Sonny?" asked Danny. He shook the marshal.

Rune's eyes fluttered open and settled on Danny. "Sonny shot me."

Rune passed out, and Danny pressed down on his chest and tried to keep him alive while Barrett did the same with the belly wounds. He'd been so stupid, Danny roared at himself inside his head. He'd had it wrong from the beginning. Sonny had made him dance like a puppet, and what a puppet he'd been. He'd followed every breadcrumb, believed the man because he liked him, felt sorry for him, and because of it, one more man was dead, and another was dying.

Something deep inside him hardened, and he wanted to scream in fury, but this wasn't the time. First, they needed to save Rune, then he'd fucking take care of Sonny.

Danny heard the ambulance's sirens, and red flashes of lights soon invaded the hallway through the open door.

Paramedics burst through the back door and rushed in with cases in each hand. Danny heard the footsteps of one man stop at Soto.

The second paramedic was Rosebud Hills. Young, fresh-faced, she usually wore a toothy grin, but not now. She entered the cell and pushed Danny aside as she knelt at Rune's side.

Danny heard the arrival of a second ambulance and saw the intensity of the flashing red lights double. Danny listened as a third paramedic rushed in and apparently dropped to help Soto as well. He was quickly followed by a fourth paramedic who entered the cell and took over duties from Barrett. Danny saw the name BLACKMORE on the man's nameplate. He wondered if it was the same Blackmore who'd had his dog stolen by his ex-wife. Barrett joined Danny outside the cell door, both coated in Rune's blood.

Edmund had stirred and sat with his back against the wall, his head leaning forward. Blood ran down the side of his neck, and his eyes remained focused on the floor in a thousand-mile stare.

Danny didn't know if Edmund could hear him, let alone answer, but he had to ask, "Who did this, Edmund?"

The man's eyes were still staring off, but he stated in a hoarse voice, "My fault."

Janine took her key ring out and, with Barrett's help, went and unlocked the basement door to free Winnie and Maggie. Both appeared unharmed but traumatized and scared out of their wits. Danny glanced at Edmund as the work continued on Rune. His eyes moved to the man's holster and saw it was empty.

Winnie gasped at the carnage and moved to treat Edmund, who was climbing to his feet.

"I'm fucking fine," he said. He gave her a hard look. "Go take care of somebody else."

Edmund walked forward, unsteady on his feet. Janine moved to him and slid a shoulder under his arm to support him. They stopped in front of the cell and watched Rose and the other paramedic try to save the marshal's life.

Danny watched the hurt in Edmund's eyes, but the worst was still to come. The man turned to see the body of Soto being lifted onto a gurney and hustled out the door.

Edmund turned to look at Danny, then to Janine. "Is he…." His voice trailed off.

"We don't know," answered Janine.

Danny wanted to reach out and touch him, tell him it wasn't his fault. Edmunds's eyes drifted slowly to the empty hallway. Tears filled his eyes. Words failed Danny. Janine wrapped her arms around Edmund, and the man went to pieces.

The medics got Rune as stable as possible and brought a gurney in to move him. Janine had gotten Edmund to sit in a chair and squatted before him, whispering as he wiped his tears.

Danny, Barrett, and Mike followed Rune out and watched as he was loaded into the ambulance. Soto and the other two medics were already on their way to the clinic.

"Will he make it?" asked Danny.

Rose jumped up in the ambulance as Blackmore moved to the driver's door.

"He's alive right now, best I can give you," she said.

"What about Soto?" asked Danny.

"No idea, not my patient," snapped Rose. "Close the doors."

Danny slammed the ambulance doors shut, pounded on the back window, and the ambulance pulled away. The clinic was only blocks away, and Dr. Benteen would already be working on Soto if they were lucky. As for Rune, Danny had to believe he had a chance, a slim chance maybe, but a chance, nonetheless.

Mike put an arm around Danny's shoulders, and along with Barrett, they walked inside.

Janine was on the phone with the clinic and arranging to head over. Winnie and Maggie had sequestered themselves in the TV room, too shaken to talk about what had happened. And Barrett went to check on Joe Niland, who had been forgotten in all the chaos, and found he was missing.

"A fucking goat rodeo all the way around," said Danny as he walked up to Barrett and Mike.

He'd walked Edmund to the TV room and talked to the man for ten minutes. He'd then asked Winnie to make him some coffee, keep him company, and watch him for a bit. Janine wanted to drive him to the clinic and have him checked out for a concussion.

"How's Edmund?" asked Barrett.

"Fucked up six ways to Sunday," replied Danny. He sipped on a soda he'd grabbed from the fridge in the TV room. "Jesus H. Christ, what a mess."

"What the hell happened?" asked Barrett.

"Edmund says Redwing met him at the front door as he was bringing in supper. He wanted to talk to Sonny, so Edmund took him back," replied Danny.

"Then what happened?" asked Barrett.

"He says Soto was on cell duty and stood up to take some of the food. The next thing Edmund remembers is waking up on the floor," said Danny. "He might remember more later, but right now, he's pretty fucked up."

"Mind if I go talk to him?" asked Mike. A pained look was on his face. "I got experience in living with yourself after things go wrong and people you care about get hurt."

Danny gave a nod as a look of unspoken understanding passed between them.

Mike put a hand on Danny's shoulder, squeezed it, and then let his hand drop as he walked down the short hallway and disappeared into the TV room.

"Interesting man," said Barrett as he watched Mike disappear. "What'd he do in the Navy?"

"Diver," answered Danny.

Barrett waited for more, and when it wasn't forthcoming, he said, "I guess we figured out who's who." He pointed down the hallway at the empty corner cell. "Except for Niland."

"I'm not in a trusting mood," said Danny. "Niland gets put in the same basket as Sonny."

Janine walked up with a face like thunder.

"Fuck no, Soto's not?" asked Danny, dreading the answer.

"No. He's alive, stable, and sedated," she said with an effort. "The marshal is touch and go. They got your girlfriend coming from Darwin. Benteen says he needs a second surgeon in the room before he'll operate."

"What now?" asked Danny.

"I'm taking Edmund to the clinic, whether he wants to go or not," replied Janine. She fished her keys out and threw them to Danny. "It came to me that if Redwing took Edmund's gun, he might also have taken his keys. So, check the evidence room and see if it's been cleaned out."

"Roger that," said Danny.

Janine didn't move.

Danny paused, "Something else?"

"Why'd you give Mike a gun?"

Danny blinked. He hadn't even thought about it. He'd done it on instinct. "We needed more backup. Especially if the shooter was still here."

"He's a civilian," stated Janine.

"And a retired Navy Seal," said Danny. "If anybody deserves a gun in a firefight, it's him."

Janine mulled it briefly, then said, "We're short-staffed. Give him a badge to make it legal." She turned on her heels and headed down the hallway to the TV room. She yelled over her shoulder as she went, "I'll call when we know something about Soto or the marshal."

"Just how many of you whites are we going to hire?" asked Barrett as they watched her go.

Danny just shrugged, and they headed to the evidence room.

Ten minutes later, it was clear that the money, the coffee tin, and all the evidence inside it had disappeared. They made a side trip to the supply room, then joined Mike, who they found alone in the TV room. Winnie and Maggie had gone with Janine and Edmund to the clinic. Janine because she had an officer down, Edmund because he needed medical attention, Winnie, because she was a nurse, and Maggie because Winnie didn't want her out of her sight.

"The money from Niland's trailer, Goodnight's basement, and the vault in Long Hope is gone. Plus, the coffee tin and necklace," Danny said to Mike.

Mike handed Danny and Barrett mugs filled with Winnie's strong-brewed coffee.

"Redwing and Sonny walked out with over four hundred thousand dollars and all the evidence," said Mike. "This night is getting shittier by the minute."

"We got nothing now," said Barrett.

"We still got what DCI collected," said Danny. "Everything from Niland's trailer, the Goodnight shootings, and the Salamanders' place."

"That means we still got the medicine bag with the dog figurine," added Barrett. "That at least points a finger still at Redwing."

"Maybe, maybe not. Who the hell knows? Sonny has been playing us from the start," said Danny. "Manipulating evidence, sending us down false trails. Who's to say he didn't slip the figurine into the medicine bag? He might be the one that killed the Goodnights."

"I thought he said he didn't have killing in him anymore," said Mike.

Danny gave him a stern look and replied, "Sonny has been lying the whole time. Who says giving up killing isn't just another lie." He pulled a spare badge he'd gotten from the supply room. "Janine wants you to have this. Consider yourself hired for the duration."

Mike took the badge. "She sure about this?"

"Says you got to have a badge if you want to keep the gun I gave you."

"I'm not giving the gun back," replied Mike.

"Then I guess you're out of excuses," finished Danny.

The phone rang on the desk beside the television, and all three men flinched at the sound.

"It might be Janine," said Barrett. He walked over and picked up the phone.

"Barrett," he said.

As Mike pinned on the badge, he asked, "Are all investigations guesswork like this?"

Danny gave a cynical smile and answered, "I don't know. This is only my second one."

Barrett hung up and rejoined them. He had a strange look on his face, and Danny was guessing the phone call had been more bad news.

"Was it Janine?"

"No, it was Joe Niland," said Barrett. He glanced at Danny, "He wants to turn himself in, but only to the Wasi'chu."

Chapter 22

Joe had given the location where he'd meet Danny and turn himself in. They didn't know where he was calling from or if this was a trap being set by Redwing or Sonny. They also had no choice, so it was a waiting game until twilight.

To keep busy, they spent the rest of the night and most of the next day running down the one loose thread they had in the investigation and dealing with the collateral damage of the night.

The loose thread was the address the Salamanders' magazines had been sent to in Tennant Creek. It turned out the house had been owned by Lilly Iron Kettle, the mother of Ethan Iron Kettle and the daughter of Sonny. Sonny had inherited it after her death, and according to all concerned, he'd never stepped foot inside the place after her funeral.

The rest of the day was dedicated to keeping vigil over both Soto and Rune. Soto's wife had arrived and joined him as he was treated in the emergency room. Rune had been rushed into surgery to stabilize him, and Darwin General had been called and was sending a surgeon.

They returned to Tribal Police Headquarters to find that Joanna and Ethan's death certificates had also been delivered. Janine added them to the file since, by all evidence, they had identified their killers.

Also delivered was the veterinarian's report on the steer found with John Goodnight. It had been tested positive for bovine tuberculosis. The report stated that the remainder of the Goodnight herd must be quarantined and tested for possible depopulation.

Janine tossed the report onto her desk. "Not sure why the vet can't just say 'put down.'"

"I reckon it just sounds better than kill," said Danny.

"Maybe so," replied Janine. "Still means more dead things in the world."

"You're in an ugly mood," said Danny. He held his hands up as Janine gave him a harsh glare. "Don't worry, we're all there with you."

As the sun dipped below the skyline, Danny drove toward the meeting with Niland. Mike sat beside him in the Power Wagon. He had argued with Janine, Barrett, and Mike that he needed to go alone since Niland had said he

would only surrender to the Wasi'chu. They'd countered
that he hadn't specified which Wasi'chu or how many
Wasi'chu. Danny had countered their counter by saying he
thought Joe had meant him and only him.

"I don't give a shit what you think," Janine had
said. She'd moved in front of him and, standing nose to
nose, had laid down the law. "We got dead bodies all over
the Rez like it's raining fish and a marshal who will most
likely join them." She jabbed a finger in his chest. "Mike
fucking goes with you, or I lock your ass in a cell. You
told me if anybody deserves a gun, it was his Seal ass, so
him, his gun, and his new badge go with you. Got it?"

Danny had acquiesced since it seemed he had no
choice, so Mike sat beside him in the Power Wagon. The
man was still armed with the Beretta, but an M4 lay on the
seat behind them, with Danny's M4 removed from the rack
and lying beside it. Six magazines lay on the seat, and each
rifle had a seventh one already locked and loaded.

"Where are we going again?" asked Mike. He
worked the action on the Beretta.

"Crazy Buffalo Canyon," answered Danny. "Joe
said he'd meet us at his burned-out trailer."

"Don't we pass the spot where you got ambushed?" asked Mike. He'd holstered the pistol and now stared at the side of Danny's head.

"Yeah, why?" said Danny.

"Nothing, just thinking," said Mike. "Poetic if they hit us again at the same place. Correcting a missed opportunity."

Danny took his eyes off the road to glance at Mike for a second. "Why are you here?"

Mike half grinned, "I was the only other white guy retired Seal available."

"No, I'm serious," said Danny. "You could have punched out a long time ago."

Mike's half grin disappeared, and Danny saw a shift in the man's eyes.

"Farming is what my family has always done, but to me, it's just a job," he said. He stared out the windshield and motioned into the darkness ahead of them. "But this. Making a difference. Saving lives and bringing a small amount of justice to bad men. That's why I'm here."

"You should have stayed in the Navy," said Danny.

"I have no doubt, but I did what I did for Margery and Ruth. I got no regrets," replied Mike. "But I want to thank you."

"Thank me for what?" He slowed and turned onto the road that would take them to Crazy Buffalo. "You're supposed to be on vacation."

"Thank you for allowing me to make a difference again," said Mike. "And for letting me see who Danny Coogan really is." He turned, and the grin was back again. "You're a damn good man, Danny. And I'm proud to have you marry my daughter."

Danny didn't say anything back and glanced out his side window so that Mike didn't see the mist that had come into his eyes.

They silently traveled the remainder of the journey until they were just short of where Joe's trailer had been. Through the trees, they could see a small fire and a lone figure sitting beside it on a kitchen chair.

Mike had Danny slow the Wagon to a crawl as he reached back and grabbed one of the M4s from the rear seat. He told him to hit the override switch that killed the dome light when the doors were opened.

"Do you think he's got someone else here we don't know about?" asked Danny as he hit the switch to kill the light.

"You do," said Mike. "And as I remember, you aren't in a trusting mood right now."

"Be safe," said Danny. "Ruth will kick the shit out of me if you get hurt."

"If I were you, I'd be more scared of Margery," said Mike. "Where do you think Ruth gets it from?"

"Let's try not to kill anyone else," said Danny.

"That will be up to Niland. I'm going to come up through the woods and get the drop on anyone Niland might have invited to the party," said Mike. He eased his door open. The dome light stayed dark, and he dropped out of the truck, closed the door behind him, and disappeared into the shadows of the sparse trees.

Danny sped up and pulled off the gravel road and into the grass beside the burnt-down shell and melted tires that had once been Joe's home. He saw that the man had started the fire with parts of the trailer that had not completely burned previously and then used some of the surrounding deadfall to get it going. It wasn't quite a bonfire, but it leaned in that direction.

Joe didn't look the worse for wear since his disappearance from the Tribal Police cell, and Danny wondered what his game was and how many friends might be waiting in the dark. A thin smile came to his lips as he shut the Wagon off and thought to himself that he also had a friend in the dark.

Fuck it, he thought. He reached behind him and picked up the M4. Trust has to be earned from this point forward, he rationalized. He climbed out of the Wagon, slung the rifle across his back, and drew his pistol.

"Here we go," he said in a quiet voice and walked into the light of the fire.

Joe looked up at him and nodded. "Thanks for coming."

"What's this all about, Joe?" asked Danny. He kept the pistol alongside his leg, but he panned his head back and forth and strained his ears for any sounds coming from the dark. "Why escape just to turn yourself in?"

"'Cause lots of folks want to kill me." He gave Danny a frown. "I'm broke and too tired to run. Back in jail seems like my best option for staying alive."

"So, you want police protection," said Danny. He thought he heard a twig snap, and his pistol wavered but didn't come up. "What are you offering?"

"The truth," answered Joe. He dropped his gaze and watched the fire. "Or at least all the truth I know."

"The truth hasn't been your strong suit so far," replied Danny. "Why would I trust you now?"

"'Cause it's the only way you'll catch him," replied Joe. "He's leaving the Rez, but he's got a couple of things to do before he disappears."

"What's that?" asked Danny.

"Bury his grandson," said Joe. "And kill Redwing."

"Sonny said Prince never told him where Ethan was buried," said Danny.

"Sonny lied; it's what he's best at. Prince told him, and he went and dug Ethan up. He wants to give the boy a proper burial."

"Why kill Redwing?" said Danny. "He broke you and Sonny out of jail."

"He broke Sonny out of jail," corrected Joe. "I slipped out in all the confusion when the shooting started. Before somebody put a bullet in me."

"I see killing you as a loose end, but why kill Redwing?"

"'Cause Redwing caused all this. He killed that girl years ago. Sonny's grandson saw him do it," said Joe. "Prince was already thieving for Redwing and was told to shut the boy up."

"Jesus Christ," swore Danny. The extent of Redwing and Prince's crimes overloaded his mind. "They were just kids."

"Kids, women, whatever. It doesn't matter to Redwing. He's a cold bastard."

"So, Sonny wanted revenge on Prince for doing the killing and Redwing for ordering it," said Danny. "But how did killing Goodnight figure in?"

"Goodnight didn't have the belly for all the killing," replied Joe. "He got scared and wanted to go to Whitepipe and tell all he knew for immunity. But Sonny doesn't trust the white man's courts. He wanted Redwing and Prince dead, not in jail."

"So, he got added to the list as a liability."

Joe didn't say anything.

"Does Redwing know about Sonny's plan to kill him?" asked Danny.

Joe laughed at the question, then answered, "Course not. He's a scared rabbit right now. He's got no idea all the evidence you got on him came from Sonny. Shit, he thinks Sonny will help him get back to Canada."

The final piece fell into place. "He thinks he's Edmond Dantès," said Danny.

Joe looked at him funny.

"*Count of Monte Cristo*," said Danny.

Danny saw Mike step out from the tree line and into the far reaches of the firelight. Mike lifted his hand, held up one finger, and then pointed at Joe. Danny understood he was saying that Joe was alone and had no one waiting for them in the surrounding woods.

Joe looked up from the fire and stared into Danny's eyes. "Now that your backup is here, we can head back to town," he said.

After the silent drive back to town, Niland was again secured in cell number three and seemed content with the arrangement. Bringloe had been roused out of his bed and was now the full-time jailor with both sidearm and shotgun. The entry door to the Tribal Police Headquarters was also locked, and Stan sat at the front desk with a shotgun pointed at the double doorway in case of uninvited visitors. The rear door had been chained shut, and short of an armed assault by superior numbers, Joe was safe.

Janine returned from the clinic and joined Danny, Barrett, and Mike in her office. Two deputies from Sheriff Johnson in Beckwourth County were at the clinic entrances to ensure nobody who didn't belong there got inside.

She settled in behind the desk, and an uncomfortable silence filled the office. She's raw from the goings on tonight, thought Danny. Shit, we are all a little raw.

"How's Rune doing?" he asked as she ran her fingers through her hair.

"He's in recovery but still critical. Dr. Benteen and Dr. Beebe removed the bullets and patched him up the best they could," said Janine. "The Marshals Service has been notified. They're arranging air transport to St Patrick's in Missoula for Marshal Jacobsen and Soto."

"They doing more than that?" asked Barrett.

"A shit-ton more," replied Janine. "By mid-day tomorrow, we'll be ass deep in feds of all flavors. Marshals, FBI, ATF, Homeland Security."

"What about Soto and Edmund?" asked Danny.

"Soto's stable, but the eye was too far gone to save," said Janine. Danny could see the slow burn in her at the mention of it and could tell from her red-rimmed eyes that she'd been crying. "I don't know about Edmund. I left him with Winnie, who was trying to talk to him, but he blamed himself. He stares at the wall and won't talk."

"It's going to be a hard road back for him if Rune doesn't make it," said Danny.

"Then let's say a prayer, light a candle and hope for the best," said Mike. He glanced at Janine and Barrett, embarrassed. "Or whatever your religion says to do for intercession from a higher power."

"We got a high percentage of churchgoers on the Rez," said Janine. "I'm not one of them, but I appreciate the sentiment. Moving on, tell me about Niland."

Danny filled her in on everything Niland had said to him around the fire, with Mike and Barrett listening to every detail.

When he finished, Janine asked, "Do you believe him?"

"I'm not sure I believe anybody anymore," answered Danny. "But given that he called us to give up and seems honestly scared that Redwing wants to kill him. I think we can risk a little trust."

Janine gave it a moment of thought. She drummed her fingers along the side of the desk, finally shook her head, and blew out a breath before saying, "I should have stayed with barrel racing where life was easy."

"Same with the Army," added Danny with a smile.

"Ditto with the Navy," said Mike. He stretched a leg out to kick Danny's boot.

"And I'd rather be on the back of a horse watching cattle graze, but none of that will happen in the next twenty-four hours," said Barrett. He pulled his cigar out but still didn't have a lighter, so he put it back in his shirt pocket. "Right now, we got a decision to make. What's your call, Chief Whitepipe?"

"I want to look Niland in the eye and have him tell me his story," said Janine. "I understand Sonny's vengeance, with the death of his grandson and his daughter's suicide and all, but I don't understand why Redwing is part of any of this."

"I got a feeling Redwing got tricked by Sonny, just like everyone else," said Barrett. "It still hurts my heart to find out that old rancher was walking the wrong road this whole time."

"I second that emotion," said Danny. An odd mix of sorrow and anger churned deep in his gut. He considered the tragic deaths of Ethan and Lilly and could understand Sonny's thirst for retribution. But it all changed when his thoughts shifted to images of Rune fighting to stay amongst the living or Soto being disfigured for life. The pity he felt for the man and the hell he'd been through evaporated like morning fog in the day's heat.

Hating the man for what he'd done would be much easier if the old rancher wasn't so likable.

Janine stood and said, "We best get to the rat killing. The clock is ticking on Sonny putting a bullet in Redwing's head and heading north."

The four left the office and headed down the hallway toward the cells. Janine told Stan the plan and not to let anyone in the front door, no matter who they were.

"Just buzz me, and I'll come back and decide if they get in, understand?" she said.

Stan nodded and said, "Whatever you say, boss." He moved the shotgun closer to him, took a bite of his sandwich, and returned to reading the Darwin newspaper.

"You think someone will come after Joe while we got him locked up?" asked Mike.

Janine shook her head and added, "No, but I didn't think they would try to break out Sonny or shoot a U.S. marshal, so my opinion doesn't mean shit right now."

The hallway opened to the wide room with the three cells on the far outside wall. Bringloe sat at the desk with a bottom drawer pulled out and his feet resting on it. He was watching his computer where a war movie was playing on Netflix. He had the sound turned down and glanced up as they arrived.

"How's Soto?" he asked.

"Stable," answered Janine.

"And the marshal?"

"Still alive last I knew," replied Janine. She pointed at the cell, "How's our lodger?"

"Quiet," replied Bringloe.

Danny saw that Niland was sitting on the bunk with his head slumped forward and his eyes closed. At first, he seemed asleep, but as they looked at him, he turned his head and stared at them.

Danny approached the cell bars and said, "Chief Whitepipe wants to ask you some questions."

Niland didn't move or make any indication he had heard Danny. He stared past him and watched as Janine stepped forward.

"I'm Janine Whitepipe, Ray's daughter," she said. "I met you when I was little. You ran the pony rides at the Dead Horse Days Carnival. Handed out root beer barrel candies to all the kids."

Danny could almost see Niland drift back through the years and retrieve the memory. At length, he said,

"You didn't like root beer, but your father made you take it to be polite."

"Still don't like root beer barrels," said Janine.

Niland smiled. "That's okay. I don't have any on me anyway."

"I need the truth, Joe," she said. "You might buy some consideration with the truth."

"Ain't looking for consideration, but I promised Coogan," he motioned to Danny with his chin, "all the truth I have. It was the deal I made for protection."

"What hold does Sonny have on Redwing?" said Janine.

"Fear of everyone finding out the truth," said Joe.

"What's the truth?" asked Janine.

"That he killed a girl and told Prince to kill a boy," replied Niland. "That him being a big shot in the gas fields in Canada is all bullshit."

"So, he doesn't have money?" asked Barrett.

"He has money, but it's from rustling and stealing everything not nailed down," answered Niland. "He only came back to the Rez to try to con the council into building a casino and naming him gaming chairman. He called it his retirement."

"Sonny gave him the casino idea, didn't he?" asked Danny. "He had Charlie Prince contact Redwing once Sonny found out he was the one that killed Joanna."

Niland nodded yes and smiled. "Sonny was always worried about you the most. Said you could see through people and knew they were up to no good."

"There was never going to be a casino, but it was the perfect bait to lure Redwing back home," said Danny. He turned to look at each in turn, ending with Janine. "Once Sonny had him back on the Rez, he could watch him twist in the wind as the evidence stacked against him."

"That explains Redwing," said Janine. She shifted her eyes to Niland. "But why does he want to kill you?"

"I have this," said Niland. He slipped his boot off, held it upside down, and a necklace fell into his hand. He held it up by the clasp, and a blue turtle with flecks of yellow spun lazily in the fluorescent light of cell number three. "And I was there when he killed John Goodnight."

"Then Sonny did slip the dog figurine in the medicine bag," said Barrett. "Then he put it with the body where he knew we'd find it. We had that figured right."

"It put Redwing in the trick bag and made him our prime suspect," reasoned Danny. "And it put him ever further under Sonny's thumb, who I can only guess promised to save Redwing. He played both sides. Son of a bitch that cold-blooded."

"Why did he want to kill Goodnight?" asked Bringloe from the desk.

"Like I told Coogan, John went chickenshit," said Niland. "Told Sonny about the necklace, how Prince was blackmailing Redwing with it. He wanted to take it to the Tribal Police and buy immunity, then leave the Rez with Ellen."

"That would ruin Sonny's revenge," said Danny. "Killing Goodnight kept the plan going, plus he got the bonus of framing Redwing for it. But he got sloppy and killed Goodnight before he knew where the necklace was hidden."

"So why was Ellen killed if she didn't know anything?" asked Janine.

"That was Charlie," said Danny. He glanced at Niland, who nodded he'd guessed right. "Sonny sent him there to find the necklace, but he'd seen the bankruptcy sale notice. He knew Goodnight didn't use the money to save his ranch, so it had to be hidden someplace."

"But Ellen didn't know where it or the necklace was, so even if he tortured her, he got nothing," said Barrett. He walked over and leaned on the deck beside Bringloe. He closed his eyes and said, "She died not knowing the reason, just scared and alone."

"Collateral damage," said Mike. Everyone turned to look at him. "It's a bullshit term the government uses to feel better about itself when innocent people die."

"Why did you do all this, Joe?" asked Danny. "You saw it going off the rails. Why did you stick with Sonny?"

Niland gave Danny a hangdog look and said, "Sonny's my friend. Never had one 'til him." He dropped his gaze to the floor. "Reckon I'll never have another one again, now."

Danny glanced at Barrett and Mike and then back to Niland. He stared at the man, solitary and locked in a cell, and his heart broke for him.

"Do you know where Sonny took Redwing?" asked Janine.

Niland kept looking at the floor, shook his head no, and said, "Sorry."

The list of questions hit a brick wall with Niland's last answer, and each looked at the other for another tack to take.

Suddenly, Mike asked, "What were the last things Sonny wanted to do before he left for Canada?"

"Bury his grandson and kill Redwing," said Janine.

"Goes to reason that since Redwing ordered Ethan killed, Sonny would want to make him feel pain before he finished him," said Mike.

"The grandson," said Danny unexpectedly. He walked to the cell and grasped the bars. "Where's Sonny's daughter buried?"

"In her family's cemetery, over on Table Mesa," said Niland.

Danny looked over his shoulder at Barrett. "Where is that? I never heard of it."

"It's a miniature hill eight or nine miles northwest of town," replied Barrett. "It doesn't have a name, but some folks call it Table Mesa. Got a passel of old family cemeteries up there. But nobody has been buried up that way for a long time unless it was done illegally."

Danny returned to Niland. "You sure that's where she's buried?"

"Positive. Went last year on her birthday. Sonny laid flowers. He told me he goes up and talks to her every so often when he gets lonely."

Danny rolled on his heels to look at Janine and Barrett. "That's got to be it. Sonny wanted to bury his grandson. Where else would he bury her but beside the boy's mother."

Directing his question at Niland, Mike asked, "Is it a quiet, out-of-the-way place?"

"Uh-huh," replied Niland.

"Then it's the perfect place to finish Redwing," said Mike. "And poetic. Executing Redwing for killing Ethan, and beside the grave of Lilly, the mother, he drove to suicide."

"I would have never believed Sonny had that much cruelty in him, but in his mind, it's all justified, I guess," said Barrett. He glanced at Janine. "I say we go. What say, Chief?"

"It's a guess, but the best one we got," said Janine. She checked her watch. "It's just short of ten, and I don't think Sonny will want to dig a hole in the dark. I want to be in position an hour before sunrise."

"I think he will dig at night. Folks bring flowers during the day. The dark gives him more privacy," said Danny. He shrugged, "He's outthought us so far."

"I agree with Danny," said Barrett. "Ain't no more trouble to get in position before midnight and wait."

Janine gave the argument a tumble in her head, frowned, then said, "All right. But we set up in pairs and ensure at least one is awake."

Barrett shook his head. "Unbelievable. We're trying to save a murderer from a second murderer. We could let it play out without butting in. Maybe we'll get lucky, and they'll kill each other."

"No, we need them alive to stand trial," said Janine. She gave Barrett a harsh, angry stare and, with an edge to her voice, said, "Someone's got to go to jail for the innocent folks that got caught up in this."

Chapter 23

The group headed out at a quarter to midnight in personal cars and trucks. Danny had suggested it to Janine to prevent having the trap detected due to parked Tribal Police cruisers and SUVs scattered around the top of the butte.

Janine decided that Stan and Bringloe would stay at their posts. Stan would continue to watch the front, and Bringloe would keep an eye on Niland in cell three and the back door. Neither was happy with the decision.

Danny followed Janine to the medical clinic, where she parked along the front. She left the Jeep running, got out, and walked back to the Power Wagon. Danny lowered his window and asked, "What are we doing?"

"I got a pick-up to make," she said.

As she turned and began to walk toward the entrance of the clinic, Danny saw she carried a second Glock in a holster with her off hand.

They watched the automatic doors open, and a uniformed Beckwourth sheriff's deputy put his hand up to stop her. They spoke briefly before she was waved forward, and the automatic doors slid shut.

Barrett sat in the back of the Wagon while Mike had the shotgun seat. Nobody spoke for a full five minutes.

"You think it's a good idea to hand a gun to Edmund right now?" asked Barrett abruptly. The silence had been so overpowering that Danny jumped at the man's voice.

"It might be his only chance," replied Mike.

"You mean like get back on the horse that threw you?" asked Barrett.

"Pretty much," said Mike. "The more time he spends blaming himself, the less chance he has of seeing past it. Seen it ruin men in the Navy."

Another minute went by, and the automatic doors swished open. Janine walked out with Edmund trailing slightly to her right and a step behind. She waved for him to continue to the Jeep while she walked to the passenger side of the Wagon. She tapped on the glass, Mike hit the button, and the window slid down.

"Everybody ready?" she asked. All three men nodded in the affirmative. "Follow me, then, and stay close."

They watched as she walked away, climbed in the Jeep, pulled away from the curb, and headed out of town.

They drove northwest for three miles on a hardball road. They got to Five Points, an intersection where five roads converged. They took the sixth one that was dirt and hadn't made the cut to be considered a road.

The dirt road devolved as they traveled through the dark on it, and after two miles, it was little more than a path with wheel tracks and a strip of grass running down the middle.

"Does this trail have a name?" asked Mike as he grabbed the crash strap above his head and braced himself with his other hand on the dash.

"You're driving on history. This road is a remnant of the auto trails from the early twentieth century," said Barrett. He pointed at a telephone pole as they passed it. It was weathered, cracked, and had faded red and yellow strips on it. "Those banded poles marked the way so tourists from back East didn't get lost."

"Where did it come from, and where did it go?" asked Mike.

"This was just a branch off the geysers to Glaciers Highway. A side trip for wealthy tourists who had time to spare," replied Barrett. "The highway's southern start was Flagstaff, Arizona, while its northern finishing point was the Canadian border, near Babb."

Danny looked in the rearview mirror and saw Barrett smiling in the moonlight. "Ain't you a fountain of information. What about the mesa itself?"

"It's a half-mile long by three-quarters mile wide. The sides are steep-sloped or cliffs, and the only way to the top is on the road we're driving on," replied Barrett.

"How come you know so much about it?" asked Danny.

"What can I say? I like history," said Barrett. "And my wife has ancestors buried up there."

"Anything else you want to tell us before we get to the top?" asked Mike.

"Nothing much more to tell," replied Barrett. "Supposed to be haunted. Legend says dead warriors rise and defend the burial grounds against any white man stupid enough to step foot on it."

Mike turned to stare at Barrett. "You're kidding, right?"

"That's the legend," answered Barrett with a shrug. He turned to look out as they drove past another telephone pole. With a teasing smile, he added, "Guess we'll find out when we get there."

Mike shifted his eyes to Danny, who glanced at him and frowned.

"Don't look at me. You had to ask," said Danny.

The road steadily climbed over its last mile before it leveled out, and the top of the mesa was thrown open to them. A sprinkling of trees stood sentinel here and there across the horizon, and a carpet of grass covered the ground as far as the moonlight let them see.

The headlights of the vehicles illuminated a cluster of assorted headstones, and Danny followed suit and shut his lights off when Janine did.

They exited the two vehicles and met in front of the Jeep. Danny saw Mike staring at the headstones and couldn't help saying, "Legend must not be true. We're still alive."

Mike gave him a dirty look, and Barrett smiled at them both.

Edmund pulled the pistol from the clip-on holster and slid it into the empty holster hanging around his hips. He glanced up and saw everyone staring back at him. He looked at Danny and said, "Don't worry about me. I'll do my job."

"Never thought you wouldn't," replied Danny. He turned to look at Barrett. "So, where is the cemetery we're looking for?"

"According to Niland, we go by the Raincloud cemetery first. That must be the one we lit up when we topped the hill," he said. "Next, we go by the Long Soldiers, the largest on the mesa. Then Kicking Dog and finally to the daughter's family."

"What family are they?" asked Danny.

"Iron Kettle," answered Edmund. "My father's mother was from Iron Kettle. It's a cursed family."

Janine patted Edmund on the shoulder, then looked at everyone. "Keep the lights off and drive by the moonlight. Once we get to the cemetery, we'll stow the vehicles the best we can, find the grave, and set up. Everybody got it?"

They reloaded the vehicles and headed down the road at a pedestrian pace. They followed the road to the left and passed the Raincloud cemetery. Most headstones leaned at angles, and devil thorns choked the grass.

They stayed to the left and passed the lengthy lines of Long Soldier graves. The Long Soldier family cemetery was easily three times the size of the first one they had passed, and the headstones looked well cared for, and the grass thick and thorn-free.

They cut hard to the right so that the last cemetery they passed before reaching their destination passed them on their left. It was smaller than the second but still more extensive than the first. The headstones formed concentric rings around a garage-sized tomb in the center. The year 1919 was carved above the doorway.

"What's with the crypt?" asked Mike.

"That's Dan Kicking Dog. He was chief when he died in a flood outside Brokenrope," answered Barrett. "He, his wife Jonette, and his five children were killed. My grandfather told me stories about how the entire Rez was up here for the funeral."

The crypt faded into the shadows as they drove farther down the road, and soon, a gathering of mismatched and tilting gravestones came into view. Janine passed the cemetery and found a stand of a couple of dozen red maples one hundred meters beyond to stash the vehicles in. It wasn't perfect, but the Wagon and Jeep were hidden unless you looked just right.

Danny was armed with an M4 and his Sig. Mike had the other M4 and the Beretta. Barrett borrowed the .308, while Janine and Edmund had Glocks and shotguns. If nothing else, thought Danny, nobody would die from being under-armed.

They hiked back to the cemetery and searched through the markings until they found the one they sought. It was unlike any other and, from the back, had looked like a medium-sized solitary boulder. It was waist-high and made of black basalt. It had the name LILLY IRON KETTLE inscribed on it. A running horse with its mane and tail flowing in the wind was carved in low relief below the birth and death dates.

Janie ran a quick scan of the ground with her flashlight. "We didn't miss him." She pointed at Lilly's grave, the thick grass covering it, and the nearby area. "No dirt's been turned here for a long time."

Janine checked her watch. "Just after one," she said. "Edmund, Barrett, and I will move to the north side of the cemetery," she pointed at a large tree approximately two hundred feet away, "and camp out by that large oak."

"Where do you want Mike and me?" asked Danny.

She scanned the area and pointed to the east along their driven route.

"See those ponderosas with the thicket of juniper to the left? Settle into that and keep hidden," she said. "That way, you can cover the road out of here in case it all goes to shit."

Danny looked at the trees and juniper. It was only forty or fifty feet from Lilly's grave. "A touch close, don't you think?"

"No other cover unless you want to cozy up behind a headstone," said Janine.

He scanned the area and found she was right.

He thought about it and decided that cozying up behind a headstone was an excellent way to get seen or shot. "I think we'll take the juniper," said Danny, and with Mike in tow, he stepped off.

"Hold up," said Janine. She unsnapped her radio from her belt and handed it to Danny. "Better reception than cell phones. Edmund has his, so both teams have comms."

"Checks on the hour?" asked Danny.

"Make it the half-hour," said Janine. "I think you and Barrett are right, and Sonny will be early."

Twenty minutes later, everyone was in position, and the long hours of waiting started. After an hour, with not even a rabbit or coyote wandering by, Danny remembered why he disliked hunting. After two hours, he and Mike were stiff from lying beside the pines and took turns standing and massaging the kinks out. The lawmen gathered after the sun came up, and no Sonny or Redwing.

"I say a couple of us stay put in case he shows, and the rest head into town to pick up food and water," said Barrett. He shifted to look at Janine. "What say, Chief?"

"Agreed," she replied. "Danny, you, your bodyguard, and Edmund stay here. Fan out, don't get seen. We'll be back in an hour with chow and to spell you."

An hour later, they returned. Janine hid her Jeep with the Power Wagon, and the food and water were divided. She'd also brought binoculars, which made keeping eyes on the mesa easier. The day wore on, and they alternated sleeping and keeping watch on the single road Sonny would have to drive on.

Twilight came and went, shadows lengthening until they joined together at nightfall. The moon appeared in quarter form, and they could see the hazy band of the Milky Way stretching out above them.

"Any movement?" came Janine's voice on the radio.

Danny pressed the button on the side of his brick. "Nothing here. I'm starting to think Sonny out-thought us again."

"We'll give it until midnight and then reevaluate, but you may be right," answered Janine. "Whitepipe, out."

"Dammit," Danny said as he dropped the radio in the grass. "I've got to piss." He got a thumbs-up and smile from Mike, then moved to the far side of the trees, unzipped and had just started to empty his bladder when he heard the sound of a vehicle climbing the road just below the mesa.

"Shit," he whispered. He pinched his stream off, reeled in his tackle, and raced back to drop beside Mike.

"God's got a helluva sense of humor," said Danny. He pulled out the radio. "We've got incoming." He checked his watch. It read three twenty-two.

"We hear it," responded Edmund. "Chief says to keep your ass down. Radio when you get a positive ID, that it's Sonny and Redwing and not some kids looking for trouble."

"Will do," replied Danny. He tossed the radio onto the ground beside him. "Now we wait."

They lay in the juniper and watched headlights dance across the sky as the vehicle climbed the hill. Three minutes later, two pinpricks of light materialized over the lip of the mesa and rumbled in their direction.

The vehicle skirted the first two family cemeteries, followed the road to the right, and passed the crypt. It came within fifty feet of their position, then pulled off the road and drove straight at them. Both men attempted to melt deeper into the bushes, and each turned their face away to avoid having the light illuminate their white faces.

Danny squeezed the M4 tighter. Every muscle in his body vibrated with adrenaline. He readied himself to react. The vehicle got closer. He imagined its tires running over him. He drew a leg up for purchase with the ground, and just before he sprang to his feet, the vehicle veered off to travel between two rows of headstones and stopped beside the black basalt boulder.

"That was almost really bad," hissed Mike. Danny glanced over. He had his rifle extended and was covering the vehicle that sat idling.

Danny shifted his eyes to the vehicle and recognized it immediately. It was the green Jeep that the shooter had used to escape from the Goodnight house after shooting at him and Mike. He mentioned this to Mike, who said, "Nice when things come full circle. Gives closure."

"Not the time for Zen shit," whispered Danny. He picked up the radio and said, "It looks like the green Jeep the Goodnight sniper used."

"ID yet?" returned Janine's voice.

The passenger door opened on the Jeep.

"Stand by," said Danny. He squinted as a figure climbed out of the Jeep and moved in front of the vehicle to be illuminated by the headlights.

It was Jonathan Redwing. He looked rough, and it was clear he'd been battered since the jailbreak. He wore a blue denim shirt that was torn open, and blood caked the left side of his head. The blood had run down his neck and stained the shirt.

Redwing's hands were tied at the wrists and hung before him. Abject terror interspersed with hysterical confusion mingled to contort the man's face. As a human being, Danny felt no pity for Redwing since he knew the man's sins, but the lawman in him put it aside, and he prepared himself to try and save the bastard.

The driver's door opened, and Sonny stepped out into the grass. He held an AR-15 loosely in his right hand, letting it dangle beside his leg. On his left hip was an M1911 Colt with its butt forward for cross-drawing with the right hand. Behind the Colt hung a knife in a leather sheath.

Danny radioed Janine and Edmund that he had eyes on both Redwing and Sonny. Janine responded that they were working on a plan.

"How do you want to do this?" whispered Mike as Danny finished with the radio.

"Rather not kill them," replied Danny.

"Neither of them deserves a chance, you know?"

"That's exactly why we can't kill them outright," said Danny. He looked at Mike. "The Law's got to be better than the Lawless."

"Rules of engagement on the battlefield were so much clearer," said Mike. He sighted down the rifle.

"Preach it, brother," replied Danny.

Janine called to say that they would move closer and try to get in a position to encircle Sonny and force a surrender. Danny said they would stand by and only engage if it looked like Redwing was in danger.

Sonny reached behind the driver's seat of the Jeep and drew out a shovel. He tossed it at Redwing, and it landed between his feet. Next, he walked to the back of the Jeep, keeping the rifle on Redwing the entire time, and gently lifted out a large duffel bag. He carried it to the side of the Jeep and laid it down with care.

Sonny walked forward, and as he did, he reached back with his left hand and drew the knife. He got to Redwing, and with his left hand, he used the knife to cut the ties from the wrists.

That done, Sonny stepped back and motioned with the AR-15 for the man to pick up the shovel. Once he had, Sonny pointed at a spot beside Lilly's grave, and Redwing began to dig.

"Must be Ethan in the kit bag," whispered Mike. "We got till the hole is finished to figure out our play here."

Danny watched Redwing continue to throw dirt. He stood in the hole now, and Danny guessed he was down a foot.

"We're as close as we dare," said Janine over the radio. "Still over a hundred or so feet away. We can see Redwing. Is he fucking digging a hole?"

"A grave," replied Danny. "We got eyes on the bag that's holding the grandson."

"We don't have a clear view of Sonny. He'd kill Redwing if we moved," said Janine. "It's on you to figure something out. Sorry, Danny."

There wasn't time for Danny to reply. Redwing had dug deep enough to satisfy Sonny, and he yelled at him to stop and climb out of the hole. Redwing climbed out of the grave but kept the shovel in his hand.

Sonny shifted the rifle to his left hand and reached across to draw the Colt. He extended his arm and aimed at Redwing, who quailed and pleaded loud enough for Danny to hear.

"Shit, shit, shit," said Danny. He glanced at Mike. "Shoot the fucker if he shoots me."

"What?" asked Mike. But it was too late. Danny had stood up.

"Sonny Siebert, Tribal Police, you're under arrest," said Danny loudly. He had the M4 up and tight against his shoulder.

Sonny spun and raised the rifle while the Colt stayed aimed at Redwing.

Danny heard radio static and then overheard Janine's disembodied voice say, "What the fuck are you doing?"

"Coogan," said Sonny. He rested the butt of the AR on his hip but kept it aimed at Danny. "Is it just you, or did everybody come?"

Danny moved forward two steps with the M4 locked on Sonny's chest. "You're surrounded, Sonny. I need you to lose the rifle and pistol, drop to your knees, and interlock your hands behind your head."

"He wants to kill me," shrieked Redwing.

"We all want to fucking kill you, you child-murdering son of a bitch," yelled Danny. He rolled his shoulders to vent his hatred for the man and all the evil he'd brought to the world. "I ain't doing this to save your piece-of-shit life." Then he directed his following words at Sonny: "I'm doing this for Lilly and Ethan."

"Don't say their names," said Sonny. The rifle barrel stayed steady, but the Colt dropped and was no longer aimed at Redwing. "It hurts too bad."

"None of this will change things," said Danny. He took another three steps. "Let me arrest him. Let him go to prison and live in hell the rest of his life."

"What do you know about hell?" asked Sonny. "I've spent a lifetime living in hell."

Sonny turned to look at Redwing, and he let the AR-15 slip from his hand and clatter to the ground.

"Sonny," said Danny. "You don't want to be remembered this way."

"Don't matter," said Sonny. "All I ever wanted was a family; he took that from me."

Danny dropped to one knee, steadied his aim, and yelled, "Dammit, Sonny, put the weapon down. I don't want to shoot you, but I'll have to if you don't lower the weapon. Do you want to die today, Sonny? Yes or no?"

"Yes," said Sonny. He lifted the Colt and aimed at Redwing, who stood before the shallow dug grave. Redwing raised the shovel to protect himself as Sonny fired. The bullet struck the blade of the shovel. The striking angle caused the slug to ricochet and disappear into the stratosphere, saving Redwing. But the force of the strike forced the shovel rearward. It smacked Redwing in his face and flattened his nose. He dropped the shovel, howled in pain, stumbled back, and fell into the grave.

As Sonny fired, Danny pulled the trigger on the rifle three times, and red blots appeared on Sonny's belly and thigh, and he went down in a heap beside the Jeep. The Colt flew from his hand and landed on the edge of the freshly dug hole.

Figures charged from the north, and Danny saw Janine, Edmund, and Barrett running toward him. Janine yelled orders at the other two. All had their weapons out, and chaos reigned supreme.

Danny ran to Sonny, who lay at the side of the Jeep, his arms wrapped around the duffel bag.

"I'm sorry, Ethan, I'm sorry," he sobbed as Danny approached him.

Danny laid his rifle on the ground. He reached for Sonny as the man's strength faded, and he rolled him onto his back. He'd been hit twice in the belly and once in the thigh. The thigh wound was a through-and-through and had missed the artery, but the two in the gut had caused massive damage, and he was bleeding out.

Danny heard Redwing shout behind him, "Tried to kill me, huh? Now it's your turn, motherfucker!"

Danny reached for the rifle, but it was too late. He snapped his head and saw Redwing standing on the grave's edge holding the Colt. It was aimed at both him and the dying Sonny. Danny didn't hesitate. He leaned over Sonny, using his body to shield the old rancher.

"No-good bastard," said Redwing. The muscles on the back of his hand rippled as he squeezed the trigger. Whether from being dazed from a shovel to the face or unfamiliar with the Colt kick, Redwing's aim went to the left. One slug burrowed into the ground, while a second struck the gravestone of SSG Donald Spotted Elk, showering both Danny and Sonny with shards.

From far off, Danny heard Janine and Edmund order him to drop the weapon.

Redwing's eyes shifted to look in the direction of the voices. He fired three shots from the Colt into the darkness. Danny heard the return fire of both rifle and shotgun, and a few pellets found Redwing, who staggered but did not go down.

The man abandoned his effort to kill the targets farther off and rotated the Colt to aim back at Danny and Sonny.

But Janine and Edmund had bought Danny time to snatch up the rifle. The realization of his mistake came to Redwing as Danny squeezed the trigger. He pumped three bullets into the man's chest, and Redwing was blown off his feet and back into the grave. A single foot rested on the grave's edge and twitched as Redwing died. It was a Rocky brand working boot, and Danny reckoned it would be a size ten.

He stood, ensured Redwing was dead, and then glanced down at Sonny. The man's eyes were open, and he stared at the night sky, but they were vacant. Sonny was now with his daughter and grandson.

Danny knelt beside Sonny as Janine, Edmund, and Barrett rushed up. He looked up at the three of them. The headlights of the Jeep illuminated them.

"It's over," said Danny.

Epilogue

Danny pulled his truck off the road a mile outside of town. He was preoccupied with the past and wanted to think it through before the day's festivities.

It'd been two and a half months since Table Mesa, and the ramifications still rippled through the Rez. The murderers of Joanna Parker and Ethan Iron Kettle had been identified, but since they were both dead, the residents of the Rez felt unsatisfied and empty.

As it turned out, Redwing's fortune was a house of cards and collapsed after he died. He was buried in a pauper's grave in Tennant Creek Cemetery along with his medicine bag, which DCI had returned. The money for the pool and theatre he had promised at **Two Moons Tribal Hall and Sports Center** evaporated, and construction halted until a mysterious four-hundred-thousand-dollar donation was made.

Everyone knew it was the vault money from out in Long Hope, but everyone also figured it was a debt payment from the Salamander brothers for a lifetime of misery they had visited on folks on the Rez.

Beloved in the community, Sonny had been revealed to be a stone-cold killer. But he was dead also, so no case beyond that of public opinion was ever brought. To many Nakota, he remained beloved and was considered a martyr who had taken the law into his own hands to get justice for his daughter and grandson.

The Tribal Police and BIA had been cast as the villains in events, along with Jonathan Redwing. The Tribal Police and BIA were villains because their perceived inaction, ineptness, and inattention had forced Sonny to go vigilante in the first place. Redwing, because he had killed Joanna, and ordered Ethan's death, which led to Lilly's suicide.

Danny had been painted with the same brush as the Tribal Police, and sentiment on the reservation gradually turned against him. He had put Redwing down, but he'd also been the one to shoot Sonny. It was never hostile or overt, but questions were asked about his suitability for service, and echoes of Redwing's claims of not needing a "white savior" began to make the rounds.

Those who made these claims had quickly forgotten a few points. First, Redwing was a murderer, and second, Redwing had only made the claim to eliminate Danny as a threat to himself. But the whispering campaign continued to grow, and pressure had been brought on Barrett as the council chief and Janine as acting police chief to fire Danny.

Barrett and Janine refused, but the writing was on the wall. So, on Labor Day, Danny walked into Tribal Police Headquarters and resigned. It had not been easy for him, but he respected Barrett and Janine too much to watch them be ruined by carrying his remaining on the Tribal Police into battle.

So, Danny found himself unemployed for the second time in the last few months.

He received phone calls from the sheriff's departments of Beckwourth, Teton, and Cascade counties asking about his availability. The Montana DOJ rang him about the still-open investigator job, and even Brand Enforcement contacted him. Edmund had talked him up to Charmayne, and she'd made some phone calls after hearing he was back on the open market.

Ruth told him there was no hurry and to take his time deciding, so he did.

Fall arrived in Beckwourth County, and the turn in the weather and his unemployment fueled a wanderlust in Danny. Either by himself or with Ruth along for company, Danny had taken to driving in the backcountry of the county and the Rez.

He enjoyed the aspens along the swift-running Spoon River as they flashed their golden hues. He marveled at the red maples scattered across the landscape, painted in colors that ran the spectrum from glowing yellows and oranges to brilliant scarlets and maroons. When he drove higher, he saw the needles of the Western Larch as they were beginning to transition from green to gold.

But still Sonny, his life and death, and the Rez, where for a brief time Danny had felt at home, would return and ride point in his thoughts.

He'd taken a pre-dawn drive today to shake off his melancholy. He'd circumvented the Rez, counted the miles, and watched darkness give way to light. As the Wagon rolled to a stop, he shifted into park, leaned back, and reached for his thermos.

He filled his cup as the eastern skyline blushed with the sky-blue pink of the morning. John Denver's "Song of

Wyoming" played low, and he blew the heat off his coffee and drank. He was dressed in jeans, boots, and a denim shirt. The straw cowboy hat still rode on the Power Wagon's dash and seemed to have become a permanent fixture. A garment bag hung in the backseat along with his good boots. He had a date in town later and needed to be appropriately attired.

He looked down at Tennant Creek, its population of cars, trucks, and school buses beginning to stir. He lifted his eyes to stare past the town. Past the buildings, past the houses, beyond the surrounding prairie. His eyes gazed out at the far mountains as the light grew more robust and the day gathered strength.

He sat, drank his coffee, and took the tally of all they'd won and lost.

After the investigation was closed, Sonny's body and Ethan's bones were released to the Iron Kettle family. Barrett pushed through an exception with the council, and a week later, father, daughter, and grandson lay together. Danny figured that being together put this in the win column.

Ray walked out of the hospital in Darwin on the last Thursday in July. The nerve damage had not improved, and he would need to walk with a cane from now on. Always searching for a silver lining, he told everyone he'd lost weight and that his knees didn't hurt for the first time since he could remember. After talking it over behind closed doors with the council, he retired as Tribal Police chief, and the crown was passed to Janine officially.

Sotomayor had been released from the hospital on the first of August without his left eye. He came back to limited duty as Danny was resigning. The eyepatch and new beard gave him the appearance of a Spanish "Snake Plissken," which appealed to him. He dinged his patrol cruiser twice on the yellow poles at the fast-food drive-through but was adjusting to the dead zone created by being a cyclops, as he put it. He had to call this one a split decision. It was a loss when it came to the eye, but Soto was alive, and who doesn't want to be Kurt Russell?

Deputy U.S. Marshal Rune Jacobsen had spent a month recovering in Missoula, then was transferred to a rehabilitation facility in Northern Virginia close to the Marshals Service Headquarters. The last time Danny talked to him, Rune said he was improving but that the Marshals Service had scheduled a fitness-for-duty board, so maybe he would soon be unemployed. This was a loss, figured Danny. But Rune said he wasn't dead, so it was a loss he could live with.

Bringloe recovered completely and transferred from Medicine Hat to the big leagues in Tennant Creek. Edmund forgave himself for the jailbreak after he and Soto had a long talk, a few tears, and a case of beer. Teenaged Andrea moved in with her Uncle Barrett and Aunt Nina, broke up with Becca, and got hired as the new Tribal Police chief's assistant.

Winnie Whitefeather resigned from the council to concentrate on caring for her daughter, Maggie. Demitta took her council seat in a unanimous vote. Janine charged Maggie Whitefeather for her actions during the road ambush. Danny testified in her defense, and due to extenuating circumstances, the charges were reduced to the destruction of police property, and she was sentenced to two years' probation and the price of a Ford Interceptor in restitution. Danny considered this a win-win-win.

Joe Niland was the recipient of a slew of charges. He cooperated with the feds and filled in the blank spots for them. He told how he was present when Sonny killed John Goodnight with the captive bolt stunner and how he'd overheard Prince confess to killing Ellen.

After the dust settled, Niland received a twelve-year sentence for the cattle thieving and vehicular assault on Danny and Edmund. If he served it out, he would be eligible for Social Security when released.

When it came to Sonny, Danny thought the man had won, but at a horrific price. He'd taken his revenge on the men who destroyed his family, but he'd lost his humanity and violated every virtue given to his people by the **White Buffalo Calf Pipe Woman.**

The rancher had left a detailed account of his revenge against Charlie Prince and Jonathan Redwing. Janine found it folded in an envelope, tucked between the pages of a hardcover edition of *The Count of Monte Cristo*. The book sat on a small table in the living room beside his recliner, and passages had been highlighted and notes written in the margins.

Danny had been right about Sonny seeing himself as a modern-day Dantès. The rancher had read the book and used it as a blueprint for revenge.

In the letter, Sonny hadn't asked for forgiveness or understanding. He'd wanted to kill the men who'd killed his grandson, plain and simple. His thinking went no further than when the final bullet was fired. Consequences and repercussions never occurred to him. In the final paragraph, he wrote that he was sorry about Ellen. She'd been innocent, but so had Joanna, Ethan, and Lilly, he argued. He accepted the blame for her death since he had sent Prince to the house but finished by saying he had no regrets for the things he'd done.

Danny sipped at his coffee. He didn't feel bad about Charlie Prince, the Salamander brothers, or Redwing; they'd lived a violent, outside-the-law life, but it bothered him that he could be so callous. The death of John Goodnight ate at him sometimes, though. The man had, in the end, tried to do the right thing and go to the police. But he'd told the wrong man, thus sealing his fate. An inevitable victim of Sonny's march to retribution.

Also found with the letter was a scrap of paper. On the paper, in looping cursive writing, Sonny had written Northern Plains Savings and Loan. A key was taped to the top right corner of the scrap. The key ended up being to a safety deposit box at the Northern Plains branch in Darwin. In the box, they'd found eighty thousand dollars, Sonny's Last Will and Testament, and the deed to his ranch.

The will explained that the money was proceeds from the stolen cattle and mushrooms. Sonny had never spent a dime of the dirty money and wanted it to do some good in the world, so he asked it to be donated to the medical clinic to use as they saw fit.

The Iron Kettle family would inherit the ranch, with the exception of the two horses. Sonny wanted them to go to Bringloe since he was a true horseman and would appreciate good stock.

And like the last chapter in a book, and in an act overdue by decades, the ghost town of Long Hope burned to the ground. It was unknown if it had been through a lightning strike, arson, or divine intervention, but in the last week of August, a bright glow had been seen on the horizon. Stan had been on patrol and responded. He radioed in the fire, but Long Hope was too far from any waterlines to save it.

Danny poured more coffee into his cup as his phone rang. The theme music from *The Magnificent Seven* filled the truck cab. He put the cap on the thermos, sat his cup on the dash, and picked up his phone.

He unlocked the screen, and a picture of Ruth in running shorts and a tank top appeared. The photo was his phone's home screen and had been taken during the Bitterroot Mountain Marathon back in March. Ruth was beautiful and glistened with sweat. An ear-to-ear smile was fixed on her face, and a starburst-shaped medal hung around her neck. She was toasting with a bottle of yellow-and-gold-labeled Carta Blanco and giving the thumbs-up.

As he looked at the picture, he smiled unconsciously, and the past slipped into the shadows and disappeared. She was his lifeline and the Starshine that drove away the demons.

"Morning, sleepyhead," he said. "How are you feeling on the big day?"

"Woke up and thought you were still in bed," she answered. She laughed as she continued. "Turned out it was that small pony you call a dog."

Danny could just picture Sunka, their huge, black-faced, brindle-coated Great Dane, spooning Ruth, and he smiled. As he did, the past receded even further.

"I made coffee before I left. Pop-Tarts are on the counter for Mike, and your mom's muffins are warming in the oven," said Danny.

"You don't have to bribe them," replied Ruth. "They already like you better than me."

"Well, I love you, and that's all that matters," said Danny. He closed his eyes, and the past stayed where it belonged. Only the future remained in his thoughts.

He listened as she shifted the phone. She then asked, "Ready to get married, cowboy?"

"Been ready since I met you, Doc," replied Danny.

"See you at the Tribal Hall," she said. "I'll be the one in the white dress."

Danny laughed and replied, "I love you, Ruth."

"I love you too, Danny," she answered.

The connection dropped, and Danny returned his phone to the empty cup holder.

He would have to get going soon. He needed to stop by Tribal Police Headquarters to sign some papers for his final pay, then head to Edmund's house. Edmund was his best man, and he would shower and get dressed at his house before heading to the Tribal Center.

The wedding would be held in the small park beside the Two Moons Tribal Hall and Sports Center. The reception would be in a large, open-air shelter house with the catering done by the Dan-Dee Diner from the Rez and the Dream Bean Coffee Café from Darwin.

The mothers, Molly and Margery, had advocated for the Catholic Church in Darwin, but Ruth and he had held firm. Ruth had a pronounced hippie streak, and the outside venue and casual wedding were what she wanted. Mike and Ben counseled him to follow the Happy Wife, Happy Life adage. So outside and casual was what Ruth would get.

He leaned forward, started the truck, and had just reached to put it in drive when the phone rang again. He picked up the phone, glanced at the number, didn't recognize it, but figured it might be important if they were calling this early.

He hit the answer button and said, "Coogan."

"Morning, Danny," came a voice he recognized. "Shit, I just realized what time it must be out there in the sticks. Hope I didn't wake you up."

"No worries, Rune," replied Danny. "Farmers and ranchers are always up before dawn. How have you been?"

"Physical therapy is coming along, but I'm done with field duty. I got the board's decision yesterday."

"Sorry, Rune," replied Danny. "Does that mean you are unemployed like me?"

"Not quite. They retired me with a decent enough pension so I wouldn't go hungry," he said. "But that's not the reason for my call."

"Are you wanting to congratulate me on getting married later today?" laughed Danny.

"Damn, I had no idea. Congratulations," said Rune. "I guess you could classify my call as a wedding present."

"I don't understand."

"Can you be at the Marshals Office in Billings the first week of October?"

"We get back from the honeymoon the last week of September, so I should be able to make it," answered Danny. "What gives?"

"When the board retired me, they asked if I had any suggestions for my replacement. I gave them your name, and they are requesting an interview."

"Bullshit," said Danny. "They don't even know me."

"No, but I do. And Pete Buckwalter, the U.S. marshal for all of Montana, has heard of you and is impressed. He says Fish & Game were wrong to let you go."

Danny sat stunned. The U.S. marshal for all of Montana knew his name and was impressed. This could be a game-changer chance to still work in Montana and not be tied down to a single geographic jurisdiction. A smile slowly spread across his face, and possibilities flooded his head.

"Are you still there?" asked Rune.

"Yeah, I'm still here," said Danny. "The first week of October sounds great."

"Fantastic. I'll find out the date and time and let you know," said Rune. "Best wishes on the wedding. See you soon."

Danny hung up the phone and laid it on the center console. The smile stayed on his face as the thought of Deputy United States Marshal Danny Coogan flashed through his mind.

He shook his head and dropped the Wagon into gear. That thought would have to wait until later.

He had a beautiful woman to marry and a new life to start.

Made in United States
Orlando, FL
04 April 2024

45436247R00280